The
Concealers

The Concealers

JAMES J. KAUFMAN

Downstream Publishing

New York   Florida   North Carolina

Downstream Publishing, LLC
1213 Culbreth Drive
Wilmington, NC 28405
downstreampublishing@gmail.com
℞ ® a registered trademark of Downstream Publishing, LLC

FIRST EDITION 2013

Hardcover Edition: ISBN 978-0-9825873-6-2
Softcover Edition: ISBN 978-0-9825873-5-5
E-book Edition: ISBN 978-0-9825873-7-9
Audio Edition: ISBN 978-0-9825873-8-6
Large Print Edition: ISBN 978-0-9825873-9-3

Publisher's Cataloging-In-Publication Data
(Prepared by The Donohue Group, Inc.)

Kaufman, James J.
  The concealers [electronic resource] : [a novel] / James J. Kaufman. -- 1st ed.
  1 online resource. -- ([Collectibles trilogy ; bk. 2])
  Issued also in print, audio book and large print editions.
  ISBN: 978-0-9825873-7-9 (ebook)
  1. Women journalists--Fiction. 2. Fathers and daughters--Fiction. 3. Bank fraud--Fiction. 4. Electronic books. I. Title.
PS3611.A846 C66 2013eb
813/.6

Library of Congress Control Number: 2013936447
Library of Congress Catalog - in - Publication Data
Kaufman, James J.
e-book edition ASIN [As Per Data Base Assigned]
The Concealers/James J. Kaufman
Printed in the United States of America
10 9 8 7 6 5 4 3 2 1

For Patty

Special dedication to my granddaughter
Annabelle Lewis

ACKNOWLEDGMENTS

First is Patty, for her love, graciousness, keen eye and ear, and for always believing in what I can do, and our daughter, Kristine, and son, Jeffrey, for their love and support.

I thank my editor, Barbara Brannon, for her input, edits, and critiques, and I thank my friend, author Brooks Preik, for her sharp eye in line editing and content.

Thanks to my agent, Richard Barber, Richard Barber & Associates, and to my marketing team, Peter Berinstein, Wild Onion, and Michael Sloser.

I acknowledge my indebtedness to those consultants who generously provided invaluable information in specific areas:

Douglas Love, for his considerable knowledge of and experience in the field of investigative journalism and his contribution in editing;

Bill Corwin, president of the Clarke Schools for Hearing and Speech, Dr. Catherine Bartlett, Dr. Ted Mason, and audiologist Emily Bambacus for contributing their time and professional expertise in the field of hearing and speech;

Joe DeCicco, author of the Michael Romano series, former New York Police Department detective and current private investigator, for helping me understand the intricacies of the NYPD and private detective world;

My friends Rod Graybill and Ron Skudlarek and Craig Parsons for their input as to skeet and trap shooting and the Newark Rod and Gun Club.

With deep gratitude, I express my appreciation to the following for their contributions:

To Emma Mahn, for her patience, research skills, and uncommon devotion and assistance in making this book possible;

To Jeanne Devlin, for her friendship, brilliant design talent, and knowledge of the publishing industry;

To Pat Rasch, for her industry, energy, and solid formatting skills combined with a keen eye for design;

To my friend Patricia Roseman, an outstanding photographer;

To Debra Datesman-Tripp for walking into the hornet's nest with patience, skill, and humor;

To my long-standing friend, Paul T. Miller, thanks for your generosity and valuable input;

To what has become my reader group, to whom I am indebted for their countless hours of reading manuscripts and their valuable input: Ann Kalkines, Diana Holdridge, Andy Miller, Steve and Marty Braff, Carol Pulizzi, Harley Sacks, Betty Mahn, and Christopher Navarro;

To George Kalkines, with whom I have, for more than fifty-six years, talked, listened, laughed, and shared life, appreciating his friendship, generosity, intellect, and wisdom.

I express my deep appreciation to the members of associations and book clubs with whom I have conversed in person and via Skype throughout the country and to those who have taken the time to write to me about *The Collectibles*. Your input has been generously given, instructive, and of immense value.

≇

Morton's Fork: John Morton (c. 1420–1500),
Archbishop of Canterbury, was tax collector for
England's King Henry VII. To him is attributed
Morton's fork, a neat argument for collecting taxes
from everyone: those living in luxury obviously
had money to spare, and those living frugally must
have accumulated savings to be able to pay.

—*John Jones, Catalogue of Ethical Dilemmas*

∞

One of the most striking differences between a cat
and a lie is that a cat has only nine lives.

—*Mark Twain, Pudd'nhead Wilson*

PROLOGUE
JUNE 1988

Beth Kelly's heart raced as "CODE TRAUMA 3" blared over the speaker. She rushed into the trauma room, narrowly avoiding a collision with the young medical resident, but quickly recovered her rhythm. She joined him and the emergency service assistants, slipped into a gown and gloves, applied glasses, and, following the protocol she'd been practicing, helped move the patient from the paramedic stretcher to the hospital gurney.

Beth studied the bloody, battered figure under the cotton blanket. Both of the young man's legs were mangled and the back of his head was bleeding profusely. She tried to catch everything the paramedic was saying, over the commotion and clatter: "... tractor-trailer jackknifed ... overturned—driver nonresponsive at the scene—head trauma indicated." The ER team worked quickly, and in less than half an hour the man's vital signs were stable. The resident began a full-body assessment under the attending physician's scrutiny; the patient was on his way to surgery—and, to Beth's wonderment, likely to survive.

Finally on duty in a big city emergency room, Beth Kelly was ecstatic. She felt like she was reliving the documentary *A Day in the Life of an Emergency Room Nurse*. Undeterred by the past two days of exhaustive orientation and training in preparation for her six-week nursing residency program at Roosevelt Hospital, she was a working nurse at last, in a busy New York City hospital to boot. Her recent graduation from The State University of New York at Plattsburgh behind her, she could now look forward, if with anxiety and even fear, to the excitement of the real thing.

In her first four hours on duty she'd already witnessed more life-threatening cases than she'd seen in all her previous training. Besides the truck accident victim, there'd been the fifty-seven-year-old obese white male in cardiac arrest; a four-year-old black girl with a blocked airway ultimately determined to be the result of an allergic reaction; a thirty-eight-year-old Latino who'd severed his left arm using a table saw; and an elderly lady, exact age unknown, stabbed in the neck by a deranged passerby.

The initial challenge, of course, was to get the diagnosis right. Some situations were transparent; others required comprehensive blood analysis and other tests. Many required radiology. During triage that afternoon, one twenty-three-year-old white male (wrist band Wilson, 3/13/65) seemed to have even the doctors stumped. He had arrived with stable vital signs but acute abdominal pain. The resident suspected appendicitis, only to be overruled by the ER physician's tentative diagnosis of diverticulitis. After radiology, Wilson was sent upstairs for further observation and treatment.

Beth, who had assisted Wilson in the ER, was directed by the charge nurse to assist the nursing station on his floor once they'd finished with the accident victim. "We need you here, but go to Station Eleven. Bigwigs are always doing this."

Beth found her patient in a large, well-furnished, private room in the hospital's VIP section, surrounded by so many flowers she was afraid he had died. To her great relief, Wilson was awake, alert, and free of pain—but something clearly had him in a sour mood. She smiled and was about to introduce herself but was interrupted mid-sentence when a silver-haired matron in a chic Nancy Reagan-style red suit burst into the room, followed immediately by a clean-cut, young, tired-looking doctor dressed in scrubs.

"Diverticulitis? At his age?" the woman said.

"We can't rule it out—symptoms are indicative. The CAT scan did eliminate appendicitis."

"At least you didn't send him right into an unnecessary surgery!" The woman gave the doctor a withering look and at last turned to acknowledge the patient. "Are you feeling any better, dear?"

"I'd be fine if this nice nurse would just bring me a cold beer," said Wilson, winking at Beth.

"No food and drink until we are certain of your diagnosis," the doctor said.

"Which I do hope will be forthcoming soon," the woman said, "especially in light of the generous donations we've made to this hospital over the years. I'm going to speak with the chief of internal medicine."

Wilson looked over at Beth with a frustrated sigh. "My mother," he explained.

Unsure whether it would be proper to commiserate, Beth reached for the young man's wrist and began taking his pulse. "She has your best interest at heart," she said. Beth checked Wilson's chart.

"I didn't like hearing that GI specialist talk about a colostomy. That's where they cut a hole in your intestine and attach a sack here, right?" Wilson said, pointing to his right-side midsection. "Let's talk about something more agreeable, like where you're from and how long you've been working here."

Beth deflected all his questions with a snap of the chart and urged him to rest. She knew his type—the flirting was just bluster to mask the fear he wouldn't show. Nice guy, really.

★ ★ ★

Two days later, after his attending physician determined Wilson had suffered a mild case of food poisoning and his mother was satisfied he was on the mend, Beth returned to check her patient's blood pressure and temperature and help him prepare for discharge. He'd been easy to look after, watching baseball games on TV, taking Jell-O meals and doctors' rounds in stride, never complaining when she had to wake him at odd hours for his medications.

"Hey, could we talk for a few minutes?" he asked her when they were alone in the room.

"We've been talking for the past three days," Beth said.

"I know," Wilson said. "What I want to know is whether you'll let me take you to dinner tonight, you know, to thank you."

"Are you hitting on me, Mr. Wilson?"

"Absolutely," he said. "It's your deep blue eyes."

"It's not the eyes. It's the medicine," Beth said, patting him gently on the shoulder. "You'll get over it. Besides, I have a boyfriend."

"Really? What's he doing?"

"He's in the Air Force—based in Plattsburgh, where I went to school."

"Are you serious about him?"

"It's a long story. He's a pilot and ... that's what he's really into. I have to attend to some other patients now," Beth said. "I'll be back to check on you when your discharge paperwork is ready."

When she returned an hour later, he continued the campaign. "All I want is to take you to dinner—say thanks. I'm sure your boyfriend wouldn't object to that."

"I can't. Besides, I won't be done here until eleven."

"Okay, I'll be waiting for you in front of the hospital, Tenth Avenue and Fifty-Eighth Street," Wilson said.

Beth laughed. "I hope you're feeling better. It was nice to meet you. Take care of yourself."

★ ★ ★

Exhausted at the end of her twelve-hour shift, Beth struggled down the stairs to the street, anxious to get to her apartment and rest. She raised her arm to hail a cab only to be greeted by a long black limousine. A driver in suit and tie came around and opened the door for her. Beth hesitated, then looked in at the bright face of her patient, raised her arms in surrender, and stepped in.

She closed her eyes, immediately absorbing the scent of leather and wood in what seemed to her more a luxury den than a motor vehicle, eased back in the seat, and extended her tired legs and feet fully before her. She had no idea where the limo was taking her—but she was too tired to care.

Beth imagined a hot bath and sleep. She wondered where Larry was right now, what he was doing, whether he was even alive. She could only surmise that her unreturned phone calls meant that his group of the 380th was gone—somewhere. No good-bye, no word, as usual. And then he'd come back full of descriptions of his adventures. Whatever he was doing, she was sure that he was reveling in it and not thinking of her.

The next thing she remembered was Wilson's hand on her arm, gently shaking her.

"Where are we going?" she asked.

"Wherever you like. Hungry?"

"I don't know ... but first, how are *you* feeling?" Beth asked.

"Great. Worked out at the New York Athletic Club, took some steam. Got the hospital out of me. Still hungry though."

Wilson pushed a button to lower the privacy window separating them from the driver. "The Flame Restaurant, Jimmy," he requested, as though accustomed to giving orders. "Fifty-Eighth and Ninth."

The restaurant was not crowded. Wilson picked a table in the back and ordered a hamburger, fries, and a milk shake fountain delight. Beth followed suit, now realizing how hungry she was. She found Wilson, who she thought would be stuffy and arrogant, to be earnest, forthcoming, and funny.

She answered his questions about growing up in a small upstate town, attending nursing school at Plattsburgh, being selected for the residency program, and experiencing the big city for the first time. He told her about his sailing during summers at Martha's Vineyard, his love of fast cars and golf, and his intent to be a successful chief executive officer of a big company someday.

The limo was waiting for them when they finished their meal, after midnight.

"Where to?" Wilson asked.

"I'm at the West Side Residence—that's where the Roosevelt put us up, 340 West Eighty-Fifth."

Wilson gave the address to Jimmy, said something to him about later at The Limelight, and the limo moved on.

"What's The Limelight?" Beth asked. "Is that a private club?"

"Yeah, a place to hang out, dance, drink . . . should be rockin' about now."

When they pulled up in front of the West Side Residence, Wilson again told Beth how much he appreciated everything she had done for him, how much he had enjoyed the evening. "I owe you for getting me back up to speed."

"So . . . are you going to The Limelight tonight?"

"That could happen."

"Can you give me about ten minutes?"

"Absolutely," Wilson said.

Beth rushed to her room, took a quick shower, and chose a spritz of cologne and the right outfit. She dashed back downstairs and greeted Wilson with a kiss on the cheek, unable to hide her excitement. "I know you think I'm just a rube, but I've never been to a real New York club before!"

He hit the down button. "The Limelight, Jimmy."

About ten minutes later, Beth was surprised to see the limo pull up in front of a large stone church. She began to wonder again what she was doing, whether her forwardness had been a big mistake. There was a barricade on the street side and a black wrought-iron fence on the church side, with young people jammed in between, forming a long line. In front of the big doors to the church were two large men dressed in black, surveying the crowd and choosing the anointed that would be allowed in.

"You have to be kidding me," Beth said.

Jimmy opened the door and one of the club's guards came over.

"Good to see ya again, Mr. Wilson."

They were ushered up the stairs, through what looked like a

vestibule, and into a gigantic room with a revolving mirror ball on the three-story-high ceiling. Colored lights were moving everywhere, in sync with the loud, pulsating music. The dance floor was packed with young people laughing, dancing, and singing, soon joined by Wilson and Beth. Beth was in a different world, far from the seriousness and surgical precision demanded of her at the hospital, liberated by the brash sounds and sights, and freed by Wilson's lack of command and control—so different from being with Larry.

After an hour or more—she'd lost track after the second Bloody Mary—Beth asked to go home. "I love all of this, but I have to get some sleep. Big day tomorrow."

"You got it," Wilson said, and led her strategically through the crowd, out the door to the limo.

Wilson directed Jimmy back to the West Side Residence. Almost subconsciously as she recalled the excitement of the evening, Beth moved her body languorously across Wilson's. What had come over her? She reached for the switch to the window. "Jimmy, please take the long way home."

Sitting crossways to Wilson, Beth took his face in her hands and murmured, "This has been wonderful."

She turned her head toward the gentleman who'd been her patient only a few hours earlier and locked his gaze in hers. She could smell his well groomed hair, breathe in the earthy scent of peanuts and beer on his breath, and feel the smoothness of his skin. He was taller than Larry though not as muscular. She found his trim good looks and urbane manner intoxicating.

"By the way," she said, "in all this time, I forgot to ask your first name."

Suddenly she found herself doing something she could hardly have imagined that very morning: she kissed him deeply—and he responded in kind.

Somewhere in there she heard him say, "Preston. It's Preston."

Beth's head was still filled with the piercing, pulsating music as she felt Wilson unzip the back of her dress, and she yielded to the freedom from its release. She felt the cool leather on her skin and the heat rising from his body.

She knew this was having sex, not making love, but right now she didn't care. She felt appreciated, and it felt good.

She would deal with the rest of it in the morning.

CHAPTER ONE
APRIL 1, 2012

As she lined up for check-in, helmet cradled under her arm, Katherine's thoughts were not on the race as she knew they should be, nor were they about some academic question or multiple intertwined facts in a research project. This time it was personal, her mind wrestling with an old dilemma, one she'd come to think of as *Incomplete Reconciliation*. In her heart she felt a hole. It stemmed from her phantom father, killed while serving in the U.S. Air Force before she was born.

April Fools' Day? The irony was not lost on her. What kind of fool had she been, to get herself into this sort of commitment? But there was no time for second-guessing now.

Instead she compartmentalized, counting the things she was certain of: number one, that she had more questions than answers; two, that her mother's love was unconditional; and three, well, that nothing in life was certain.

Most questions were easy, thought Katherine. Others plagued her, crying out for answers, particularly the big ones. She always worked hard to find the answers, applied herself, did her homework. But to do so meant asking more questions, including finding the right ones to ask. And some answers simply eluded her—chief among them, to get to the heart of it, was *what would my life have been like with a father?*

Nothing like facing your own mortality to bring up the big questions. As to the second certainty, of course, she was grateful and felt
blessed. Her mom loved her, had raised her while working long hours
as a nurse, and had been there for her every step of the way.

As to the third, Katherine had learned that some things happen—
good and bad—no matter what she did. They were beyond her
control. She accepted that reality.

Another, timelier, question. Had she lost her mind? As she
approached the check-in stand, her New York driver's license showing her motorcycle endorsement in hand, Katherine counted her
blessings, prepared for the worst, and hoped for the best.

After check-in, Katherine struggled to straddle-walk her CRF-
450X Honda trail bike into position. That Sunday morning the spring
clouds hung low, spreading a thick fog over the Berkshire range, and
she could make out little of the trail ahead.

She checked out the racers, the words of her motorcycle coach
circling through her mind: *Find your man—the right Class A rider—
and follow him.* Katherine settled on 6A. She sized him up at about
six-foot-two, with broad shoulders and sandy-blond hair slightly vis-
ible from the back of his helmet. From the front, she'd seen him only
for a few seconds, when they were lining up, but like hers, his face
had been mostly obscured by helmet and goggles. Still, there was
something about his posture, the way he sat on his bike as if he had
nothing better to do.

Katherine glanced down at the newly purchased sports watch on
her wrist: Four past eight. Rows of five riders had been departing
every minute since the 8:00 a.m. start; one more to go before hers.

Only at that moment did Katherine have second thoughts about
the wisdom of her project. *Worst case: I'm going to go off a cliff,
injure myself or die . . . if I don't get stuck in a swamp or drown in a
river first.* An unfamiliar burn took hold in her stomach, and her heart
began to pump like mad. Had her drive for perfection overtaken her
good sense this time? Watching would have been enough to write the
paper. It still would be.

As the fifth row of riders surged forward, leaving nothing ahead of her but the yawning void of the starting line, Katherine hung back. Her mother had totally understood her junior-year trip to work with at-risk women in Uganda, but she'd almost had a stroke when she learned about Katherine's first parachute jump. What would her mom think now if she got herself killed in a motorcycle race her first time out, just so she could cover it firsthand?

As if that were the one incentive she needed, Katherine shoved the bike forward to rejoin the pack. In her lessons, she'd worried that if her bike went over, she'd lack the strength to pick it up, especially given the heavy boots, the race suit, and all the protective gear. Five-six and 127 pounds was no match for 440 pounds of steel, aluminum, and rubber. Too late to dwell on that now. Odometer, *check*. Roll chart, *check*. Race computer, *check*.

The flag dropped. Katherine fumbled to put her bike into first gear, still trying to get used to the metal shank and the massive O'Neal boot. She swore and then recovered, shifting to second and then moving quickly forward to catch up.

Katherine Beth Kelly, wearing number 6D, was in the race.

★ ★ ★

She wasn't looking to win, of course. And besides, the riders were racing against the clock, not one another. If she could maintain the target twenty-four-mile-per-hour average between the checkpoints, she hoped only to avoid a wipeout and complete the 75.6-mile course. *If you finish, you win,* she had reminded herself in her practice sessions. She understood that the Berkshire Mountains Enduro would test all the riders' skills under an incredible array of conditions.

Riding in the race hadn't been on the course syllabus—that was all Katherine's idea. Self-aware and confident at twenty-three, she never did anything halfway. And on this assignment, which she expected to help seal her master's degree from New York's select Fletcher Thomas School of Journalism and a top job in her field, she was convinced that firsthand participation was the only way to learn about

Enduro racing and discover why people pursued it so passionately.

By now 6A was already well out in front, as Katherine lagged behind all the other racers in her group. *Follow the arrows, don't overpower the bike, and pay attention to the trail,* her instructor had told her. *Pick your spots and stay out of trouble.*

The signs led through deep woods, around sharp turns, and over ridge tops. On the downside, the narrow trails were steep and slippery. The riders in her own group were now out of sight, and others were passing her on the trail. She knew she was falling behind, but she wasn't sure by how much. She couldn't read her watch, which jumped around on her wrist. Katherine wished she had thought to mount it on her handlebars. She glanced at her bike's computer but was too nervous and excited to read it.

An hour in, Katherine was becoming accustomed to the rhythm of the trails. The open areas were easy and gave her a chance to catch her breath. Somehow, she had managed not to get stuck or fall off. *So far, so good. Now, where the heck was 6A?*

Ahead, Katherine could see a slight opening. It was a checkpoint, a clearing about the size of a small house, surrounded by tall walnut and pine trees. Three race officials checked in racers stopping for a water break, and a couple of riders had pulled off to the side to inspect their bikes.

She caught a glimpse of 6A cleaning his chain, but as she came closer, he remounted and sped down the winding trail. She rejoined the trail and followed as quickly as she could, each turn sharper and steeper than the one before, branches hitting her on each side. After a punishing few minutes that seemed like hours, she suddenly heard a thunderous noise. Just ahead was a wide creek filled with large angular stones. Crowds of spectators on both sides shouted encouragement and guidance to the riders. "Over here, enter over here . . . stay away from there."

Katherine spied 6A through the trees, his motorcycle powering down the middle of the creek. She hesitated at the creek bank, aware of other riders behind her as they yelled, "Move it! Go, go, go!" She headed down the steep bank and froze. Riders swerved around her, plunging into the water like horses fording a swollen river, almost knocking her over. There was no room to turn around. Bikes kept coming. One rider sailed over her and into the creek. Katherine's face burned; her legs shook. She took a deep breath and revved the throttle. The front wheel jumped up, almost smashing her face. "No!" Katherine screamed as she struggled to regain control of the big bike. The coach's words came back to her: *Let the clutch out slowly and twist the throttle, giving it power gently at first, and then put the hammer down.* Her bike lurched forward, and she was in the creek.

As she fought to keep the bike in balance, Katherine could feel the cold water seeping into her boots. *Keeping the water out of the engine's air intake was what she needed to worry about,* she thought, recalling her preparation. Scanning the creek, she looked for the shallowest parts that would make passage easier. She was losing time and she knew it. Riders were whizzing by, drenching her and the bike. She could barely see through her helmet's face shield, but she had to keep pushing.

Katherine blipped the throttle carefully and turned to avoid slipping on the rocks or hitting a submerged log. Finally, she spotted the next arrow, on a big log pointing up the slippery creek bank. She turned her bike, gunned the powerful 449-cc four-stroke engine, and flew up the bank. "Yes!" she cried, as she regained the trail, reveling in the cheers of the crowd behind her.

After several more checkpoints and close calls—she had lost count of how many by now—Katherine guessed she must be past the halfway mark. And 6A was long gone, she figured. She was tiring fast, and thirsty.

Rounding a sharp corner, she encountered mud, a slough too wide to avoid. There was nothing to do but power through it. Katherine twisted the throttle, but in her speed, she failed to look ahead, where a large log lay directly across the trail. She hit it and flew over the handlebars and somersaulted onto her back. At first she felt as if she were floating, and then she felt pain shooting through her chest, right arm, and lower back. She opened her eyes and nearly saw double—*this would not be the time for a migraine,* she thought. The bike was leaning against the log, still running.

A rider came along, stopped momentarily, looked in Katherine's direction, and yelled, "You all right?"

"Just fine," Katherine muttered to herself as she shook her head, painfully lifted her right arm, and gave him a thumbs-up. The rider turned his bike around, rode about twenty feet back up the trail, and then wheeled around again to face the obstacle. Gunning his motor, he jumped the log on the left side where it was narrowest. Katherine could feel the heat and smell the exhaust of his bike as he flew over her shouting, "Give it up, girl—this ain't for everyone!" and disappeared down the trail.

No way, she thought as she willed herself to a sitting position. *But I see why they insisted on all the body armor.*

She presumed that no bones were broken. The bike was another matter. Banged up, its engine still running, it had become wedged into an offshoot of the log. She rose, walked over, and killed the ignition. Much as she tried to pry the bike loose, though, she didn't have the strength to free it.

Katherine pondered her vulnerable position as she heard the approach of another motorcycle behind her. To her surprise, the rider downshifted and pulled to a stop behind her. He stood his own bike on its kickstand, and without removing his helmet, motioned to a stout limb on the ground nearby. Dragging it over, he helped her jam it between her bike and the offshoot. Together they pried the wheel loose, bending one of the spokes but leaving the tire intact, and righted the bike again. The rider waved her on as she rode about fifty feet back up the trail, turned around, picked her spot, gunned the engine, and sailed over the log as she had seen the earlier rider do.

Two hours and two more checkpoints later, Katherine noticed more light coming through the surrounding woods. The trail was flattening out, too, and she could feel her speed increasing. Suddenly, as if she had passed through an open door, she found herself on a large grassy field, just a few hundred yards from Tucker's Pub, where she had started the race. She stared with disbelief at a huge sign: *"IF YOU FINISH, YOU'RE A WINNER!"*

People of all ages were gathered at the finish, the children cheering and clapping. Some riders who'd finished long before her were standing around their bikes talking; others were sitting or lying on the ground, looking up at the sky. Several tents lined the north side of the field, the largest surrounded by flags and streamers. The tantalizing aroma of hamburgers and hot dogs filled the air.

Katherine parked her bike alongside the others and walked into the big tent, where she pulled off her gloves, lifted her face shield, and gulped down a bottle of cold water. She struggled with the chin strap on her helmet, her fingers throbbing with pain after the ride. Finally, she got the strap loose and pulled the helmet off, throwing it on the table. Grabbing another bottle of water off the table, she poured it down the back of her neck. She was already soaking wet with sweat and dirty creek water. She was sure she looked dreadful, but frankly she didn't care. She'd survived.

"Glad to see you made it," a voice behind her said.

Katherine turned around and looked into the muddy face of the six-foot-two guy with the sandy hair, who held out a gloved hand to shake hers. "Sean O'Malley. Don't see many women on the trail. Your first time at the Berkshire?"

"Yep," she said. "Katherine Kelly. I think I owe you one," she added. "At last I get to meet the man behind the number."

"How's that?"

"It's my very first race—ever," she said, pouring more water on a napkin and then using it to wipe some of the grime off her face. "My coach told me to pick a top rider to follow. I did. But I couldn't keep up with you. I saw you at a checkpoint, but you took off like a shot." Katherine was aware of her messed-up hair but too tired—and exhilarated—to care.

"Yeah, there's a three-mile free zone after that stop, so I turned it on," said O'Malley.

"Free zone?" Katherine asked, reaching into her pocket for her notepad and pencil. She'd seen "free zone" in her research but apparently had missed its strategic significance.

"It's when they don't take points away for arriving too early."

"Oh," she replied, detecting a reaction from O'Malley as she wrote. "Hope you don't mind?"

O'Malley nodded his assent. "Checked out your bike when you walked in the tent. Honda four-stroke was a great choice. Low-end torque. Takes the hills like a tractor, and you don't have to lean forward to compensate. And it's set up right."

"Really?" she said, continuing her note-taking. "How's that work? Low-end torque, I mean."

"Gives your bike the power to dig in going uphill ... otherwise, depending on how steep it is, the front of your bike can flip over your head. The important thing is, you got through it," O'Malley explained. "Who turned you on to Enduro racing in the first place?"

"I'm not turned on to Enduro racing. At least not yet. I'm writing a story about it."

"You're a reporter?" O'Malley asked.

"Not yet, exactly—still a raw apprentice. I'm finishing my master's in journalism in New York."

"Cool. So you got your motorcycle license, joined the American Motorcycle Association and the New England Trail Riders Association, all of that?" O'Malley asked.

"I had my license, but ... yeah, a lot of hoops."

"All for a story," O'Malley said, shaking his head.

"An assignment—a paper on an action sport. Where I grew up, off-road anything was a big deal for the guys, as long as there was mud or dirt. They'd drive old cars up hills and race motorcycles. Motocross. Enduro."

"Did you race?"

"No, but my boyfriend did. That was years ago. I did think it was neat, particularly the cross-country enduros. There were races all over. When I got this assignment I went to the IDR Speedsville Enduro to see what it was like. Couldn't see much, though. I decided the only way to be able to write about it was to do it," Katherine said.

"Where was ... where'd you grow up?"

"A tiny village in upstate New York. Marion."

"Amazing," O'Malley said. Then he stood. "I'm going for a beer, Katherine. Want one?"

"No, but I'd love a Gatorade. I'll go with you," she said, trying to keep up with O'Malley as she registered the pain in her back, right arm, and left leg. She was relieved to see the guys from the shop loading her bike onto their truck along with a few other customer bikes. She was sure she didn't have the strength left to move it herself.

While they were waiting for their drinks, O'Malley looked at Katherine and said, "How'd you get the bike, if you don't mind my asking? It's a pretty sophisticated machine for a rookie."

"A friend of mine from home has a motorcycle shop, and he knows a motorcycle dealer in the city. Are you sure *you're* not a reporter?" Katherine joked. "Let's talk about you. Besides being a Class A rider, what's your story?"

He parried. "Let's just say, I'm in a line of work like yours—where I usually ask most of the questions."

"Let me guess. You're a lawyer."

"Close, actually," said O'Malley. "I did finish a year of law school."

"And then?"

"U.S. S—" Just as he was about to tell her more, a voice over the loudspeaker announced that the scores were being posted.

Katherine's curiosity shifted into high gear. There was a great deal more that she wanted to know about Sean O'Malley, but their private conversation came to a halt when three of his buddies, still in racing gear, came to their table, full of high fives. They said hello to Katherine and then one shouted to their friend, "You did it again! Time to get your trophy. Besides, we're starving."

"Nice talking with you, O'Malley," Katherine said. "I should go. I'm tired, soaked, and a little sore ... heading back to the city. Good luck with your job—whatever it is you do."

O'Malley appeared more than a little disappointed. "I'd like to see you again, 6D. How do we do that?" he asked.

"I'd like that, too," Katherine said. She got up from the table. "But it's going to be crazy for the next few weeks, graduation."

"How 'bout a phone number then?" he persisted.

Katherine kept walking, thinking about her paper and Sean O'Malley's experience as a racer. And he wasn't exactly ugly. She wanted to talk with him at length to learn what had prompted him to start riding, get a sense of what he enjoyed about it, find out how much time he spent on the hobby, see what kind of bike he had and where he rode it, discover what other sports he was into. At bottom, she wanted to know what motivated him. She knew she needed time to get the information she wanted, but she felt it was too late to try to do it now. Besides, she was exhausted. It would have to wait.

Then she stopped, took out her iPhone, spun around, and snapped a picture of Sean. She scribbled on her pad kat.journ@gmail.com, ripped off the paper, and handed it to him. "Going to be really tied up for a while … but I definitely would like to stay in touch."

"Me, too. Have a good trip back to the city," he said, turning and walking away to join his friends.

Once again, Katherine was looking at the back of 6A.

Katherine caught a ride back to the cabin she'd rented at Prospect Mountain Campground so she could shower and pick up her bag, and then headed back to New York City. She dropped off her rental car and took the subway to Union Square. At her second-story walk-up apartment a block away, she struggled with the two locks on her door, heard Hailey bark, and was thankful that her friend Susan Bernstein, who'd looked after Hailey, was able to drop her off earlier that evening. Inside Katherine romped with Hailey on the floor and after a flurry of kisses perched herself on a kitchen stool and sipped some soup. Katherine scribbled some memories of the race while they were still fresh, and made a note to set up a meeting with her journalism school mentor for early Wednesday morning. She took out her cell phone and studied Sean's picture. *Just another uncertainty,* she decided, and fell into bed.

CHAPTER TWO

"Hey, P.J., see if you can make the horn blow?" Preston prompted, his expression telegraphing his frustration and pain in not knowing how much, if anything, his thirteen-month-old son could hear. P.J. smiled and bounced around, his energetic little hands hitting everything in sight.

Preston could see that Marcia relished the moment. She got down on the floor and joined their son. Preston was proud of the way his wife applied her psychology background, always reinforcing their young son's opportunities for new learning experiences. Not wanting to get into a fight with Marcia, though, he refrained from talking about the hearing issue.

Preston lifted P.J. high above his head, delighting in his son's giggles but unable to quell his anxiety over his son's hearing impairment. At forty-seven, he remained conflicted. On the one hand, he felt incredibly lucky—he'd pulled his marriage back from the brink, even though he'd nearly given up on fatherhood. When P.J. came into their lives soon afterward, he knew he had closed the deal. Marcia was thrilled to finally have a child, and he was, too. At last, their home, while not a model of domestic tranquility, appeared to have at least settled down, and they'd put the turmoil of the preceding decade behind them. Still, there was P.J.'s disability and Marcia's concurrent uneasiness. And secretly, he was still struggling with the sudden death of his mother two months before P.J. was born.

In Preston's excitement bordering on euphoria at the hospital at P.J.'s birth, he either was unaware or did not notice the equipment the technician was using. He barely focused on the doctor's concern that P.J. had not passed the hearing test.

Preston didn't know that an infant's hearing could be tested so quickly after birth. It was later, in discussions with the doctor, that Marcia and Preston learned about measurement of an acoustic reaction produced by the inner ear that bounces back in response to a sound stimulus from a small probe with a microphone and speaker. It was all too technical to Preston, who knew lots about business but little about science—something about electrical stimulus sent from the cochlea to the brain stem and a second and separate sound that does not travel up to the nerve but returns to the infant's ear canal, the otoacoustic emission.

During the weeks following P.J.'s birth, there was much discussion with Marcia's gynecologist, and numerous pediatricians and audiologists, concerning the causes of hearing impairment, its varying degrees of seriousness, and the need for continued assessment. The good news was that with early detection, depending upon the cause and type of loss, much could be done to increase P.J.'s access to sound. Notwithstanding many consultations since, however, Preston still couldn't understand how P.J.'s hearing could ever be normal.

Marcia saw things differently. "P.J.'s hearing will never be normal." The audiologist had explained that hearing aids amplify the sounds that would reach an infant's brain and stimulate it to produce the architecture that will allow him to hear and speak normally with aids or cochlear implant depending upon the severity of the loss. "If you can't accept our son's disability, Preston, at least I have—and I thank God every day that it was not worse," she pleaded as she gently rolled the baby over to face them and leaned down to cuddle his cheek. "He can be fitted with hearing aids right away. Don't you think it would be worth trying?"

All year Preston and Marcia had argued about whether to fit their growing son with hearing aids. When Marcia chided him for his unwillingness to make the decision, Preston only procrastinated further. She feared now it might be too late.

For Preston's part, he was totally supportive of full exploration of all efforts to correct P.J.'s hearing, but worried at the time it was taking and whether his son's hearing would ultimately be normal. Besides, the pediatric specialist he had consulted counseled patience, telling Preston that he had seen many cases in which hearing ultimately developed on its own—as late as year two or three—and to wait and see.

Preston had worked hard over the years to develop automobile sales franchises—Porsche, Audi, BMW, Mercedes—that were upscale, unique, and more durable. His success hadn't happened overnight. Now it was a bit like having a cartel. On the business side, his stores appeared to have recovered from a previous setback and were even showing spurts of growth; most of his dealerships, in part because of the nature of the franchises, were far ahead of the dealers he knew who had struggled more to achieve much less. Of his ability to lead Wilson Holdings, Preston was certain. Accumulating wealth and managing relationships, however, were another story.

Preston's thoughts were interfering with his playtime with P.J. He pushed them out of his mind and lifted P.J. into his circular bouncer, where he could play with all the buttons and colored animals.

"Daddy's got to get back to the office," Preston said for Marcia's benefit.

Marcia looked up at Preston and said, "We'll never get another chance to build our early relationship with our son. This time is so important."

"It is," Preston said, kneeling down beside her. "But I have a meeting at two. Maybe we can all go to the park—or even the zoo—tomorrow."

"Are we still on for dinner with Mary and Bill tonight?" Marcia, Mary, and Marcia's old roommate Ann, had been close friends at Smith College. Mary and her husband, Bill, lived in Soho, and

Marcia had been trying to get together with them for some time. She reached for her cell phone to call the nanny. "I want to make sure Nadine comes early, so P.J.'s fed and asleep before we leave."

"As far as I know," Preston replied.

"I have to get Ann up here. I miss her and I know Mary does, too. I wish she lived in New York. Speaking of relationships, what's going on these days with Missy? And Tommy?"

Preston thought for a while. "Uh, they're fine. I guess."

"When's the last time you spoke to either of them, Preston? I'm getting a bad feeling here. Slipping. Remember who we named this little guy after?"

They'd chosen their son's middle name, Joseph, to honor Joe Hart, an attorney friend who had helped Preston overcome some thorny financial and banking issues that had nearly toppled Wilson Holdings, Preston's automotive and real estate firm—and empire. It was hard to believe Joe Hart had been gone for more than a year.

"Don't do that," Preston said, seeing the expression on Marcia's face and knowing he was in trouble the minute the irritable comment left his lips.

It wasn't that Preston didn't appreciate all Joe had done for him. Facing enormous debt, Preston had been sure his automobile business was doomed to bankruptcy. Worse, because Marcia had personally guaranteed the notes, she, too, was at risk.

What bothered Preston deep down was Joe's requirement that Preston fulfill an unspecified condition in the future before he would undertake the case. Preston could not understand how anyone could commit to do something without knowing what it was. When he'd raised the question Joe had simply replied, "Some men can and some men can't," which Preston had interpreted as "my way or the highway." Faced with a Hobson's choice, Preston had made the commitment.

Joe Hart had delivered. He'd worked hard in preparing and carrying on negotiations with Preston's banks. He had also showed Preston how to stabilize, restructure, and grow his business. Preston had to admit he'd learned a lot from Joe, and he was grateful.

"Look," he said to Marcia, more amiably, "I am well aware of my promise to Joe, and we both know all he did."

"I just think you have to remember the promise to Joe regarding the Collectibles never really ends," Marcia reminded him gently.

When Joe had called in the IOU, he'd revealed his conditions: he wanted Preston to meet, earn the trust of, and care for several friends of Joe's, including a battered wife, a photographer with a bipolar condition, a man suffering from Alzheimer's, a gambling addict, and a mentally challenged man.

Preston had at first hated and resented the assignment. He could not figure out why Joe would have taken on these people and their issues in the first place, much less pawn them off on someone else. Still Preston felt he had no choice but to live up to his side of the bargain, and he'd set out to find his charges.

Preston had been in the process of tracking down Harry Klaskowski, Joe's photographer friend, when events in his own life took an unexpected turn.

That was a little over a year ago. Life was indeed good for Preston now. And here he was, again being tied by his wife to past commitments. *Why now?* He asked himself, afraid to ask Marcia. *How long do you owe a duty to the dead?*

Preston's automobile stores were booming with business and his real estate was holding its own. He had ample time for golf, the club, and travel, and Marcia was consumed with being a mother. They enjoyed the occasional dinner out, thanks to their godsend of a nanny, and they'd hung onto the home in the Hamptons, where they had taken P.J. a few times to experience the country and to see the ocean. Apart from Marcia's disappointment and occasional nagging, Preston felt that he and his wife were in a better place than ever, except for the P.J. issue. And now there was that accusatory word *slipping*. It left a wrench in his gut and spoiled his afternoon.

He had thought many times about calling Tommy and Missy in the past year, but something always seemed to either come up at the office or appointments with P.J.'s doctors got in the way. As for Harry, Preston had certainly let him know that he'd intended to get together ... it was just that he'd been so busy.

"I'll give Bill or Mary a call about tonight," Marcia said, interrupting Preston's thoughts.

Preston gave Marcia a perfunctory kiss good-bye and headed out the door.

CHAPTER THREE

Katherine rolled over to find Hailey sniffing expectantly at the window, where sunlight was streaming past the gauzy curtain. The chilly spring storm that had brushed the city was past, and she knew Hailey would be eager for an outing. Her mother had warned that Katherine's beloved golden retriever would be a distraction during grad school, and, of course, Susan—who loved dogs—thought anyone who wanted to keep a dog in a cramped apartment in the city was completely nuts. But Katherine couldn't imagine getting through graduate school without Hailey's companionship and moral support.

Four days after the race, Katherine finally felt rested—and hungry. She hopped in the shower, as always appreciating the tremendous water pressure and instant hot temperature inherent in these old Manhattan buildings. She welcomed the pounding of the water on her body, particularly the strained muscles in her neck, shoulders, and back, as she thought about her meeting this morning. She toweled off in front of the mirror. Dissatisfied with what she saw—thighs too big, breasts too small, legs too thick—she renewed her pledge to eat less and work out more, and picked out a pair of khaki pants and a light tan collared blouse with small red flowers.

"C'mon, Hailey, Dr. Gerry's waiting!" Katherine said as she grabbed a scarf, looped it around her neck, and bounded down the twenty-five stairs and around the corner to the coffee shop, her favorite hangout morning and night.

After hot coffee and a bagel with lox and cream cheese, another New Yorker habit she'd been happy to adopt, she hoisted her backpack, took Hailey's leash, and headed north toward Broadway, but not before noticing all the tents already in place in the square. She loved NYC's street fairs, festivals, and farmers' markets, especially the artists and vendors they drew. The fresh produce of the farmers' market always reminded her of home.

When Katherine first came to the city, she had been overwhelmed by the crowds—people rushing everywhere all at once—and the cacophony of honking horns, sirens, jackhammers, traffic, garbage trucks, and street sweepers. A world away from the rural peace and quiet of Marion, New York. But Katherine had quickly absorbed the energy of the city, and now, on her rare trips home, the slow pace, absence of crowds, and quiet felt like forced re-acclimation.

Entering Broadway, Katherine heard a man playing a saxophone beneath the silvery statue of Andy Warhol, as she passed under a block-long scaffold, portending renovation, but without ever seeing a single workman. When she got to East Twentieth, she could just make out the side of her destination, the iconic Flatiron Building and the fourth-floor office of Professor Gerald Simpson, her mentor at the Fletcher Thomas School of Journalism.

She had studied the history of the Flatiron Building and, like so many others, had fallen in love with its architecture and culture. In sharp contrast to the city's grid of modern skyscrapers and office buildings, it seemed a throwback to a different era, a relic of a golden age.

The park was already filled with people as Katherine entered the building from the Broadway side with Hailey and ran her security card through the turnstile.

"Service animal, right?" said the building's voluble superintendent, grinning.

"My very survival depends on her," said Katherine, slipping past.

"How'd Adam's softball team make out?" She hardly waited for the answer. As usual she took the wooden-railed stairs, pausing at the bottom momentarily to admire the view straight up through all twenty-two stories. All trace of muscle pain had vanished.

Anxious to hear the evaluation of her project and turn in her Enduro exposition, Katherine knew Simpson wouldn't care that she was late; she'd waited for *him* countless times, and during the past ten months they'd overcome the initial tension inherent in their professor-student relationship.

Grateful to have such a talented and well regarded teacher, Katherine had come to think of Gerry as a good friend and mentor. While her academic performance was in the top tier of her small class, Katherine appreciated that his teaching her was more important to him than his grading. She knocked, then breezed into the small triangle-shaped office with the smell of old books and narrow tall windows overlooking the junction of Broadway and Fifth.

Professor Simpson, a thin African-American man in his forties with the face of an intellectual, glanced up from his computer monitor. "Miss Kelly and Miss Hailey," he said in a slightly mocking tone, glancing at his watch. "I've been expecting you."

Katherine seated herself in the high-backed wooden armchair in front of his vintage desk, pulled out the thin wooden writing tablet, and sighed, "Okay, let's have it." Hailey lay down at Katherine's feet, nose resting on outstretched paws.

Simpson began slowly, carefully, addressing Katherine in a deliberate manner, as a master chef might prepare a delicate dish. "People should know—and will likely care—about the fraud and abuse in our Medicaid and Medicare health-care delivery systems, and your narrow focus on foreign doctor fraud made the issues easier for the everyday reader to understand," Simpson said, spinning his chair around to the shallow black shelf in front of the window and pouring himself a glass of water. "Would you like some water, Katherine?" he asked.

"Why the formality, Gerry?"

Simpson poured a glass for Katherine, turned his chair back around, rose, handed it to her with a smile, and returned to his seat, taking his sweet time.

"I particularly liked the explanation of the way you got some of those physicians to talk to you—the FBI immunity angle."

"That's the first question you asked me," Katherine said. "'How are you going to get them to talk to you?'"

Katherine knew Simpson would ignore her interruption. "Tying this to billions of dollars of fraud in the '97 Florida Medicaid tobacco litigation, while historical, seemed a bit musty. Your approach worked, however, largely because the tie-in to cost containment made it relevant. In short, you went through the green light and all the way to the finish, with your story reaching its maximum potential, sacrificing neither your integrity nor your credibility. The writing was clear and professional, the research solid, the reporting in-depth and fair," Simpson said, gesturing to emphasize his point.

"I have the feeling there's a 'but' coming," Katherine said, beginning to sweat.

"Your writing is technically good on paper ... excellent, in fact. *But,* what you haven't shown me is *inspired.* Where's the emotional core? Why the distance? Clinical, factually correct, but dry. You're holding back, shying away from driving to the heart of the story, from your point of view. People who follow reporters follow them from *here,*" he said, patting his heart. "Not *here,*" pointing to his head.

"Wow," Katherine said, feeling queasy and rubbing her nose and forehead, "I sure didn't expect that." She reached over and nudged her foot against Hailey for reassurance. She fought the urge to be defensive; objections would be futile and ill-received, she knew. Instead she asked, "Where is this going?"

"Don't fret. Your master's project is done and accepted. But you have the capacity to be more than a good reporter, Katherine. You have a shot at being a great one."

"Thanks, I think. So ... "

"I have an additional assignment for you. Whether it's helpful will be up to you. I want you to have the experience of writing a story in which you necessarily will be emotionally involved."

"I thought the whole idea was *not* to be emotionally involved. Objectivity and all that stuff," Katherine said. "Where's the emotional core in Medicaid fraud?"

"That's the point. Find it. It may be the story of the people committing the fraud. Or their victims. Don't confuse objectivity with impartiality."

Katherine leaned forward, momentarily resting her head on her left palm and then running her hand through her light brown hair. "Got an example?"

Simpson thought for a minute. "You talked about a Haitian doctor practicing in Florida. Undetected for a while. Not licensed. Under the radar. What drove him to game the Florida Medicaid system? Greed? Mistreatment in Haiti? How does he justify his misconduct? Was he a victim of fraud back home? What did he do with the money—give it to poor people, or buy a flashy car?"

Katherine sat back in her chair, dizzy, intersecting thoughts buzzing in her head like a busy railroad switchyard. She also felt conflicted, but there was no question that her mentor had touched a chord. She reached in her handbag, took out a notepad, and started jotting some notes. Simpson smiled and sat down, not saying a word.

When Katherine stopped writing, he continued. "I want you to write a story about a person, living or dead—though not a relative of yours—who has had a substantial influence on someone in your family. This person's influence may have helped your family member overcome a major life obstacle, set a strong example, or assisted in some other way. While you may talk with the family member, also interview others."

"Why?" Katherine asked, her surprise apparent in the tone of her voice. Hailey perked up.

"I know you came in here thinking you had this nailed. You did, of course. You did all the things a good reporter should do. I have no doubt you'll be a good reporter. But for you, that's not enough. Or shouldn't be. If you don't push through 'clinical' to 'inspired,' you will be good, but not great. And you have a chance to be the real thing," Simpson said, standing again. "I hope you understand."

Katherine looked at Simpson intently for a few beats, and then said testily, "Here's my Enduro paper. I thought it was the last."

"I'm eager to read it," he said, taking the paper. "I know this may have you puzzled, even upset. It's just one more paper. This has nothing to do with your graduation. It's not for me; it's for you."

"If it's just one more paper ... for me ... with no grade ... then it's an option, right, not a requirement?"

Simpson smiled. "That's right; it's an option, not a requirement. You don't even have to turn it in ... but if you do, I'd love to read it."

Katherine's head was spinning. She stood up, shook his hand, and, with a tight smile and a tight grip on Hailey's lead, waved good-bye. She walked out of the room more slowly than she had entered it, trying to sort out her emotions. She felt pushed and hurt, but she trusted Simpson, at least as much as she could trust any man. He was drilling too deep, but she also knew he would not have bothered if he hadn't believed in her.

Katherine stared at the tiny square tiles in the old floor, thankful there were no other people in the small elevator vestibule. She couldn't push the button. She walked over to the stairway, putting one hand on the round metal ball atop the square corner of the rail on her left, her other hand on the metal ball on her right, and looked down. As always, she was mesmerized by the symmetry of the rails and the stairs, and the straight view down. Hailey strained at the leash.

Once again Katherine thought of the father she'd never had. *What would it be like if she could talk with him now?*

She moved to the stairs on her left, placed her right hand on the rail, and she and Hailey descended one stair at a time. They finally reached the bottom of the stairway, went through the door, waved to the man behind the security desk as she passed through the turnstile, and merged into the crowds on the street, lost in thought. *A person, not a relative, who has had a substantial influence on one of the members of my family. Mom is my family. Who influenced her? Her old friend . . . her nursing colleagues? This is so stupid.*

Katherine blended into the crowds on Broadway and let Hailey lead. *Living or dead.* She was confused. The person doing the influencing could be living or dead but was not to be a family member. The person being influenced was supposed to be a family member. Where did Simpson come up with this stuff? And what was the tie-in with her holding back? She had never held back with Gerry. Or had he just not asked these kinds of questions?

Katherine found herself thinking about her past boyfriends. Not the casual ones, but the two who had come close. Why did she shut them down? And what about Sean O'Malley from the race—why had she chosen not to call him, either? She'd had a perfectly legitimate reason. Hadn't she? Was there something wrong with her? Was she antisocial, a loner who would end up aloof and apart for the rest of her life?

She reached for her cell phone, found Mother at the top of the favorites, but opted not to tap the screen. She knew her mother would be in the middle of her nursing shift, and she didn't want her to hear her voice right now. Her mom would know in an instant that something was amiss. Katherine kept walking, surrounded by hundreds of people, yet feeling very alone.

CHAPTER FOUR

By nightfall, after a long walk with Hailey, Katherine's anxiety had lifted and she was in a better frame of mind to tackle the problem. This time she dialed the number, and a beloved but tired voice answered.

"Hi, Mom," said Katherine. "Bad time?"

"No, dear, just got home. Are you all right?"

"All good. I got the details on graduation. Are you still sure you want to go through the hassle and expense of coming down?"

"Absolutely! I wouldn't miss it. Go ahead."

Katherine read from the page of information in front of her. "'The ceremony will be held at Lincoln Center, May 1, at 2:00 p.m., with a reception following outside ... the whole process shouldn't take more than an hour.' Have you checked flights?"

The line went silent for a beat, then Katherine heard the clicking of her mother's keyboard, and knew she was scanning a travel site online.

"It looks like I can get a round-trip for under three-hundred dollars, into LaGuardia—leave at nine, arrive about two hours later. Do you think that's too close?" Beth asked.

"No, that'll work. How are you, Mom? Your voice sounds funny."

"I'm ... oh, you know how crazy the shift nurse's position is."

"Okay ... get some sleep," Katherine said. "Are you going to eat at home?"

"I had dinner at the hospital. Are you all done with everything? Did you get your master's critique or whatever it's called?"

"I did. My project's accepted; I'm essentially done. Now, I have to get serious about a job—hope to have some interviews in the next few weeks."

"I know you're dying to get started. I'm so proud of you."

"Thanks, Mom. Listen, before you go, I want to ask you one question. Who would you say has influenced some member of our family? I know it sounds weird, but my mentor, Professor Simpson, has suggested that I do a special paper on a person—not a relative—who has had a positive influence on someone in my family."

"Why does he want to know that?" Beth asked.

"It's complicated. He thinks I have the potential to be a really great reporter."

"Of course, he does. My God, look how well you've done."

"It's about finding what he calls the 'emotional core' of the story, something I'm not objective about or at least involved with personally. Who's influenced you, Mom? Who made a difference in your life? Or Grandpa Adrian or Grandma Colina? I know it's a little weird."

The phone went silent for a while. "Well," Beth said, "you know how close I am to Joan. We've been friends since nursing school. She's done well ... I feel like I'm missing something here. As far as my mother or father being influenced by someone else—other than family—I can't think of anything out of the ordinary. Just good people, who worked hard and led a decent life. I guess Father Patterson has been something of an influence on your grandfather, but not very much on me."

"That's all right, Mom, forget it," Katherine said.

"Are you all right, dear?"

"Fine, Mom. Lot on my mind. By the way, I saw a documentary on television last night about a Navy SEAL operation in Panama having to do with capturing Noriega. The general was actually captured in '89, but the operations apparently started in '88—going into ... hang on a minute, I want to check my notes ... here it is ... Palmerola Air

Base, as it was known then, Operation Golden Pheasant. Was my father ever at Palmerola Air Base?"

She waited for a response from her mother, but none came. Katherine could feel the unwanted angst and, perhaps, animus build in her. She began to feel trapped, out of control, like being in a taxi without air-conditioning on an insufferably hot New York summer day, hopelessly stuck in traffic, late for an important meeting, too many blocks away to walk.

"Mom, are you there?"

"Yes, I'm here," her mother replied in a clipped manner. "As I've told you, I was dating Larry while he was in the Air Force and stationed at Plattsburgh Air Force Base. One night when we were together, he hinted that he'd be receiving deployment orders. I asked him when and how long he'd be away, but he said he did not know, and couldn't say if he did. That was the last night I saw him. I never knew exactly what happened . . . couldn't get it. All I know is that he died during the mission."

"Were there any newspaper accounts of what happened? Do you have anything in writing about my father's death?" Katherine hated herself for pressing so boldly, but in light of her professor's assignment, she was even more consumed by the desire to know more.

"Not much. I'm sorry. That was a long time ago. They closed the Plattsburgh Base, I believe, in 1995 . . . I'll go through my stuff upstairs and see if I can find any newspaper clips or whatever. If I find something, I'll send it to you."

"Sure, Mom. Sorry to bother you with that. I can't wait to see you. Won't be long now. It's beautiful here. You'll love the square."

"See you soon, dear. Good night. I love you," Beth said, and clicked off the phone before her daughter could ask any more probing questions.

★ ★ ★

Once her daughter hit on a topic, Beth knew, she'd persist until she turned up answers—but she honestly had nothing to offer about

Larry Manning's mission or the details of his death. At the time, she'd thought about calling Larry's mother, whom she'd never met, but elected not to. She had never had the woman's address or telephone number, and she wasn't sure that Larry had even told his mother about them.

Beth had noticed a newspaper story about a military operation overrunning Contra rebel supply caches in the San Andrés de Bocay region and deployment of the Seventh Infantry Division Quick Reaction Force. The article talked about support by the Air Force to secure the Honduran Military Base, but didn't mention Larry's Air Force group or anything to do with the Air Force at Plattsburgh, only references to the Army's 82nd Airborne stationed in North Carolina. Beth wasn't sure why she had clipped those articles—except that there were things she'd always wondered about, herself.

Beth knew her daughter and could tell from Katherine's sudden shift from intensity to a light-hearted tone ... *sorry to bother you ... won't be long now ... beautiful here ... you'll love the square ...* that it was not adding up to her. Katherine would not let it go.

Tears in her eyes, Beth rushed to the bathroom and threw up. The time had come. She had to tell Katherine the truth somehow. The whole truth. She was sure she would be punished by God for having lived a lie. She prayed that God would give her time to try to straighten it out.

Beth took a hot bath, then climbed into bed, rolled onto her back, and tried to fall asleep. But Katherine's questions played over and over in her head like a broken message over the hospital intercom.

CHAPTER FIVE

lbows propped on his Italian marble-top desk, Preston went over the operating statements for each of the automotive franchises for the third time, and he wasn't sure he liked what he saw. He buzzed his chief financial officer. If anyone could explain arcane finances in a way ordinary people could understand, it was Casey Fitzgerald, who'd started with Preston more than twenty years ago as a tax accountant fresh out of Wharton and was at his side through the company crisis in 2009. "Casey, I'm looking at the statements. Can you come in? Ask Austin to come, too."

Casey, looking battle-worn and munching on a Snickers candy bar, ambled into Preston's corner office overlooking Ninth Avenue and settled his girth into one of the two tan leather chairs in front of the boss's desk. Austin Disley, tall and dapper in a seersucker suit and bow tie, bounded in and took the other chair. Preston always got a kick out of seeing his longtime pal from prep school, whom he'd hired six months earlier to lend Casey a hand.

"What do you need, Pres?" Austin asked, notebook at the ready.

Casey rolled his eyes.

"Just looking at these figures," Preston replied, "especially the bottom line. Mercedes is okay, but the Bentley numbers are in the basement."

Casey peeled the wrapping from his second Snickers, still chewing on what was left of the first. "We've talked about this," he reminded

Preston. "Either it's a loss leader or you sell it. In a recession, buyers don't want the luxury image—they're stepping down to Porsches and BMWs."

Austin jumped in. "But we can use the loss to offset the gains in the other stores. Right?"

Preston glanced in Casey's direction and rubbed his chin. It was an idea.

★ ★ ★

After a few hours of uneasy sleep, Beth rose, had breakfast, and called the hospital to report that she would not be in that day. She then went to her desk, pulled out the thin pocket file secured with a string closure, and retrieved the Manhattan business phone number she had obtained from her Internet research. She calmed herself and dialed.

"Preston Wilson, please."

Beth gave her name when asked by the receptionist, and as to the nature of the call, simply replied that it was a personal matter. He would know. She waited what seemed like an eternity, fighting the urge to hang up, when a man's voice, polite and pleasant as she remembered, but deeper, came on the line. "This is Preston. Beth Kelly, is it? How may I help you?"

Beth could not speak.

"Hello? Are you there?" Preston asked.

Beth replied faintly but steadily, so as not to be mistaken, "Yes, I'm here. My name is Beth Kelly. It has been a long time, Mr. Wilson. How are you?"

"Do I know you?" Preston asked. "Forgive me, but I don't recognize your name."

"Yes, you know me, but as I said, it's been a long time," Beth said in a trembling voice, reading from the script she had written out for this moment. "I appreciate your taking this call. Close your eyes and think back to when you were twenty-three years old—"

"This is ridiculous," Preston said. "Tell me why you are calling me or I'm going to hang up."

"You need to hear this. Roosevelt Hospital. June 1988. Misdiagnosis of diverticulitis. Actual diagnosis, food poisoning. Your mother was there with you in a VIP room. You were discharged two days later, and you insisted on taking a young nurse to dinner ... in a limousine."

Beth waited a bit for Preston to make the connection, but not hearing a response, continued. "We went to The Flame Restaurant for a bite to eat, to temporary living quarters for a quick change, and on to a club called The Limelight. Any memory of that?"

The phone was silent for several beats, but Beth did not hear a click on the other end. He was still there.

"Yeah. I do sort of remember that. And you were that nurse? Yeah, *Beth.* That *was* a long time ago. Are you in town? How're you doing?"

"I'm fine."

Preston laughed. "Great. So, why are you calling me?"

"I'm in Marion, New York. I live here and work as a nurse at Rochester General Hospital."

"Okay," he said. "I'm trying to figure out ... how I—we—can be of service to you? Are you looking for a car?"

"That's not why I'm calling ... I mean ... I don't want anything, this is not about me. I have a daughter, Katherine, who lives in New York City. She went to Columbia University and is about to receive her master's degree from the Fletcher Thomas School of Journalism."

"Well, congratulations. You must be very proud," Preston said.

Beth then heard him tell someone the conference was over, to leave the room, shut the door, and not disturb him.

"I am," she said, "and you should be, too. She's a fine young lady, Preston. Smart as a whip and with a heart of gold."

Again Preston did not speak for a few seconds, but Beth could hear the sound of his breathing. Finally he asked, "What are you saying?"

"I know this comes as a shock, and I'm sorry about that. What I'm telling you is that you have a wonderful daughter. I've done my best to raise her," Beth said unsteadily, tears flooding her eyes. She paused for a moment, blew her nose, and looked at the ceiling. "I'm really all she has. My dad does what he can at this point, but she needs a father.

She has always needed a father. She needs one now more than ever."

Silence. Then Preston spoke in a low, firm tone. "This makes no sense. Forgive me, but if I'm hearing you right, how do I know that I'm the father?"

"You don't, but I do ... and you will."

"What's that supposed to mean?" Preston asked. Beth heard incredulity, and irritation, rising in his voice.

"It means that I know you're the father because we had sex in your limousine after we left The Limelight. My boyfriend at the time was in the Air Force—off somewhere—classified. There was no one else. You *are* the father."

"Why should I believe you?" Preston shouted, truly angered now.

"You know that, or will, because I am sending you a DNA sample taken from Katherine as well as a sample of my own. You can have a paternity test to confirm the truth."

"That sounds fishy. How do you just happen to have DNA samples?"

"I know this is difficult. It's not easy for me either. If I weren't ... if ... I have DNA samples because I have the beginnings of macular degeneration, and the last time Katherine was with me I wanted to run a test on her to determine whether she was genetically inclined to develop the condition as well. My ophthalmologist took several scrapes from each of us, and I preserved a couple of each. I'd like to send them to you. Do you have a cell phone number, an e-mail address?"

"You're crazy if you think I'm giving you that information. My wife—"

"Believe me, this is hard on me, too. Why don't you think about it—meanwhile write mine down?"

She spoke the information clearly for him.

"I don't want to talk about this anymore now," Preston said. His voice edged with frustration. "I'm married, with a son. If I'm your daughter's father, why didn't you ever let me know you were pregnant? To call out of the blue nearly a quarter of a century later ... "

"I understand. I'm sorry. I'm telling you this now. I'm trying to give you a heads-up. Katherine wants to learn about her father—and she won't let this go. She's like a dog with a bone, and she's a sharp researcher. Sooner or later, she's going to discover that my boyfriend was not her real father. And knowing her, she's also going to figure out, somehow, who is. I wanted you to know first. I don't want this to be any worse than it is. And I don't want Katherine to be hurt any more than she has to be."

"Listen, I don't wish any pain on you or your daughter either—"

"*Our* daughter," Beth managed to say before choking up entirely. "You know where to reach me, Mr. Wilson."

★ ★ ★

Preston marched out of the office, telling his secretary only that he would be gone for the rest of the day, and barked at one of the salesmen to drive him to Trump Tower. In the back of the Bentley demo, Preston uncharacteristically did not speak to the driver. At the Tower he went directly to his thirty-eighth-floor condo, without a word to the doorman either. He hoped he'd find the place empty, if Marcia had taken P.J. in the stroller to the park, but no such luck.

"Hey, surprise," said Marcia, "P.J.'s asleep. Isn't that great? What's going on?"

Preston poured himself a scotch, double, neat, and sat down slowly on the leather love seat. "We have to talk," he said.

Marcia walked over, sat down beside him, and put her arm on his shoulder. "You look like the end of the world has come," she said. "Is it something with the firm?"

"No, I got a phone call today, out of the blue, from a woman named Beth Kelly. It was a strange call. I asked her what I could do for her. She told me ... This is not good, Marcia. She told me that ... that I have a daughter."

"You're right," Marcia said, maintaining a steely cool. "Not good. Go on."

"She said she's a nurse up in Rochester, that I'd met her twenty-four years ago ... apparently at Roosevelt Hospital in Manhattan. I vaguely remember being in the hospital, something that turned out only to be food poisoning. My mother made a big stink, insisted on a fancy room and all of that. I remember her arguing with the doctors."

"Pres, tell me about the *your daughter* part."

"I'm trying to, Marcia. This just happened, for God's sake."

Preston got up slowly, replenished his drink, and sat down again, looking like a deflated version of one of those roadside hot air balloon figures. Marcia had moved to the far end of the love seat, wearing her iciest expression. Preston confessed the circumstances of his brief encounter with Beth Kelly twenty-four years earlier.

"For God's sake, Preston, did you have sex with this woman or not? Or don't you remember?"

"She says we had sex ... in the back of a limo."

"That sounds about right," Marcia said, convinced now. "You were what ... twenty-three at the time? Of course, you had sex. Did you?"

"Yes. It was her idea, if that helps."

"This is the first time you're hearing from this woman in all this time? Something's wrong here. I wouldn't be surprised if an extortion threat wasn't next."

"She ... she was warning me so I wouldn't be blindsided. Or at least that's what she said. And she's trying to shield her daughter from hurt when she discovers the truth about the man she thought was her father."

"So she lied to her daughter then," Marcia said. "And now the wheels are coming off. You know, I can understand how awful it must be for this Katherine, whoever her father is. What are you going to do?"

"I don't know. I don't know if I'm the father."

"Are you going to find out?"

"What do you think I should do?"

"Don't put this off on me, Preston. Just tell me what *you're* going to do."

★ ★ ★

Preston left the tower and took a long walk in Central Park. He passed the joggers, people walking their dogs, parents pushing kids in baby carriages, people sitting on the park benches, all of whom seemed blurred and otherworldly. He came to the lake and sat down on a bench, staring first at the water and then at the sky, as though answers might be found there. Two hours floated by without any.

Preston fought the confusion in his mind, to find a sense of order and peace. He'd grown weary of the conflict with Marcia over P.J., and now this. He hated to be in a box. How in the world could he decide what to do without knowing whether, in fact, he was the father? One part of his brain argued for finding out—making sure. Another part clamored for caution. *Will I be admitting something just by having a test? What kind of record does that leave? Who sees it?* He came to one conclusion: he needed some confidential advice from the right lawyer. Again.

Preston called his corporate counsel, said he had a close friend with a serious matrimonial problem, and asked him to find a sharp, discreet lawyer in that field. Preston dismissed his lawyer's inquiry as to what was really going on with a "just do it" admonition, and directed him to set up an appointment as soon as possible, preferably first thing in the morning.

CHAPTER SIX

Preston walked into the law offices of Forsyth and Forsyth, on the twenty-third floor of the Empire State Building, for his 9:00 a.m. appointment, pleased that his corporate attorney was able to set up the meeting and that he'd thought Benjamin Forsyth was the right lawyer.

Ben greeted Preston on time and warmly in the waiting room, making Preston feel as comfortable as he could under the circumstances. They walked to Ben's office, where the attorney closed the double doors, turned, and stood facing Preston, appearing to take his measure. He then gave Preston a brief summary of his practice and they agreed on the ground rules, including the understanding of the protections, application of privilege, and strict confidentiality of their communications and relationship. Preston suggested they move to a small table and chairs.

After they settled in, Ben said, "What's going on, Preston, and how, specifically, can I help?"

"I assume you have knowledge of my background?"

"Yes, to the extent your corporate counsel has filled me in, what I see on your website, and what you have told me today. I understand you want to talk about a matrimonial problem that concerns ... a friend of yours."

"Actually, I told my lawyers that because this is very personal. It's

not a matrimonial problem, but it is a surprise event in my life."
Preston told his new lawyer about Beth Kelly's phone call. "I guess
at this point I need to know if I'm in the right place. Is this the kind
of thing you handle?"

"Yes," Ben replied. "Paternity cases often go hand in hand with
domestic relations, as you may imagine. You've obviously given this
some thought. Do you believe this woman?"

"Well, after the shock of the call, I did remember the ... encounter.
Whether that makes me the father? I don't know. And why she chooses
to tell me twenty-four years after the fact is beyond me."

"It's usually driven by money. But I didn't hear you say that she
asked you for money."

"Not in so many words. She did say she didn't want anything, that
it was not about her. But I don't know this woman. Money changes
people. She may be setting me up. Maybe this is all a scam."

"Let's separate the issues," Ben said, looking at his yellow pad full
of notes. "First, is there sufficient evidence to conclude that in all
probability you are the father? DNA, assuming the samples are correct and the procedures are followed, is probative of paternity. From
what you've told me, she has a sample—and is willing to provide it.
What we don't have is proof of the chain of handling of this sample.
In other words, what is the scientific proof each step of the way from
the taking of the sample from your alleged daughter to your receipt
of it? We can only assume that the sample is what this woman says it
is, and how she took it from her daughter and so on."

"Do DNA samples have to be refrigerated or kept in a certain way?"
Preston asked.

"No, they don't have to be refrigerated. But if the sample could
be confirmed as coming from the young woman, genetic profiling of
DNA establishes paternity with a ninety-nine percent or higher probability. In short, if those things hold true, it's almost certain you're
the father—and the court would agree."

Preston's jaw tightened as he considered the implications. The
lawyer continued.

"The daughter, however, is, as I understand it, of maturity—over twenty-one years of age—and emancipated. That would lead to the next piece of analysis: what are your financial and/or legal obligations to this young lady?"

"What are my options?" Preston asked.

Ben Forsyth spelled them out in careful lawyer-speak. "This woman, Beth Kelly, and her daughter, Katherine Kelly, have the burden of proof as to paternity and any support obligation. Practically speaking, Beth Kelly would not be in a position to assert such claims against you for herself at this late date. Your options include: one, doing nothing and waiting to see what action, if anything, is brought against you; two, engage in negotiations with Beth and/or her daughter to determine what claims, if any, are being contemplated. From what you have told me, initially, an optimistic read would be that Katherine's mother wanted you to know so you could determine what, if anything, you felt you might like to do."

"That's sort of what she said. I don't know if I can believe her. But I will say, I felt like I could. Actually, she was really being ... she was ... I thought she was looking out for her daughter, who needed a father, and she wanted me to know before her daughter found out. She thought that would be better for her daughter and for me."

Ben nodded and continued with his options. "Three, you could have a DNA sample taken, have it compared to the one you have, and see whether you are the father. And, finally, you could also ask the mother to have her DNA taken."

"Beth says she has samples from herself and her daughter." Preston quickly explained the mother's recent diagnosis and concerns.

"Obviously, the mother in this case is either incredibly clever or otherwise being quite helpful," Ben said.

"She's apparently a good nurse."

"Look, if she has the samples, and sends them to you, the tests will tell you whether you are the father or not. If you aren't, you could either forget the entire matter, or let Beth Kelly know the results. If she does not accept the results, she could still claim paternity on behalf of her daughter and sue you—or have her daughter sue you—and you would have a defense. If you are the father, then you'd be in a position to evaluate how you want to handle the situation going forward."

Preston fell back on his favorite decision-making strategy. "What do you advise me to do?"

"Make the decisions based on the input I've given you."

"What would you do?"

"I'm not in your situation, and I hope I never am. I'd rather you make the decision after you're fully informed. It sounds to me like Beth Kelly now believes, for whatever reason, her daughter needs a father and wants to make it easy for you by sending the samples. Sometimes things are as they seem and people do the right thing in life. If you trust her and think you may be the father, I'd have the test done and rule it in or out. But, it's up to you."

"If I have the test done, is the result confidential?"

"Yes."

"Thanks for your input," Preston said getting up, walking around the room, and stopping to look out the window. "I have to process all of this. Can't believe I'm in this situation. I have a one-year-old son—who can't hear—and now I may have a twenty-three-year-old daughter I've never seen."

The lawyer put his hand on Preston's shoulder and told him that he understood and was sorry he was going through all of this. Ben picked up one of his business cards from the desk, wrote his cell phone number on the back, and told Preston to feel free to call him at the office or on his cell phone anytime.

Preston continued to stare out the window, not wanting Ben to see the tears in his eyes.

He reached for his iPhone and tapped out a message to the address he'd been given: *Send the samples.*

CHAPTER SEVEN

The limousine was waiting, of course, by the time Preston reached street level. He waved it away. "I'll walk. Need the fresh air."

Preston welcomed the twenty-one-block walk to home but dreaded facing Marcia. At Thirty-Seventh Street, his blood still pounding in his ears, he took a right turn, increasing his pace as he considered the comforts of the Union League Club. Yes, that was the ticket.

Preston entered the club through the Thirty-Seventh Street doorway, waved at the blue-uniformed doorman, and immediately wrapped himself in the familiar invisible cloak of protection. He climbed the bilateral marble staircase on the right and proceeded past the pool tables and up the two steps to the bar. With a nod to Eddie, a Chivas Regal, neat, appeared on the old mahogany bar top. In one swallow it disappeared.

The turnaround of his dealerships had allowed Preston to finally push back, if not completely overcome, his fear of failure. He'd put aside the dread of repeating the mistakes of his father, the insecurity he had carried since hiding as a fifteen-year-old in the butler's pantry off the kitchen, where he had listened to his mother tell his father, *You have failed to deliver on every significant business matter you have ever undertaken,* and learned that his father had nearly exhausted the money his grandfather had left to his mother with nothing left for his son. That he was an abject failure. *An abject failure.*

He knew he owed Joe Hart for the turnaround. Still, Preston told himself he had earned his success, achieved it with skill sets Hart did not possess, and that he had fulfilled his obligation to his rescuer. Besides, Joe was gone. And Preston had named his son after Joe. At what point was enough enough? He recognized he'd never be able to satisfy Marcia on this subject.

Enough of the Collectibles. His thoughts turned to P.J., but that only made him more somber. *I finally have a son and he's born deaf.*

He tried to look at the bright side. The boy could hear some sounds. And the pediatrician Preston had sought for a second opinion had counseled a wait-and-see approach about P.J.'s hearing, feeling that P.J. might gain hearing as he developed. That advice conflicted sharply, however, with the collective opinion of the ear-nose-and-throat specialist, the audiologist, and P.J.'s original pediatrician, the team Marcia's maternity doctor had marshaled for consultation.

That trio of doctors had emphasized the value of early screening and, having found significant loss, wanted P.J. fitted with hearing aids in his first six weeks. They stressed the critical importance of stimulation to P.J.'s brain from various sounds, without which they argued the brain would not develop the necessary speech, language, and cognitive functions.

Preston desperately wanted his son to have the best medical treatment possible, but he also believed the physicians he'd consulted and he wanted to at least give his son the chance to develop his hearing.

The conflict opened old emotional wounds between him and Marcia, and Marcia's intensity combined with her confidence in the rightness of her position made Preston once again doubt that she viewed him as her equal. He feared she saw him as lacking the horsepower upstairs to fully understand the situation. He sensed he was losing Marcia once again.

The second and third scotch didn't mend matters at all, and Preston hadn't even gotten to the third theater in his head—whether or not he had a daughter, and whether he should take the test to find out. He ordered a fourth scotch. Eddie complied.

Preston pushed back from the bar, looked at the tables behind him, and then glanced around the corner into the wood-paneled dining area to see how crowded it had gotten.

"Would you like anything to eat, Mr. Wilson?"

"That's a good idea, Eddie—all the way around. I'll have a steak sandwich and some potato salad, please. I'll be in there. Thank you."

"Of course, Mr. Wilson."

Drink in hand, Preston carefully lowered himself into his seat at the wooden table alongside the wood-paneled windows overlooking the majestic rising marble staircase and entrance to the grand room and elevators. He fidgeted with the silverware. He stole glances at his watch, his restless legs moving up and down more than usual.

Suddenly Preston pushed his chair back, rose, and charged out through the entranceway, past the bar and the billiard tables, through the doorway, and headed toward the phone booths. He chose one on the far left, entered, closed the door, pulled out his cell phone and called Marcia. He loved the Union League Club's rule barring the use of cell phones anywhere but in those old-world booths, and even in his distressed state he respected it.

"Hi, honey," he said when she answered. "How are you?"

"I'm fine, Pres. Where are you? I tried to reach you at the office but they thought you were AWOL. Is everything all right?" They were adept at this evasive dance by now.

"I'm at the club. Everything's fine. How's P.J.?"

"Are you sure? P.J.'s adorable. He's sleeping at the moment. Are you having a business lunch? You sound a little funny."

"No, I had a—meeting earlier, and I just felt like grabbing a bite at the club alone."

"Well, that sounds good. Maybe you could get some steam while you are there, and a massage. Did you have anything specific in mind when you called?"

"No, nothing specific. I just wanted to hear your voice. Lot on my mind to sort through."

Preston could hear Marcia breathing, but not saying a word. His mind was racing. He wondered how much he should tell her. How much more did his wife really want to know?

"I went to see an attorney this morning ... about ... the phone call. I know this is an awful situation, Marcia. I'm trying to determine what to do."

"What did the lawyer tell you to do?"

"He just gave me options."

"Imagine that. And?"

"He can arrange a paternity test." He latched onto the attorney's precise language. "Ninety-nine percent accurate. At least."

"You got yourself into this mess, Preston. For what it's worth, it seems to me the first step is to take the test and find out how real all of this is. But it's your decision. I doubt if any more scotches will help."

He pondered that for a long moment.

"Just let me know if you'll be home for dinner. And by the way, Tommy Greco called here looking for you."

Marcia gave Preston Tommy's number. He thanked her, thanked God for having her, returned to the dining room, devoured his lunch, and headed for the exercise room. Yes, a workout and a massage. That should help.

CHAPTER EIGHT

Refreshed, Preston went back to the phone booths and returned Tommy Greco's call, feeling guilty that he had not spoken with him for several months.

"Hi, Tommy, what's up?"

"I'm in New York and I wanna talk to you. It's about me and Missy."

The last time Preston had seen Tommy and Missy was at Joe's funeral. Tommy had actually met Missy through Preston; Tommy had helped Missy work through a nasty situation with her abusive ex-husband.

Tommy, who grew up in the Italian-American community in Niagara Falls, New York, knew all about abuse from his own youth.

"How's Missy doing?" Preston asked.

"She's good. We got married."

His mind in a cloud, Preston struggled to shift his thoughts from his own problems to find the right response. He vaguely remembered receiving an invitation; he assumed Marcia had covered for him.

"Hey, you there?" Tommy said. "Am I getting you in *a interruption?*"

Hearing Tommy's voice and his unconventional way with English jarred Preston back into focus. "No, you're fine, Tommy. Sorry, a lot on my mind. Congratulations. Missy's the best!"

Preston thought about his first meeting with Missy in Las Vegas, and how insightful and helpful she was with his own difficulties with Marcia.

"Where are you?" Preston asked. "Do you want to get together?"

"I had an important appointment. I'm downtown. Forlini's, Baxter Street. Quit screwing around. You free or not?"

Preston could not help but smile. He could picture Tommy, the master of mixed metaphors and garbled words, sitting in a restaurant, beefy, broad shoulders, tie loosened around his size twenty-inch neck, staring into Preston's eyes. Tommy's bluntness made Preston feel warm. Just what he needed.

"Be there in fifteen." Preston heard Tommy hang up.

★ ★ ★

Preston entered through the door leading to the restaurant—not the bar—and found Tommy sitting alone at the end booth on the right side beneath an Italian painting. Tommy leaned forward, his five-four solid frame pushing against the table, and warmly crushed Preston's hand with his own as Preston slid into the booth.

"Good to see you, Tommy. You're looking great. How do you do it?"

"*Genetikets,*" Tommy replied.

"What?" Preston said.

"Y'know, family. And olive oil."

Preston finally smiled as he figured it out. They ordered wine, talked for a while, and then looked at the menu.

"What would you like, Tommy?"

"Linguini and *clams shells.*"

Preston started to laugh but caught himself. *Close enough.* "I guess I'll have the veal parmigiana."

After talking with Tommy for more than an hour, and downing two bottles of Chianti and a marvelous dinner, Preston felt the best he had all day. He told Tommy all about his stores, how he had assembled a remarkable sales team and hired a new vice president of finance, and how well the company was surviving under the circumstances. He talked about Marcia and told him about their son.

"Hey—that's great. P.J. How d'ya like that? The 'Joseph.' That comin' from where I'm thinkin'?" Tommy clapped his hands and then opened and lifted them, palms up.

"It is, in honor of Joe," Preston said.

After the waiter cleared the main course, Tommy put his huge hands on the white tablecloth and looked into Preston's eyes. "I've gotta important situation to ask you about," he said.

"Sure. Go ahead, Tommy."

"As I told ya, Missy and me got married in Vegas."

"Where were you married?"

"I just told ya."

"I mean, in a church or what?"

"The Wedding Chapel, ya know, not the Little White one. We went for the Viva Las Vegas. Real classy. Missy's mother, Mrs. Scarlatti, came all the way from Lyons, New York, and some of Missy's show-girl friends were there. My friend Frankie Vittarone from Chicago was my best man, and his guy, Jimmy, and a few of their friends were there, too. Oh, and Harry showed up and followed through."

"How about your family, Tommy? Were they there?"

"They've never been there. The ones there were my family."

Tommy had dropped out of high school and taken a job working at the Corner, a neighborhood bar where the patrons became his family and teachers, and the lessons learned were how to bet and fight, and the rules for survival. His de facto home was a far cry from the tourist image of Niagara Falls. Tommy had gone to Vegas to start a new life and become a better man.

Preston pictured the scene at the chapel in Las Vegas, those present, and how important they were to Tommy and Missy. Other than introducing Marcia to Tommy and Missy at dinner during a business trip to Las Vegas, and arranging for Missy to have an audition as a dancer at the MGM Grand, Preston had had no contact with either of them since Joe's funeral, an omission Marcia had reminded him about frequently.

Preston thought about Harry. He still hadn't even met the man.

"What did you mean about Harry showing up and following through?"

"We didn't know Harry until Joe's funeral. He didn't say a lot, but I tell ya ... he was close to Joe, and he's a stand-up guy. That's enough for me. Missy and me made a point of getting to know him. He's something else. A photographer. Professional. A musician—plays the piano, plays that squeeze box thing. And he has a band. He calls it something funny. Oompah or somethin'. When he heard Missy and me were tying the knot, he offered to come out, take pictures, and bring his band to play at the reception. We couldn't believe it. And he did, brought his guys with him, and it was outta this world."

"That's great," Preston said. "Where did you guys go on your honeymoon?"

"That's what I wanna talk to you about. We went to Elko—near the Ruby Mountains. Missy and I like it up there. She's always been crazy about kids. Me, too. We decided to have a camp up there for kids. Ya know what I mean? Kids that have had it tough. Total naturalization. It's in foreclosure, and I think we can get enough to buy it," Tommy said.

He went on to describe Missy's plan to open a dance studio for girls with special needs, and his plan to make sports available to boys and girls, including basketball, baseball, and soccer—and even an indoor-outdoor swimming pool.

Preston was surprised at the thought that Tommy and Missy would leave Las Vegas—but even more amazed that they would want to start a camp for children with special needs. Still, he could see that Tommy came alive talking about it. He tried to be careful.

"That's quite an ambitious undertaking," Preston said. "How much is this going to cost?"

"We think we can get a sixty-eight-acre ranch with a view of the mountains for just under a million. It needs a little work, you know, fixing up."

"Where are you going to get the money?"

"We're working on that now. Maybe the ponies'll be good to me,"

Tommy said. "I coulda got all the money I need from certain friends of mine. It woulda been easy, but, like I learned from Missy, sometimes it's better to leave the strings off."

Preston thought about when Missy got in trouble with her ex-husband, and how Tommy knew someone who made the problem go away. He could see the influence Missy was having on Tommy.

"Missy's quite a woman," Preston said. "She's obviously been a big help."

Tommy smiled, pulled out a cigar, and then mumbled something derisive about New York's Mayor Bloomberg and put the cigar back in his breast pocket.

"Missy and me have been saving all we can. There are some legitimized organizations which are interested, and we will be hittin' them up for donations. It'll be tough. We can use all the help we can get."

"If you want, my financial people can look over the land and the project. I have some talented staff on the real estate side. If your camp projects a positive cash flow, I may be interested in investing in it."

"This is somethin' Missy and me believe in. It don't have to make money, just enough to keep it going. We both know what it's like to be knocked around as a kid and, thanks to Joe, we know it's okay to chase our dreams."

Preston didn't really know how to respond to that, fearful that Tommy and Missy were headed for financial disaster. His mind drifted back. Preston had found the day overwhelming—and his attempted escape to the club helpful but incomplete. Now, here he was talking with Tommy in Little Italy about a camp in Nevada for children with special needs.

Only then did Preston regain focus and remember to call Marcia—belatedly—to tell her of his surprise dinner partner. He excused himself and made the call. The fact that it was Tommy got him out of the doghouse, and he returned to the table promptly.

"What kind of improvements are you going to need, and what will that cost? I'm assuming the infrastructure—water, sewer, electricity, roads—are all in and the zoning is appropriate for what you want to do. Is that right?"

"Missy and I have penciled it. You own a lot of real estate. Been through this before. That's why I wanted to talk to you, y'know, get the business angle. And, if you wanna, you could donate some money to the camp. Sort of start-up. Get a little vigorish."

"I can have my people look at it," Preston said. "Send the workup to Casey, my CFO."

"What workup?"

"The information you have about the real estate, its cost, the improvements, how much will be financed, the terms, and the pro forma, P&L, and balance sheet for the camp, all that stuff."

"I ain't an accountant, but I got some go-to guys on the numbers. I'll get it together."

Tommy reached over the table and shook Preston's hand again. "Thanks for looking into this. I appreciate it," he said. "And I think it's a special thing you got with your kid, P.J. Makes me think about Joe." Tommy crossed himself. "You gotta be proud."

Preston looked down at the table for a minute and then back up at Tommy. They finished off the wine and ordered dessert. But nothing could make the conflict Preston felt go away.

Finally, Preston blurted out, "P.J.'s hearing-impaired."

"So?" Tommy said. "Kids need special attention. Besides, we all got something. He may turn out okay; you said he's only one year old, right?"

Preston was surprised by Tommy's reaction and wondered if he appreciated the full import of the problem. "Let me explain. They tested him at birth. They can do that now. He didn't pass. But I agree with you. I talked to a pediatrician who told me his hearing may develop, but it's too soon to know. Marcia's pushing for having him fitted with hearing aids now. Can you imagine that?"

"Yeah. I mean, if that's what it takes. Important thing is let 'em know you love 'em." Another hand clap and a big smile.

★ ★ ★

Preston awoke that Saturday morning with a slight headache. Over breakfast with Marcia, he described his previous day to her—from the visit to the lawyer's office to his dinner with Tommy, leaving out nothing except Tommy's feelings on the hearing-aids issue. Preston knew on some level he must be testing his wife's patience, but he'd never held anything back.

He spent some time with P.J., but felt restless and a bit irritable. He tried watching television but soon became bored and decided to take a walk. Maybe that would help clear the fog that had settled over his head during the past forty-eight hours.

As he was leaving the lobby, the doorman handed him a Federal Express envelope. "Just signed for this, Mr. Wilson," he said. "I was about to call and let you know. It must be important."

One glance at the Marion, New York, address told him it was. He dialed Ben Forsyth's cell number.

"Look, I'm sorry to bother you on the weekend," he told the attorney, "but the package I mentioned is here already. I don't want to open it and risk damage or contamination or anything—what should I do?"

"Here's my home address. Bring it by, and I'll take care of things from here."

Preston at first felt a shock at how fast this was all moving, but he had to admire Beth's determination and the integrity of her follow-through.

After taking a cab to Ben's apartment and giving him the package, Preston decided to go to the Manhattan store, even though it was a Saturday, to take a look at how the sales team was operating and try to put this matter out of his head. He knew he would never have peace until it was determined, one way or the other, whether Katherine Kelly was, in fact, his daughter.

CHAPTER NINE

Katherine checked her mailbox at the bottom of the stairs and found everything she didn't want, but still no letter from her mother. Graduation was only a week away now; maybe she was just holding onto information to bring it in person. But Katherine's need to know something, anything, was gnawing at her.

She went back up, sat down at the tiny bistro table, fired up her Mac, and Googled obituaries for Lawrence M. Manning, realizing she had never even known her father's rank. After exhausting that thread on several dead ends, and prompted by the Navy SEALs documentary, she typed in Operation Golden Pheasant—Honduras—1988. While the results provided considerable detail, they yielded nothing about Airman Manning nor his unit from Plattsburgh, New York.

After another two hours of exploring leads and getting nowhere, Katherine felt like she was lost in a corn maze, desperate to find her way out—time for a walk in the park. Hailey was happy to get out, too. It was midday, the tents were up, and the crowds were milling around the park—a sight that always helped clear Katherine's head and made her feel better. Katherine browsed the display of mushrooms in one tent; racks of fresh, organic whole wheat bread in another; apples, peaches, plums, and other fresh fruit in the next, delighting in the smells and sights. An impromptu quartet was singing in one corner across the street from Barnes & Noble, while a magician was performing on the east side of Union Square. Lots of people were walking their dogs. The smell of fresh flowers was in the air.

As Katherine tagged along behind Hailey, it hit her. What about the Plattsburgh Air Force Base personnel files? Why hadn't she tried that?

She raced back to her apartment, pursued that lead, and once again, came up empty. But she had a hunch: what if former Plattsburgh personnel communicated with each other, to trade gossip and old memories? If classmates used the Internet to keep up, surely military units did, too.

It didn't take long to locate several bulletin boards and identify one that allowed visitors to post queries. She composed a short, simple message. "Did anyone know my father, Larry M. Manning, who was stationed at Plattsburgh Air Force Base around 1988? kat.journ@gmail.com." Maybe this would be the breakthrough—if she could make contact with someone who'd known him, maybe it would lead to hard information.

Before she'd even finished making a sandwich for lunch, she heard the chime announcing new e-mail.

The answer was brief. "I knew Larry Manning and served with him in Central America. I was on special ops in his unit when he was killed 3 April 1988. He was a good man. I'm so sorry for your loss. I can't say any more than that, so please don't contact me." There was no signature, only a cryptic e-mail address in the header.

Katherine nearly leapt off her seat. A connection, at last. She felt for her crimson pen in the outside pocket of her handbag, and not immediately locating it, rose in a panic and began to search frantically for it. She was relieved when it dropped to the floor but examined its thin shell carefully for any cracks. Satisfied that the only pen that would do had survived intact, she grabbed a pad and scribbled out the figures, hoping that what she came up with in her head was wrong. But what if . . . Katherine thought about all her mother's hedging, her failure to send the newspaper article, and the peculiar change of tone the subject imposed on her voice.

Katherine reread the guarded e-mail, this time focusing on *"specials ops ... can't say any more than that, so please don't contact me."* She was seeing a black hole and digging it deeper. This was not just the truth she was seeking in one of her academic investigations. This was *her* truth, with no certainty that once known, it would set her free. It was as if she were experiencing tremors increasing in strength, projecting an earthquake, and threatening her very foundation. Katherine knew she had to talk to her mother, she had to do it soon, and she had to do it in person.

CHAPTER TEN

Beth's plane from Rochester was late, causing her to arrive at LaGuardia with only about an hour to spare. To save time, she had packed light and carried her bag on the plane. When she arrived, she had stopped in the ladies' room to freshen up, but spent far longer there than she had intended, not counting on her nerves causing gastric implications. She'd heard nothing in response to her package to Preston Wilson. Now that she was about to see her daughter again face to face, would she be able to keep her composure? Or keep her secret until she was ready to tell it?

Beth appreciated Katherine's making arrangements for her to stay at the Empire Hotel across from Lincoln Center, and even though it had been many years, she remembered the area well. She knew Katherine's tiny apartment had only a bed and a couch, but she thought that setting might make the talk easier somehow. At the hotel, she felt like a nurse being called before a peer review committee to explain a patient's death.

As Beth rehearsed in her mind her rationale for withholding the truth—that it was best for everyone—she felt her blood coursing through her body, overwhelmed by the emptiness of the justification. In the next moment, she thought, *it was not an attempted justification, but rather an act of kindness to my father and mother. They had*

already reached the conclusion that Larry was the father. They had
already accepted Larry's death. And they were committed to helping
her raise her child. What good would it have done to take all that
away from them? And Katherine?

As Beth struggled with all of these conflicting thoughts, she felt
dizzy and recognized the onset of another splitting migraine. She
fought the urge to take more ibuprofen, knowing she had already
exceeded the limit. She prayed her daughter wouldn't hate her, that
Katherine could somehow get over this.

Beth worried in the cab ride all the way in from the airport, checked
her bag with the doorman as Katherine had suggested, tried to calm
herself, and headed for Lincoln Center. She was scared. She knew
how strong-headed her daughter could be, how driven. She would
say she understood, but would she really? Could she?

★ ★ ★

Katherine, in dark glasses, sat near the iconic fountain in front of
the Metropolitan Opera House, keeping an eye out for her mother.
She knew the ceremony, with only eighteen graduates, would be brief,
which was fine with her. She'd anticipated this event for what seemed
like forever but now, on this clear, bright day, she saw only a dark,
threatening sky.

The cloud of her suspicion had hovered over her all week. No new
information had arrived to confirm it or sweep it away. She'd thrown
herself into job-search mode to avoid any all-out storm that might
have completely ruined her graduation. She'd made it a point not to
call Gerry Simpson. She'd discouraged Susan, her best friend from
Columbia days, from taking time off to attend the ceremony—Susan
would have taken one look at her face and demanded her to spill. And
she certainly hadn't called her mother.

At her graduation from Columbia, she had thought wistfully about
the father she never knew, imagining what it would be like to have
him standing quietly by, holding her hand, smiling with pride. Those
thoughts were now wiped out, as if she had hit the delete button in

the computer in her head. Now, she found herself avoiding the pockets of students and their parents and friends hovering in the square.

She spied her mother walking up the steps, wearing a white dress with large yellow flowers and a lightweight yellow sweater, with a matching handbag over her shoulder. Katherine thought for a fleeting moment of standing up and lifting the hem of her master's gown to reveal the yellow dress under it. But she couldn't fake her mood that far.

Instead she waved, made herself smile, and stood to meet her mother's long embrace—long enough to fix her resolve, settle down, be grateful, and remember everything her mother had done to make this day possible.

"I haven't missed out, have I?" Beth asked.

"No, you're fine, Mom. You ... look beautiful ... love your dress. I'm so glad you're here." Katherine sensed her words sounded hollow.

"Come on, Katherine. This is huge. I'm proud," Beth said, hugging Katherine again.

Katherine led her mother into Avery Fisher Hall, up the stairs to the narrow second floor gallery on the right, and selected a seat with the best view over the high barrier overlooking the auditorium.

"I'm not sure how long you'll have to wait, but once the pomp and circumstance starts, it should be over fairly soon."

"Hope not. I want it to last," Beth said.

"We'll meet downstairs in the lobby after the ceremony," Katherine said, kissing her mother, and leaving the visitors' area as others were filing in.

★ ★ ★

After the formalities, speeches, and diploma ceremony, the small group of graduates, parents, and well-wishers gathered in the front lobby and then moved to the reception in the square. Katherine took the opportunity to introduce her mother at last to Gerry Simpson.

"Pleased to meet you Professor Simpson," Beth said, offering her hand, which Gerry shook with obvious enthusiasm.

"I'm very glad to meet you as well," he said. "Your daughter is a star in the making. It has been my honor to teach her. I know how proud you must be."

"Thank you. My daughter has always been special."

There was silence for a beat, and then Beth lightly laid her hand on Professor Simpson's arm and said, "There is one thing that has me puzzled, though."

"Yes?" Simpson asked.

"I don't understand why you would ask a student to write a paper about a family member ... especially when it wasn't required for graduation?"

Professor Simpson stared in silence, first at Beth, then at Katherine. "It's nuanced, and I thought, private. I meant what I said about Katherine. She has the rare capacity to be a great reporter. I thought the request would help."

"Help how?" Beth persisted.

Katherine felt ill. She didn't register the next thing her mentor said, or what followed. The faces in front of her became distorted in waves of movement. Another ocular migraine was coming on. Her mother's ophthalmologist had told her the best way to deal with them was to eliminate the triggers, starting with avoiding stress. *Life plays cruel jokes,* Katherine thought, as she tried to signal her mother that it was time to go outside to the reception.

"We really have to leave now, Gerry," Katherine said, taking her mother's arm and ushering her to the door. "We don't want to be impolite and miss the reception," she said, though that was exactly what she knew would happen.

"I agree," Professor Simpson said with a nod and a warm smile. "I'm happy to have met you, Ms. Kelly. I hope you'll see the potential of the assignment in time."

★ ★ ★

In the few minutes it took for them to cross the street to the hotel and take the elevator to Beth's room, Katherine's vision had returned to normal and the walls had very nearly stopped spinning.

"I'm so sorry one of these episodes had to spoil your big day," said Beth, laying a cool cloth across her daughter's forehead. "I'm afraid you've inherited that from me."

"Or maybe from someone else," Katherine said acidly. "But then, how would I know?" She immediately regretted her words. Her mother was silent.

Katherine sat up on the corner of the bed in the tiny room. "Mom, I need to ask you some questions I probably should have asked you long ago. If I've learned anything in all this journalism stuff, it's that assumptions are dangerous. You know I love you. You've been everything for me. I know I've pestered you for more information about my father ... "

"Katherine, I've ... "

"Please ... let me finish. When I talk with someone during an investigation and she seems reluctant to give me the answers or let me see the documents she says she has, I get an uneasy, queasy feeling, the same feeling I have about our conversations about my father. I need to know all you know and have not told me about my father, including the date of his death."

"I know, I don't have a lot, I've tried ... " Beth said.

Katherine put up her hand, signaling her mother to let her finish.

"When I didn't hear more from you about Operation Golden Pheasant, I did some further research. I stumbled on a chat site for folks involved in one way or another with what was going on with my father's unit back then. I got an e-mail from a man who served with my ... with Larry Manning. Mom, do you know when Larry Manning died?"

The room seemed to grow even smaller.

Finally, Beth said, "I loved Larry, but I was not his wife. As I told you, one of his buddies, I didn't know him, called me to tell me. I was shocked. I cried long and hard. I don't remember any more about the conversation."

Katherine could see the pain in her mother's eyes, but also the slight twitch in her lower lip, her flushed cheeks, and her eyes blinking more than usual: the cluster of multiple behavior telltale signs she had learned to recognize when a person is lying or holding back the truth. Katherine knew there was more.

"It's too—close in here," said Beth. "Is there somewhere we can get some air?"

They took the elevator to the roof, where they searched for refuge from the afternoon sun.

"After you called me, I went up in the attic and found the article," Beth admitted, eyes blinking more rapidly than ever. "I didn't bring it because it doesn't make any difference."

"Actually, it makes all the difference in the world," Katherine said. "The man who responded to my e-mail said that Airman Larry Manning died on April 3, 1988—eleven months before I was born. I'd like to know if that is accurate. If it is, then he's not my father. That makes a difference to me, Mother. A *big* difference."

CHAPTER ELEVEN

The slanting sunlight was blinding. Both women reached into purses for sunglasses, then spotted an unoccupied canvas cabana, away from the poolside sunbathers. Katherine lowered the curtains on both sides and kicked off her shoes. She called the waiter over and ordered two vodka tonics, double.

"I never knew how much of what little information I had was true. It was military. Who knows what really happened? Or when? I didn't ... not being Larry's spouse meant I had no standing. It was awful, not being in a position to demand answers. I was the one who loved him. The article didn't refer to Larry at all. I know why it matters to you, and I know why it doesn't matter to me, except that it matters to you."

Katherine watched her mother rub the back of her neck, and the tears form in her mother's eyes—the dam broke as Katherine could no longer hold her own tears back. She felt her body move over to her mom, and her arms reach out and hold her. They stayed locked together arm in arm for a time, not saying a word. Finally, Katherine heard herself say, "It must have been terrible. I can only imagine."

"I loved Larry and he loved me. But he loved the Air Force more," Beth blurted, reaching for the box of tissues on a nearby table. "I tried to get him to marry me, I really tried. And then he was off, gone. Some men would rather fly and fight than ... if he didn't want me ... I thought it was wrong to try to keep him. I don't expect you to understand."

"This much I understand. Larry Manning was not my father. But you know who is."

Katherine watched Beth's head and shoulders drop, as if her mother were shrinking before her eyes. Then Beth sat up, straightening her back as if raised by an imaginary rope from a pulley in the cabana frame, removed her sunglasses, and brushed the hair back from her face with her hand. Katherine decided not to say a word.

"I was twenty-one and had just graduated from Plattsburgh. Larry had been gone for weeks. Not a word. I was starting a residency program at Roosevelt Hospital, not far from where we are today. One of my first patients was a young, rich guy who wanted—after he was discharged—to take me to dinner. Of course I refused, but when I finished my shift that night he was waiting in a big black limousine. I was exhausted and hungry. And afterward, I persuaded him to ride around for a while."

"What does that mean?" Katherine asked, removing her own glasses.

"Well, the club had been great; the limo was luxurious; I'd had a few drinks; and he had been a perfect gentleman. I ... "

"Came on to him?" Katherine said.

Their drinks arrived, and Beth paused long enough to drink half of hers at once. "And more," she admitted. "By the end of the summer I knew I was pregnant. I was scared. What would I say to Larry when I saw him again? And what would I tell my parents?"

"What did you do?"

"I went to confession and talked with Father Patterson. He was no help. He told me God would understand, that He would provide a way if I would just listen to Him. I resolved to keep the baby—from the start—and I made up my mind to tell your grandfather about my indiscretion in the city. I wanted to talk with my father, but I just couldn't do it."

"Then what happened?"

Before we could have that talk, I got the call from Larry's buddy that he had been killed in action—months earlier."

"Wow," Katherine said.

"I was a wreck. Coming apart. I told my mother and father about Larry. And then I blurted out that I was pregnant. You know Grandpa and Grandma—they told me not to worry; they'd stand behind me, help me as best they could. They just assumed Larry was the father. I knew I didn't love your father, he didn't love me, and I didn't think it would be fair to bring him into it. I'd met his mother, and I feared she would think I wanted his money. I decided to raise you as a single mom, and let everybody think whatever they would think."

Katherine worked to process what her mother had just said, trying to force her mind to be objective. She downed the rest of her vodka and waved for another.

"What is my father's name?" she asked, her voice trembling.

"Preston Wilson."

Katherine's mind was spinning out of control. In the heightened reality of the heat and the bright blue sky and now this unexpected information, she felt as though she and her mother were in a movie stuck on fast forward. Preston Wilson. It could have been just another name being called at graduation. She repeated the name, forcing it from her throat. "Preston Wilson." Then she heard herself ask, "Where is he? Who is he?"

Her mother waved a hand vaguely over the city scene below them. "Right here," her mother said. "He lives in New York. Trump Tower. He's a businessman."

"What? Trump Tower?" Katherine couldn't believe it. This was not happening—except that it was. Her mother soldiered on with details, something about cars and real estate and a wife. Katherine instinctively pulled out her notepad and recorded the information as fast as she could. The problem was she was not writing about somebody else this time. She threw her pad down on the padded bench. She could see that her mother was tired, drained, and a little tipsy. She wasn't doing so well herself.

"This is ridiculous. I don't want to talk anymore. Actually, I don't want to listen anymore either," Katherine said softly, trying to push back her emotions but finding the hole in the dam too big to block.

Beth nodded, either in agreement or resignation. Katherine accompanied her mother back to her room, waited for her to change and lie down to rest, and went down to hail a cab. But first she placed another call, to the only friend she knew she could count on at such a time.

Susan picked up on the second ring even though Katherine knew she hadn't yet left her office for the day. "What's up, Masters Kelly? How'd it go?"

"Hennessey's. Now. Ground rules: darts, drinking, no questions."

"Sounds serious. Give me half an hour," Susan said.

CHAPTER TWELVE

Katherine stopped by her apartment just long enough to change clothes, freshen her makeup, and give Hailey a reassuring pat before meeting Susan. The dark, old bar with its familiar woodwork and dim hanging lamps was just the antidote she needed to soften the day's revelations. She looked up and forced a smile as she watched her thin, tall friend Susan, dressed in a green empire-waist dress, stride in, pull up a chair, and sit next to her. They embraced as though their separation had been a matter of years, not weeks.

"What are we drinking?" Susan asked. "Or is that a prohibited question?"

"Guinness for me. Blue Moon for you? But I must tell you, I've had a head start."

"You look absolutely awful," Susan said.

"Thanks. You look like a grasshopper."

"Thanks."

"Are you hungry?"

"Always. Are you?"

"Well, I never even had lunch, now that I think about it."

The waiter led them to a booth in the back, where they ordered beverages and burgers.

"So, I know you wanted to come to my graduation," Katherine

said. "But the truth is I also knew you'd think I looked awful, and you'd want to know why."

"It's all right. You still look awful," Susan said. She held up both hands, like a school crossing guard. "Hey, no questions, no problem. Let's just hang out and play some darts."

Susan had been Katherine's sidekick, sounding board, and sometime rival throughout college. She, however, had also been her staunchest ally when it came to making a difference in the world. Their career plans differed, but they shared common ground. Both women had been moved by a guest lecturer's description of the state of diagnostic health care in underdeveloped countries. The speaker, Dr. Kristen DeStigter, co-founder of Imaging the World, explained that many pregnant women in Uganda died in childbirth—their pioneering program using portable ultrasound identified risky pregnancy situations so the women could get help in time for safe deliveries. The success rates were impressive, and Katherine and Susan both wanted to be a part of it.

Katherine was impressed with the depth and diversity of Susan's interests and talents. A drama and theatre arts major, a talented pianist and singer, and a fluent speaker of French, Susan was also fun, always able to make Katherine laugh. It was during their month-long volunteer stint in Uganda that Katherine discovered Susan's talents as a photographer. Katherine marveled at her ability to capture the feelings and character of the people she photographed.

But Katherine had also seen Susan's dark side and at times had witnessed changes in her behavior when drinking.

They devoured their food, talking about Susan's family, Katherine's job search, anything but the elephant in the room.

Finally, Katherine could hold back no longer. "I wasn't sure what was going on, Susan. I needed to talk to my mom. But I didn't want to screw up the day for her, and she didn't want to screw it up for me, either. She loves me, and she's proud of me," she said, finishing the Guinness and signaling the waiter for another.

"It's deep, isn't it?" Susan said.

"Yeah, it is. We had a long talk," Katherine admitted.

Susan picked at her fries, letting Katherine take her time.

Katherine drank deeply of the second beer.

"I've mentioned to you from time to time some of my feelings about wanting to know more about my father."

Susan nodded and kept eating.

"Well, lately, I found out a lot more about him."

Susan nodded and emptied her glass.

Katherine took out her pen, grabbed a napkin, and drew a couple of boxes. With her pen she pointed to the box on the left. "This is about a man named Larry who died during an Air Force special op before I was born and who I thought—until a few days ago—was my father," she explained to Susan. Pointing to the box on the right, she said, "This is about a man named Preston, whom my mother met as a twenty-one-year-old nurse in the city—and a few hours ago I learned is my father."

Susan dropped the French fry on her plate. "Oh, my God."

"This gets a little complicated," Katherine said.

"You think?"

Katherine retold the story in as much detail as she knew. It helped to say the facts out loud, to try and make sense of so much new information. "My mother didn't lie outright to anyone. She just let everyone go on believing what they assumed was true. She made the call to leave it that way. I'm not sure how I should feel about that— but right now it makes me angry as hell."

Susan nodded. "Darts?"

★ ★ ★

Katherine woke up with two mad roofers competing to see who could pound the most nails into her head. Hearing the noise from the garbage trucks outside and the heavy rain against the windows, she knew she would pay for last night. She also knew that her mother would have to return home that afternoon, and their conversation was far from finished. She groped for her iPhone and hit the speed-dial number. She was amazed at how clear her mother sounded.

"Good morning, Kat. Have you had breakfast?"

"Uh, no, Mom, no ... having a little trouble getting going this morning. Listen, I'm really sorry about leaving you in the lurch for dinner—"

"It's okay, I understand. I ordered room service and then slept for twelve hours. I'm guessing whatever you did, you needed to do."

"I just bent Susan's ear all night, that's all."

"I'm bringing you a bagel and coffee. Black, one Splenda, right?"

"You don't have to do that, Mom, I'll come—"

"I'm right here at the Starbucks around the corner. I'll be right up."

Katherine fell back in bed but then forced herself to open her eyes again. *Mom made a real effort to be here and open her heart. I match that with a litany of questions, give no response to her answers, get drunk, and now leave her alone.* She showered and managed to pull on jeans and a Columbia T-shirt before the doorbell rang.

Her mother stood at the door, umbrella and overnight bag dripping, coffee tray and bagel sack in hand. Katherine showed her over to the small round table, where they unwrapped their bagels in the gray light of the apartment's lone window. Hailey followed them expectantly but lay down at Katherine's feet when she saw no treat was forthcoming.

Beth spoke first. Her words were measured and deliberate, and Katherine suspected she was struggling to keep control. "I know I've hurt you deeply, Katherine. I'm sorry. Really sorry. I hope somehow you can forgive me."

Katherine fumbled in her handbag to retrieve her pen, and drew a straight vertical line on the Starbucks paper napkin. "You don't want to hear this, but I have to ask you more questions."

"Ask." Beth Kelly sighed, like air released from a punctured balloon.

Katherine drew two small circles on the left side of the line on the napkin. "I know why you didn't tell Grandma and Grandpa and why you didn't want to tell Preston. But did you ever feel that they had a right to know?"

"I had a lot of feelings. I was three years younger than you are now, unmarried, pregnant, and the man I loved was dead. I was scared to death, wondering how I could survive. What kept me going was the thought of raising my child—raising you. I couldn't see how telling Preston would make that easier. Deep down, I was afraid he would want to ... make the situation go away. I couldn't do that. I decided to raise you myself, whatever it took."

Katherine put a check in one of the circles. "So you've never tried to reach him? Have you ever thought about him?"

"I did reach him, finally," Beth said.

The rain beat down harder on the window.

"When? How?"

"A little over three weeks ago, April 5 to be exact. On the telephone."

"Why? Why then?"

"Because I knew you wouldn't let it go. I thought if I told him, it would be better for both of you."

"How did you know where to reach him?"

"I'd thought about him over the years. I knew where to find him."

"What did you tell him?"

"That he had a wonderful daughter, living in New York, that he would be very proud. And, that you could use a father."

"A little late for that, don't you think?" Katherine said, sorry the second she said it, then, not sorry at all. She chose a different tack.

"Did you ever feel Grandma and Grandpa had a right to know?" Katherine asked, drawing a third circle on the napkin.

Beth seemed to think about the question but continued nibbling on her bagel.

"Did you ever feel *I* had a right to know?" Katherine asked, her lip beginning to tremble.

Beth stopped eating and turned her gaze directly at Katherine. "Let me ask *you* a question. Do you want a father?"

"Will you *please* just answer me? Did you feel I had a right to know that I had a father?" Katherine said, crying in earnest now.

"Of course you had a right to know. My mother and father had a

right to know, too. And so did Preston. And I didn't have the courage to tell them or you. I've been living a lie for twenty-four years,"
Beth said, her face distorted with a twisted half smile. She wiped tears
away from her eyes.

Katherine put her pen away and tore up the napkin. "I'm exhausted.
Don't know what else to say. Do you want another cup of coffee? I
can make some."

"No, no thanks. But there is something else I'd like."

"What?"

"I'd like you to try to forgive me," Beth said, blowing her nose,
tears returning. "I need to know that this will not ... that we ... that
you will get over this, at least as to us."

Katherine thought about her mother's bottom-line question.
Would their relationship survive? How could it not be affected by a
lifetime's worth of lies? Not only lies to her, but to her grandmother
and grandfather, her teachers, her friends, everyone. Not to mention
what this meant to Mr. Wilson, wherever he was at this moment and
whatever he was thinking.

Katherine felt like a car hitting a huge pothole, not only wrecking
the tire but also forcing a realignment of the car's body. Only it was
her body, her mind, and her heart. She knew this would take time to
sort out—for each of them. A lot of time. More than her mother had
today. More than she would have for a lot of tomorrows. She decided
to change the subject. She knew she had ruined her mother's trip and
wanted to try to end on the best note she could.

"What's going on with your eyes?" Katherine asked, sensing her
mother's relief at the shift in conversation. "You seem to be doing
well."

Beth relaxed into nurse mode. "There is a notable drusen increase
in both eyes, crowding the maculae, but they're still dry. So far it
hasn't interfered with my work, but that may change."

"You're in the best place to get excellent care, though, right?"

"So far, so good. What about you, your headaches? The commotion
brought on yesterday's, I'm sure. But have you had more?"

"Only a few recently ... mostly when I was working on class deadlines or my job search."

"You're worried about a job. I hate that I'm adding to the worry," Beth said.

"I told you about the Career Expo in March, and the three best choices. An internship would be a foot in the door, and there are some very good ones, but the ones I've looked into don't pay much, maybe a thousand a month. Starting salaries in the City, fresh out, are better—maybe $58,000 or so—but it costs a lot more to live here. If I stay, I'd have to move to Brooklyn and commute. If I go to D.C. with *Mother Jones*—the magazine—my living expenses would be less—but so would the pay. Other than that, I've put out resumes, filled out a lot of applications, and had some phone interviews, but nothing else seems interesting yet."

"What's Professor Simpson's advice? Didn't he want you to go to the *Times*?"

"I'm meeting with him in the morning."

"Say hello for me," Beth said, looking at her watch.

"You're okay for LaGuardia. How's Grandpa?"

"He's fine. He's missed you this year—it's not like when you were an undergrad at Columbia and could come home for breaks or long weekends."

"I know. It's been pretty intense. The Fletcher Thomas program drives you hard, but the professors say in the end it'll pay off. Maybe once I get settled—wherever that will be—I can come back up for a real vacation."

"That would be nice." The rain hammered down. Beth went to use Katherine's closet-sized bathroom to repair her makeup, while Katherine phoned the car service.

Downstairs, Katherine, barefoot, held the umbrella and saw her mother into the sedan as the driver put her one small bag in the trunk.

"You didn't have to spring for luxury on your budget," Beth chided her daughter.

"It's only a small thing. You'd have waited forever for a cab in this downpour."

"Some things are a long time in coming," she replied. She put her hand on the door to leave, and Katherine put her hand over it. "Wait, Mom, there is one more thing. I love you."

"I love you, too," Beth said, patting her daughter's cheek and climbing in. "LaGuardia, please," she said to the driver.

For hours later, watching the rain outside her window, Katherine replayed in her mind the conversations of the last two days. She was trying to absorb the disturbing realization that the idyllic construct of her father as a hero who died serving his country—and from that fact, a man of presumed strength, character, and purpose—was a myth. The foundation and architecture of his image, and her genetic connection and identity, a complete fabrication. Her desire, no, *compulsion,* to not disappoint this larger-than-life father—which had so driven her to excel in all she did—was a house built on quicksand.

Katherine had always wondered whether she was worthy of the love of her father, the love she never got. She saw now that worry was misspent, wasted, and likely in some way she was yet to understand, destructive. Worse for her, there were new worries, deeper worries. How would she react to her newly discovered father? Could she successfully rebuild the house she had mentally lived in all her life? Did she want to? This time the image of her father would be tested against reality. Would she be disappointed in her new father? In herself? The raw nature of these core questions ignited a fire in her mind, creating unbearable heat and little light. She was lonely. More lonely than she had ever been. And more scared.

CHAPTER THIRTEEN

"Hey, Gerry," Katherine said, setting her briefcase and handbag on the floor and settling Hailey into her customary spot. "Sorry my mother pressed you on the assignment. Moms."

"Your mother's proud of you. She's just protecting her cub."

She felt the sting of her mentor's words. Katherine knew better. Her mother was not protecting her; she was protecting herself. Katherine had never seen this crafty side of her mother, or if she had, it had not registered. Or maybe it was irrelevant. Her mother had always been there for her, and Katherine was grateful for her mother's scrappiness. Katherine hated the lens through which she was now looking at the only parent she'd ever known. She pushed these thoughts as far back as she could, mindful that she needed money, had to get some pieces published, and had to get a job. As soon as she stopped thinking about herself, she registered Gerry's perplexed but patient look.

"Jobs," Katherine said, pulling a list from her briefcase.

"I don't handle jobs," Gerry said with a smile. "How'd it go at the Career Expo?"

"I'm in at *Mother Jones,* but I would have to go to San Francisco or D.C., and the stipend is only a thousand dollars a month. *American Banker* is a possibility, along with the *New York Times.*"

"*American Banker* gives its readers financial information."

"Yeah, but I still have to look for the human side of the story."

"It seems to me you have to make some threshold decisions—newspaper or magazine—and freelance or payroll."

"I've thought about that. Most of these entry-level opportunities involve fact-finding and editing, not reporting. I want real reporting," Katherine said.

"The question is how does an editor know you can be trusted to deliver? That comes from experience—their experience with you. You can submit freelance articles to them now. See what they'll accept, what they like. And if they bite, it's a source of money."

Katherine sat silently, rubbing the back of her neck, and absorbing her mentor's words. She nodded, and Simpson continued. "You might have a better shot at establishing yourself through a six-month internship, and a magazine might be more inclined to give you the chance to prove yourself."

"I'm feeling a lot of pressure about money, Gerry—student loans to repay, living expenses—but that's my problem, not theirs. I'm thinking about going to D.C. to talk with *Mother Jones*. And yes, I am going to write some articles and send them along."

"Yes, unfortunately, money matters. You appear to be on track," he assured her. "Forgive me, Katherine, but I have another appointment."

"No problem," Katherine said, standing up, gathering her briefcase and handbag, and heading for the door. As her hand reached the doorknob, she heard her mentor say, "How's your assignment coming?"

Katherine froze and thought about what she would like to say to Simpson. *Well, Gerry, I've found your emotional core and I hate it. I'm broke. I need a job. My mother lied to me, a big lie. I now have a father, a different one, whom I need to investigate, which I don't have the time to do. I already know the influence he's had on my mother, and twenty-four years later, the impact he's having on my life.*

Instead, Katherine turned her head and said, "I'm working on it . . . believe me, I'm working on it," and then turned and walked to the stairs with her canine companion. She grabbed the corner post and waited for the staircase to stop moving.

★ ★ ★

The sight of people in sparkling metal chairs at the tables under the colorful umbrellas, taking advantage of a bright spring morning in the city, eased Katherine's spirits somewhat. She stopped, looked up, and smiled as she saw the top of the Empire State Building against the clear blue sky.

She went into Argo Tea, ordered her favorite brew, and found a seat under an umbrella. As she put her briefcase and handbag down on the table, she took a sip and turned to stare up at the Empire State Building, as if to draw down some of its magic into her soul.

Suddenly she felt a tap on her shoulder and heard Hailey's cautious growl. Startled, she whirled around to see the burly bulldog face of a thick man maybe her grandfather's age, his large round head gone partly bald.

"Gotta be careful setting your handbag down on the table and looking the other way," he said with a toothy smile. Hailey backed down and began wagging her tail.

"Are you going to steal it?" Katherine asked.

"No. Twenty years on the force. Old habits die hard." He pulled out a chair. "Marco Angelo Bertolini. My friends call me Angelo. Mind if I join you?" He didn't wait for her permission.

"You're a cop?"

"Retired. Private investigator now. I like Argo Tea, and now that Bloomberg's created all these great seats, I like parking myself here."

"Suit yourself," Katherine said. "I'm leaving soon anyway." She decided that any human Hailey trusted was okay with her, at least in a crowd in full daylight.

"I saw you come out," Angelo said with a gesture to the Flatiron Building. "I love that building."

"Me, too," Katherine said. "So how's the PI business? What are you doing here?"

"I have a meeting in a half hour with a professor friend who I've done investigative work for, for years."

"Really? Who?"

"Gerry Simpson."

"No way. You've been doing work for Professor Simpson? He's one of my professors and my mentor. I just graduated from the Fletcher Thomas School of Journalism."

"Small world. Congratulations. Now you can join the ranks of the unemployed."

"If you're going to be a wiseass, I'm not going to let you sit at my table."

Angelo laughed. "It ain't your table. It's the City's table. But I'll be good. Besides, you probably already got a job. You got the look."

"Yeah? What's that look, Angelo?"

"Hungry. Inquisitive. Don't-mess-with-me look. The kind that gets you employed—if you got the talent."

"Maybe I'm just in a lousy mood."

"That helps, too. So, do you or don't you have a job?"

"I have offers. I'm thinking about it."

Angelo seemed to swallow the seat he was sitting in, swirling his straw around in his drink and then slurping what was left of it. Rumpled white shirt, narrow dark tie stopping three quarters of the way down, belt a notch too tight. Not a trace of self-consciousness. Katherine found him interesting, even compelling. Looking into his face was like reading a complicated, worn roadmap.

"You like dogs?" Katherine asked.

"I love big quiet ones like yours. Hate little yappy ones," Angelo said.

"How about bulldogs? You look like a bulldog."

"I am a bulldog." They laughed together.

Angelo's smile fascinated Katherine. She felt that Angelo could make it warm or cold depending upon the effect he wanted.

"How's your PI business these days?"

"You asked me that."

"I know. You gave me an evasive answer. How about a real one?"

"Retired recently after I got my twenty. I'm no longer a detective, but retirement is for the birds. So I'm building up the PI work. So far, it's been a bunch of crap. 'See if my husband's screwing around.'

'I need some dirt on my boss so he'll stop hitting on me.' Nothin' I can get my teeth into yet. It's drivin' me nuts. Maybe you can send me some stuff."

"I did my master's thesis on Medicare and Medicaid fraud. As a detective, you have to know a lot about fraud."

"I do."

"The *Village Voice* is interested in some short articles I've written on the banking industry. Do you know anything about bank fraud?"

"I imagine I do."

"There are some bad guys in the banking business."

"There are some bad guys in every business," Angelo said with one of his smiles, this one lukewarm. "Sometimes you need a bad guy for a good friend."

Katherine thought about that for a minute. "Are you a bad guy—or do you want to get the bad guys?" she asked.

"I'm a good guy who sometimes does bad things for good reasons to get the bad guys."

Katherine pondered that as well, and wondered what sort of bad things he'd done for Gerry Simpson. "I've really got to get going," Katherine said, finding the conversation interesting and not without potential, but at the same time feeling something deep inside her telling her it was time to move on. "I've enjoyed talking with you, Angelo, and my instincts tell me we should keep in touch."

"I agree." Angelo handed her his card. "If you need something, give me a call."

Katherine took the card, looked it over, and placed it in her bag. "Thanks, Angelo," she said. "I may just do that. You never know when I'm going to need some special information."

"I figured that," Angelo said.

Katherine got up, patted her new friend on the shoulder, and waved good-bye. As she ambled down Broadway, she realized she was smiling. She'd gotten a kick out of Angelo and would check him out.

Before long, she had reached Union Square, people everywhere. Amid the everyday bustle she thought she caught the incoming e-mail beep on her phone. No telling what news it might contain today. She sat on one of the large granite blocks lining the sidewalk.

How's the newest racer on the circuit these days? What are you up to? Sean O'Malley

She quickly responded. *Sitting in the entrance to Union Square, people watching and now reading your e-mail. How's the best racer on the circuit?*

They traded mobile numbers, and in seconds Katherine's text alert sounded.

How r u, Kat?

OK. Sort of. Crazy things in my life right now.

Did you get your master's?

May 1st—What r u up to?

Finished my Secret Service basic training—finally in the field.

Wow. My racing hero is a Secret Service agent?

An agent who wants to get to know u better!

I u 2. How does that work?

Based in Washington. Any plans to come here?

Actually, I may be in connection with a job. Working on it. Will let u know.

Great. We'll make it work. Got 2 go.

☺

Ha—maybe she'd move that *Mother Jones* interview up the list. And quickly.

CHAPTER FOURTEEN

Katherine's cell phone buzzed, with Susan's name. "Hey, Susan. What's up?"

"I have a peculiar request, Kat. It's a best friend request."

"You want me to fix you up with the latest guy I didn't like, but you would think he's gorgeous?"

"No. This is sort of serious."

"Oh. What?"

"I want you to come to an Alcoholics Anonymous meeting with me tonight," said Susan.

"Why? Are you writing a paper? What's going on?"

"I'm going because I've reached bottom and need to go."

"Are you telling me you're an alcoholic?"

"Yes."

Katherine was silent for what seemed like several minutes. She knew that Susan liked to have a good time and that certainly included fun at their favorite pub, but she had never considered Susan an alcoholic.

"Of course, I'll go with you tonight. How about getting together right now and talking about this . . . if you feel like doing that."

"I'm working today. I'll pick you up at your apartment at 5:30 p.m. We can have dinner at the diner and then we'll go to the meeting at 7:00 p.m. I know this is a shock to you. I'd been sober for more than

five years, stopped going to meetings and working with a sponsor—
but during the last year, I've been drinking. I may be a functioning
alcoholic, but I have a problem and I need to go back to AA. I just
wanted to tell you, because I know you'll be there for me."

"Of course I will. Thank you for calling me. I'll see you at 5:30."

★ ★ ★

As usual, Susan was on time, the diner was not crowded, and they
found a comfortable table in the back. Katherine mostly listened and
in the process learned considerably more about her good friend.

Susan had mentioned her family in the past, but Katherine had no
idea that both her father and her mother were alcoholics. Katherine
had met Dr. Bernstein and his wife on a couple of occasions at
Columbia a year earlier and had seen no signs of either having a
drinking problem. In fact, Katherine had had the impression that Dr.
and Mrs. Bernstein, when not traveling around the world, were busy
all the time—her dad with endoscopies, colonoscopies, or whatever
gastroenterologists do, and her mother with charitable work helping
children and hosting events at their country club.

As Katherine would learn in greater detail, however, in talking with Susan that night at dinner, later at the AA meeting, and
afterward, many alcoholics don't fit the out-of-touch dysfunctional
stereotype, and yet they struggle on a daily basis to deal with the
disease. While she knew that many people had drinking problems
and had generally understood that there was a genetic component
to the disease, she had not realized how many functional alcoholics
there were nor the strength of the genetic proclivity and the statistical
probability of children with one or more alcoholic parents, themselves becoming alcoholics.

Katherine was moved by the openness and honesty of those who
spoke at the meeting, and admired the courage it must have taken.
When she saw Susan step up to the podium, she felt a burning in
her throat and pain in the back of her neck. As Katherine listened to
Susan say the obligatory opening, go on to explain her problem and

what she had done and intended to do again to deal with it, she had to fight back tears.

Katherine's in-depth awareness and understanding of the universe of alcoholism had been considerably expanded, and she was grateful to her friend for allowing her inside. She found Susan's conversation about the alcoholic's relationship with her sponsor to be insightful, particularly with respect to how honestly each would speak with each other and the degree of trust, in some cases making their relationship stronger than the ones they had with their spouse or family members.

She wondered whether her thoughts were colored by the questions of maternal candor and trust she herself was currently facing. In any event, she knew she would look at alcoholism differently, with a more nuanced appreciation going forward. She also thought about the extensive experiences her mother had as a nurse and wondered how many alcoholics she had treated. Thinking about the genetic connection, she was glad that for her mother and grandfather, and to the extent she could remember her grandmother, drinking had not been a problem.

Now, she had a father. She wondered about him. *What is he like? What are his parents like?* She found her mind running through the possibilities—alcoholism included.

CHAPTER FIFTEEN

Katherine followed what had become her daily ritual: wake early, shower, take Hailey for a walk, head back to the apartment, pick up her iPad, go across the street, order breakfast, and check ire.org for the latest job opportunities. On this morning, she spotted an investigative reporter listing by a newspaper called the *Twin Forks Press*. What it described piqued Katherine's interest: *We're looking for a reporter with strong writing, reporting, and computer database skills, willing to relentlessly pursue government and bank institutional wrongdoing to join our award-winning investigative team. The candidate must possess strong initiative, creativity, and the ability to break through the filter and find real answers.*

While Katherine had never heard of the *Twin Forks Press*, the job description was what she was looking for and she felt that she possessed the required skills. Besides, she had to get a job—and soon. She liked the idea of *Mother Jones*, particularly the intern program with the nationally respected magazine, but knew a thousand dollars a month would hardly scratch the surface of the cost of living in Washington, much less begin paying her debts.

She Googled the *Twin Forks Press*, copied all the information to her iPad, and read it as fast as she could. A small weekly in Southampton, a town on the eastern end of Long Island ... too small, she determined, except that further digging revealed that the

Twin Forks Press reported to the Northeast Print and Media Group, which she knew was growing rapidly and garnering a lot of attention. Owner Solomon Kaplowitz was a Pulitzer-prize winning author and editor with a remarkable prior history—but why had he left Gannett and the *Rochester Democrat & Chronicle* for a weekly newspaper in a resort community of 55,000 year-round residents?

The only way to know, Katherine decided, was to ask him.

★　★　★

Katherine's cell phone rang, showing her mother's number, just as she finished making notes in preparation for her call to the *Twin Forks Press*. "Hey, Mom, what's up?"

"Hi, Kat," her mother said.

Katherine detected trouble in her mother's voice. "What's wrong?"

"Nothing. I'm fine. I'm on shift, but it's quiet and I wanted to hear your voice. That's all. How are you?"

"Okay, a little stressed about finding a job, paying my bills, Susan ... stuff like that. But I have some ideas about work I want to check out ... too soon to talk about them."

"What I really wanted to know is how you and I are doing," Beth said so softly Katherine could hardly hear her. "Even though you're trying to be nice to me, I know you are really pissed ... about the lying thing. I want to know how you are dealing with it . . . and if you are getting through it ... if you are?"

Silence for a few beats.

"Mom, I don't want to deal with this right now," Katherine said. "I'm trying to focus on getting a job, starting my career, paying my bills, and maybe even having some fun."

"Well, I need to know. I'm worried sick about all of this. It's all I think about. I'm distracted at work, and it's getting old."

More silence.

"Why does this always have to be about you?" Katherine said at last, not liking the tone of her voice or her mother's and immediately becoming angry with both her mother and herself.

"I'm sorry, Katherine. You know I can't change what happened. Neither can you. We have to move on."

"I'm not doing this. Not now," Katherine said. "We've discussed all of this. You've explained it all. You decided to lie. You felt it was the only way to go."

"Are you going to try to talk to your . . . father?"

"Mother, for God's sake, leave me alone. You've done your part. You made the call. It is what it is. What I do or don't do is complicated, but it's up to me. Not you."

Katherine could now hear her mother crying, and was fighting a battle not to cry herself.

"I'm sorry is all I can say. I know it's not enough. Maybe someday you'll have your own call to make, and maybe then you'll understand," Beth said.

Katherine heard the line go dead.

★ ★ ★

Katherine stormed out of the apartment and ran into the square. The day had turned colder and rainy, matching her darkening mood. She walked around the square to Fourteenth Street at a fast clip, watching the vendors pack up their small booths, and then covered the same ground again. She stopped at the pizza parlor, devoured a single slice, and gulped down a steaming hot coffee. She tried to reach Susan, left a message, and went back to her apartment, which, like her universe, was fast growing way too small.

Why didn't she have a boyfriend to call at a time like this? Why didn't she have a boyfriend in any event? She liked men. In fact, she loved men. Too much at times. Why did these relationships never seem to work out? Okay, she was too busy with school. But that was over now.

Katherine gathered her composure, sat down at the kitchen table, and took out her cell phone. She pulled the *Twin Forks Press* phone number from her contacts, picked up the phone, dialed, and asked for Mr. Kaplowitz.

She was surprised to hear the response, "That's me."

"Mr. Kaplowitz?"

"Yes. To whom do I have the pleasure of speaking?"

"Katherine Kelly, sir. I read your ad online at ire.org. I'm a recent graduate of the Fletcher Thomas School of Journalism, and I would appreciate the opportunity to talk to you about the position."

"Good. Talk."

"Well, I have the qualities and skill-set you're looking for."

"Either that or a lot of *chutzpah*."

Katherine smiled. "Well, I did poke a little beyond the ad, about you, the *Twin Forks Press*, and its affiliations. May I come out and meet you?"

"Of course. When?"

"Whenever is convenient for you. I'll rent a car and drive."

"How about sending me some information first so that I may have the benefit of learning about you before we meet? Résumé. Background. Perhaps a first-person piece about what you learned in your master's program, how you liked it, what kind of reporter you want to be and why. And most of all, what you think sets you apart from other candidates. Can you have all of that e-mailed to me by this afternoon?"

"Yes, no problem."

"Okay, then. We'll make it tomorrow. It will be a little more quiet on a Saturday. If you get an early start, you might be able to get here by 11:00 a.m."

"I'll see you in the morning. I look forward to meeting you, Mr. Kaplowitz. Thank you."

"Call me Sol. I look forward to meeting you, too."

CHAPTER SIXTEEN

The overcast skies and wind-whipped Trump Tower matched Preston's foul mood, made worse when his cell phone buzzed and displayed the name "B. Forsyth." To say that Preston hadn't been looking forward to this moment was an understatement. With every day that had passed he grew more apprehensive and less eager to learn the answer. Maybe if enough time passed, the matter would just miraculously go away. He froze, feeling equal parts fear and excitement, and then gritted his teeth and took the call.

"Hi, Ben."

"Preston. I just found that I have the report. It actually came into the office a week ago, but there was some confusion because it was marked 'Personal and Confidential' and I have been out of town. Would you like to come down to the office?"

"You've read it?" Preston rose from the couch, tiptoed past P.J.'s room, where Marcia was occupied with their son, and stepped into his den and closed the door for privacy.

"Yes."

"It's confidential?"

"Yes."

Preston could feel his pulse pounding through his veins.

"No, just tell me."

"Congratulations. You're the father of a beautiful twenty-three-year-old girl."

Silence.

"Preston, are you there?"

"Yeah. I'm here," Preston said in a barely audible voice. "Thank you, Ben. I hope my daughter likes me," he said before hanging up.

Preston sat down at his desk and stared blankly at his collection of tastefully framed pictures. A headshot of Marcia before they were married, Marcia and Preston together, Preston and Casey in the mountains (snapped by their guide when they went looking for Joe), and P.J., the day after he was born. Preston got up and found Marcia in the kitchen.

"Honey, we need to talk."

"In the closet?" Marcia asked with a slight smile. For some reason that Preston knew Marcia never understood, whenever he had a particularly sensitive subject he wanted to discuss, he would drag Marcia into his walk-in closet as if his suits and pants and shoes could somehow insulate him and what he had to say.

Preston nodded, as Marcia followed him to the bedroom. Once inside, Preston turned to his wife.

"I just got a call from the lawyer I consulted about ... the paternity issue."

"And?"

"I'm the father—her father."

"How long do we have to stay in the closet, Preston?"

"What do you mean?"

"Well, there is some duality to the question. Can we leave this closet now, go to the kitchen, have a cup of coffee, and discuss this situation? I mean, how are you going to handle this? What are you going to do? What are you going to say? To whom? Stuff like that. And maybe you can tell me what you know about her, starting with her name?"

Preston and Marcia returned to the kitchen, took their seats around the fancy butcher-block table, and Marcia poured coffee.

Preston told his wife what little information he had about Katherine. "I don't have to do anything. No one knows about this except my lawyer and you," he said.

"And you. You know about it."

"I mean ... I'm talking about burden of proof and all of that. It's not on me. On the other hand, honestly, while I'm anxious about all of this, I'm also intrigued. Katherine's apparently done very well. I'd like to know more about my daughter."

"I can understand that," Marcia said.

"What do you think I should do?"

"We've covered this ground. Again, don't go there. Just make a decision. Then I'll make mine."

"That's not fair. Back when we were having problems you were always complaining that I didn't open up and talk to you ... that I was ... distant. Now, I am talking to you, and you're pulling back. What I decide, obviously, involves you."

"Don't put this on me. I was not involved when you created this situation. This is, after all, *your* daughter, not *our* daughter. You have to determine whether you are going to reach out to your daughter or not. You don't know how any of that is going to turn out, nor do I."

Preston stood and started pacing. He ended up looking out the window at Central Park. He was tired of the conversation with Marcia and disappointed in her response, but he also knew that she hadn't created this quandary. He turned to Marcia.

"I'm going to meet Katherine, talk with her. I'm going to tell her that this is a shock to me and must be a shock to her as well. I want her to be aware that I didn't know until now that I am her father, that I don't want her to think that she was abandoned by me."

"I understand," Marcia said. "I really do."

★ ★ ★

Preston dialed the cell phone number Beth had given him.

"Hello," Beth answered.

"Beth, this is Preston."

"Hi, Preston. Can I call you back? I'm at the hospital, but I'll be off my shift in about thirty minutes."

"Sure, call me on my cell," Preston said and gave her the number.

A little over a half hour later, Preston's cell phone rang. He quickly answered.

"Sorry I couldn't talk earlier," said Beth. "Occupational hazard."

"I'd like to talk to your ... our daughter. Can you tell me where I can reach her?"

"Thank God, Preston. I can't tell you how much that means to me. I'm not sure how she's going to respond. She's upset with me at the moment. Why don't you contact her through her e-mail first and let her decide whether to give you her cell number?"

"That sounds like a sensible idea, under the circumstances. Go ahead with the address—I have a pen and paper." Preston recorded the information.

CHAPTER SEVENTEEN

On a gray and soon-to-be rainy day, Katherine fed and walked Hailey, picked up a rental car at the agency five blocks away, drove to Susan's apartment, dropped Hailey off, and drove up the FDR Drive, through the Queens-Midtown Tunnel and onto the Long Island Expressway, I-95, heading toward the Hamptons. It seemed as though every resident of Manhattan was headed the same direction, even on a Saturday morning. This was Katherine's first trip to Long Island, and she'd heard about the traffic congestion on the LIE. She almost wished she'd brought Hailey and buckled her into the right front seat so that she could use the fast High Occupancy Vehicle lane.

As she inched along, she caught up on her phone calls. She retrieved the private investigator's card and after some thought, gave him a call.

"Hi, Angelo, it's Katherine Kelly. We met outside the Flatiron Building."

"I know. What d'ya need?"

Katherine laughed. "You really know how to smooth-talk a lady, Angelo."

"Come on, let's have it."

"I'd like to have you get some information on someone, but I don't have any money to pay you right now."

"Don't worry about that. We're both just starting out—me as a PI, I mean."

"I'd like you to find out what you can about a man named Preston Wilson. A Google search presents his extensive automobile dealer-ships, and I have information that he lives at Trump Tower."

"How deep?"

"I'd like to know what there is to know."

"What's your interest in this guy, if I may ask? He giving you trouble?"

"No, it's not like that, Angelo. But it's complicated. That's all I'd like to say about it at this point. I have an exit coming up."

"Gotcha. No problem. I assume you want this yesterday?"

"Today will be fine," Katherine said with a laugh. "Actually there's no deadline on this, Angelo. Since you're doing it pro bono, you probably should work me in when you can."

"I get that. You and me will help each other. If you like my work, you can refer me business. I figured that was sort of a given when we first met."

"Thanks, Angelo."

"You got it," he said.

Katherine noticed the congestion had disappeared as she got closer to the Nassau County line. She checked her iPhone for direc-tions as she continued east. The GPS wanted her to continue on the LIE all the way to Manorville, exit seventy. But she decided to get off the expressway early, taking Route 112 south to Montauk Highway to explore some of the little towns along the South Shore, many of them with Native American names. She drove through Patchogue and continued east through Shirley, and Speonk. She detoured off Montauk Highway, slowed down to admire some of the charming old houses in the Remsenburg area, and other sections of rural farmland. The scenic countryside reminded her, surpris-ingly, of Marion, the Finger Lakes, and rural sections of upstate New York. She eventually reached the Hampton Bays area and the entrance to Long Island's South Fork, and the Hamptons, a playground for some of the world's richest and most famous people.

The closer she got to the Hamptons, and to the ocean, the more she recognized the hedgerows and the mansions behind them that she had heard and read so much about, with fewer rural patches in between. Katherine was surprised by the swift changes between farming country and trendy little towns or villages. The highway veered northward to Shinnecock Hills, and then turned southeast again. Finally, she reached Southampton, noting the upscale nature of the community: stately colonial-style expansive homes behind more carefully trimmed hedgerows and interesting shops with artistic signs and catchy names.

On her right, she passed the Southampton Town Hall and the Bridgehampton National Bank. She found the *Twin Forks Press* on the southeast corner of Hampton Road and Lewis Street, in a three-story wood frame house with a barn-style roof covered in Shaker shingles. The ground floor front consisted of two large windows with a wooden door in the middle; the house as a whole had an Early American feel. Clearly, this was not the *New York Times*.

It was only 10:15, so Katherine turned around, drove a few blocks, and found a Starbucks, where she freshened up and ordered a cup of coffee to go. Returning to the address she'd verified earlier, Katherine grabbed the black leather Tumi briefcase her mother had given her for graduation and briskly entered the newspaper office.

She was greeted by a man of average height with curly black hair, a warm smile, and an outstretched hand. He wore thick horned-rim glasses with round frames and appeared to Katherine to be in his fifties.

"Hi, Katherine. Sol. Welcome."

"Thank you, sir," Katherine replied, thinking he looked a little like Lou Grant in the old *Mary Tyler Moore* television show.

Sol led her past the reception area to his office at the end of the hall.

"You made good time. Would you like some coffee?"

"No, thank you, Mr. Kaplowitz, I just grabbed a cup down the street."

"Call me Sol. If you were Southern you would agree and still call me Mr. Kaplowitz, but you're from New York. By the way, where are you from in New York? You don't sound like the city, certainly not the Bronx."

"I'm from Marion, a small village in upstate New York, north of the Finger Lakes Region and south of Lake Ontario."

"I know where it is."

"I was inspired reading your biography. It's one of the reasons I'm here."

"What are the other reasons?"

"I'm eager to start my career, and I need money. I have an internship offer from a highly ranked magazine in Washington, D.C., and the chance to work in the nation's capital would be great, but frankly, I'd prefer a tougher challenge. Besides, I can't live on a thousand dollars a month, and my research indicates that my chances of being allowed to run with a good story in today's economic and journalistic environment, before I have proven myself as a reporter, are slim to none. I'm impatient and eager to be given a real chance to show what I know I can do."

Sol pushed his chair back and went to a credenza where he poured himself some coffee. He looked at Katherine to see if she had changed her mind about coffee, and she shook her head.

"Your assessment of the industry is correct," he explained. "Major daily papers are folding, with literally thousands of journalists losing their jobs. Investigative reporting is no longer seen as a good investment. Papers can't afford to take the risk. They're under immense pressure to cut back on print and shift their focus to the Web. I worry about how discouraged our young people are not finding jobs—the whole jobless issue," Sol said.

Katherine nodded in agreement. "I've talked with journalists-to-be in and out of Fletcher, and many of them are worried not only about whether they will get a job or have to freelance, but if they do get a job, how little they'll be paid, the way their pay will be calculated, how long their jobs will last, and whether their pay will be based on page views or other metrics."

"Yes. So let me tell you a bit about the *Twin Forks Press*. Fortunately, I had the money and the desire to make the investment. It also helped to be connected to the Northeast Print and Media Group."

"For me, this really comes down to security or opportunity," Katherine said.

"Which do you choose?" Sol asked.

"It's a false choice. I have to be practical and live with reality, but if I'm given a chance and enough money to live on, I'll forego security in favor of expanded opportunity."

Katherine and Sol talked for a few more minutes about issues in newspaper management, before he invited her to stay for lunch. They walked west on Hampton Road a few blocks to the Fish Tank, a charming little restaurant featuring a large tank filled with live lobsters.

As they entered Katherine took in the delicious aroma of fresh seafood cooking. Several diners, she saw, were enjoying steamed clams and crab legs. She could not resist having a closer look at the lobsters.

"This place is an institution in Southampton," Sol said. "Owned and run by the same family for three generations. I was introduced to it by Donald Louchheim shortly after he bought the *Southampton Press* in 1971 at the age of thirty-four. He is one of my heroes. It's sort of like a senior law partner, tired of dealing with all the management issues in a huge firm, throwing away the support system and following his romantic dream to practice his way."

"And that's you, too—why you bought the *Twin Forks Press*?"

Their waitress brought water to the table, interrupted their conversation, and took their orders. Katherine was tempted to have the lobster but settled for the crab sandwich.

Sol ordered flounder and then continued.

"Yes. At some point, the idea of being an editor and publisher and having the ability to decide what stories were truly worth pursuing, aside from the anticipated reader reaction, seemed more meaningful to me. Fortunately, I had enough money to not only purchase the *Press* and fund the operations, but to take the inherent risk of developing and following through with stories whether the subjects liked it or not."

"The inherent risk of telling the truth?" Katherine asked. "Such as being sued?"

"All of that. We're in the business of the truth, and we're being challenged more every day."

"I understand," Katherine said.

"I was intrigued reading your story, particularly your description of what your mentor, Simpson, asked you to write about— the influence of someone outside your family on a family member—and why. Do you agree with him that you are holding back and need to learn how to find the emotional core of the story?"

"No. I thought he was off his tree," Katherine said with a laugh. "But I'm taking it seriously, because I respect him and there probably has been some holding back. It's all about balance. I'm working on it."

Sol smiled and seemed to approve. He asked more questions about Katherine's master's program, probing in detail about her Medicare/ Medicaid fraud project and how she'd gotten her sources to talk. They finished lunch, Sol paid the bill, and they returned to his office and took seats in the conference room.

Katherine peppered Sol with her own nuanced questions about himself, his family, his newspaper days, the history of the *Press*, and his acquisition of it. Sol patiently answered each of her questions and told Katherine his own story, the stuff not in his biography, including what led up to his winning the Pulitzer Prize. He talked about his family, his upbringing first on Long Island and then in Palm Beach, Florida, about his wife, Rachel, and their two children, Sandra and John. Katherine took notes as fast as she could write.

The more Sol talked, the deeper Katherine drilled. She wanted to know as much as she could about the *Twin Forks Press* and his relationship to it, its circulation, how many people were employed, what they did, and specifics about the relationship with the media group, economically, control-wise, and otherwise. She'd heard plenty of stories from graduates about the difficulty of finding a job in journalism that would provide sufficient pay and security and knew from her research the pressure the print medium was under. She was reassured to learn how large and well-staffed this weekly was—and well-funded.

For his part, Sol inquired in equal depth about Katherine's background, Marion, what it was like growing up there, what she did, who she did it with, what she liked, what she didn't, how she felt about her undergraduate studies, and how she felt about living in New York City, having been raised in such a small village.

"I've never been to Marion, New York," he admitted, "although I am aware of it. Coincidentally, we have an East Marion on the North Fork, just a few miles away."

Their conversation continued, thorough on both sides, never missing a beat—at least until Sol noted, "In all of your discussion about your mother and grandfather, I don't recall you saying anything about your father."

"I didn't," Katherine said. "That's a complicated subject, Sol. Do you feel it's necessary for me to go into it at this point?"

After a considerable pause, Sol looked straight at Katherine. "No, I don't," he said. "You've been frank and open with me about your situation, what you want, and where you'd like to go. I appreciate your coming down here so quickly and spending this time with me. As I see it, investigative journalism is more than a business. It's an insatiable, never-ending pursuit of the truth. That path can be arduous and even painful, requiring at times, enormous discipline."

Katherine decided to simply listen and not say a word. She waited.

"I've talked to and read e-mails from a number of candidates who have responded to my ad," said Sol. "You told me on the telephone that you had the qualities and skill-sets I was looking for. I agree."

Katherine nodded modestly in thanks. Again she held her silence, her heart beating so loud in her ears that she was sure Sol could hear it across the table. So far, so good—he was saying the right things. She was in the middle of crossing her fingers, mentally, for a phone call back, when Sol Kaplowitz said the words she almost couldn't believe she'd heard. "I'll pay you three thousand a month and cover your moving and business expenses, Katherine. And I have an assignment in mind that should be just the challenge you're looking for."

"That sounds interesting. And what about work hours?"

"Long and unpredictable," Sol said. "Why don't you go back to New York, think about my offer, and let me know by Monday?"

Katherine knew she'd done all the thinking she needed. "I'll tell you what I'd like to do, Sol. I'd like to go back to my apartment, find a way to get out of my lease, pack my things, go to Marion—my Marion—spend a few days with my mother and grandfather, find an apartment I can afford, move to Southampton, get settled, enjoy Memorial Day, and the day after go to work for the *Twin Forks Press*. How do you feel about that?"

Sol considered that for a long minute. Katherine had begun to wonder whether she'd said something wrong when, finally, he said, "We could use the help now, but three weeks isn't a deal breaker. I can use that time to remodel a little. So, I feel good about that." He came around his desk and gave Katherine a warm hug. "Really good. Welcome aboard. Let me know if you need help with anything and have a safe trip home."

"Thank you, Sol," said Katherine. "I feel good about it, too."

CHAPTER EIGHTEEN

Katherine sat at a choice table in the Gramercy Tavern devouring a delicious flatiron steak. She'd decided to splurge, still basking in the glow of her visit to Southampton, and the excitement of finally having a job—one she was truly excited about to boot. She called Susan to share the news and see if she might be able to ride with her to Marion, and maybe even to Southampton. Susan agreed to meet her along the way to Southampton, but suggested that Katherine should have time alone to visit with her mother and grandfather.

She knew she should call her mother, but decided to wait until she had more information about getting out of her lease and finding an apartment, thinking that it would be easier to answer all the other questions her mom would ask. Katherine was working on her to-do list when she felt the buzz from her phone. A new e-mail had arrived from an unfamiliar but unmistakable source: Preswil21@gmail.com. This one she would save until she got home, not trusting her emotions in public.

As she walked the five-plus blocks from East Twentieth Street across the Square, she tried to anticipate the content of the e-mail and what her response would be. Whatever the e-mail said, she knew she had to deal with it, and her mind focused on her core questions first: *(1) Did Preston Wilson have the tests done, and if so, is he my father? (2) If he is, does he want to be my father now, after all these years? (3) If he does, what should I do and what do I want to do? (4) If he does, what should he do, and what does he want to do? (5) If he does not, what should I do, and what do I want to do?*

Katherine quickened her pace, and before she realized it, she was racing up the stairs to her apartment. She hadn't managed to think through even the first scenario.

She collapsed on the couch, exhaled, and opened the e-mail.

> *Hello Katherine,*
>
> *I was hoping to call you, but your mother wasn't comfortable giving me your phone number. She gave me your e-mail address instead, and suggested that I write to you. I know how strange, awkward, and horribly impersonal this must seem for you to be reading this.*
>
> *I learned from your mother, not long ago and to my complete surprise, that you are my daughter. I hope you will forgive me, but I had a paternity test done, and it confirmed what your mother told me.*
>
> *I can't imagine what learning all this now must be like for you, and it breaks my heart to think about it. What I do know is that I want to meet you, get to know you, and love you, if you're willing to let me do that. Since I have not had the chance to be your father before, I would like to make up for it now.*
>
> *Preston Wilson*

As Katherine closed the e-mail and turned off her phone, she felt hot tears on her cheeks. She got up and went to the bedroom, almost in a daze, and threw herself on her bed, where she cried some more. At some point, she realized her tears might also be harbingers of joy.

★ ★ ★

"Hi, Mom. Am I getting you at a bad time?"

"No ... give me a minute ... I can talk better in here," Beth said. "I'm so glad you called. How are you? How's it going?"

"Actually, I have great news. I have a job!"

"That's wonderful." Katherine was pleased to hear the excitement in her mother's voice. "What, where? Tell me about it."

"I'm going to be a reporter for the *Twin Forks Press*, a small but prestigious weekly on Long Island, connected to the Northeast Print and Media Group. My salary is three times what the *Mother Jones'* internship would pay, all my business expenses will be covered, I'll have the freedom to pursue and report on my stories, and most of all, I really like Mr. Kaplowitz, the editor."

The phone went silent for a few beats, Katherine knowing her mother was trying to process all of this.

"I'm so happy for you and proud. I knew you'd do it. You're on your way. When do you start?"

"As soon as I can wind up things here and find a place to live in Southampton. I asked Mr. Kaplowitz for a little time to visit home, too. I want to come spend some time with you and Grandpa, pack, and talk with Grandpa about buying a good used car. Then, I'm off to Southampton. Susan may join me, help me move in."

"You're right, this is great news. Let me know when you'll be here. I want to change my shift around so we can have some real time together. I love you, Katherine, and I'm very proud of you." The noise from the garbage trucks and handlers on the street below distracted her and made it hard to concentrate.

After a moment's hesitation, Katherine said, "I love you, too, Mom. See you soon." She'd held back telling her mother the other big news of the day. There'd be another time for sharing that, after she had time to think it through herself.

The walls of her crowded apartment suddenly felt too confining for her mood.

"Come on Hailey girl, let's get some sunshine," she called out. "Clear our heads." Katherine got the leash, and together they bolted down the stairs. The world suddenly looked bigger and more colorful.

At the Square, she stopped at a park bench, smelling the fresh fruit and produce from the vendors' displays, and expanded her to-do list to include all the people she had to see and talk with, and the new tasks she had to do. On her to-do list was a visit to her mentor, Professor Simpson. She wanted to tell him about the job in person, and to again thank him for all he had done and been to her.

At the top of the list, though, and coloring every other thought, was the issue of how to respond to Mr. Wilson. That was the problem, really, she determined. It was *Mr. Wilson.* Apparently, he was indeed her father, but how should she approach meeting him? It was the scariest meeting she had ever contemplated, and perhaps the most important. What should she do or not do? What should she say or not say? She again played out the scenarios in her head.

In the end, she realized there had to be two people on the stage of this drama. She would have to determine what to say and do depending on what her father said and did, and like any interview, she would gain more by listening than talking. But this wasn't any interview for which she'd been trained. This was coming face-to-face with a ghost. This was meeting the phantom she had dreamed about all her life.

Whether she liked it or not, the next line in the script was hers. Her father had taken the first step up a steep stairway with too many stairs to count. She had to respond. She wanted to respond. And she was scared to respond.

Katherine thought about calling him at work, at the number she'd already looked up, but she couldn't imagine what the telephone conversation would be like. She contemplated waiting until she heard from Angelo, but she decided that would hardly be fair to Preston. She decided to answer his e-mail and suggest a meeting. The last thing she wanted was a protracted discussion via e-mail. This had to be done in person. She had to hope he would understand that. Perhaps he was as nervous as she was. Or maybe he wasn't nervous at all.

Katherine had read his brief message over and over. Preston had written that he wanted to be her father, to meet her, to get to know her ...

and love her, if she was willing. But what did that mean? Certainly, she wanted to meet him, too, whether she was anxious or scared or whatever. She had to meet him. She also wanted to get to know him, and so she knew they were in agreement on that part. They would each have to see about the rest.

She reached for her iPhone, hit Reply to Preston's e-mail, and typed:

> *Preston,*
>
> *Thank you for your e-mail. This must be difficult for you as well. I certainly want to meet you and get to know you. I'd rather not continue on e-mail, though. If anything is personal in my life, it is this. Where and when can we meet?*
>
> *Katherine*

She read and re-read her response. Satisfied, she hit Send.

His response was as quick and satisfactory as she could've hoped.

> *Hi, Katherine,*
>
> *Can you meet me 12:30 tomorrow afternoon at the 21 Club?*
>
> *Preston*

Katherine responded, *"See you then."*

CHAPTER NINETEEN

Katherine walked down the stairs and into the 21 Club at 12:30 p.m., and knew as soon as she spotted him that the tall man with a full head of thick black hair and piercing blue eyes waiting in the front room to the left of the lounge was her father.

"Hi, Katherine," Preston said.

At that moment the maître d' walked up to them.

"Mr. Wilson," he said, with a nod to Katherine and a slight tip of the head, " ... as requested, Table Number Two awaits you. This way, please." He led Katherine and Preston into the bar room and straight to a corner table for two. He positioned the table sufficiently to allow Katherine to slide into the sumptuous red leather seat to the right under two brass bells separated by a bronze sculpture of a bull and bear drinking from a bucket. Preston sat facing the entrance, with his back under the sculpture of a lone bear situated under a shelf adorned with a vase and enclosed in a rich wood inset.

The waiter approached the table and asked what they would like to drink. Katherine ordered sparkling mineral water, they agreed on Pellegrino, and Preston ordered a Chivas Regal 12 on the rocks.

Katherine's eyes scanned the iconic bar room, trying to absorb it all, beginning with the expansive bar itself, the model airplanes, assortment of helmets, a number of tractor-trailers, a Goodyear blimp, outboard motorboats, and other fascinating toys and models hanging from the ceiling, as well as the playful elegance of the entire room. Suddenly she remembered she was there as a guest, and the man who invited her, the one she'd just met, was ... her father.

"I get it ... is this why your g-mail address is Preswil21?" Katherine asked with a smile, not knowing what else to say and hoping to excuse her lapse of attention and break the ice.

"Yes," Preston said. "My company sells a lot of high-end cars. This restaurant is good for business. Not just because it's famous, but the food and wine and service are superb."

Katherine wondered whether she had offended him by suggesting the address was pretentious or at least too transparent. She thought she had done a good job at starting on the wrong foot, and she wondered if he could sense her embarrassment.

"The restaurant is awesome," she said. "What an amazing bar room. Why did you request this table in particular?"

"You won't believe it," Preston said. "This is where Michael Douglas sat in a scene in *Wall Street*. Imagine, Gecko sat right where I'm sitting now."

Katherine could not figure out if Preston was trying to be funny or was sincere in his enthusiasm. She decided to just say, "Wow." That didn't help either.

"Tell me about your car business," Katherine said, while reaching in her handbag and taking out her pen and pad. "Do you mind if I take notes?"

"Well ... this is not an interview, is it?"

Katherine hesitated and then put the pad and pen back in her handbag. "Sorry, old habits die hard. Do you mind if I record this conversation instead? Just kidding—sort of," Katherine said in a shaky voice. "Please go on, I'm interested in your car business."

"I formed Wilson Holdings several years ago, principally to own and run automobile dealerships. We started out with the Mercedes franchise here in New York and as we grew that store, we expanded to Atlanta, San Francisco, Chicago, Charlotte, and Houston, and in many locations it served our purpose to buy the underlying real estate as well."

Katherine told Preston that she'd checked out his website and was impressed with the presentation and the variety of automobiles his companies offered for sale. Preston explained how it had been his good fortune to have secured at the onset high-end franchises such as Mercedes, Porsche, Audi, BMW, and Bentley, and the competitive advantage that they had provided over the years.

He talked about the franchisors' increasing requirements to improve the dealership facilities and why his decision to embrace this effort was a big part of his success, the rest being an outstanding management team committed to discipline, excellence, and understanding their market and customer base.

"You're obviously a success. Has it always been easy going for you?"

That was the first time Katherine saw Preston laugh, but she noticed the smile on his face did not include his eyes, and the sound of the laughter had a bit too much push. She wished she had been able to take notes.

"No, it has not always been easy. The car business is cyclical; by its nature, there will be ups and downs. We got into trouble a couple of years ago or more, and we were facing bankruptcy. Our big-shot lawyers saw no way out, but fortunately, we found one lawyer who was able to turn it all around."

"How did that work?"

"He understood the automobile business, the banking industry, and, most importantly, people. He saved my business. He was amazing."

"Was?"

"His name was Joe Hart. Unfortunately, he died a year and a half ago—an inoperable brain tumor."

Katherine detected honest emotion in Preston's face and body language. She had no doubt that he had strong feelings about Mr. Hart and what he had done for him.

"He obviously meant a lot to you."

"We—my wife, Marcia, and I—have a one-year-old son named Preston Joseph Wilson. We call him P.J."

"Mr. Hart being his namesake?"

"Yes. Some would call us sentimental, I suppose."

"Not me. It sounds like the perfect name," Katherine said slowly, trying to wrap her head around this newest idea of a half-brother. "How's P.J. doing? What's he like?"

"Oh, he's a great little guy, full of smiles, starting to pull up now. He's doing fine ... except that he was born with a serious hearing impairment."

"I'm so sorry. I hope something can be done."

"Working on that," Preston replied.

Katherine hoped that Preston would elaborate on P.J.'s condition and possible treatment, but she was reluctant to pry. In the awkward gap when Preston didn't continue, it dawned on Katherine, and she hoped on Preston, that they'd not ordered their meal. She was ravenous. She needed food to quell her sour stomach, which was in knots, and she hoped not apparent to the man sitting across from her.

"Preston, could we order? I'm starving."

"Of course, I'm sorry," Preston said, motioning for the waiter, who quickly came to the table and asked for Katherine's order first. She skipped the appetizers and selected the Vermont pulled-pork sandwich. Preston ordered lobster and fennel salad, to be followed by the maple-glazed Long Island duck breast.

"Tell me about you, Katherine," Preston asked his newly discovered daughter. "You're obviously a good reporter. You've had me doing all the talking. I know, from a conversation with your mother, that you went to Columbia University on a scholarship, and that you're now getting your master's degree in journalism. I also know how proud your mother is of you."

Katherine told Preston about growing up in the tiny town of Marion, between the Finger Lakes Region and Lake Ontario in upstate New York. She talked about her time at Columbia and adjusting to the big city, her tiny, noisy Sixteenth Street apartment off Union Square, and how much she enjoyed graduate school. She leaned forward and told Preston in nearly a whisper about the job at the *Twin Forks Press*, and that after a quick trip home to see her mother, pack, and buy a used car, she planned to drive to Southampton, find a place to live, and finally, go to work as a reporter.

By then, they had finished their entrées and were indulging in desserts.

Finally, Katherine pursued what was most on her mind. "There's something I've been wondering about. When and where did you meet my mother?"

Preston laid his fork on his dessert plate and complied. "A long time ago. Here in the city. I woke up with a lot of pain in my abdomen one morning and went to the hospital. Your mother was one of the nurses in the ER and later took care of me in my room. My doctors thought it might have been diverticulitis or whatever—something serious—but it turned out to just be food poisoning, and they let me go."

Preston and Katherine ordered coffee, and he continued.

"I wanted to take your mother to dinner to thank her for taking care of me. She turned me down, but I met her when she got off her late night shift, and we went for a bite to eat. She wanted to go with me to a club, so we did that and then ... I took her back to her apartment."

Katherine tried to imagine the scene, her mother coming out, exhausted after a late night shift, and being talked into going to dinner. She wondered what she looked like in those days, how she wore her hair, did she change out of her uniform, what she would have worn. She forced herself to focus, catching the end of Preston's saga: "... and that's the last time I saw her."

"But she called you?"

"Yes, a little over a month ago—out of the blue—and told me about you, and that I was ... am ... your father."

"And that was the first time you had any contact with my mother, since ... "

"Yes. It was a complete surprise."

"And quite a shock," Katherine said.

"Yep," Preston said, again with a half-smile. "I know for you, too, this must be—I don't know the words. I've thought about it ever since your mother called me. I was twenty-three at the time. I never knew."

Katherine became silent, trapped in a self-imposed prison, consumed by her thoughts. She recognized the same sincerity she felt when Preston was talking about Joe, and she was intrigued by the range and control he appeared to have over different sets of emotions. In the business and car discussions, he seemed to be one person; when talking about Joe, Marcia, and his son and now this, another, separating business and transactional issues and personal issues, and placing them in distinct boxes. She wondered if she was being overly analytical, and if so, was that her defense mechanism?

Katherine found herself listening to Preston and at the same time, replaying in her mind parts of what he'd said already, particularly the part about the attorney—Hart—who had saved Preston's business and obviously had been an influence on him—enough for Preston to name his first son after him. *A substantial influence . . . on one of the members of your family.* Bingo.

"Are you all right? Have I offended you in some way?" Preston asked.

Katherine was jarred back into the universe of the table, realizing she had strayed far out and more than a little annoyed with herself for having done so, yet aware she could not have helped it.

"I'm fine, thank you. Sorry—my mind drifted off. I didn't mean to be rude."

"I hope I can see you again soon," Preston said, and Katherine knew he meant it. "What can I do to help? Forget buying a car, I'll take care of that. What kind would you like?"

Katherine, who had never had an offer like that in her entire life, was caught completely off guard, still processing the *influence on a family member* hook.

"Oh my God," she blurted out, her feelings comingled with her excitement at the prospect of finally seeing a path to fulfilling her last assignment required by her mentor. Katherine's face flushed, she hoped Preston could not read the confluence of thoughts, impressions, and ideas swirling and spinning in her brain like a tilt-a-whirl at a carnival. She heard the words, "Thank you, but I can't let you do that," come out of her mouth, and while relevant, they didn't seem to match all that she was thinking and feeling.

"Why not?" Preston persisted. "Please, let me help, you can't know how much that would mean to me."

Katherine unconsciously squeezed the fingers on her left hand with her right, feeling the pain. Preston had just made an amazing offer to give her a car, and she was struggling with an answer.

"Can I think about it?" Katherine said, not knowing what else to say.

"Of course, the offer stands," Preston said as he signed the check. "Would you like anything else, Katherine, more coffee?"

"No, thank you. And thank you so much for meeting me, for this lunch, and especially all of our discussion. I've never been in this restaurant. It's wonderful."

"You're welcome, Katherine, believe me," Preston said.

They were among the few diners left in the room, and Katherine was feeling uneasy about taking so much time from Preston, from his business and his family. They got up from the table, Preston straightened his tie and sports jacket, and they walked a few steps. Katherine again marveled at the curved benches finished in red leather, the tables, red-and-white tablecloths, all the color from the pieces hanging from the ceiling, and the large, curved wooden bar.

"Do you see that table?" Preston asked, pointing to the table at the end of the row and closest to the bar.

Katherine followed his direction, noting the empty table for two, and said, "Yes."

"That's where Humphrey Bogart proposed to Lauren Bacall—Table Number Thirty."

"Really? That's awesome," Katherine said.

They turned, Katherine briefly running her left hand along the edge of the bar, and walked slowly from the bar room to the entrance.

Preston lightly placed his hand on Katherine's arm and seemed to Katherine to be locking his eyes on hers.

"You know, I'm the one who is thankful to you," he said. "I've truly enjoyed every minute, and I hope you'll call me and tell me when we can get together again, the sooner the better."

"I'd like that, too. I'm fascinated by all you told me about the attorney who helped you, Mr. Hart. I'd really like to learn more about him. Would you mind discussing your relationship with him further, and if so, when could we do that?"

"I'll talk with Marcia, and if you are free, we could go to dinner tomorrow night. Marcia will want to make sure P.J. is settled for the night. We live at Trump Tower. The entrance is on East Fifty-Sixth Street. You could come by our place at six. How does that sound?"

"Sounds wonderful," Katherine said with a warm smile, returning a light touch to Preston's left arm, while eluding his eyes.

Preston and Katherine exchanged cell phone numbers. "You can see my office when you pick up your new car. I'd recommend a BMW 325 convertible. Just let me know what kind you'd like," Preston said with a wide grin.

"You've given me a lot to think about," Katherine said, uncomfortable with the feeling of being overwhelmed.

Preston nodded and said, "I understand."

By then they were outside the restaurant, and again said good-bye. Katherine could sense that Preston wanted to do more than shake her hand, perhaps hug her, and she thought that maybe there should be more, and on one level wanted more, but she remained uncertain. In the end, they just stood there staring at each other for what seemed to her like a long time.

Finally, Katherine thanked Preston again, warmly offered her hand, which Preston took eagerly, and said, "Thank you, I'll see you tomorrow night," and she briskly walked west on Fifty-Second to the nearest Starbucks, took out her pen and pad, and began to make lengthy notes.

★ ★ ★

Preston headed east to his condo, reliving the time just spent and assessing all that he was feeling. He could see Katherine was bright, energetic, and focused. Her mother was right: she wasn't going to let anything get by her. He'd love to have her working for him.

By the time he reached home he'd decided: *If a man has to find out at my age that he has a daughter, this young lady's the one to have.*

★ ★ ★

Katherine finished recording everything she could think of. She ordered a café latte and called Susan.

"Hi, you. What's happening?" Susan asked.

"Can you talk?"

"Give me a minute," Susan said. "Okay, what?"

"I just finished lunch with my father. At 21, no less."

"How did ... ? What ... ? Just tell me."

"He e-mailed me. A good e-mail. We met, had lunch, talked."

"And ... ?"

"And, I learned a lot about my father and want to learn a lot more."

"Take your work clothes off for a second. What did he look like? We know he's rich, but is he tall, dark, and handsome? Or am I being too insensitive? Yeah, probably am ... question withdrawn."

"You're just being jerky you, but I love you anyway. Actually, he is tall, trim, and handsome. If he has a dark side, it was not on display today. He was gracious and modest, and he truly seemed interested in me. He told me he wanted to get together again soon—we have a dinner date tomorrow night with his wife—at Trump Tower."

"Wow, this is moving fast," Susan said.

"That depends upon your perspective. Twenty-three years, no father. Two weeks, father."

"How do you feel about it? Did you like him?"

"Yes, I have to say, I did. This has not been easy for him either. He has a wife, a one-year-old son, and, out of the blue, a twenty-three-year-old daughter. As I said, I think he really is trying."

"Are you trying, too?" Susan asked.

"I am. I'm trying to get to know him better."

"Did you hug him?"

"That's enough, Susan. How are you doing? Are you drinking?"

"Not at the moment. I've been clean. I'm okay. Stop asking. You're not my sponsor."

"Really?"

"No."

"Do you need me? Need anything?"

"It'll be okay."

"If you're sure ... I'll call you the day after tomorrow."

"Okay. I'm happy for you, Kat," Susan said.

CHAPTER TWENTY

Katherine called Gerry to ask if she might be able to see him later in the day for a few minutes. They agreed on 3:00 p.m., and she arrived at his office on time.

"Hey, Katherine. How goes the battle?" Simpson said, motioning for her to sit down.

"I'm here to report. I answered an ad on ire.org from a small weekly in the Hamptons."

"*Twin Forks Press?*"

"No way. How do you know that?"

"Sol Kaplowitz called me. You didn't think he'd pass on checking references, did you? We worked together a few years back on a Gannett paper in Rochester. He knew that I joined Fletcher Thomas after I left Columbia, and he called to ask about you."

"And you committed perjury?"

"Of course," he said.

"I should have known; it seemed too good to be true when Mr. Kaplowitz offered me the job on the spot."

"Cut it out. He's excited about you, and he should be. You've worked hard, and you've done well. He knows a good thing when he sees it. What drove your decision?"

"Well, it would have been tough to make the internship route work out. More importantly, as you know, I would never get the chance to report the way I want to unless I freelance or find the right editor with deep pockets who owns a weekly."

"I agree. Congratulations. You look great, by the way. You have a boyfriend or something?"

Katherine hesitated and then dropped the bomb. "I have a father."

Gerry sat quietly, then put his feet upon his desk and waited.

"As you know, my father died in the Air Force before I was born. At least, that's what I was told by my mother, and, of course, what I believed but I have always longed for more information about my father. I felt incomplete in some way, and I always wanted to know more. I pestered my mother for details of his death but never received them, which just made the hole deeper. Recently I saw a documentary on a military mission in Central America involving Noriega—with U.S. Air Force support. I wondered whether the air support could have been from the same unit my father served in."

Katherine explained how she discovered that Airman Manning could not have been her father—and how she discovered who was.

Gerry put his feet on the floor, walked around his desk, and put his hand on Katherine's shoulder. "I guess I can't know how much you have missed having a father all these years, and now discovering that you have one. What must that be like? Where do you go from here? Have you talked to him? Have you met him?"

"He e-mailed me. I was moved by what he said and how he said it. We had lunch yesterday, and I'm going to have dinner with him and his wife tonight. Stay tuned." The moisture in Katherine's eyes contradicted the flippant tone of her last remark.

Gerry nodded and returned to his desk. "Would you like some coffee? Some whiskey?"

Katherine rose from her chair, reached for her briefcase out of habit, and laughed at the realization that this was the first trip to her mentor's office without it. She looked at Simpson with an expression of deep gratitude.

"I'll pass on both, although the whiskey sounds good. I have to go. You've been a great teacher and a wonderful friend. By the way, I have not forgotten the last assignment. In addition to finding a father, I think I have found the person of influence. I'll get you the paper."

"That's great, Katherine. Remember, the paper's for you, not for me."

Katherine gave Gerry a big hug. "Thanks for always being there for me, Gerry."

"Get out of here. This is getting too mushy," Gerry said.

CHAPTER TWENTY-ONE

Katherine walked back to her apartment and tried to figure out what to wear for dinner. Preston had not told her where they were going, but she guessed it would be heavy upscale. Unfortunately, her clothing selections in that department were slim, and it would be quite a while before she would have the money to build them. Finally, she decided to wear her burgundy mock-wrap jersey dress accessorized with a gold serpentine necklace, small gold earrings, and black pumps.

Dressed up more than usual, Katherine took a cab from Union Station to Fifty-Sixth Street. She had been in the lobby of Trump Tower a couple of times, window-shopping the expensive stores. She had marveled at its over-the-top, pink-white vein marble, its brass and mirrored entrance, its seven-story retail atrium, and the waterfall. But she had never until now had reason to enter one of the exclusive condominiums.

In accord with Preston's instructions, she walked to the private entrance on East Fifty-Sixth Street, where a tall doorman in his late thirties dressed in tails and a top hat peered through the glass door wearing on his face what could only be called a "what-do-you-want?" expression. He opened the door slightly, as if to protect the lobby against even the eyes of anyone without the right to be there, and unkindly asked Katherine what she wanted. She explained that she was a guest of Mr. Preston Wilson and that he was expecting her. He told her to wait outside and in a minute or two he returned. This time with a broad, insincere smile, he opened the door with considerable ceremony and ushered her in and to the elevators, which she took to the thirty-seventh floor.

Marcia answered Katherine's soft knock and welcomed her with a warm hug. Nonetheless, Katherine, taking in Marcia's dark-haired good looks, designer outfit, and classic jewelry—the real stuff, Katherine guessed—felt distinctly shabby. She wondered how in the world this was going to work.

She appreciated Marcia's smooth manner, which helped dispel her anxiety. "Finally," Marcia said, "I get to meet the young lady Preston has been talking about nonstop since your lunch yesterday. Preston is saying goodnight to P.J., and he will be out in a minute. I'm so happy you are here. Would you like a drink?"

"Are you having one, Mrs. Wilson?"

"I'm having wine. Please call me Marcia."

Marcia led Katherine from the elegant foyer to the living room filled with antique furniture, a solid cherry built-in bookshelf along the wall to her left and floor-to-ceiling windows facing her. "Come, sit down next to me," Marcia said, sitting on an expansive striped satin couch and pouring glasses of merlot for Katherine and then herself. "Preston has told me so many nice things about you." Katherine commented on the condominium, the view, and particularly the bookcase. She asked Marcia what she liked to read, and they each shared their feelings about their favorite books and authors. Ten minutes later, Preston joined them in the living room and greeted Katherine.

"You look beautiful," he assured her.

"Thank you," Katherine said, thinking that she had waited twenty-three years to hear those words.

"Would you like some wine, Pres?"

"Yes, but I'll have it at dinner," he said. "The nanny is here. P.J. is settled."

Turning to Katherine, Preston asked, "What is your favorite food?"

"Unfortunately—everything. If I had to pick one, it would definitely be Italian."

"I knew it. I've made reservations at Armani's. It's just across the street, Katherine, and inasmuch as it's Thursday, I'd like to get there before eight so that we can take the stairway to the restaurant."

Katherine, having read an article about the Armani Store and Restaurant, felt a twinge of excitement. Marcia and Katherine rose from the couch.

"We can continue this at dinner, my dear," Marcia said, and the three of them left the apartment and took an elevator to the lobby.

They walked across the street, around the corner, entered Armani's through the store entrance, and walked slowly up the magnificent circular lighted stairway to the third floor.

They passed the retail clothing section to the left, turned right, passed by the elaborate display of fine chocolates on one side of the corridor, with other fine items displayed on the right, and headed for the reception area across from the elevators. There they were warmly greeted by two ladies and a gentleman. One of the ladies picked up three menus and ushered them into the dining room, past the bar on the left and to a corner table by the floor-to-ceiling windows in the far right.

Katherine was immediately taken by the ultra-modern décor, with its mixture of black, brown, and white, which seemed to her at once elegant and mysterious. As Katherine walked to the table, she felt the effect of the soft carpet, matching table settings, and furnishings, the indirect in-point ceiling lighting, followed by the breathtaking view through the special window covering. Preston held her chair and then Marcia's, as they sat for dinner.

"This restaurant is delightful," Katherine said.

"We love it," Marcia said. "The food is good, and it's so convenient. We're so happy you could join us."

A thin young waiter with a pleasing manner and a strong Italian accent explained all the choices and specials, while an attendant poured water for everyone at the table. After ordering wine and examining the expansive menu, they each made selections from the antipasti, salads, and entrées, leaving the decisions about elaborate desserts for later.

"I know you and Pres have talked a great deal, but if you don't mind, I'd really like for you to tell me about yourself," Marcia said. "I already know that you had the good sense to go to Columbia, and they had the good sense to grant you a scholarship. I used to teach at Columbia, by the way—psychology. Why did you not go to Columbia's School of Journalism for your master's?"

"I thought about that, but in the end, I was intrigued with Fletcher Thomas, particularly because of its small size and the opportunity for one-on-one learning. I was fortunate to have Professor Simpson as a mentor, and honestly, I loved the program."

"What was your master's project?"

"An exposé of fraud and abuse and cost containment within Medicare and Medicaid."

"What piqued your interest in that?" Marcia asked.

"I was fascinated by the 1997 big-tobacco litigation throughout the United States, and particularly, in Florida, the first true arena for the battle with tobacco firms. Florida's legislature had eliminated the traditional legal defenses, leaving only fraud and abuse and cost containment, therefore causing these areas to receive extraordinary attention. I hated the fraud and abuse, yet was intrigued by its multiple moving parts and Medicaid's gross insensitivity to the need to contain the cost. It was like looking inside a complicated watch to determine why it had stopped working."

"Very interesting," Marcia said. "Quite analytical."

Their appetizers arrived and they ate, after which Preston excused himself from the table.

"I must tell you, Katherine, that color looks stunning on you, and your necklace is perfect," Marcia said.

"Thank you, Marcia. I don't mean to be rude, but is your dress a Valentino?"

"Why yes, it is."

"I thought I remembered seeing it in a magazine ad. It's really beautiful."

Preston returned to the table and explained that he wanted to say hello to a friend, just as the salads were being served. They sat quietly for a while, enjoying the food.

Katherine scanned the dining room, noticing the two stylishly dressed, thirty-something women at the table to the right and an older group seated in the leather couches at the larger table in the middle of the room, obviously enjoying their meal and having fun.

"I love this city," she said.

"Well, it has its merits. What was it like growing up in a small upstate village?" Marcia asked.

"I liked it. Everyone knew each other and helped each other. Cheerleading, dances after the games, skinny dipping in Canandaigua Lake, boating, water skiing at Sodus Point. I had an eighteen-foot Penn Yan with a Johnson 25. There was lots of snow, big hills, skiing, and ice skating on a frozen pond under the moonlight with my boyfriend."

Katherine, warming to fond memories, was on a roll and didn't want to stop. "It's one of the most beautiful areas in the state—the heart of the Finger Lakes, rolling high hills, vineyards, deep clean lakes, hiking in the summer, snowmobiles in the winter. Have you ever been upstate?"

"We New Yorkers think of upstate as Westchester," Marcia said. "But Preston, as a young boy, spent some time with his father hunting in the Adirondacks and made a trip back there not long ago. Right, Preston?"

Before Preston could answer, their next course arrived. Katherine sensed that Preston welcomed the interruption and that he looked forward to an opportunity to say a few words himself. They all watched as their dishes were expertly prepared and served and then were quiet for a while as they delved into the succulent food.

As they delighted in the dinner and the continued replenishment of the wine, Preston said, "Marcia is referring to my trip to the

Adirondacks with Casey Fitzgerald, my CFO, to find Joe Hart, the one I spoke to you about yesterday at lunch. You seemed to want to know more."

"Joe helped my husband and me out of a big mess," Marcia said, interrupting Preston.

Katherine sensed for the first time some tension between Marcia and Preston and wondered what drove it.

"Preston told me about that," Katherine said, "and he's right. I did ask him if he would tell me more about Mr. Hart, what he did for him ... for you both."

Katherine was pleased to see Marcia retreat, momentarily at least, and allow Preston to provide some backstory, to recount how his lawyers were convinced that bankruptcy was the only option and how Casey's search had come up with Joe as an attorney with the unique skills to save his business.

He told Katherine about Joe's wife being murdered, how he had escaped to the mountains, how Preston had found him and practically begged him for help. He explained that Joe agreed to take his case, providing Preston would commit to fulfilling an unspecified condition in the future—to which Preston, out of desperation, reluctantly agreed.

Preston outlined how Joe miraculously accomplished a turnaround with the banks and businesses and then, when Joe called in the IOU, how Preston had to find, earn the trust of, and care for a group of Joe's friends—"the Collectibles"—each flawed in some way. Preston gave a brief summary of Missy, Tommy, Johnny, and Corey, four of Joe's friends he had met, and the challenges they each faced. He then described Joe's funeral, seeing them and Harry, a fifth damaged soul, at the funeral.

Katherine could feel the intensity in Preston's remarks and could tell he had been moved by the experience. Marcia was apparently also moved, but Katherine's intuition suggested in some other way, how she could not fully understand. She wondered whether it was the subject, their relationship, or both, and perhaps more.

Preston signaled the waiter, who promptly brought the dessert menus, explained the elaborate choices, and made recommendations. They made their selections, and the course was soon served. After finishing and ordering coffee, Katherine thanked Preston for sharing all of that with her.

"What a story," she said. "And I guess if I understand this right, the story is not over. What is your relationship like with these folks? Are you still seeing them and caring for them now? How did you feel about reaching out to Missy, Tommy, Johnny, and ... "

"Corey and Harry. Those are good questions," Marcia said, "and a subject I've explored with Preston many times. I can tell you, Preston did help Johnny, who is mentally challenged. Preston arranged for a speech therapist to work with him, and it made a big difference. Alice produced a lot of background that helped in that effort."

"Alice?" Katherine asked.

"Marcia, please, let me answer the questions," Preston said, clearly annoyed. "Alice Hawkins was Joe's legal secretary. Joe's wife, Ashley, had done considerable work in education and helping mentally challenged people, including helping Joe help Johnny. Alice introduced me to Johnny down in Braydon, South Carolina. She had some files of Johnny's background from Ashley's research, and some files of Joe's, that helped point me in the right direction." He nodded at his wife. "Marcia helped me as well."

Preston explained to Katherine how he'd met Missy and Tommy in Las Vegas, Corey in South Carolina—but that he had not been able to connect with Harry since the funeral. "I was informed that Tommy and Missy got married in Las Vegas," he added.

Marcia responded to Preston, "We were informed by an invitation. You chose not to attend."

"I gathered from what you told me yesterday, Preston, that Joe had a substantial influence on you and your life. Is that correct?"

"Yes, he did," Preston said.

"That's an open question," Marcia inserted. "Preston's evolving on the subject."

Katherine knew she had struck a nerve. *There it is.* She had to know more. How had Joe influenced Preston? At least, she wanted to hear what he had to say about that. And she wanted to hear the other Collectibles' responses to that question as well. Alice sounded like the gatekeeper; Katherine thought she would start with her and decided to ignore—for the time being—Marcia's comment about Preston's *evolving.* As Gerry had often said, "Some stories never end." She wondered whether she would ever be able to complete the assignment.

"I would like to meet these people. Would you be willing to help me do that? I'm totally blown away by what Joe asked you to do. It's sort of a pay-it-forward thing."

Preston appeared to be in thought for a minute and then replied, "Of course, I would."

They all decided some light conversation was in order as each had a second cup of coffee. Eventually, they went back to Preston and Marcia's condo. Marcia showed Katherine around, they peeked into P.J.'s room, where Marcia told Katherine how sweet P.J. was and about his hearing problems.

Preston showed Katherine his den, picked up a business card, wrote a number on the back, and handed it to Katherine. "This is a direct line; you can reach me on it anytime." He reminded her about the car.

"I don't know, I appreciate the offer, but I feel really odd about accepting it. You're right that I do need a vehicle to take Hailey and move my stuff. Maybe—maybe you could come shopping with me and give me some guidance about a used SUV?"

"Not a bad idea. Why don't you come down to my Manhattan store tomorrow about noon? You could also meet Casey and Austin. I'd like them to meet you."

"Do they know about ... me ... and you?"

"Casey does. I was too excited not to tell him."

Katherine thanked her hosts—she still hadn't quite figured out what to call them—for a wonderful dinner and lovely evening. She especially thanked Preston for his willingness to openly discuss all of this with her, and for the generous offer of car help, to which he replied, "That's what fathers do."

As Katherine rode the elevator down to the main floor and walked out of Trump Tower, she felt tears running down her face, and she made no attempt to wipe them away.

CHAPTER TWENTY-TWO

K atherine bounced out of bed early after the best night's sleep she could remember in a long time. She showered, dressed, and flew down the stairs and across the street to the coffee shop. While having breakfast she checked her to-do list. She went back to her apartment, took Hailey out, called her landlord, explained the situation, and asked him if there was any way she could get out of her lease. The rental agent told her she could, with thirty days' notice, because the rents in that building were being raised, and they had someone who wanted the apartment. One down. It was time to check-in with her mother, a call that was, in fact, long overdue.

Katherine caught her mother mid-shift. "Hey, Mom. Can you talk?"

"Hi, Kat. Yes, for a couple of minutes. What's going on?"

"Give me a call when you can talk longer. Two minutes won't do it this time. I'll give you the headlines. I met Preston and his wife, and I'm going to look for an apartment on Long Island before I come up to see you."

"You what? Hang on. I have more than two minutes." The line went silent, and Katherine could picture her mother hurriedly requesting one of her nurses to cover her.

"I'm back. Sorry ... you're coming home. Great. When? You don't know yet. Tell me more about the job. Your lease?"

"I'm thrilled. I'm okay with the lease; the landlord's anxious to get more rent and has someone waiting."

"That's good."

Beth's rush to talk about the job and the lease, while genuine, was to Katherine, her mother's attempt to buy time and allow her to absorb what she had just heard. *She puts this whole thing in play. Preston makes his move, I respond, and she can't figure out if she's happy or sad about it all.* Katherine decided to pierce her mother's cover.

"As to the Preston part: he e-mailed me. I liked what he said and how he said it. We met for lunch. At the 21 Club, can you imagine? He invited me to his condo last night to meet his wife and then have dinner. It was an amazing experience. Bottom line: he's all in, really trying, and I like him. A lot."

The line went silent.

"Mom, are you there? Mom?"

Finally, Beth answered quietly. Katherine could hardly hear her. "I'm here. I can't talk more now. It's not work; I just can't talk right now. I'm glad you met him. We'll talk more later. I love you."

The line went dead. While there was a lot more to discuss, Katherine had at least broached the difficult subject. Two down.

Katherine took the subway to Grand Central Station and the shuttle across to Times Square. Then she transferred to the uptown train to Columbus Circle and walked to the twenty-story, block-long building displaying the lighted Manhattan BMW-Mercedes Auto Plaza sign on two sides. She walked in the Fifty-Seventh Street entrance, noting the enormous windows admitting the sunlight onto a bevy of shiny new European cars. She gave the receptionist her name and asked for Mr. Preston Wilson.

The young woman told her that Mr. Wilson was not in the building, that he had left a message for her to see Mr. Fitzgerald, and ushered her to a second floor corner office with the door open. "This is Mr. Fitzgerald, and he is expecting you. Please go in."

Katherine found Casey slouched behind his desk piled high with files, and munching on a Snickers bar. Aside from the spectacular view, the only items adorning Casey's office walls were his framed CPA license and photos of his wife, kids, and German shepherd.

Casey coaxed his 250-pound body out of his chair and waddled over to greet her.

"So you're Katherine. I'm delighted to meet you. Preston's told me a lot about you. Please, come in and sit down."

"Thank you, Mr. Fitzgerald. Mr. Wilson has told me a little bit about you. I gather you are his right-hand man."

"I don't know about that," Casey said with a twinkle in his eye. "I'm Wilson's CFO."

Scanning the wall across from the windows, Katherine said, "I assume these are your family? And you have a beautiful German shepherd, I see."

"They are," Casey said, looking at the pictures, "and Spike is a great dog. Are you a dog lover?"

"I am. I have a three-year-old golden retriever, Hailey."

"Preston tells me you went to Columbia University and just received your master's in journalism. Congratulations."

"Thanks. A lot is going on right now. Exciting times."

"Well, Preston tells me he's assisting you with your vehicle needs today. You couldn't wish for a better adviser—or father—to help with that, I'll tell you! Do you mind letting Judy, my secretary, get a copy of your driver's license and information? As for meeting Austin Disley, that'll have to wait for another day. He had to go out to one of the properties at the last minute this morning." They walked over to Judy's desk, where Katherine submitted her license and signed the papers she was given.

"Thank you, Mr. Fitzgerald. I really enjoyed meeting you. Maybe I'll see you again soon."

"Cut out the Mr. Fitzgerald stuff. We dog lovers have to stick together. Call me Casey and give me a hug," he said with outstretched arms.

Katherine immediately fell in love with this man, sensing intellect, warmth, and understanding. She gave him the hug he asked for. He went to his credenza, where Katherine would later learn he kept his private stash, pulled out three Snickers bars, and gave them to Katherine. "If my G2 is correct, you'll soon be driving out to Southampton. You'll need these along the way."

Casey took Katherine down to the showroom, where she expected to meet Preston. Instead, they were promptly joined by a young, well-dressed salesman wearing the name plate John Riddle, who walked them over to a shiny vermillion metallic red 2012 BMW X5.

"Here she is," Casey said. "All yours."

"There must be a mistake, Casey, my . . . Mr. Wilson and I talked about going to look at used SUVs."

"No mistake, Katherine, believe me. This is the car Preston wants you to have. He's still tied up in a meeting. Once you gave Judy your information upstairs, the title and insurance were processed. Don't screw it up. Take the car."

Katherine struggled to find words. What finally came out was, "Yes sir, thank you, Casey."

"Well, get in," Casey said. "See how she feels. There is plenty of room for Hailey. John will answer all your questions."

Katherine felt light-headed and dizzy with excitement as John opened the driver's door and she slid into the sand beige premium leather seats. She looked at the dash, put her left hand on the leather steering wheel and her right on the leather-covered gear shift, breathing in the new car smell. She had never sat in a car like this, let alone driven one. Or owned anything remotely like it.

"Why don't you wait in my office until the car is road ready?" Casey said. "It'll give us a chance to talk a little more."

"I'd love that, Casey." They walked upstairs and back into Casey's office. "You were in on this all along, weren't you?"

"Well, I don't mind admitting to a little deception—of the happy sort. Would you like anything to eat or drink, Katherine?"

"No thanks. I'm good. But I would like to ask you something."

"Shoot."

"Preston told me about Joe Hart. It's an amazing story. Especially the part about the Collectibles. I haven't been able to forget it. I've heard Preston and Marcia talk about Mr. Hart. You knew him. What was he like? Did he have a major influence on Preston?"

Casey sat back in his swivel chair, hands behind the back of his head, and put his feet up on the desk. "Joe Hart. He had one hell of an influence on me. I learned so much from that man, listening to him, watching him perform, watching the way he cared for others."

"How old was he when he died?" Katherine asked softly.

"Forty-five or so. Way too young. And his wife was killed in a drive-by shooting only a year before, and his mother and father died when he was a young boy. Joe Hart had seen more tragedy than any man deserves."

Casey went over to a table in the corner and poured himself a cup of coffee. He looked at Katherine, but she shook her head.

"What can you tell me about these Collectibles? And what is Preston's relationship to them?"

"I'll leave those questions for Preston," Casey replied. "I can tell you that I recently received some materials from one of Joe's friends, a Mr. Thomas Greco, who is interested in buying land in Elko, Nevada, and starting a camp with Mrs. Greco for children with special needs. He and Preston have apparently talked about this. I don't know how interested you are, but you might also check with Alice Hawkins, who was Joe's secretary and right-hand, as you might put it. She lives in Braydon, South Carolina." Casey wrote down Alice's telephone number and handed it to Katherine.

Their discussion was interrupted by Casey's intercom telling him that Miss Kelly's car was ready. Katherine felt another jolt of excitement.

Casey put his hands in the air and said, "Let's go get 'er."

★ ★ ★

Katherine went over the controls and details with John one more time. He synced her cell phone, reviewed the automatic shift, the steptronic and manual sport shift options, and showed her how to work the stereo, the GPS, the Bluetooth, and countless other options. She tried to concentrate and absorb it all, but she was sure she would be reading the manual many times.

Finally cleared to go, and with her GPS set for Southampton, she drove her new SUV slowly away from the dealership into Manhattan traffic and headed back toward Long Island. The luxury SUV drove like a dream. Once off the freeway, and more comfortable with its features, she accessed her communication system and directed it to call Preston's cell phone.

"Hello?"

"Hi, Preston. This is Katherine. Am I getting you at a bad time?"

"Actually, I'm just going into a meeting. Is everything all right? Can I call you back?"

"Everything's fine. You don't need to call me back. I just wanted to tell you how much I'm enjoying driving my new car and how much I appreciate your giving it to me. It's awesome and I wanted to thank you."

"So you've wrapped up your little surprise meeting with Casey and John? You're quite welcome. It's my pleasure. I'll talk to you soon. Thanks for the call," Preston said.

★ ★ ★

An hour later, Katherine was enjoying a midafternoon coffee at the Princess Diner, going through the real estate ads in *Newsday*. Lots of expensive homes for sale, scads of vacation rentals. Apartments were harder to locate, especially in her budget range. But soon she spotted one that seemed to fit her needs: an 800-square-foot, one-bedroom, one-bath furnished apartment for lease just off Post Crossing in Southampton Village with parking and pets okay. Twelve hundred dollars per month. She called the number listed, and within twenty minutes, was doing a walk-through with the rental agent. It was small but clean and efficient, and the furniture was in good shape.

Katherine called Sol to ask his take on the apartment, valuing a local's opinion. He liked the location, recognized and felt good about the rental agency, thought the price was right, and encouraged her to take it. She gave Mr. Kaplowitz and the *Twin Forks Press* as a reference, signed the one-year lease, and told the agent she would send in the deposit in the morning.

As the sun began to set over Long Island Sound, Katherine contemplated her good fortune. How many lucky people would end up with a diploma, a job, a new car, and an apartment all in the same month—not to mention a father in the deal?

Time to call Susan. She gave instructions via the car's hands-free input and heard Susan's voice, crystal-clear, over the speaker system.

"Hi, you," Susan said. "What's happening? Where are you?"

"I'm sitting in my new BMW SUV, driving back from Southampton, having just spoken with my new employer, Mr. Kaplowitz, owner of *The Twin Forks Press* . . . "

"Oh, my God," Susan said. "Unbelievable. Knowing you, there's more. Keep going."

Katherine did, for two straight hours. It was late by the time she got back to the city. Afraid to park on the street, she found a garage close by where she could put her new BMW overnight, deciding to pay the twenty-five bucks for peace of mind.

Katherine dined on an inglorious dinner of leftovers, cleaned out her refrigerator, packed her belongings, took a hot bath, and fell into bed. Hailey, thrilled to see her, lay down at her feet. It had been a most productive day.

CHAPTER TWENTY-THREE

Katherine awoke at 6:00 a.m., dressed, grabbed a quick breakfast at the coffee shop, retrieved her vehicle, parked in front of her apartment, gathered her few portable belongings, lugged them down the steep stairs for the last time, packed them in the car, said good-bye to the noisy dumpsters in the alley next door, and set her GPS for her mother's address in Marion. At last she and Hailey were headed home.

As soon as she was through the Holland Tunnel, and the traffic had thinned a bit as she headed west on I-80, she told her communication system to dial Susan again.

"Hey, you," Susan answered.

"Hey back. Got time for a question?"

"Sure."

"What do you think I should tell my mother?"

"Let's see, 'Hi, Mom, I met your lover's wife.'"

"Are you serious?"

"Yes."

"Have you been drinking?"

"Yes."

"Really?"

"Yes"

"Why?"

"It makes me feel better."

"Are you messing with my mind?"

"That, too."

"So you're not drinking?"

"I am drinking."

"Can I help?"

"No."

"Why are you messing ... "

"Because you're full of yourself."

"How?"

"You've gone a lifetime without a father. Now you have one, he's rich, gave you a new car, and you're worried about what to tell your mother? Get over yourself. But, I'll help you move into your apartment anyway."

Never in all their years of friendship had Susan talked to her in that manner. It scared her to hear Susan slur her words.

"This is not a good conversation," Katherine said. "Do I need to turn around and come back?"

"No, this is good for me, and I think it's good for you, too."

Katherine went quiet for a while and then said, "Maybe I'll become an alcoholic."

"Not possible," Susan said.

"Why?"

"Because you don't hate yourself."

"I hate the way I look. Does that count?"

"A little."

"Do you hate yourself?" Katherine asked.

"At times."

"Why?"

"That's what I'm trying to figure out. Could be I'm too tall ... or could be that my mother and father are drunks ... and so am I."

Katherine could hear the pain in Susan's voice but felt inadequate and powerless to do anything about it.

More silence. "Why didn't you want me at your graduation?"

Susan asked. Katherine knew Susan's comment was rhetorical and could feel the hostility in her tone.

"Because I didn't ... "

"Exactly," Susan said.

"This conversation sucks."

"I knew we could agree," Susan said.

★ ★ ★

After thinking—worrying—for an hour about Susan and her parents, Katherine decided it was time to call her own mother.

"Hi, Mom."

"Hi, Honey. How are you doing? Where are you?"

"I'm headed home and should be in Marion in time for dinner. How's your shift?"

"Good. Timing's perfect. You know where the key is if you get to the house before I do. I can't wait to see you."

At that moment, Katherine's sound system began making a faint beeping sound. Was it an alarm? Something malfunctioning? She ended the conversation with her mother and looked for a chance to pull over.

The beeping didn't stop, and it seemed like it was taking too long for her to pass the eighteen-wheeler to her right. She fumbled with the dials and pushed a few buttons until the beeping stopped, and she could see the truck in her rearview mirror. She heard a voice through her speaker system.

"Kat? Are you there?"

"Yes ... Hello ... I'm here. Who is this, please?

"6A."

"Really? Sean? Is it really you?"

"Affirmative. Can you talk?"

"Absolutely. It's good to hear your voice. How are you?"

"I'm good. What are you up to?"

"I got a job at a great weekly in Southampton. At the moment, I'm driving to upstate New York to see my mom and grandpa. After that I'll move into my new place and take a brief vacation before I start work."

"Cool. Where're you going?"

"Well, it's a long story, but I'm going to drive to Braydon, South Carolina, talk to a woman there—don't know for how long, and then make my way back up the coast."

"Unreal. This could be good. Any idea when you'd be making this trip?"

"Probably spend two days in Marion, then a day to get to Southampton and unload my stuff . . . so I'd say I'll start next Monday, assuming I can confirm the arrangements. I'm guessing it's fourteen, maybe fifteen hours to Braydon. Why?"

"I'm traveling a lot these days myself. You won't believe this, but I'm going to be working in the southeastern part of North Carolina about that time. I've been trying to figure out how we could get together, after you couldn't make it to Washington. So, maybe on your way back might work out. Have you ever been to Wrightsville Beach?"

"I've never heard of it. Is it nice?"

"More than nice. Check out Wilmington, North Carolina, and Wrightsville Beach. As your personal travel representative, I strongly recommend that you secretly meet a certain agent there so that you and he can finish a conversation that was started in April in the Berkshires."

Katherine could feel her heart pounding. She tried to sound casual, but she knew her success would be limited.

"I certainly would like to get to know that agent better, and I love the beach. I should warn you that I'll have Hailey with me."

"Is she your girlfriend?"

"Yes—my four-legged girlfriend."

"Sounds like a good plan," Sean said. "I'll set you up in a condo on Shell Island, the north end of Wrightsville Beach, if you don't mind. I'll text or call to give you the arrangements."

"I'm on a tight budget, Sean."

"I'll handle the lodging," Sean quickly offered.

"Not sure I want you to do that. We're just having a conversation, right?"

"Relax, Katherine."

"Will you protect me?"

"There's nothing I'd like better," Sean said. "See you soon."

Katherine could see on her dash that the call was over, all too soon as far as she was concerned. Her conversation with Sean was settling over her, caressing her like a warm summer breeze. She pictured him the way she saw him in the mountains after the race, mud on his face, sweaty, clear-eyed, and adorable. Suddenly she was hungry. She pulled off at the next exit, refueled her SUV, freshened up, and bought a sandwich and a diet Coke.

Katherine's conversation with Sean was toggling between the right and left hemispheres of her brain, with the analytical quadrant getting the most attention. She felt like a worried director examining dialogue in a screenplay for unintended meaning. One thought survived with clarity: if she intended to follow through with the idea of a trip to Braydon—the first vacation she'd taken in four years, and likely the last she'd get for a while—she needed to make the arrangements with Alice.

Katherine looked up the number Casey had given her. She scanned the BMW's telephone section, found it, and made the call. A female voice, soft and Southern, answered.

"Hello," said Katherine, and introduced herself. "Casey Fitzgerald gave me this number. I'm trying to reach Alice Hawkins. Are you Alice?"

"I sure hope so. I've been using that name for a lot of years. If Mr. Casey gave you my number, it must have been for a pretty good reason. What a dear man. How may I help you, young lady?"

"May I call you Alice?"

"Of course."

"Am I interrupting you?"

"Not at all. It's a good time. I just finished planting my beautiful impatiens, and I'm sitting on my front porch having some sweet tea."

"It's a long story, Alice ... and the reason I'm calling. I'm twenty-three years old, on the cusp of becoming a reporter, and ... this is going to sound strange ... I recently discovered that Preston Wilson is my father."

"Oh, my dear. Preston Wilson, the automobile dealer from New York?"

"Yes. And he told me about Joe Hart, and that you were Mr. Hart's secretary."

"I know your father. He visited me in Braydon and helped a friend here named Johnny. How is Mr. Wilson?"

"He seems to be doing well. He and Mrs. Wilson have a one-year-old son named Preston Joseph. They call him P.J. He was named after Mr. Hart."

"I didn't know any of that. I wish I had."

"I hope I'm not intruding, Alice, but I was so captivated hearing Preston, his wife, and Casey talk about Joe Hart and the way he helped his friends ... I'd like to come to Braydon to meet you and learn more about Mr. Hart. He must have been an amazing man."

"I would be happy to have you visit with me, Katherine. When would you like to come?"

"I know this is short notice, but I have a window of opportunity before beginning my new job. Would Tuesday or Wednesday of next week be possible?"

"Possible? Dear, I'd welcome the company. That will be fine. Are you going to fly or drive?"

"I'll be driving. Besides, I'll have Hailey, my golden retriever, with me."

"Oh, how delightful. She'll have to meet Buck, Joe's dog—now, my dog."

"What kind of dog is Buck? How old is he?"

"He's a German shepherd. A gem, nearly as old as I'm feeling these days."

"You don't sound old to me," Katherine said.

"Oh, bless your heart. You might like to stay at the Live Oak Inn. It's a lovely old place. If you like, I can talk to the folks over there, get you a discount. And I'll tell them not to give you any nonsense about Hailey."

"That would be wonderful, Alice. I think it's going to be about a fifteen-hour drive. I may get in late and I don't want to disturb you. Could we meet on Tuesday morning?"

"Sure. You and Hailey can come to my house, visit a while, and then have lunch if you like." Alice gave Katherine her e-mail address, and they agreed to touch base once she left for Braydon. Katherine was elated at the prospect.

As Katherine worked her way north on Interstate 81 through Pennsylvania and into New York, she was increasingly aware that morning of the changing colors and shading of light, as the rays of the sun rippled through the evergreens, occasionally bouncing off the waters of the creeks, rivers, and lakes along the way. She wanted more, and reset her navigation system, heading west from Binghamton along Route 17 and then north through Horseheads to Watkins Glen.

Katherine's grandfather followed the development of racing at Watkins Glen, and often talked to her about the old days, his excitement when the Formula One cars came in 1961 for the first Watkins Glen U.S. Grand Prix, a tradition that continued through 1980, the financial difficulties at the track that ended in bankruptcy, and how upset he was when the track was allowed to deteriorate. Adrian Kelly had followed the racecourse's later rebirth just as eagerly with NASCAR and the Winston Cup Series; today he kept pictures of Jeff Gordon and his Number 24 race car all over his den.

Katherine's interest increased when the Budweiser at the Glen, which her boyfriend called *the Bud*, grew to become New York State's largest motor sports event, and compelled the attention of all the guys in Marion. Katherine would never forget her grandfather taking her to Watkins Glen years ago to watch the races and explore the Glen.

She loved the trip, riding in her grandfather's pickup truck to the end of Seneca Lake, seeing the track she'd heard so much about, exploring the Glen, and staying at the Seneca Lodge, where her grandpa knew the owners. She could still see the tavern room in her mind: a real nickelodeon, laurel wreaths from the Formula One races that her grandfather talked about hanging behind the bar on arrows shot into the wall by ace archers and those lucky enough to bag a deer when hunting with the owner. She prayed it was still there. She asked her communication system, the number rang, and she heard a pleasant female voice.

"Seneca Lodge, this is Gloria. May I help you?"

"Hi, Gloria. My name is Katherine Kelly. My grandpa, Adrian Kelly, and I stayed at your lodge years ago and really enjoyed it. I'll be coming through Watkins Glen—probably early afternoon—and wondered if you are open for lunch."

"Sure, Katherine. I think we can find something for you. We look forward to seeing you."

Katherine arrived at the lodge just after 2:00 p.m. and met the owners at the reception area to the left of the entrance. Gloria and Jim escorted her through the dining room to meet their son, Brett, who was tending bar. The room was pretty much as she'd remembered, the oak floor, with pegs in the planks, and the wide oak bar with the laurels and arrows. After taking in the whole room, she went straight to the nickelodeon, deposited a nickel, and clapped her hands for joy when the honky-tonk music began to play.

After a delicious and surprisingly inexpensive lunch, Katherine thanked everyone, said good-bye, and once again headed north along the west side of Seneca Lake. She could see and smell the rolling green hills to her left, covered with evergreens, red and silver maple trees, silky dogwood among them, and occasional vineyards, and the sun shining through them all the way to the deep clean waters of the lake to her right.

As Katherine drove through Geneva, passed Hobart and William Smith colleges on her left, and proceeded along the narrow roads and through the small villages of Phelps and Newark on the way to

Marion, she contemplated how different her life would have been if she had accepted William Smith College's offer of an academic scholarship, and if she'd stayed in upstate New York. She pondered the New York City directness and dimensions of Marcia's question at dinner ... *What was it like growing up in a small upstate village?* That thought intensified as she proceeded along Hydesville Road, County Road 220, Mill Road, and into her hometown of fewer than six thousand people, the genesis of so many wonderful childhood memories.

Katherine thought of the changing demographics of America, the country she loved, and the stark contrast between Marion, a rural community, ninety-seven percent white, and the cultural diversity of the city of more than eight million people that she had just left that morning, which she also loved. She turned onto North Main Street, drove past the elementary school on her left, and soon turned right, pulling into the driveway leading to the large white two-story wood frame house with the country porch, a house her great-grandfather had built, where her grandfather still lived, where her mother was raised and still came home to, exhausted after taking care of patients at the hospital, where Katherine had grown up. The place she still thought of, and would always think of, as home.

CHAPTER TWENTY-FOUR

"Hi, Marcia. It's Ann. My one-day editor's conference I told you about finished much earlier than expected, and I have a few hours before I leave for LaGuardia. Have you and P.J. got time for a quick visit?"

The last time she'd seen her college roommate, Marcia had left Preston, discovered she was pregnant, and spent the whole visit unloading on her best friend.

"Absolutely. You have to come over. Can you stay a couple of days?"

"What's wrong?"

"Nothing. Everything."

"I'm hungry."

"I'll feed you. How long before you can get here?"

"I'm in your lobby now," Ann said. "Talk to the concierge, I'm handing him my cell phone."

Marcia asked the concierge to send Ann up, and in a minute was at the door waiting for her with a big hug. While Marcia called the Trump Grill and ordered lunch, Ann was busy talking to the airline about changing her return flight to the next day. Soon their lunch arrived. They moved to the stools at the marble countertop, ate lunch, and drank wine, and Marcia listened to Ann's colorful description of the speakers and interactive exercises at the editor's conference.

After an hour or so, Marcia could see and hear from the monitor on the counter that P.J. was starting to wake up.

"I'll introduce you to His Majesty in a moment," Marcia said. "I'd like to make him presentable first."

Marcia went into P.J.'s room, cuddled with her son, changed his diaper, and brought him out with considerable fanfare and presented him to Ann, who took him in her arms.

"Look at him. Those eyes. Wow. Marcia."

"I agree," Marcia said, taking him back and placing him gently in his bouncer with wheels. "He's a bit wobbly, but he'll be walking soon. We've baby proofed the whole condo. Our nanny will be here in half an hour to take him to the park."

Marcia and Ann sat on the floor and played with P.J. for a while.

"How's his hearing coming?" Ann asked.

"It's not. That's one of the five thousand things I want to talk to you about before Preston comes home. You'll have to keep extending your flight."

"Tell me."

"Remember our phone conversation about the nature of P.J.'s loss, the architecture issue, and the Clarke Schools for Hearing and Speech?"

"Of course."

"P.J. needs hearing aids. The window is about twelve to fourteen months. Preston loves P.J., but he doesn't get it. He thinks because P.J. hears certain sounds, everything will work out—that P.J. just needs time for his hearing to develop—and the pediatrician he consulted for a second opinion agrees with him."

"It's good that P.J. hears certain sounds, right?" Ann asked.

"Sure. But the audiologist has tested P.J. His loss is moderate at certain frequencies and severe at others. Even though he hears sounds, he's not hearing all the letters. It's gibberish. And it's harmful." Marcia felt a sense of dark despair, like the sky had suddenly been overtaken with heavy black clouds blocking out all the light. She reached for a box of tissues. "I'm sorry, enough of this."

"How are you and Preston doing—apart from the hearing stuff?" Ann asked, curling up on the couch, her legs and feet beneath her.

Marcia followed her to the couch. "Do you remember when we talked at your house last year and I told you about my conversation with my dad when my favorite doll broke?"

"Yeah—well, not word for word, but the idea was he could either fix it or get you a new one ... "

"That's right," Marcia said. "If he fixed it, it wouldn't be perfect, and if he got me a new one, it wouldn't be my favorite."

"And if I remember correctly, you said that's the way you felt about Preston, that deep down he was a good man, but you couldn't wait forever for that to surface. You said you'd lose yourself in the process."

"Right. It's complicated. Preston's father was not a good guy. He was always chasing rainbows, waiting for the next big deal—to make up the losses from the last one—and that's not all he chased. He wasn't the most attentive father either. Finally Preston's mother had enough of the squandering and womanizing and divorced him. Preston was just fifteen at the time. He's always been scared that he, too, would be a failure."

"I thought his business problems were turning around."

"It looks that way. I never know, but that's another problem."

"I'm missing something," Ann said.

Marcia got up, walked to the credenza, and poured herself bourbon, neat. She looked at Ann, who shook her head and held up her half-filled wine glass. Marcia looked out the window to the park, sighed, and returned to the couch.

"He has a daughter."

"*What?*"

"He recently found out that he's the father of a twenty-three-year-old. Her name is Katherine; she lives in New York. Just finished her graduate studies and is about to begin her career as a reporter."

They both sat quietly for a few moments, staring at each other. Then Marcia looked down and ran her foot across the soft carpet.

Ann broke the silence. "Has he met her?"

"Yes, we both have. Preston had lunch with her not long ago, and the three of us had dinner together across the street at Armani's last Thursday."

"Do you like her?"

"Yes. She's smart and thoughtful," Marcia said, taking comfort in their symmetrical exchanges and her ability to read the analogical codes. "This has been difficult for her, too. She'd been told by her mother that her father was killed in the Air Force before she was born. There was a man killed in the Air Force—her mother's boyfriend—but, recently, Katherine discovered that he was not her father, and that Preston was," Marcia said in a soft, distant voice.

"How's Preston doing with all of this?"

"He loves it. He's got a new sales campaign."

"What does that mean?"

"He's got to win her over—going all out."

"And you're pissed."

"I don't know what I am anymore. Preston didn't ask for this. He was twenty-three, for God's sake. He never knew ... until the girl's mother called him out of the blue about a month ago. I thought he handled it pretty well for the most part."

"So you're not upset?"

"I'd like not to be. Okay, I am upset. But I'm not ... pissed. I'm okay with his having a daughter, and, in a way, I admire his reaching out to her. She needs a father. And she's a good kid. My problem is with Preston, his inability to truly understand P.J.'s impairment. Passive-aggressive procrastination. Maybe even embarrassment. He'll use his newfound daughter as a welcome distraction. I've already seen him pulling away from me and P.J., and I hate it."

"Embarrassment?"

"I'm not sure, but he's always wanted a son. Now he sees imperfection in the mirror."

"Sounds like a psychology paper. Does he know you feel that way?"

"I haven't told him in so many words. He knows I'm upset. And it's likely to be fueling his fears about my leaving him again. He's never gotten over that. And you know what? I may do it. I don't know."

"How long has this been going on—your thinking about leaving him?"

"If you're asking whether it started after I found out about Katherine, the answer is no. Everything was going well while I was pregnant. Preston was attentive; his business was getting back on track; he was talking with the Collectibles—you know that group of Joe Hart's friends I told you about—and he seemed headed back to the Preston I fell in love with."

"That sounds like a, Yes?"

"No."

"Okay, so what was the trigger? P.J.'s hearing?"

"Probably. His lack of response then hurt me … but even before that. It's a pattern. He didn't follow through with Joe's friends. He and I see his commitment to Joe differently."

At that moment, there was a knock at the door, and a pleasant-looking woman walked in.

"This is Nadine, our nanny. We love her to death. Nadine, this is my dear friend, Ann."

"I'm pleased to meet you, Ms. Ann," Nadine said with a Jamaican accent, smiling at them both and picking up P.J. "How's my little man today? Are you ready for a stroll in the park?"

They all laughed when P.J. thrust his arms in the air and smiled.

"He responds readily to smiles and laughter," Marcia explained to Ann. "C'mon, Ann, let's get you settled in the guest room while P.J. and Nadine go out and get some fresh air."

★ ★ ★

P.J. and Ann were asleep when Preston came home and found Marcia sitting on the couch, staring at the bookcase.

"Ann's in the guest bedroom, Preston. Her conference ended early and she came over to talk—she's leaving in the morning."

"That's fine. I'm sure you two have had a good time. How's she doing?"

"Quite well, it sounds like. Her newsletter has taken off."

"Great."

Preston looked in on P.J. for a minute and then, back in the living room and seeing Marcia's glass of wine, poured himself a scotch, and sat down in one of the leather wingback chairs across from the couch.

"Have you had dinner?" Marcia asked.

"Yeah. At the club."

"We need to talk."

"We are talking."

"I'm serious. This can't wait."

"What can't wait?"

"Your son."

"How much wine have you had?"

"Not enough. It's not the wine. I'm going to have P.J. fitted with hearing aids as soon as the audiologist can do it."

"We've been through this," Preston said.

"This is important to P.J. and to me. My way can't hurt him. Your failure to see the need—or your procrastination—could."

"But P.J. *is* hearing. You know what my pediatrician says. These are honest differences of viewpoint."

"I don't care about honest differences of viewpoint anymore. There's the big 'D' school of thought, too. Is that what you want?"

"I'm just saying give it a few more months," Preston asked.

"I'm not doing that, Preston. I'm having him fitted with bilateral aids as soon as possible."

"I thought we were a team on this," Preston said.

"Then I'm resigning from the team."

"What does that mean?"

"You figure it out. I'm going to bed."

CHAPTER TWENTY-FIVE

A large man wearing a plaid shirt under overalls and moving with agility defying his seventy-eight years took the stairs two at a time to meet his granddaughter.

"Hi, Grandpa," Katherine shouted, throwing her arms around him.

"Hi, Kitten," Adrian said, hugging her long and hard.

"I've missed you so much," Katherine said. She loved hearing him call her Kitten, the only one who ever did so. Katherine let Hailey out of the SUV to run. Hailey ran to the open backyard and beyond.

Katherine walked with her grandfather around the house to the back porch, talking all the way, and they sat down in a pair of old wooden rockers. She saw Hailey way up on the hill, but one call was all it took to bring the dog running back, flat out toward Katherine's voice.

"Your mom will be home soon. She's called three times already. Let me help you with your stuff."

"Just leave it all there, Grandpa. We'll get it later."

Joined by Hailey, they walked back up the steps and into the hallway leading to the kitchen on the right and the living room to the left.

"Hungry?" Adrian asked.

"Not really. Guess what, Grandpa?" It's a game they used to play when Katherine was a child.

"What?" Adrian replied.

"On the way home, I had lunch at the Seneca Lodge."

"Well, I'll be. Did you see 'em? Jim? Gloria?"

"I saw them both. They send you their regards." She could see the twinkle in his eyes.

"Did you play it?"

"Luckily, I had a nickel."

"How's the track?"

"They said it's fine. I was in such a hurry to get here, I didn't have time to see for myself," she explained. "Grandpa, I want to go up to my room, rest for a while. You think that would be okay?"

"Of course. You've had a long day—coming all the way from New York City. You go ahead," he said, giving her a kiss on her forehead.

With Hailey at her side, Katherine climbed the wooden stairs to the second floor, passed her mother's room and her grandfather's room, and continued down the hall and through the door on the right. She marveled at the size of the house, how clean it was, the smell and warmth of the wooden floors, the wooden stairs, and the wooden railings. She thought about the 650-square-foot apartment she'd occupied in the city the past ten months, and the two flights of steel stairs she had to climb, and the noise, and the dirt. She reckoned a house like this would cost at least five million dollars in Manhattan—if you could even find one.

When she strolled into her bedroom, she felt transported in time, back to another world. She ran her hand up and down the smooth, carved spirals of the high, four-poster, antique mahogany bed, its laced-trimmed white duvet and matching dust ruffle still in place, and the antique dresser with square mirror nearby.

Katherine sauntered over to her old desk, sat down on the straight chair, and stared at the bare top. The more she looked, the wavier the desktop became. Soon the whole room was uneven and blurry. She knew something was missing from the desk—a framed photo that had been there her entire life. Her mother must have removed it. She knew her migraine would pass. What she didn't know was whether what caused it would ever go away.

She rose from the chair slowly and made her way to the bed, deciding it was time for a nap. Hailey jumped up on the bed and snuggled up to Katherine, still licking her face. Katherine was asleep in less than a minute.

★ ★ ★

It seemed to Beth that the twenty-two-minute drive from Rochester General to Marion had taken hours. As she pulled into the driveway, she was excited to see that her daughter was finally home. Beth looked over at the brand-new SUV, filled to the brim, and wondered momentarily how her daughter had been able to afford such luxury. She ran into the house and said hello to her dad, who pointed upstairs. A minute later, Beth found her daughter stretched out on top of the bed, dead to the world. She knew Katherine was exhausted and decided to let her sleep.

Beth went downstairs and found Adrian.

"How's she doing? How does she look to you? What did she say? Did she seem happy?"

"She's fine. Let her rest," he said. "Let's eat."

"You go ahead. I'll wait."

★ ★ ★

Katherine opened her eyes, looked at her watch, and looked again, not believing she'd slept for three hours. She looked out the window, saw her mother's car, and bounded out of the room and down the stairs. Katherine found her mother getting up from her favorite chair in the living room and moving to greet her with open arms.

"Hi, Mom."

"Hi, Honey. I didn't want to wake you. You must be hungry."

"I can't believe I slept that long."

"Pancakes?"

"How'd you know?"

They gabbed in the kitchen while Beth made fresh coffee and cooked blueberry pancakes and bacon. Katherine described her day in detail—packing her belongings, the drive, and the stop at the Seneca Lodge.

"Is that a rental car?"

"It's mine. Preston insisted on giving it to me. Tried to talk him out of it, but Casey, his CFO, persuaded me to take it."

"I need a father like that."

"No, you don't. You have the best father in the world."

"I heard that, Kitten," Adrian shouted from his den.

After dinner, Katherine got her suitcase and a few other items, figuring she'd tackle the rest tomorrow, carried them to her bedroom, and joined her mother in the living room.

"What time do you have to leave for work?" Katherine asked.

"I moved some things around, took tomorrow off," Beth said. "Thought you might need a hand."

"Thanks, Mom."

That evening things were like always—sort of. Beth and Katherine talked into the night, covered all the ground—everything except the two most contentious issues. Katherine saw the lines in her mother's face, how tired she was, and thought it better to deal with all that after her mother had a chance to rest.

CHAPTER TWENTY-SIX

Katherine was up early, ahead of her mother, but not Adrian. She could smell bacon and eggs cooking, and hear the coffee percolating. She joined him for an old-fashioned power breakfast, topped off with two fresh cinnamon buns for dessert. After they finished, and Katherine had fed Hailey, Adrian told her that he was going for a walk, and invited her to come.

"Where're you headed?" she asked.

"Where I go every morning—to say hello to your grandmother. Want to come along?"

"Absolutely," Katherine said. "Let's go, Hailey." The dog was already waiting at the door, wearing her *Why the drama?* look.

Adrian, Katherine, and Hailey walked north on Main Street, passed a gray house with a white picket fence, and turned left on Cemetery Lane. Katherine could hear the sounds of children playing at the elementary school as they ambled down the lane to the well-kept cemetery grounds. Soon they arrived at the gravestone marked Colina Bethany Kelly, 1934–2003. Adrian spoke softly to his wife for a minute or two, while Katherine and Hailey waited quietly a few steps away.

"Thanks for coming with me," Adrian said. "As long as you're keeping me company, before we go home, what d'ya say we make a stop at the church?"

Katherine knew that was coming. "Sure," she said, "I'll stay outside with Hailey."

In about a half an hour, they arrived at Saint Gregory's Church. Adrian went in and returned a few minutes later.

"You know, this church is connected to Saint Katherine. That's where your mom came up with your name—with a little help from me," Adrian said.

"I guess I heard that somewhere along the way," Katherine said.

She stopped walking, told Hailey to sit, and took hold of her grandfather's arm.

"Grandpa, may I ask you a difficult question?"

"You can try," he said. "And I will, too."

"Did Mom tell you that Larry was my father?"

"She didn't have to. I knew he was . . . or thought he was . . . he was her boyfriend."

"Why did you say *thought* he was?"

Adrian was silent for a few minutes. He pointed to a bench along the quiet street, and they walked to it and sat down.

"I know this must be painful for you. I spent a lot of time back there trying to ask for His forgiveness about all of this."

Katherine didn't really understand what he was saying, but thought it best to just listen.

"Your mother is a wonderful lady. She'd do anything for you. Anything. She figured your grandma and I would assume Larry was your dad. And we did. Or at least I did. Your grandma is . . . was smarter than me, in these things."

"What did Grandma think?" Katherine asked, in some ways wishing she hadn't.

"She may have known more than I did, or more than she wanted me to know. Women are funny that way—they just know things. Larry had left with the Air Force, and your mother was busy with her nursing in New York City. All I knew then was my daughter's heart was broken, her boyfriend was dead, and she was pregnant—and she had to have her baby. She knew that, too—on her own."

"Did Mom ever tell you the whole story?"

"About a month ago."

"What did she say?"

"That Larry was not your father. Larry didn't want to marry her—was gone in the Air Force—and that she got together with a young man when she was working in that hospital down there. She said that she knew she wanted to raise you as a single mom, and after we got word Larry was killed, she thought it would be easier for everyone if she said he was your father."

"Did she say why she didn't tell you and Grandma sooner?"

"She didn't want to upset us."

"Would you have preferred her to tell you?"

"I said I'd try, but that question doesn't seem to be going any-where . . . or at least anywhere good."

"Fair enough, Grandpa. Fair enough. I love you."

"I love you, too, Kitten. We better get home before we're all in the doghouse," Adrian said, as he slowly got up from the bench.

Katherine put her hand on her grandfather's shoulder. "Sit down, Grandpa, there's something else I want to say to you." Adrian sat and looked at Katherine. She could see the thoughts swirling in his head.

"You've always been there for me, Grandpa," Katherine said in a voice choked with tears. "You've taught me so much. One of the things you taught me is that it never hurts to say *thank you*. Thank you, Grandpa, for fixing my dolls, for cheering for me when I was cheering for our guys on the field, for teaching me how to drive, for telling me how beautiful I look—when we both knew better. For making me feel that I'm smart, that I can do anything, be anything, and shoot for the moon. And thank you for always telling me the truth."

Adrian sat without saying a word for several minutes. Finally, he put his arms around his granddaughter and gave her a warm, long hug. "Thanks, Kitten. I'm too old to turn down a thank you like that."

At that moment, Hailey jumped on the bench and started licking Katherine's face. She and her grandfather started laughing.

"Get down, Hailey, it's time for us to go," Adrian said.

★ ★ ★

Back at the house, Adrian went to his den to watch a recording of the last NASCAR race. Katherine saw Beth at the kitchen table sipping coffee and reading the newspaper. Katherine poured herself a cup and sat down.

Katherine handed her mother a small gift-wrapped box with an envelope under the bow.

"What's this?" Beth asked.

"Open it."

Beth surgically cut the bow and removed the paper as if she wanted to preserve it for all time. She opened the box and pulled out a lavender Norm Thompson scoop-neck bamboo nightgown with puckers at the yoke.

"This is beautiful," Beth said in a velvety soft voice. She opened and read the card, stood, walked to Katherine, and gave her a hug followed by a kiss on the cheek. "Thank you," she whispered.

"You're welcome, Mom. Happy Mother's Day."

"You've made my day, for sure. How long are you going to stay?"

"As long as it takes for me to pack my car as full as I can—leaving room for Hailey—and to decide what to leave behind."

"That shouldn't be hard."

"I don't want to leave you behind—that's what makes it hard."

"What does that mean?"

"Picture a twenty-three-year-old house exposed to serious tremors from an earthquake. At first, it looks like the house survived, but a survey shows structural damage—the foundation has shifted and the entire house, including the roof, has moved out of alignment."

Katherine could see a look of bewilderment on her mother's face, as if rain had suddenly fallen from a blue sky illuminated by a strong sun.

"I know you love me. You've taken care of me—been there for me—all of my life. That has been one of the cornerstones of my foundation. Another, however, is trust. I never thought that you'd lie to me, especially about something so fundamental. I know why you did it. I understand why you did it. But that doesn't rebuild the house."

Katherine could see her mother's hands were shaking and had turned white. Beth began to cough and rub the back of her neck.

"I know this is painful for you," Katherine said. "It's not fun for me either. But we have to deal with this. I don't want to leave without our at least trying to set the framework for rebuilding the house."

"How do we do that?" Beth asked in a shaky distant voice.

"The foundation has to be the truth. Promise me—and more importantly, promise yourself—that you will never lie to me again."

Beth nodded her head and mumbled some words that Katherine could not understand. Katherine got up and put her arm around Beth, and hugged her.

"I love you, Mom."

"I love you, too—and in the spirit of telling you the truth—I hate that you won't forgive me."

That stopped Katherine cold. *I hate that, too.* Her mother had just put her finger on the one burner on the stove in Katherine's mind that she hadn't been able to turn off. But it was a start. "What else do you hate?"

"I hate that I'm losing my eyesight and there's nothing I can do to stop it. I hate that I won't be able to help your grandfather when he needs me most. And when he's gone, I'll be alone."

Katherine knew her mother's macular degeneration was progressive, but she didn't know how far it had gone. Her mother was at her core a nurse, and with all her problems what she was worried about most was not being able to care for someone else.

"Hey, Mom, let me take you and Hailey for a ride in my new BMW before I pack it up. It's a beautiful day. Let's go to Sodus Point and have lunch on the bay."

"Let me check with Grandpa," Beth said.

"He can come, too."

"No, I think he'll be fine. Besides, I want to ask you some questions about Preston."

★ ★ ★

Beth went into the den to tell Adrian of their plans.

"How're you doing, Dad?"

"Fine. Better now that you two are talking. I've been purposely leaving you alone. She's a fine girl, your daughter. And you've been a fine mother."

"Stop it, Dad, stop it. I've done enough crying today. Do you want to ride with us? You'd love the car."

"Another time. I just want to be alone right now. And you two have more talking to do I'm sure. Be with her while you can."

Beth gave her father a kiss on the cheek.

"We'll be back in a while."

"Take your time."

★ ★ ★

Katherine punched the button on her remote, opening the back of her SUV just in time for Hailey to clear the hatch as she jumped in, tail wagging. Beth hopped in the right front seat, marveling at the finely stitched leather seats and dashboard and all the gadgets. Katherine set the GPS for Sodus Point, mainly to show her mother how the feature worked, and they were on their way, with Hailey's head practically in the front between them.

"Okay, let's have the questions about Preston," Katherine said.

"Just tell me. I want it all. How does he look? What's he like? How did you feel when you were with him?"

"Well, it started with his e-mail to me. He said he couldn't imagine what this must be like for me, and it breaks his heart to think about it. Here's a middle-aged man who finds out he has a daughter and he's thinking about how hard this is for me. Then he said he knew he wanted to be my father, to meet me, and get to know me *and love me*. I knew then that I wanted to reach out to this man."

"So you got in touch with him."

"I e-mailed him back and told him I wanted to meet him. He responded by inviting me to lunch the next day at the 21 Club. Have you ever been there?"

"No, but I've heard of it. Keep going."

Katherine described the lunch meeting in detail, down to the last morsel of food and the last word of conversation. "He told me he was married to a woman named Marcia and that they have a one-year-old son, who, unfortunately, has a hearing problem, Mom. They named the son after Joe Hart, a lawyer friend. That interested me because the lawyer obviously had been a huge influence on his life."

"Does this tie into your assignment?"

"It may. I'm working on that."

"He asked me about my career and all of that. It was a long lunch. I told him I wanted to learn more about Hart, and he invited me to his place to meet his wife and son and then go to dinner. So the next night, I found myself in Trump Tower meeting Marcia and P.J. and then when the nanny came, the three of us went to dinner across the street at Armani's."

"Armani's on Fifth Avenue?"

"Yes."

"I never knew they had a restaurant."

"That was wonderful. It was a great dinner and I enjoyed meeting Marcia."

"What did she look like?"

"Younger than Preston, dark hair, thin, smart—stylish. She was a professor of psychology at Columbia."

"What did you talk about?"

Katherine took the curves along the road with little effort in the powerful SUV. Almost on autopilot, she recalled the meeting with Preston and Marcia, and learning about Preston's charges.

"They were called the "Collectibles" and each was flawed in some way. Fulfilling that promise apparently had a big impact on Preston."

"Really? That's a twist. Why do you say *apparently*?"

"Just a hunch at this point. Something Marcia said when talking about this group of people and the influence Hart had on Preston ... I tried to pin Preston down, but Marcia called it an open question and said Preston was evolving on the subject."

"I'm not sure what that all means, but I know you'll figure it out."

Katherine thought about that and changed the topic. "Mom, what's the latest on your MD?"

"It's still dry MD, but my drusen are increasing fairly rapidly in both eyes, and I have slight central vision blurring in my right eye. My doctor thinks it could develop into wet, which is worse—new blood vessels under the macula leak blood and fluid—and that could damage my macula rapidly. For some people, shots to stop new blood vessels from growing can help—but there's risk with that, too. I worry that I won't be able to work down the road."

"I worry about that, too. I'm so sorry you're going through all of this," Katherine said, feeling the rising anxiety in her mother.

Now it was Beth's turn to change the subject. "How's your friend Susan?" she asked "She's such a sweetheart."

"I don't think I've told you this, Mom, and it's not for publication. Susan is an alcoholic. She's been sober for years, but recently has been drinking again. I spoke with her on my way home."

"I'm sorry to hear that. Tell her I asked about her."

Katherine drove along the shoreline of Lake Ontario as they continued to catch up, and Katherine knew her mother was enjoying the day as much as she was. Hopefully, she'd struck the right tone in their earlier discussion, and was glad that her mother seemed to be more at ease. On the way back from the Point they stopped to let Hailey leave a few messages and run around a bit, had a good lunch at a small bayside restaurant, where Beth indulged in two glasses of chardonnay before they began their trip home.

The rest of the day Katherine played with Hailey, did laundry, sorted what she would take to her new apartment, packed a small bag for her trip to Braydon, and talked some more with her grandfather. Beth was busy marinating the steaks and preparing Katherine's favorites, garlic mashed potatoes and green bean casserole.

After dinner, with their bellies full and the dishes in the dishwasher, the three generations of Kellys repaired to the porch. Adrian, Beth, and Katherine sat in rocking chairs, Hailey spread out on the floor close to her best friend, enjoying the cool breeze. For Katherine, it was just the rest she needed. She hoped it had done them all good.

CHAPTER TWENTY-SEVEN

Preston put aside the acrimony arising from his discourse with Marcia over the weekend, went to Wilson Holdings, skipped the routine morning meetings, and called Casey into his office. "Good morning, Casey. Is it not ever too early to eat a Snickers bar?"

"Goes good with coffee. You should try it. Might keep you from being so grumpy," Casey said.

"Goes well," Preston snapped.

"Who cares? Why'd you call me in here?"

"I'd like you to book me for the National Automobile Dealers Association and JD Power meetings in Vegas next week."

"I thought you were done going to those."

"It's been a while. I think I should join our team—good for morale."

"Okay."

"By the way, do you have Missy's contact details?"

"All I have is the e-mail for Mr. Greco."

"Forward that to me."

"Okay."

"How's Austin doing?"

"He's a regular tornado."

"What's that mean?"

"He's your buddy, Preston."

"Is he being helpful to you?"

"Not really," said Casey, between bites of candy bar.

"Why not?"

"Why are you drilling me on this?" demanded Casey, who was generally not easy to rile. "You bring this guy in a half a year ago, supposedly to help me. If you want him to be CFO, be my guest."

"Whoa. What's that all about? I thought you'd come around."

"You thought wrong."

"Why don't you like him?"

"How long you got?"

"Give me the short version," said Preston.

"He's long on the salesman, short on the brains."

"You're hopeless."

"Maybe this will help: he's gonna get you in trouble one of these days."

"Have you got any specifics?"

"Yeah. You got time to actually listen to this?"

"Yes."

Casey launched into the story he'd been holding back on. "He comes into our sales meeting yesterday, twenty-five minutes late." He described the scene with Bill Lamb, their new car sales manager; Antonio, their parts manager; Loreen, in charge of F & I; and Sam, their used car sales manager; all seated and waiting.

"Disley asks them for their reports," he continued. "They give them. He doesn't listen. Tells them his meeting with the folks at Mercedes could not have gone better, that they love us. He stresses we're a team—united—on our way to the moon. All the guys are rolling their eyes."

"And that's what's bothering you?"

"No, that's what should be bothering you. What's bothering me is, he comes into my office after the meeting—tells me he ran into Teddy Thomson, Bank North America's lease manager, at the New York City Athletic Club playing racquetball. That Teddy wants some kind of financial backup to support the next extension of our lease. And he wants my file."

"What happened to Brad Whitestone, BNA's loan officer in the commercial real estate division? He's handled our account for more than twenty years."

"Exactly. I told Disley that we leased the building from General Contractors and Holdings, and we sublet six thousand feet to BNA. General got in trouble, BNA took the building, and we became the Bank's tenant—that I figure Thomson probably wants our year-end operating statements—and that I'd handle it," Casey said.

"And?"

"He pushes back—wants to take it to Teddy—says it fits in with his sales outreach, and Thomson's a heavy hitter—I told him that was not a good idea. I'd handle it. He says he wants to look over the statements. I told him I'd send him copies."

"Is that all he said?"

"Yeah, other than his views on how the Packers are doing and telling me I need a big flat-screen television in my office."

"I don't get it," Preston said.

"I'm not done. I pulled the most current operating statements for the four franchises being run out of the Mercedes store. Seeing they were not consolidated and in their present condition failed to accurately reflect our true financial condition, I tossed them on my credenza and called Jane for updated, accurate, consolidated statements. She said they'd be on my desk the next morning."

Now Casey had his boss's undivided attention. Preston knew how carefully Casey had trained Jane, the company's bookkeeper, and how Casey stressed the necessity for all reports to portray the company's situation—good or bad—as precisely as possible.

"What happened?"

"When I got back from lunch, the statements on my credenza were gone. I immediately called Disley and asked him if he'd taken them. He said he'd picked up the copies to save me the trouble. I reminded him that I'd told him I'd handle it. I told him he'd picked up the wrong statements."

"Not good," Preston said. He buzzed Austin on the intercom and asked him to come down. A few minutes later, Austin sauntered into Preston's office, nodded at Preston, and sat in the chair next to Casey without looking at him.

"Hey guys, what's up?" Austin asked.

"You picked up copies of our operating statements last week? What did you do with them?" Preston asked.

"Yeah. I got them from Casey."

"No. You took them from my office," Casey said.

"You told me I could have them," Austin said.

"You picked up the wrong papers. I told you I'd handle it."

"Hang on," Preston said. "Austin, I asked you what you did with them."

"I gave them to Teddy Thomson, BNA's lease manager."

"Thanks for coming in, Austin. I'd like to talk to Casey alone."

Austin left the office, and Casey closed the door.

"Fix it," Preston said.

"You mean I can fire him?"

"He didn't know they were wrong. Fix the statements and get them to the bank."

"I've already corrected the statements, Preston, and sent them to the bank—with copies to you. Have you ever looked at them?"

"That's your job. I'm glad you straightened it out."

"You don't get it. What I'm worried about—and what *you* should be worried about—is not what I've corrected, but what I don't know and can't find out. What has Austin done that he shouldn't, or not done that he should? This has to stop."

"I agree. It's just that I have a lot on my plate right now. I know this is difficult, Casey, but do the best you can."

Casey scratched his head, took off his glasses, polished the lenses with his handkerchief, and reached in his pocket for another Snickers bar.

CHAPTER TWENTY-EIGHT

Katherine breathed in the familiar musty, earthy smell with the faint hint of a cigar as she climbed onto the cracked leather bench seat of the old red pickup truck and sat next to her grandfather. She hated to leave him, and was excited when he'd asked her if she wanted to go out to the Newark Rod and Gun Club to "shoot some birds." Worried about Hailey's ears, she'd left the dog at home.

It wasn't just the outing. It was being with her grandpa. Feeling his presence. Talking to him in his truck, a sanctuary where, looking back, the conversations were deeper, protected, and had exceeded the test of time.

The club was on the outskirts of the small village of Newark, some fifteen miles from home. Katherine was pleased that her grandfather was driving slowly through the winding country roads—she wanted the time with him to last as long as possible.

"I had a chance to spend some time with Mom after we talked."

Adrian looked at her, not saying anything but saying everything.

"You knew I would," she said.

He smiled.

"Thanks for taking me to the cemetery."

"Thank you for going with me. It gets a little lonely sometimes."

"There is something I would like to ask you, Grandpa, if you are by any chance in the mood for a few questions."

"I'm always in the mood for talking with you, Kitten, and that usually includes a lot of questions."

"Thanks. When we were at the church, you went in. You're Presbyterian. Why did you go in there?"

Adrian was quiet for a while.

"Your grandma was a serious Catholic. She worried about me—wondering whether I was getting enough of what I needed in the religion department. She talked me into going to church with her a couple of times. She always lit those candles . . . 'votives,' she called them."

Katherine knew her grandfather was getting around to the answer, and she wasn't sure what it would be. She was intrigued by the candles comment, but didn't want to rush him. After a few minutes of silence, just riding along, her patience was rewarded.

"Lighting those candles," he said. Katherine pondered the neutrality of his tone.

"What did you feel when you did that?"

"It's something I can do. It's what she always did. I'm just giving her a hand."

Katherine pondered his words as she stared out the window at the muddy water in the winding creek on Hydesville Road. She saw turtles on the banks basking in the sun, birds darting in and out of the foliage and trees, searching for food. The scene was bittersweet for her.

"Do you feel, then, that you're fulfilling her commitment?"

"No, she's fulfilled that. She's home free. I'm just keeping her alive for me."

"I think I understand," Katherine said softly.

"It wasn't just for her yesterday."

"Mom?"

"And you, Kitten."

"I love you, Grandpa."

"I love you, too," Adrian said, as he drove through the village of

Newark and turned onto Tellier Road. "What'd ya say we shoot some clay birds?"

The old Ford truck grunted and creaked as it passed an old hen-house on the left and made its way over the quarter-mile dirt road extension leading to the club. Getting closer, they saw a few men shooting at a trap and then a skeet field on the left. Adrian parked on the gravel bed about thirty feet from the forty-by-twenty-four-foot raised ranch building. They could see another trap field followed by a skeet field on their right.

Adrian lifted the first and then the second Remington twelve-gauge shotguns off the rack in his truck, collected two earmuffs and two eye protectors from the floor behind the seat, and then grabbed his old deerskin ammo pouch.

"They're using eleven-eighty-sevens today, but I brought this eleven-hundred for you. It's the one you fired at this club when you were fourteen." He handed Katherine the 1100, one of the eye shields, and an ear noise protector.

"I don't remember the gun, but I sure do recall being here," she said, taking the gun and protective equipment.

They walked in the door and over a vinyl floor to the first of four eight-foot metal folding tables and chairs, set down their guns and gear, and proceeded to a coffee bar where they were greeted by a burly, round-faced man in his fifties wearing green-and-grey hunting pants, a red-and-white checkered shirt, and a big smile.

"Adrian. Good to see you again. When you going to join the board?"

Adrian laughed. "Meet my granddaughter, Katherine. Kitten, this is Ronnie Randell, one of the big shots running this club."

"I'm pleased to finally meet you, young lady," Ronnie said, shaking her hand. "Your grandfather and I go way back. He talks about you all the time. You're in the big city now, aren't you?"

"Thank you. It's good to meet you as well. Yes, I'm working in New York, or will be soon."

"Katherine's going to be a journalist," Adrian said, with obvious pride. "Today we thought we'd shoot some trap for old times' sake."

"Sounds like a plan. Can I get you a coffee, soft drink, or anything from the fridge?" Ronnie asked.

"No thanks, we're all set there," Adrian said. "Where you got us set up?"

"The first trap field on the right. Gene's over there now and ready to go whenever you are."

While Adrian and Ronnie were talking, Katherine had wandered over to the wall on her left, where she was studying the trophies and pictures. Adrian thanked Ronnie and joined her.

"That's a picture of Harold Contant. He's in the Skeet Shooting Hall of Fame. Over there is Craig Parsons, a national skeet shooting champion. He shot thirteen hundred and fifty straight and never missed a bird."

"Grandpa, here's a great picture of you. Who's the man with you?"

Adrian looked at the picture for a minute. "That's Harry Klaskowski. He's a good friend and a great shooter. He shoots real good with a camera, too. Harry took the Trap and Skeet Night title a while back and was a state champion skeet shooter. He's from the Buffalo area but has been a member of our club for years."

"May I take a picture of this wall?"

"Absolutely," Adrian said. "Then let's go to the field so we don't keep Gene waiting. These fellows help out, and I don't want to abuse their kindness."

"Sorry, Grandpa. Guess I got carried away with the wall." Katherine took a few shots of the pictures and trophies with her iPhone, thanked Ronnie, and said good-bye. Then she picked up her gun, went outside, and joined her grandfather walking toward the trap field with his shotgun and pouch and protectors.

Adrian and Katherine could see the green wood house with a rubber roof slanted upward, from which the clay targets would automatically be ejected into the air upon the voice command of "pull," transmitted through the small microphone in the shell a foot or so in front of their shooting station. Behind them, sitting on a stand like a lifeguard at a beach, was the scorekeeper who would oversee the shoot, ascertaining when the shooters were ready and giving the command to proceed.

Adrian set a box of shells on a small wooden table in front of where Katherine would be starting, and they took their places at the field, Adrian at position one, Katherine at position two.

The scorer asked, "Shooters ready?" Adrian replied, "Yes." The scorer directed, "Commence firing."

Adrian took one shell from the box lodged in the pouch in his belt, opened the receiver, placed it in the chamber, pressed the latch to close the chamber, and adjusted his stance.

Adrian yelled, "Pull." A clay bird sailed into the air. Adrian tracked it and pulled the trigger, and it burst into pieces. He repeated the process four more times, hitting the bird each time, and then it was Katherine's turn.

Katherine was watching her grandfather carefully. She put a shell into her gun, wiggled a bit into a comfortable position, yelled, "Pull," shot, and missed the bird. She looked at her grandpa, who nodded slightly and winked at her. She took a deep breath, reloaded, and said, "Pull." Katherine took her time tracking the bird this time and then squeezed off a shot. The clay target scattered. She took her next three shots, hitting two out of three. Adrian smiled, giving her an okay sign. Adrian moved to position two, Katherine to position three, and the shoot continued.

When Adrian finished shooting at station four, he asked Katherine how she was feeling and whether she wanted to keep going. Katherine's face gave him the answer, and they continued until each had completed the entire round of five shots at each of the five positions.

Adrian began to pick up the spent shells, but the scorer told him to leave them, he'd take care of everything. Adrian thanked the scorer for the shoot. He gave Katherine a warm hug, and they walked together to Adrian's truck, where they placed the guns in the rack and their earmuffs, eyeglasses, and Adrian's pouch on the floor behind the seat.

"That was so much fun, Grandpa. Thanks," Katherine said giving him a hug and a kiss on the cheek.

"How 'bout a turkey burger?" Adrian asked.

"I'd love one."

Grandfather and granddaughter ambled inside arm in arm. Ronnie greeted them warmly. They ordered turkey burgers, which Ronnie grilled outside and served to them along with a couple of Cokes. Before long, the scorer came in and handed a sheet to Adrian and Katherine showing the results of the shoot: 23 hits and 2 misses for Adrian, 20/5 for Katherine.

"Look at that," Adrian said, studying the sheet. "You really shot well, Kitten. Unbelievable, given how long it's been."

Katherine beamed. "Just got lucky, I guess. You make me feel that way, Grandpa."

As they headed back to Marion, Katherine was bursting with enthusiasm. "Is there such a thing as shooter's high?" she asked.

"I think so," Adrian replied. "Just like smoking a good cigar."

He reached in his glove compartment, pulled out a Romeo y Julieta, and lit up. They laughed, Adrian told her stories, and Katherine shared her dreams with her grandfather all the way home.

CHAPTER TWENTY-NINE

Hailey seemed a bit anxious as she watched Katherine load the SUV. Tail tucked between her legs, she circled the vehicle slowly.

"Don't worry, Hailey, I'll make sure there's room for you."

Katherine said her good-byes to her mother and grandpa, with extra-long hugs and kisses. She could feel a weight building in her heart, knowing leaving this time was different. This time Katherine knew she was leaving more than the family she loved. Katherine reset her GPS to project the New York State Thruway to Syracuse and Highway 81 South to New York. It suited her mindset.

Katherine wanted to savor the good feelings she had from her visit and unbundle all the thoughts and emotions produced by the trip. Thinking about it, she felt like she had stepped on the up escalator of a large department store, each floor containing a wide variety of specific goods and materials.

First Floor. Marion. It felt so good to be with her grandfather again, and her mom. She loved being in the country. The winding roads, the trees, the creeks, the colors. But, somehow, it just didn't fit anymore—like trying to wear the clothes she wore as a child. Yes, it was quiet, but the quiet this time gave her a headache. It was lonely. And boring. She decided not to explore that floor anymore.

Second Floor. Uncertainty. How happy was Grandpa? His health still seemed to be good, but this time, when she looked into his eyes, there were pieces of him that were missing. How long would he last?

Third Floor. Her mother. She'd felt she designed the blueprint for rebuilding the house. She made clear that the foundation had to be the truth, and her mother had promised not to lie to her anymore. Her mother had always been truthful—with everyone. Until now, she'd never even thought about her mother's honesty; it was just assumed, perhaps, taken for granted. What Katherine understood, but still couldn't accept, was her mother's lying about such a fundamental and core matter. The roots of identity ran deep; when they were severed, the pain was exquisite and unbearable. Katherine understood her mother's reasons for lying, which she found practical and even reasonable under the circumstances—but the consequences were, for Katherine, catastrophic. The confidence inherent in an identity was replaced by insecurity.

The road suddenly became wavy, and Katherine knew she could not continue up the escalator. It was time for lunch anyway. She pulled off at the next travel plaza.

★ ★ ★

Three hours from New York City, Katherine called Susan to check in and see if she was still willing to help her get settled in her new apartment.

"Hey, what's going on?" Susan said.

"We're on our way back."

"Great. I am, too—emotionally, that is. How's Hailey doing?"

"She's licking my face as we speak."

"How'd it go?"

"It was quite an experience, actually. They say you can't go back."

"Uh-oh. I'd better sit down. This is gonna be one of those conversations."

"Not like our last one," Katherine said.

"I'm sure it won't. I'm sober."

"Glad to hear that."

"Are you going to tell me how it went?"

"It went well. I picked up my stuff. It was great to see Grandpa. And my mom took a day off so we had plenty of time to talk."

"So, what did you tell your mother?"

"That we needed to rebuild our relationship, from the ground up, and I asked her to promise she would never lie to me again."

"Too bad."

"Why?"

"That's a promise she can't keep."

"Well, she was pretty direct in our conversations after that."

"Everybody lies," Susan said. "Big lies, small ones, bad ones, and good ones. It's the grease that makes the wheel go around."

"You don't," Katherine said.

"All the time. Mostly to myself. Sometimes to others, depending on what I need and what they want. As an alcoholic, I've honed my lying skills to an art form."

"I think you're being too hard on yourself."

"I don't. We all need a little delusion to soften the reality. We all conceal parts of ourselves."

Katherine paused, giving that one a little thought. "Interesting comment," she said. "Do you really believe what you're saying about lying?"

"Ever hear about the monks in the Middle Ages who held there was actually a hierarchy of truth?" Susan asked. "At the top, they studied their navels over the fate of the universe—you know, whether there's a heaven, stuff like that. Next down on the rung, was moral truth—how to live. Under that was the allegorical truth—the lessons of the stories. And at the bottom—least significant—was the literal truth. Because that was irrelevant. It didn't matter whether it was truth, history, or fiction because it was supplied for signification. It wasn't about enlightenment; it was about concealment. Control. Sound familiar?"

Katherine was quiet for a few minutes while she pondered what her friend had just said. She could tell by the tone of Susan's voice that she was serious about it.

"Where do you come up with this stuff?"

"Well, in this case, fourteenth-century medieval history."

Katherine thought about sports. Alex Rodriguez. Marion Jones. Barry Bonds. And the endless questions about Lance Armstrong. Then her mind turned to how intense political coverage had become. Classified. Unclassified. Talking points. Spin rooms. She was glad Susan was her friend.

"Thanks for telling me that. Do you feel like helping me unload and get settled?"

"No. Call when you're at my building. And when we're done, let's go to Katz's Deli for a pastrami sandwich and see if I can get what she had."

"You'll never get Harry and Sally out of your mind," Katherine said. "See ya soon."

★   ★   ★

By the time Katherine and Susan moved everything from the car to the new apartment, they were too tired to go back to the city. They ordered in a pizza and sat in the midst of unpacked boxes to eat it. Exhausted, Katherine slept right on the mattress on the unmade bed, while Susan spent the night on the couch.

They woke up late the next morning, had breakfast, and took Hailey for a walk. When they returned, a friendly woman who looked to be sixty or so, wearing an apron, was waiting at the front door of Katherine's apartment and carrying a chicken casserole in a foil-covered Pyrex dish.

Hailey rose on her hind legs and gently put her front paws on the woman's arm, smelling the dish.

"Hailey, down," Katherine said. "I'm so sorry, ma'am."

"No need, my dear. I love dogs. Mine's been gone for two years now, and I still miss her. I'm Becky Bergner, your neighbor in the apartment next door. I made this casserole for you," she said, handing Katherine the dish.

"Thank you so much. I'm Katherine Kelly, and this is my friend

Susan from New York City. You've already met Hailey. Can you come in?"

"Oh, I'd love to."

They stepped inside Katherine's apartment. "I just moved in last night, Ms. Bergner. Please excuse the mess."

"Please, call me Becky. And forget the mess. What else would it be?"

Katherine put the casserole in the refrigerator and thanked Becky again.

"Please, what else would I do?" Becky said.

They pulled up chairs around the small, white round table—about the only space that wasn't filled with boxes, clothes, and suitcases. There was still coffee left over from breakfast. Katherine poured them each a cup.

Becky told them her life story. How her husband, Howie, had worked in the garment industry until he died of a heart attack. What a wonderful man he was. Why they never had children, and how Chloe, her French poodle and the smartest dog in the world, had died. All the time she talked, Becky was petting Hailey, whose head was resting on her lap.

"It looks like you've made a friend," Katherine said.

"What else? She's a beautiful dog. And smart."

"How can you tell she's smart?" Susan asked.

"Because she knows I love her. Look at her. The smart ones know."

"How 'bout taking care of her when Katherine's away?" Susan said. "That was my job when Katherine lived in Manhattan, but now she's out here."

"Forgive my friend Susan, Becky. She's always been direct."

"Please. I wanted to ask earlier. I like direct."

"I appreciate that, Becky," Katherine said. "I'd love to call on your help in the future."

"I'm going to go now. You have a lot to do. Come see me when you can, Katherine. I hope you like the dish. It was one of Howie's favorites. Nice to meet you, too, Susan. What's your last name?"

"Bernstein."

"You come visit me, too, Susan. I'm a good cook. And now I know what you like to eat."

"Thank you," Susan said. "We'd enjoy that. In fact, Katherine and I are going to Katz's this afternoon when we get back to the city."

"They're good. Howie thought their cheese blintzes were almost as good as mine."

They walked Becky to the door, Hailey trailing at her side all the way. At the door, Becky kissed Hailey good-bye, waved to the girls, and left.

CHAPTER THIRTY

Casey heard a familiar knock on his door and knew without a response Austin would be sitting before him with the latest great news on how well Wilson Holdings was doing—largely contradicted by the reports he had submitted at Casey's request. Sure enough, in walked Austin, in his seersucker suit, sporting a red polka-dot bow tie and an oversized smile.

"What did ya think of the reports, Big Guy?" Austin asked. "Pretty strong stuff, huh?"

Casey sat and stared at Austin, reached into the bottom drawer of his desk, took out a cheese sandwich, and started munching.

"Well?" Austin asked.

"I think if you had a cogent thought in your head, it would be lonesome," Casey mumbled while chewing.

"You're becoming increasingly difficult to work with," Austin said.

"You're empty," Casey said.

"You don't like the reports."

"It's not a matter of liking them or not. They clearly paint a positive position for us. The statement of assets is strong. Of course, it's made up largely of three-dollar bills. Did it ever occur to you that we have an obligation to tell the bank the truth?"

"We gotta get a lease extension. Teddy told me what he needs. These reports give it to them. We're not talking about a loan here, or floor plans. This is only real estate. I've presented it in the best light for us, that's all. Lighten up. It's not an IRS audit."

Casey finished his sandwich and a cup of coffee, and started in on his next Snickers bar.

"Say something, Casey."

"I don't like you," Casey said.

"Why?"

"Because you're an Ivy League helium balloon."

"That's not funny," Austin said.

"I agree. It's sad. Get out of my office."

★ ★ ★

Later that day, Casey noticed Preston in his office, buzzed him on the intercom, and asked if he had a minute. Preston motioned through the glass partition for Casey to come in.

"Have you seen any of Austin's latest reports?" Casey asked him.

"Just that they came in—I haven't reviewed them. Why?"

"They're all trumped up—if you'll forgive the expression. He's not giving the bank the whole picture. We've seen this movie before."

"So why don't you straighten it out?" Preston asked.

"I did that four days ago. And I'll correct these. But it's a pattern. He's not doing his job and he's dangerous. And you're in denial trying to protect your buddy."

"We've been through this before, Casey."

"Exactly. That's the problem," Casey reiterated. "Maybe I can make my position clearer. I quit."

"C'mon, Casey, settle down. You can't quit; you're an owner."

"Yeah, but you have to buy back my fifteen percent. So talk to your big-shot lawyers and get them working on it. Not going through this again. I'm leaving in thirty days."

Casey was out the door and down the hall before Preston could formulate a comeback, and Preston was left wondering if Casey really meant what he said.

★ ★ ★

Preston left his office and instructed his driver to take him to the Union League Club. He spent a couple of hours thinking about the company and Casey. Surely, he figured, he could talk Casey out of leaving. He wished Casey was not so critical of Austin, and he sensed some reverse snobbery in Casey's attitude.

After two or three scotches, however, Preston admitted to himself that he hadn't reviewed the financials in any depth, and if Casey was right, the company could really be exposed. He consoled himself with the fact that he'd been going through an extraordinary amount of stress, particularly with Marcia and P.J. The only bright spot was Katherine—but he sensed that that was not helping the situation with his wife. He needed to put his relationship with Marcia back on track. He was sure it was an alignment problem. He left the club, felt the light rain, went back, got an umbrella, and walked to his condo.

★ ★ ★

Marcia had finally quieted P.J. down when she heard Preston come in and throw his keys on the marble table by the door. She gently closed the door to P.J.'s room and went into the kitchen.

"I never heard from you as to when you'd be home tonight," she said to Preston. "I'm about to fix dinner. You've been at the club."

"Casey wants to quit," Preston said, pouring himself a scotch and collapsing in his favorite leather chair.

"Where did that come from?" Marcia asked. "I thought things were going well."

"I don't know. Maybe he's just blowing off steam. He doesn't like Austin."

Marcia saw the tension in Preston's face. She sat down in the adjoining chair. "Neither do I. He's a phony. You're the only one who likes him."

"So, how was your day?" Preston asked sourly.

"As you know, I've been consulting with Clarke Schools and taking P.J. to Betty Simpson, the pediatric audiologist, and to Dr. Triden, the otolaryngologist, for assessment. This morning, P.J. and I met with Betty for his first fitting. She is so good to work with."

Marcia could feel the floor vibrate from the rapid up and down movement of Preston's legs, and she could hear him patting his thighs.

"You mean he's wearing hearing aids right now?" he asked.

"Not at the moment. I just put him down. This is a process, Preston. We have to introduce him to the aids, and make it a happy time. I wish you were involved in this. It would be a lot easier for me and better for P.J."

"How am I supposed to do that when I'm trying to keep our business together, deal with Casey, and everything else? How's that supposed to work?"

"We're not the first family with a hearing impaired child. I love Casey, but he's not my first priority. If he wants to leave, I wish him the best and I hope he's happy."

"That's easy for you to say. You don't have to deal with the daily problems of Wilson Holdings."

"You know, Preston, I never gave any thought to the fact that I'm younger than you are until this moment. Every day you're becoming an older man. And every day, I'm feeling farther away from you. We have a child. He needs us. I'm going to take care of our child as best I can. If you can't be an involved husband, you should at least want to be an involved father."

"I am an involved father—on two fronts now. And I don't know how you can say I'm not an involved husband."

"Let's leave your bifurcated fatherhood on the table for the moment. I've stood by you with Katherine, and I like her. This isn't about Katherine. It's about you and me and our son. The fabric that binds us is stretching and it's starting to tear. We repaired it once. I don't know if we can do it again."

"What in the world does all of that mean?" Preston asked.

"Not enough to you. Not enough to you," Marcia said, tears streaming down her face. "Let's forget about dinner. I don't feel like cooking and I'm not hungry. I'm sorry you had a bad day, and

I'm sorry that Casey wants to leave—although it doesn't surprise me. He's probably worried about our company. And it is *our* company, if you'll recall. If Casey's worried, I'm worried. When you talk with your lawyers, and I'm sure you will, ask them what happens to his shares."

CHAPTER THIRTY-ONE

A s she drove slowly along Braydon's Main Street in her BMW, with Hailey's head hanging out the passenger window, Katherine was impressed by the old, two-story wooden buildings on each side, with flowers accenting the balconies and the windows, and the quaint stores, each adorned with a colorful display. Plenty of places to park. No meters. No honking horns, no sirens, just people and slow moving traffic along the clean sidewalks and streets. In a way, she was back home—in Marion again.

Katherine applied the brakes, realizing the street had come to an end. Looming above her was the largest tree she'd ever seen, with moss hanging from its huge limbs and seeming to grow out of the roof of an old, white wooden building. "The Live Oak Inn—Since 1846," read the sign.

Following the arrows, Katherine drove to the back of the inn, where she found a wide-open lot bordered by tall pine trees and cars lined up neatly on finely crushed oyster shells. She parked, let Hailey out, and took her for a walk to some trees and bushes at the edge of the lot. The two walked side by side along the stone path lined with azalea bushes to the front entrance and climbed two steps to a front porch filled with rocking chairs. Katherine opened the large oak door.

As Katherine entered the reception area, she discovered the other half of the magnificent oak tree, its large branches indeed protruding through the roof. To the left of the tree was a finely finished oak counter behind which was an office, apparently a holdover from the nineteenth century yet filled with computers, fax machines, telephones, and other accoutrements of a modern hotel. She was greeted by an energetic young lady wearing a scarlet silk scarf who welcomed her and, like everyone, immediately fell in love with Hailey.

Katherine checked in and accepted the clerk's offer of a tour, including a peek into the quaint dining room. The late afternoon sun was shining through windows with dark wood trim, accented by red velvet drapes with matching swag and jabot. A number of mostly square and a few round tables, covered with embroidered linen tablecloths and antique chairs, filled out the room, which was lighted by a large crystal chandelier in the center of the ceiling. In another room, a bar that brought to mind the pubs she imagined in Ireland, or perhaps ones her grandfather had talked about.

After thanking her host and with a long day of driving behind them, Katherine gathered her suitcase, and she and Hailey went to her room. Her quarters at the Live Oak reminded her of a larger version of the bedroom in her childhood dollhouse, complete with period furniture and an antique bed. A window overlooked a small park and allowed light to shine onto an antique desk (not lacking, however, an Internet modem and plenty of power outlets). She was happy to see a bath with a full-size old-fashioned tub and matching sink.

Katherine unpacked, filled one of Hailey's bowls with water and the other with dry dog food, and called Alice to let her know she had arrived safely. In no time she collapsed on the bed, sinking down in the fluffy covers. Hearing Hailey slurp up the water, and with a big smile on her face, Katherine fell asleep.

An hour later, Katherine woke and saw it was already 8:30 p.m. Worried about dinner hours, but not wanting to go out, she climbed in the tub, took a quick shower, changed clothes, and telling Hailey to stay, walked down two flights of carpeted stairs, hands on the mahogany railing, to the dining room, where she saw a few guests still lingering over their meals. A woman at the entrance to the dining room greeted her and showed her to a small table by the window, asking her if that would be acceptable. It was where she'd hoped to sit when she saw the dining room earlier.

After an enjoyable dinner, Katherine wandered into the taproom and sat at the thick oak bar, feeling the finely trimmed and finished wood and admiring the joints. She again thought of her grandpa, who while spending a lifetime farming and then at Seneca Foods' processing plant in Marion, had a passion for woodworking. She remembered, as a child, his hours in his workshop in the back of the garage refinishing antique furniture, not to mention making all kinds of toys for her. He would love to see this bar room and especially the bar itself. She decided to order a Guinness in his honor.

As she sipped her beer—mulling over her day's travels and wondering what her meeting in the morning with Alice might be like—she noticed a small, brass engraved plaque just inside the top curve in the center of the bar. Examining it more closely, she read *Cornelius C. Corrigan—Corrigan Yachts. 1922.* She asked the bartender, a slim, thirty-something young man with a pleasant face and *Bobby* embroidered on his uniform polo shirt, what he could tell her about the plaque.

Bobby first welcomed her to the Inn, explaining that he was the son of Robert and Mary McKenzie, the fourth-generation owners of the establishment. Katherine eyes immediately lit up.

"McKenzie? From Scotland?"

"Yes, indeed. But you won't want me to bore you with all of that."

"Actually, I'd really like to know."

"Well, it's fairly quiet tonight; I guess the short version won't hurt. We go back a ways. My great-great-great-great-grandfather, Hugh McKenzie, came to this country between 1745 and 1750. He landed in the Cape Fear area of the Carolina colony probably around Wilmington, and joined the Continental Army during the Revolutionary War attached to General Nathanael Greene. While in service, he became sick, never recovered, and was buried in Greenville, South Carolina."

Katherine, who had taken out her pad and pen, while he talked, was now busy taking notes.

"Why are you so interested?" Bobby asked.

"My great-great-great-grandfather on my mother's side was a McKenzie, and he, too, came to the Cape Fear region, in, I believe from what I could determine in my genealogy research, 1794."

By now, Katherine could see that she had Bobby's total interest. "The first major settlement of the Highland Scots in North Carolina was the Argyll Colony," she recalled from her research.

"That would have been about the time they fought the Jacobites, dealing a blow to the clans, and causing many Scots to emigrate to North Carolina and then South Carolina," Bobby continued, seemingly unaware of the customer at the other end of the bar.

"That's right," Katherine said.

"Have you been to Scotland?"

"I went during my second summer in college on a two-week scholarship exchange program," she replied. "Actually stood on the battlefield where the followers of Bonnie Prince Charles fought that battle and saw a reenactment."

Bobby excused himself to attend to his other customer and within a short time returned. "I can't wait to visit Scotland. Must have been a special trip for you."

"It was. There was so much to see, so much history. Edinburgh. The castle. All of Scotland, the highlands, the lakes."

"What was the place you remember the most?" Bobby asked.

"It was in Edinburgh, at the Greyfriars Churchyard. I was raised a Catholic in the tradition of my mother, but I loved going to the Presbyterian church with my grandfather. There is a stained glass window above the pulpit in the sanctuary, which depicts the signing of the solemn covenants. Just above the signers in the background of that window you could see the Edinburgh Castle. I stood on that same spot."

Bobby smiled. "You asked me about the plaque."

Katherine took careful notes as he spoke.

He told her about a yacht maker and craftsman named Corey, whose family owned a yacht company north of Charleston, on the waterway, for God knows how long, and that Corey knew the family and agreed to do the extensive woodwork restoration years ago at the Inn. The counter in the reception area, the railings for all the staircases, and the bar had been his handiwork. Corey, he said, was a fine gentlemen and a legend in these parts.

"Is he still living?" Katherine asked.

"I'm not certain, Miss Kelly," he replied, surprising Katherine that he knew her name. "Mr. Corey had some difficulties ... he'd be at least seventy-nine or eighty years old by now. A fine man, indeed."

Returning to her room, Katherine found Hailey up on the bed, head between her extended front legs, with a guilty expression on her face. Katherine gave her a kiss and took her for a long walk, the moon and stars lighting the way. Later, they settled in for the night. Katherine fell asleep absorbing the contrast of sleepy, southern Braydon with the city she left that morning. About "Mr. Corey," she definitely wanted to know more.

CHAPTER THIRTY-TWO

After being introduced to grits along with a delightful breakfast served at her favorite table with the morning sun streaming through the window, and taking Hailey for a long morning walk, Katherine phoned Alice.

"I'm glad you and Hailey are here safely. How was your trip?" she asked.

"The trip was long, but I love the Inn. Is this a good time for me to come over?"

"Absolutely. You can easily walk," Alice said, giving Katherine the directions.

Katherine and Hailey enjoyed the stroll to Mulberry Street. In fifteen minutes or so, Katherine saw a mailbox with two hummingbirds painted on the side, hovering over the number 203.

She opened the wrought-iron gate of the white picket fence and followed the stepping stones to the two-story wood frame house with forest green shutters and a wide front porch. Hailey followed behind. Pots full of brightly colored flowers hung from the borders of the ceiling.

"Hello, Katherine," Alice said, shaking Katherine's hand and bending down to pat Hailey. "So you're Preston's daughter. I'm delighted to meet you. I can't believe you came all the way to Braydon to see me. My goodness, you're beautiful."

Katherine thanked Alice, taken by how warm and sweet she was.

"Come in—both of you," said their host. "I'll need to introduce Hailey to Buck. He's upstairs at the moment, but he will be well aware that you and Hailey are here, and he won't take kindly to being kept in the dark. He'll want to make friends with you both."

Katherine and Hailey followed her into the small, neat living room, filled with Early American-style furniture and maple-framed pictures. Alice excused herself and went upstairs to get Buck. Moments later, she returned downstairs, followed by a hundred-twenty-five pound, solid black German shepherd with deep brown eyes, an intelligent face, and ears standing on full alert. When they reached the bottom of the stairs, Alice put an arm around Katherine and a hand on Hailey and led them to Buck. Buck stood still and stared at them for a few seconds, and then went over to Katherine, welcoming her and then Hailey with a few sniffs.

"Let's let the dogs go out in the backyard and get to know each other while we have some iced tea," Alice said. Katherine agreed, and they all went down the hallway and through the kitchen to the back porch. Alice opened the door, and both dogs bounded down two steps to the yard to play.

Alice and Katherine went back to the living room.

"Why don't you sit down, and I'll get the tea?" Alice said.

Katherine thanked her and sat down on the peach-colored Daughtry sofa and absorbed the room. When she saw the framed photographs on the black baby-grand piano, Katherine tiptoed over to see if she could pick out the one of Joe.

Alice returned with a silver tray covered by a white lace doily, containing two crystal glasses of mint-sprigged iced tea. She set the tray down on the table in front of the couch, then turned and faced Katherine. "He's in my den. Would you like to see the picture?" Alice said.

"You're a mind reader," Katherine replied. "Forgive me for being too intense. One of my many shortcomings."

"Not at all," Alice said. "You're a woman on a mission."

"First, thank you for seeing me. You're no doubt wondering why I'm interested in Mr. Hart. There are a couple of reasons. I think I mentioned that I recently completed my master's in journalism. I have one loose end to complete—an assignment from my mentor, who asked me to write about a person who had a substantial influence on a member of my family. I struggled with this until I heard about Mr. Hart from ... Preston, and also from Mr. Fitzgerald."

"How in the world is Casey?" Alice asked with a broad smile. "Not a bad man for a Yankee. I always enjoyed talking to him."

"I don't know him well, but there's something about him. I liked him instantly, maybe because he loves Snickers bars. I asked him whether Mr. Hart had a major influence on Preston. He said Mr. Hart had ... considerable influence on both of them. He told me a little about Joe's so-called "Collectibles." Secondly, I'm intrigued with Preston's involvement with that group of friends. So if you don't mind, yes, I would like to see Mr. Hart's picture."

Alice smiled, left the room for a couple of minutes, and returned with a picture of a man in his forties sitting in the cockpit of a fishing boat, petting a large, black German shepherd. "The one on the left is Joe," Alice said with a chuckle.

Katherine sat quietly, staring at the picture.

Alice broke the silence. "What are you thinking?"

Katherine did not know how to respond. "It's just that I've heard so much about Mr. Hart."

"If Joe were here, my dear, believe me, he'd tell you to call him by his given name," Alice said.

Katherine studied the picture. "I know I shouldn't say this ... I guess I expected him to be larger, more imposing ... he looks ... ordinary. Forgive me."

"If you knew him, saw him in action, you'd know he was an extraordinary man."

Katherine took out her pen and notepad and looked at Alice. "Do you mind?"

"Go ahead."

"I have so many questions about Joe."

"Feel free to ask me any questions you like, my dear," Alice said. "If I don't feel I should answer them, I'll let you know."

"Thank you. This may sound odd, but was Joe perfect?"

"Heavens, no."

"How is that?" Katherine asked.

"Well, if Joe were answering this question ... about another person, he would separate the person's imperfect conduct from the person. I'll take a chapter from his book. Joe let Buck ride in the back of his pickup truck without being in the crate. It drove me nuts. Joe took his boat in deep water, alone. Worried me to death. In fact, I still don't know how he made it back the day he got sick. He was stubborn, headstrong, convinced he was right—which I suppose he usually was. Relentless in drilling down—getting deep into the subject—and impatient when others wouldn't cooperate, especially when it was in their interest to do so. He worked hard to be patient with people who had a sense of entitlement. Joe was not perfect, God rest his soul."

Katherine wrote as fast as her Cross pen could go, and then sat up straight and looked into Alice's eyes.

After a few moments of silence, Alice looked at her and said, "He was a simple man of superior intellect and impeccable character, who made big problems small and little joys big. And you never doubted for a second he was doing it all for you."

From the expression on Alice's face, and the way she sat upright on the sofa, Katherine could feel the depth of feeling Alice had for this man. "You loved him, didn't you?" Katherine said softly.

Alice paused for a moment before answering. "He cared about people, my dear."

"Preston, his wife, Marcia, and Casey all mentioned Joe's friends," Katherine said, looking at her notepad. "I'd like to know about them."

"Joe had many friends," Alice said. "All kinds. His closest friend was Red. They were roommates at Annapolis and together in the Navy. Red was his exec officer—his right-hand man."

"What did Joe do in the Navy?" Katherine asked, continuing to take notes.

"He was a submarine commander. What he did was classified, but he was involved in intelligence gathering. He was very close to his men. A strong leader."

"How long was he in the Navy?"

"I'm not sure. I know that he had quite an illustrious career in the service, then went to law school, and afterward he and Ashley decided to move here and start his practice. That's when I came on board."

"Why didn't he stay in the Navy?"

"He felt he'd gone as far as he could go ... under the circumstances ... and would've been bored by a desk job. So he decided to move on. The Navy has its own way of looking at these things."

"What circumstances?"

"Joe's mother and father died in a lumber accident when he was a young boy. He was brought up by an aunt and uncle. He considered his men on the submarine to be his family."

"Can you tell me more about Ashley?"

"She was a true Southern lady. Remarkable. Beautiful. Intelligent. Always caring for others. Joe loved her more than life itself. When Ashley was killed, it was such a tragedy. And it broke Joe's heart," Alice said, and then remained silent for a while. "Would you like some more tea?"

"Yes, please," Katherine said, understanding that Alice needed a break.

Alice went to the kitchen, and Katherine continued with her notes. She felt that she was intruding, if not imposing, and she wanted to get back to the Collectibles. After a few minutes Alice came back into the living room with more tea and joined Katherine on the sofa.

"Thank you for all this information, Alice. I hope I'm not being too intrusive."

"You're fine. Life goes on. How else may I help?"

"As to certain of Joe's friends, ones he helped. Preston, and his wife, Marcia both mentioned Johnny."

"Johnny is what today would be termed 'mentally challenged.' He works downtown, at the Braydon Home Dairy. If you like we can have lunch there and I can introduce him to you."

"Yes, I'd like that."

"Joe and Ashley—bless her heart—invested a lot of time and thought in making Johnny's life better. Mr. Wilson took an interest in Johnny, too. That's when I first met your father. He came here, to Braydon, and Johnny showed him how to wash dishes," Alice said with a broad smile. "But it was more than that, of course. He talked with Johnny a good bit."

"Really. Can you tell me more about what my father actually did for Johnny?" Katherine asked.

"After their first meeting, Preston called me to see if I had information on educational opportunities for individuals like Johnny. I had two cabinets full of files—some Ashley had developed before she died, and others that Joe had worked on. I gave all of that information to Preston. He did a lot more work in that area."

"What area? What did he do?"

"Educational opportunities. He was concerned about Johnny's speech patterns—how Johnny used to call himself 'Donnie'—in the form of a third-person reference. Your father arranged to have Johnny tutored by a speech therapist. It made a world of difference—it built Johnny's self-esteem. I'll never forget Johnny getting up to speak at Joe's funeral. We were all amazed."

Katherine could see tears in Alice's eyes and feel the emotion in her voice. Then she realized that she, too, was starting to cry.

"There were others," Alice said. "Others Preston reached out to and helped. Missy and Tommy, for example. They're trying to start a camp for children now—somewhere in Nevada. Your father may be helping with that, I'm not sure. He also spent some time with Corey."

"Corey?" Katherine asked. "Mr. Corey, the woodworker?"

Alice laughed. "Mr. Cornelius Corrigan, and yes, he was a fine wood craftsman and a yacht builder. Have you heard of him?"

"I saw a sample of his magnificent work at the Inn, and Bobby McKenzie told me a little about him."

"Bobby's a fine young man. The McKenzies are good people," Alice said.

"You said Preston met Mr. Corrigan."

"I know that he went to see him ... Corey's not well. Alzheimer's." Alice reached for one of the tissues in the box on the end table.

"I'm sorry to hear that," Katherine said. "What a terrible disease."

"You speak as though you have some personal experience," Alice asked, touching her forehead with the fingers of her hand. "Do you know someone with it?"

"No, but I've read about the condition. My grandfather says he's sure he'll get it ... always joking about not knowing his own name."

"Yes, it's a serious matter. One that deserves much more attention."

"Do you know how I could find him?" Katherine asked.

"Yes." Alice went to her desk, found a book, wrote down the address and Barbara's phone number, and handed it to Katherine. "His daughter, Barbara, takes care of him, and she has her hands full. You're probably going in the morning. I'll call Barbara. She'll be pleased to meet you."

"Joe must have loved having you help him."

Katherine could see the strength of purpose in Alice's eyes, the developing tightness in her throat. Katherine looked down and checked her notes. "Johnny, Missy, Tommy, Corey. Have I missed any?" she said.

"Harry. Harry Klaskowski. He taught Joe how to shoot skeet," Alice replied.

"I don't believe it," Katherine said. "At the Newark Rod and Gun Club in New York State?"

"I don't know where or when, I just remember Joe telling me how they met. They were great pals, fished together. In fact, Harry visited Joe in the Bahamas during his last fishing trip—they shot trap off Joe's boat. I learned that at the funeral. Do you know Harry?"

"I haven't met him, but my grandfather knows him well. He was a state skeet shooting champion. What an amazing coincidence! So, I'm curious . . . what went on with Harry and Preston?"

"I don't know. Harry comes and goes. Preston asked me to help him find Harry, but that didn't happen. He was at the funeral, though. Bless his heart."

Katherine made more notes, and then looked up at Alice, who appeared to have a faraway look on her face. Katherine worried that she was asking too many questions at once. "Let's check on our dogs and then go to lunch. How does that sound?" Katherine said.

"Like a plan, young lady, like a plan."

CHAPTER THIRTY-THREE

Alice and Katherine were obviously delighted to watch Buck and Hailey, tails wagging, chase each other around the backyard, somehow avoiding Alice's azalea bushes and tomatoes. Alice called Buck, who quickly came to her side and sat. Hailey looked quizzical and disappointed, but ambled along behind.

"They're getting along great," Katherine said. "Can we just leave them here until we get back?"

"I think they'll be fine. There's a fence behind the thick shrubbery all around the backyard. In any event, Buck will not leave the yard; he knows to stay. You'll have to decide about Hailey. If you wish to bring her, you may."

"But what about while we're in the restaurant?"

"Stanley Neimeyer, the owner and baker, was a client of Joe's and loves dogs, especially Buck. I take Buck in all the time, and he rests at my feet while I'm at the table. Hailey seems calm and well-trained, but it's up to you."

"I've never taken Hailey in a restaurant, and it's a strange place for her. Let's leave her here with Buck."

They said good-bye to the dogs, went through the house, across the front porch, and down the walkway to Mulberry Street.

"Are these azaleas?" Katherine asked, quickly followed by, "Oh, you forgot to lock the door!"

"No need to lock the door, my dear. And the azaleas are the pink ones back there," Alice replied, pointing to the front of the porch. "These yellow flowers are Lady Banks Roses. The blooms in the hanging pots on the porch are petunias and geraniums. I suppose you don't have many front porches in New York City."

"Well, we do have Central Park, and believe it or not, people do plant flowers under their window sills. But I must admit, this is beautiful."

Alice talked about Joe all the way to the Home Dairy. Katherine listened as Alice related the excitement experienced in their years of working together, the action, the detail, and the gratification—knowing they were making a difference in the lives of Joe's clients. How Joe changed after Ashley died, how he escaped to the mountains, and how pleased Alice was when he came back to work. "It was working on your father's case that brought him back," she said.

Katherine could hear the building tension and hurt in Alice's voice. Katherine couldn't take notes and didn't want to record the conversation without Alice's permission, which her intuition told her not to seek.

Alice ushered Katherine through the front door, pointing out the five-foot case in which, on four glass shelves, the cakes, pies, cookies, and other specialties were displayed. Katherine immediately was taken by the aroma of the fresh-baked bread and pastries. They went through the cafeteria line and carried the trays full of wonderful smells to an open booth.

As they ate their lunch, Katherine could not help but notice the quiet rhythm in the quaint room and how far she was from the bustling pace of New York.

"Are you ready to meet Johnny?" Alice said.

"Yes, of course."

Alice led Katherine past the long steam table, behind the cashier dressed in a crisp, white uniform with a brightly colored handkerchief pinned over the left breast pocket, and through a swinging door to the kitchen. Over on the right side in front of a square opening where used trays and dishes were passed through stood a short, stocky thirty-five-year-old man with thin gray hair brushed across his balding head and a big smile on his face.

"Hi, Johnny. I'd like you to meet my friend Katherine. She is Preston's daughter."

Johnny stooped over and wiped his forehead on a cloth hanging from the counter, then wiped his hands on his soiled apron, sprayed them with a device attached to a large commercial dishwasher, wiped them again, and held out his hand to Katherine.

"I'm Johnny. Good to meet you. Preston met Johnny. Wash dishes. Nice man."

"It's good to meet you, too, Johnny. Alice has told me a lot about you. She tells me you are good friends with Buck. I have a dog also. Her name is Hailey."

"Buck loves me. I give Buck steaks. Buck got the bad man. Where is your dog?"

"Hailey's at Alice's house—playing with Buck."

"Johnny—I am a dishwasher. Busy now. Can't let trays pile up."

"I understand, Johnny. Thank you for taking the time to talk to me."

"Good-bye," Johnny said with a smile and went back to clearing the accumulating trays full of dirty dishes.

"I'll see you later, Johnny," Alice said.

Johnny looked over his shoulder at Alice and waved. Alice and Katherine returned to their table to have their dessert.

"Alice, we've talked a lot about Joe and many others, but we haven't talked about you. You've had quite a career. Seen a lot. How are you doing?" Katherine asked.

"I'm okay, Katherine. I'm sorry I've gotten a little weepy during this discussion … it's brought back a lot of memories. I'll tell you something. In his will Joe left me his house. I didn't want to move from my own house, so I sold his. I invested the proceeds, together with the cash Joe left me. He was very generous."

"So you don't have money worries; that's good," Katherine said.

"Well, not quite," Alice said.

"What do you mean?"

"I bought shares in our local bank, Braydon Community Bank and Trust. There was a big push back then to be supportive of our bank, and word got around that I had a little money after Joe died. Turned out that was a big mistake. Ray Smith, the bank's vice president and chief credit officer, and others at the bank were, well, less than scrupulous. Their actions eventually brought the bank down. It cost our community and me a lot. I lost my entire investment. I never saw it coming."

"Wow. When did this happen?"

"Last year. Ray Smith was sentenced to ten years in federal prison for being part of the conspiracy to defraud the bank. We'll have to see what happens with that."

"That's awful. What did he do, specifically? Can you talk about it?"

"He arranged for bogus loans for friends of his to purchase land all around here for development. He got kickbacks from the sale of the property. I kept a scrapbook that tells the whole sordid story, if you're interested."

"I really am interested. I am so sorry you suffered through all of this. I wrote my master's project on health care fraud—a crime I came to detest."

"I'm not fond of it either. I feel badly for those who got caught up in the greed or whatever moved them to do this, and I feel badly for our community. We lost more than money—we lost identity and dignity. So, you see, it isn't all just a bed of roses here."

Katherine underlined the words "lost identity and dignity" in her mind. "Are you working now? How are you managing after all of that?"

"I have some money left in savings. I've had many offers to work with other lawyers, but I could never do that. I have a brother in California who has asked me to come live with him and his family, but I'm not leaving Braydon. I'll be fine."

Katherine and Alice walked back to her house, arm in arm. Alice found the scrapbook on the downfall of Braydon Community Bank and Trust for Katherine, who studied it with laser-beam intensity.

Alice also showed Katherine her many books in the den, and talked about her current work with the Friends of the Library.

"What are your dreams, my dear? And how do you plan to realize them?" Alice asked.

Katherine looked into Alice's eyes, sparkling behind rimless glasses. "My dream is to be a great reporter, an investigative journalist," Katherine said. "I don't know how I'll realize it, but I believe I will. There're so many questions and so few answers. Like my grandpa used to say, *'you wanna know, you gotta keep digging.'* "

"Have you a job now?"

"I do, with a newspaper in Southampton, New York, working for an editor/owner from whom I have a great deal to learn. I start as soon as I get home."

"I've enjoyed meeting you, young lady. Give my regards to your father. I hope making this long trip was worth your while."

"I can't tell you how much this trip has meant to me, Alice. I'm so thankful to you for taking me into your home and sharing so openly and honestly all you have told me. It'll take me time to absorb all we've talked about today. I'll be thinking about it as I drive back tomorrow. And thank you for introducing me to Johnny. Joe must have been a remarkable man, and he surely benefited from having you at his side."

"Thank you, my dear," Alice said giving Katherine a hug and a kiss. Then she gave Hailey a big hug, too. "You take care of this young lady, Hailey. She's going places. Have a safe trip. Come back and see us, you hear?"

"We will," said Katherine. "I promise. Thanks, again."

★ ★ ★

Hailey woke Katherine up with a soft, sloppy kiss on her eyes. After feeding her dog and grabbing a quick breakfast of her own, Katherine took Hailey for a short walk, checked out of the Inn, set the GPS, and headed for Corrigan Yachts.

Katherine turned on the road leading to the house, and followed the directions Alice had given her. She approached the front through a walk-around porch directly facing the Intracoastal Waterway. She could smell the salt air as bits of sunlight broke through the branches of the old oak and yaupon holly trees. At the end of the long, sloping front lawn, she could see a small wooden dock.

Barbara, a plump woman Katherine gauged to be about the same age as her own mother, greeted her at the front door dressed in a flowered smock.

Katherine introduced herself and Hailey. "Do you mind my bringing my dog along?"

"I love dogs," Barbara said, petting Hailey, whose tail was wagging like a high-speed fan.

"She obviously knows," Katherine said.

Barbara showed her into the old two-story, wood frame house. Katherine's eye was drawn to the large, hand-laid fieldstone fireplace on the south end of the living room and the portrait hanging over the mantel.

"Isn't that Frederick Douglass?" she asked.

"That it is. We're all proud of that. My great-grandfather, a boat builder, helped build Mr. Douglass' grand house in Anacostia."

Katherine pulled out her pen and pad and made some notes.

"Alice tells me you're here to see my father. My mother died several years ago—he lives here alone—won't leave. He's happier here. I check on him every day."

"Your father's lucky to have you," Katherine said. "My mom ... lives with my grandfather ... or the other way around. I've been away at school ... not much help."

"Fortunately, I have the time. My husband works and is very supportive."

"Where is Mr. Corrigan?"

"Down by the waterway, sitting in a rocking chair, watching the boats go by. Just follow the path. He's had a good night. Not sure how your conversation will go, but he'll enjoy it. He will love Hailey, too. I will bring you some tea in a bit."

Katherine found a tall, trim gentleman with snow-white hair and beard against smooth black skin that gleamed in the morning sun.

"Good morning, Mr. Corrigan," she said as she approached. "I'm Katherine Kelly. This is my dog, Hailey."

Hailey was already sniffing Corey, wagging her tail, and begging him to pet her, which Corey, with enthusiasm, obliged.

"May we join you?"

"Who are you?" Corey asked.

"I'm ... " Katherine sat down in the rocking chair to Corey's right. "What a beautiful chair. Did you make it?" Katherine noticed Corey shift in his chair, a slight sparkle in his dark eyes.

"Cherry."

"You made it?"

"What's your name?"

"Katherine."

"Feel good?"

"I'm fine, thank you."

"The chair," Corey said, his arms flailing in the air and then rubbing the armrests.

"Yes, yes," Katherine said. "It does feel good."

"You gotta feel it."

They both sat quietly. Katherine could feel the rush of the water, and the warmth of the sun shining through the live oaks.

"You must love it here."

Silence for a few beats.

"Family. Built yachts. Right here," Corey said. "What's your name?"

"Tell me about your family," Katherine said.

Corey leaned way back in his chair and extended his long legs. "My grandfather worked with Mr. Douglass himself. He was a master turner."

Katherine thought for a minute. "Your grandfather turned wood."

"You're a smart young lady. Why did you come here?"

"To meet you, Mr. Corrigan. I've seen your work at the Braydon Inn."

Corey was silent for a while and then he leaned forward and looked at Katherine. "Oak."

Katherine was so excited she started to clap. "Oak it was. Finished to perfection."

Just then, Barbara appeared with two glasses of iced tea and key lime cookies on a wooden tray. "How are you two getting along?"

"Really well," Katherine said. "We were just discussing the oak bar Mr. Corrigan built at the Braydon Inn."

"He actually told you about that? That's amazing," Barbara said. "I think I'll join you."

Barbara sat in the rocker to the left of her father, Hailey curled up at Corey's feet, as they talked and watched boats go by for another hour. Katherine asked her all about Corrigan Yachts and the history of their family.

"Mr. Corrigan mentioned Mr. Douglass. Was that—"

"Yes, the same Frederick Douglass—the picture over the mantel. We're a proud and grateful family."

"Mr. Corrigan is an artist, isn't he?"

"He loves wood. He loves boats. And he loves people."

"Thank you for allowing me to meet him and you," Katherine said.

"Alice told me that you're Mr. Wilson's daughter. Your father came to see Dad, sat in the same chair you're sitting in."

"Cherry," Corey said.

Barbara and Katherine exchanged smiles.

"Cherry, it is," Katherine said.

"She's smart," Corey said to no one in particular.

"We have to get going," Katherine said, "I have a long drive."

"Thank you for visiting us," Barbara said. "You've made my father's day."

Barbara walked Katherine and Hailey to Katherine's car. "I really enjoyed meeting you and talking to your father. I can only imagine how difficult taking care of your dad can be."

"It's funny," Barbara said. "Your father said about the same thing to me when I walked him to his car."

"Really?" Katherine said. "Did he come back, or call, or write, since?"

"I'm sure he's a busy man."

Barbara gave Katherine a hug. "Alice says you're going places. I can see why she feels that way. Good luck to you."

"Thank you, Barbara. I've enjoyed this. More than you know."

CHAPTER THIRTY-FOUR

Katherine drove north to Wrightsville Beach, North Carolina, staying on Route 17 or as close as she could to the coastline, singing along with Adele, with Hailey, from time to time, sticking her head out of the sunroof. In about four hours they crossed the last bridge over Wrightsville Sound and arrived at the northern tip of Shell Island.

"Hi, Sean. We're here."

"Great. Where are you right now?"

"Walking around on the road in front of a place called Shell Island Resort, looking at a fantastic beach and another island."

"The other island is called Figure Eight, and it's where I am right now. I'll be where you are in fifteen minutes. See if you can talk the young guys in front of the resort you are looking at into letting you park in their indoor parking garage, and slip them a ten. Okay?"

"Yes, sir," she said.

A quarter of an hour later, Sean, dressed in a T-shirt and swim trunks, sauntered across the dunes to Katherine and Hailey; he knelt down and gave Hailey a playful pat on the head. The golden retriever immediately started wagging her tail and kissing his face. He stood and gave Katherine a hug.

"She likes you," Katherine said. "It's good to see you again, Sean."

"You, too," he said. "Dogs aren't allowed on the beach here this

time of year, so let's move fast," pointing toward the northwest end
of the beach, to an outboard motorboat with a fiberglass hull and
inflatable tubes on the sides, its bow on the sand.

"We're with you," Katherine said, running with Hailey and again
looking at the back of 6A as he headed to his boat. They hopped in,
Hailey immediately standing on the bench in the bow, Katherine
sitting next to Sean. He put the outboard in reverse, backed away
from the sand, spun the boat around, and headed west through the
narrow stream to the Intracoastal Waterway. He turned to port at
the buoy and drove down the waterway, Hailey's head into the wind,
her tail working overtime, and Katherine smelling the salt spray, her
hair blowing in the wind.

They passed by a tiny island of sand on the left with an artificial
palm tree in the center, under a bridge, by a waterside restaurant and
marinas on the left and right. Sean effortlessly maneuvered the boat,
landing it alongside a restaurant appropriately called Dockside. He
hopped out, secured the boat, and gave a hand to Katherine as she
stepped onto the dock.

"I thought you might be hungry," Sean said. "Best clams and burgers in the area. Hailey will be fine here. I'll bring her some water."

"Sounds good. Smells good, too. Neat place," Katherine said.

They dined, watching smaller boats come and go and bigger ones
wait for the bridge to open.

"How long have you got?" Katherine asked.

"My buddies are covering for me. I should be okay for thirty-six
hours."

Sean excused himself, disappeared through an alley, and came
back with a metal bowl full of water and delivered it to Hailey, who
drank with gusto. When he returned, Katherine talked nonstop about
her trip to Braydon, Alice, Johnny, Corey, and the Live Oak Inn.
Sean, listening, asked a few questions of his own along the way.

"When do you start work?" Sean asked. "I'll bet you're chomping
at the bit."

"The day after Memorial Day."

"And you are going to be living where?" Sean asked.

"Southampton, on Long Island. It's near the water, too—but nothing like this, I have to say!"

After dinner, Sean moved the boat into a nearby slip, tied it up, brought Hailey up the ramp, motioned to Katherine to join them, and they walked to a black SUV parked in a lot across the street. He drove them back to Wrightsville Beach and down a side street on the north end to a house converted into two small condos, and he showed her through the one he'd arranged for her. They ended up on the front porch, overlooking the best beach Katherine had ever seen.

"This is so cool. I can't believe how clean and clear the water is," she said. "Thank you, Sean."

"Thank you for coming," he said. "Let's take Hailey for a walk. Your car's not far from here. I'll help you gather your bags and bring them back."

"Where are you staying?"

Sean laughed. "I'm over on Figure Eight Island."

After they picked up her suitcase and two smaller bags from her car, they walked back to the condo and put her baggage inside. She opened the refrigerator to find a six-pack of Sam Adams.

"I figured you might be thirsty after a long drive," Sean said, grabbing a couple of bottles and heading for the front porch.

Katherine laughed as she and Hailey followed.

They sat in the rockers, Hailey at their feet, sipped their beer, and listened to the waves as the warm summer day faded away.

"Tell me about you, Sean."

"What would you like to know?"

"Well, when I first met you, I wanted to ask you a bunch of questions about the race, how you got into the sport, what you liked about it, the kind of bike you ride ... what other sports you're into. Now, the circle of inquiry is ten times bigger. Where you grew up. School. Secret Service."

"Lewisburg, Pennsylvania. Two things there—a prison and a university. I wanted to stay out of prison and I couldn't afford the university. But I ended up getting a student loan. My dad's a volunteer fireman and has a small motorcycle shop. My mom's a librarian. No brothers and sisters," Sean said and then took a long pull on his beer.

"I looked at Bucknell," Katherine said. "Good school."

"I enjoyed it, even though I was a townie. Played football. Wrestled and boxed intramural for Phi Gam. Worked a little part time when I could. I just missed a 3.0, which I needed for Government GL-7 grade. Another way to qualify was to get at least eighteen hours of post-graduate work. I chose law school. Got the eighteen hours, but my heart wasn't in it. The only thing I'd ever wanted was to be an agent."

"And ... the race?"

"I'd finished my training in Georgia and then Rowley outside of Washington, D.C. and was having some fun at the race when I met you."

"That answers the motorcycle stuff. What drove you to join the Secret Service?"

"Wanted to get the bad guys. Serve my country. Too late to be a cowboy. The Secret Service seemed the right fit."

"So you're liking it?"

"Loving it. Every week, every day, is different. We're down here this week doing advance work for a vacation stay by a high-ranking official and his family," he explained. "We look for remote locations and do everything from screening household staff to checking out boats and equipment to securing the perimeter—not so easy when the vacation site is an island—to checking the weather forecast. Hurricane season starts next week, you know."

Katherine tried unsuccessfully to hide a yawn, although she was completely interested in his story. It wasn't the company, she had to reassure him—it was truly the hour.

"You've had a long day, Kat. I'm going to let you get some rest. If you like, I'll pick you up for breakfast."

"Sorry. I am fading. I guess I'm more tired than I thought. I'd love breakfast with you in the morning. How does 8:00 a.m. sound?"

"I'll pick you guys up then," Sean said, petted Hailey on the head, gave Katherine a good-night hug, and left.

★ ★ ★

Sean was there at the early hour, and Katherine and Hailey were ready at the door when he knocked. "You look great," he said.

"Thank you, sir. You look pretty good yourself."

"Why don't you bring a swimsuit along, a couple of towels, and some bottles of water for Hailey—and wear a cap or hat if you have one?"

Katherine went into the bedroom, changed into a bathing suit, shorts, and T-shirt. "I'd like to have a cap from here," she said. "Do you have an idea where I could get one?" She took a few bottles of water and added them to her bag, along with Hailey's bowl. Sean walked them to his vehicle and opened the doors.

Sean drove to the Causeway Café on Wrightsville Beach. Katherine could smell the pancakes, waffles, and fresh coffee as they waited their turn on the porch. By the time they were seated, they were both starved, each ordering a huge stack of blueberry pancakes, bacon, orange juice, and coffee. Katherine loved the chairs, the tables, and the hustle and bustle of the place. Although she and Sean didn't say much, they couldn't take their eyes off each other, smiling easily and endlessly.

After breakfast, Sean bought a cap for Katherine and drove across the waterway, past some office buildings, a gated community, a bunch of roadside stores and restaurants, a big shopping center, a residential area lined with huge live oak trees, and finally into the heart of the historic city situated on the Cape Fear River.

He parked on Front Street, and they strolled hand in hand along the Riverwalk. To their left, they could see across the river, where the battleship *U.S.S. North Carolina* was permanently moored. People were everywhere, talking, hanging out, eating ice cream, sightseeing with their kids, or going in and out of neat little shops, restaurants, and bars.

When they got to the end of the boardwalk, they crossed the street. Sean showed Katherine the Cotton Exchange, a onetime mercantile building now filled with boutiques. He pointed out the spot where cotton was formerly sold—and some said slaves, as well. After they poked around in the shops, they returned to Riverwalk and ambled in the other direction nearly to the bridge. By then, it was time for lunch. Sean suggested they eat at Elijah's, which had an outside table by the river.

"What would you like to do after lunch?" Sean asked.

"This has been just great. I love seeing the downtown historic area and the river. We only have a few more hours. It's such a gorgeous day. Could we go for another ride in your boat?"

Sean drove them back to Dockside, parked in the lot, opened the back for Hailey to jump out, picked up his duffel bag, and led them to his boat. Hailey jumped in the bow, Sean threw the bag in, helped Katherine into the boat, started the engine, untied the lines, backed out of the slip, and headed south on the waterway.

Katherine sat to the left of Sean, comforted by his arm around her shoulders, Hailey with her head in the breeze. They passed boats moving in each direction and, after a bit, turned to port at a buoy and around a small beach into Masonboro Sound heading toward an inlet that led to the Atlantic. Instead of going to the ocean, Sean turned to starboard and drove along an island with dunes. He maneuvered close to the beach, set his bow anchor, and backed to the shore where he turned off the motor and lifted it up.

As Sean pulled off his shirt and shorts, Katherine watched him stand there in his bathing suit for a moment, surveying the beach and studying the water. Then he hopped into water up to his waist, grabbed a stern line and anchor, walked to the beach, and set the anchor in the sand. By then, Hailey was already in the water, swimming toward the shore.

He returned to the boat, picked Katherine up across his shoulder, and walked her to the shore. He went back, gathered an umbrella, a big blanket and Katherine's bag. He set the umbrella up and spread the blanket down in the shade it provided. Hailey immediately spread herself out entirely on the blanket. Sean and Katherine wasted no time jumping in the crystal clear water soon to be joined by Hailey.

They swam and played in the water for a while, then returned to their blanket and toweled off.

"Ironically, in some respects, our lives, as a result of what we want to do—or maybe feel compelled to do—are similar," Katherine said. "You think?"

"Time. Commitment. Pressure," Sean said.

"Of course, you are exposed to risk—life or death," Katherine observed.

"There's that, but I wouldn't overstate it. A lot of my daily responsibility is mundane, even boring, time spent checking, evaluating, analyzing, anticipating ... and hopefully, preventing."

"I get that," Katherine said. "I get the pressure part, too. I can only imagine what it's like."

"Soon you'll be investigating bad guys of your own. Right?"

Katherine told Sean the details of what happened to Alice Hawkins—how she lost the money Joe had given her and the cash she received from the sale of his house on account of the fraud and negligence of her bank's officers. "How do you come back from that?" she asked rhetorically.

"What can you do about it?" Sean asked.

"Expose it, explain it, and build a platform for others to go after those who caused it," she said.

Katherine saw Sean glancing at his watch. She sighed and took one long, last look at the beach. "Thirty-six hours are up, aren't they?"

"Not quite—I have just enough time to return the boat and take you back, but we have to go now."

Hearing "go," Hailey jumped up in sync with Sean and Katherine. They laughed at her eagerness and packed to leave.

★ ★ ★

Too soon, they had returned the boat and were back at Katherine's condo. Sean put his arms around Katherine and just held her for several minutes. For Katherine, time stood still.

"You know I'll miss you, Sean, and I'll be thinking about you. Be safe."

"I'll do my best," he said. "And I'll be thinking about you as well."

Katherine remained frozen in place, once again watching the disappearing back of 6A.

CHAPTER THIRTY-FIVE

After twelve rain-soaked hours of truck-dominated expressway and a couple of gas and Hailey stops, Katherine was finally living in her new apartment for good, and looked forward to a few days to rest before starting work. Her journey had taken her so far, geographically and emotionally; her home state seemed like a foreign country when she returned to it.

She walked into the offices of the *Twin Forks Press* at 7:30 a.m. Tuesday, passed the empty receptionist desk, and proceeded down the hall. Seeing a light under the door to Sol's office, she knocked gently and opened the door.

"Hello, kiddo," Sol said. "Welcome. Let's sit at the round table." Sol pulled up a chair to join her. "Are you ready to go?"

"I am," Katherine said, taking out a pad and her Cross pen, which, given the way things had been going, she now viewed not only necessary but also as a good luck charm.

"Let's go over expectations, Katherine. And then you can meet the rest of the staff when they come in later in the day." Her new boss ran down the routine. "You should be producing at least seven to ten stories of local interest every week—some short, two to three hundred words, others five times that. Historically, filing time is 5:00 p.m. and our paper goes to bed on Wednesday, so the work week starts Thursday morning. Theoretically, that's when Chuck, our editor, starts planning the next edition, makes assignments. This week's good timing for you—gives you three extra days to get settled and develop leads. But the Web has altered a lot of that. It's a hungry elephant—constantly demanding content. Sometimes there are more little stories, videos, and pictures to keep up; sometimes there are big stories that require work over days and weeks. And, unfortunately, it's as much about advanced media digital technology as reporting, editing, and writing now." Sol stopped there and gave Katherine a chance to finish her notes.

"How many reporters do you have on staff?" Katherine asked.

"Four at the moment, with two part-time freelancers."

"How long have your reporters been with you?"

"Three for more than five years, one for a year and a half. Long enough to develop relationships ... "

" ... which produce leads, particularly necessary for local stories," Katherine supplied, catching on fast.

"You're right. They have a leg up. And, they've earned Chuck's trust."

"But it's still a team sport. Or should be, it seems to me," Katherine said.

"That's one of the reasons I hired you, Katherine," Sol said. "Speaking of which, I'm looking forward to your picking up the pieces on a story I broke last week while you were gone, taking it to the next level."

"I'm listening."

Sol filled her in on what he'd turned up in a fraud case involving a local financial institution, Hamptons Bank. And while the piece had certainly stirred awareness, apparently he felt that initial story only scratched the surface.

"Interesting," said Katherine. "You know fraud's a special subject for me?"

"Why do you think I'm putting you on it? Don't let me down."

"May I review your file, and how do I access it?"

"Esther's our tech wiz. When she sets up your computer and goes over all the programs and interface, mention that I'd like you to have full access to my work on Hamptons Bank."

"Understood," she said. "Thank you."

"One other thing, get your requests in sooner rather than later—Freedom of Information, government agencies—these can take five business days, sometimes only to get the agency's reply confirming it has received your request—with weeks or months to get the actual material."

Katherine nodded and added that to her notes.

"Let's go meet people," Sol said, standing up. "Follow me."

Sol led Katherine to the office next door, where the door was open. He waved at a large man in his fifties with thick glasses and thicker hair who returned the wave and beckoned them in.

"This is Charles T. Bumgardner, our editor. Chuck, this is Katherine, the newest member of the team."

"I'm happy to meet you, Katherine. Sol's told me a lot about you. Welcome aboard, we'll talk later. Could you come back in about fifty minutes?"

Katherine glanced at Sol and, seeing his nod, said, "Yes, of course."

Sol continued down the hall, introducing Katherine to the assistant editor, the sports editor, calendar editor, and on the other side of the hall the people in sales, circulation, accounting, and finally, Esther.

At the end of the hallway, they came to a large, open room with individual work stations each containing a desk, chair, computer, printer, and credenza, and separated by five-foot gray fabric partitions.

"This is the Den, where our reporters work," Sol said. "I'll let you meet each of them at a time convenient to them and you."

They walked back to Sol's office, along the way he showed Katherine the break room, a surprisingly large comfortable room equipped with a sub-zero refrigerator, elaborate sinks, a microwave, several coffee machines—in effect, a fully equipped kitchen with two round tables and chairs and a large straight table and chairs.

"This is where the work really gets done," Sol said, and then they returned to his office.

"Well, so far, so good?" Sol asked.

"Fine," Katherine said. "Just fine. You all have made me feel very welcome. Thank you."

"Do you have any questions?"

"Just one at the moment. I am sure I'll have plenty later."

"Shoot."

"I have a well-behaved, quiet, three-year-old golden retriever named Hailey..."

"And you want to bring him to the office?"

"Her, and yes, if that's okay? I promise she will not get in the way. I tend to work late, and if she's here, I won't have to drive back to my apartment to let her out."

"Not everyone loves dogs, Katherine. I do. So do my kids. We'll give it a try. See how it goes. Fair enough?"

"Thank you so much, Sol."

"Make yourself at home, Katherine. We're happy to have you here. Good luck."

Katherine left Sol's office and found Esther, who showed Katherine her cubicle and reviewed her computer, passwords, codes, and other office systems, including how to access Sol's Hamptons Bank file. They walked together through the Den and met two of the reporters. Esther showed Katherine where the ladies room was and finally introduced her to Evelyn, the bookkeeper and office manager. The woman, who might as well have had "efficiency" written across her forehead, had her sign some employment forms, gave her a card to enter the building after hours, and took care of other first-day details.

Looking at her watch, Katherine saw nearly an hour had passed, proceeded to Chuck's office, and seeing him at his desk took one of the two seats opposite.

Chuck finished a phone call, set the receiver back in its cradle, and studied Katherine as if he were trying to read a detailed architectural design. Katherine waited, pen and pad in hand.

"Nothing more painful for a reporter than having nothing to report." He assigned her to write an obituary and to cover a local school board member recently arrested for DWI. "Flesh these out, and I'd like you to submit them no later than 5:00 p.m. tomorrow. On the obit, you can call the funeral home. They work with us. Try to speak with one of the deceased's family members. Any questions?"

"Not on the assignments you've given me. Has Sol told you about my work in systemic fraud?"

"I understand you're interested in our Hamptons Bank stories."

Katherine could feel a coolness in the office, as if the fan from an air conditioner had just slammed on. She quickly decided to drop the subject.

Katherine returned to her desk and sat for a moment, absorbing the new environment she had so long dreamed of, and at the same time, allowing the reality of the challenges she faced to sink in. She fired up her computer and placed a call to the funeral home. The director was friendly and helpful, but was reluctant to give her the name of a family member. "We'll send over everything you'll need," he said. Katherine set up an obit file, made some notes, and then, through the Internet, quickly accessed the arrest record for the errant board member, including a crazed, Nick Nolte-esque mug shot. The school board website was already buzzing with conflicting opinions about the man's drinking problems in the past and the impact or not on his job. Local politics would judge this guy long before he had his day in court, Katherine guessed.

Katherine wrote a first draft of the drunk driving story—with parenthetical reference to concerns of some board members that he should be removed from the board. By lunchtime she felt she had that story and the obit under control, and she turned her attention to Sol's Hamptons Bank file. She flagged various sections and sent them to her printer. Only then did she pick up the phone and dial Susan.

"Hello?" her friend said.

"This is Katherine Kelly reporting from partition station seven at the *Twin Forks Press*. I'd like to interview you to determine the state of your mental competence and whether you are willing and able to spend time listening to the life and times of a hyperactive and overly excited woman."

"Why would I want to do that?" Susan replied.

"You wouldn't, ordinarily, but when you hear about my trip to Braydon, and perhaps of more interest to you, my stop in Wrightsville Beach on the way home, you will."

"I'm not sure what all of that means, but I'm convinced. Where would this interview take place?"

"That question has tactical and strategic implications. We could meet at Hennessey's unless that would be uncomfortable for you. I'll meet you anywhere you like. I have to feed and walk Hailey. What's best for you?"

"I'm not drinking, but I don't mind going to Hennessey's. Why don't we wait until the weekend—see what the weather is like? Maybe I'll come out there. Do you have a deadline for the interview?"

"That makes sense. Just got a little excited. Are you doing okay?"

"I'm fine. Really. Can't wait to hear about it."

"Okay. I'll call you Friday," Katherine said and hung up.

She picked up the pages she had printed and studied them. The areas she had flagged dealt with what happened when one bank fails and another takes over—precisely what had happened to the Hamptons National Bank and Trust of Long Island, New York, on Friday, April 13.

As Katherine read the material, she tried to imagine the brutal efficiency exercised by the team of Federal Deposit Insurance Corporation agents who had walked into all three branches at once and taken over. The FDIC's motives were pure, if shocking. The overwhelming majority of the employees apparently didn't know that the bank was in trouble and about to close before the FDIC's receiver in charge and the closing team manager walked through the door and took total control. Reading further, Katherine saw that the FDIC's plan was to have Commack Community Bank take over the following Monday.

Katherine tried to imagine the fear, angst, and insecurity the Hamptons Bank employees must have felt, particularly those without knowledge of the bank's impending failure. Presumably, they, at least, were not part of the problem, and while the customers would be protected, their fate would be less certain. She thought of the tellers, the security guards, the janitors. *Would the new bank continue with them? If not, what would they do?*

You're holding back, shying away from driving at the heart of the story from your point of view. People who follow reporters follow them from here ... not from here.

Katherine left the office and walked to CCB, sauntered into the first floor lobby, sat in a chair along the wall as though she were a customer waiting to apply for a loan, and studied everyone and watched everything she could for more than an hour. Then she went to a teller's window, with a plaque bearing the name Theresa Leary.

From behind the wide bars separating the counter, a young woman about Katherine's age asked, "May I help you?"

"My name is Katherine Kelly. You're Theresa?" she asked.

"That's me," she said with a smile.

"I'm a reporter with the *Twin Forks Press*. I recently learned that this bank took over when the Hamptons Bank and Trust failed. I'm glad your bank did, because, otherwise, the Hamptons Bank's customers would be in a lot of trouble."

"I'm sorry I can't help you. I don't know anything about that bank, or why it closed."

"So you weren't a teller before the takeover?"

"No, I've been with CCB since I started, more than two years."

"I understand," Katherine said. "I'm not going to ask you anything about the Hamptons Bank. What I'm interested in is what happened to those tellers and others who were not lucky enough to continue on after the takeover."

"I know. It must have been horrible."

"Did you know any of those tellers, Theresa?"

"Only one. Constance Shipman. She was a friend of my mother's. Worked here—for Hamptons Bank—twenty-seven years. I don't know where she went after the—transition."

"I worry about that," Katherine said. "I hope she was able to find another job."

"I'm sorry, Katherine, but I see a couple of customers waiting. Do you mind if I take care of them?"

"Of course not. Thank you so much," Katherine said, handing her a sheet of paper with her contact information. "Please call me, text me, or e-mail me if you can locate Constance ... I'd like to see if I can help."

"Sure thing," Theresa said and motioned to the waiting customer.

CHAPTER THIRTY-SIX

———————————————————————————————

Wednesday afternoon, a week later, Katherine was at her desk, her afternoon coffee cooling fast and Hailey curled at her feet, reviewing drafts of the half dozen stories she would need to file by the 5:00 p.m. deadline. For a solid week she had scrambled to keep up with the regular assignments Chuck had thrown at her, working hard to learn names in the community and develop sources. On top of that, she'd been organizing notes and gathering material on the bank failure and its takeover. And each evening, at home, she had cranked out another section of the assignment Professor Simpson had given her so many weeks earlier. She'd begun to feel as though she were caught in a hailstorm without an umbrella.

After giving her stories one more look and making some final minor revisions, she sent them on to the editor, then sat back and exhaled a sigh of relief. Now it was time to deal with that other file, the one she'd finished as soon as she returned from her trip south but rewritten three times since then.

Dear Gerry,

I have just completed my first full week of work at the Twin Forks Press *and am looking forward to seeing my byline in print tomorrow. Thank you sincerely for*

everything you did to get me to this point.
I have something for you, probably a bit overdue and
I fear incomplete, but I hope it fulfills the requirement.

Submitted to: Professor Gerald Simpson
From: Katherine Kelly
Date: June 5, 2012

This paper, consistent with the ground rules, is written for me. Accordingly, I am foregoing the customary format, and presenting it to myself (with a copy to you) by e-mail.

You asked me to write a story about a person, living or dead—not a relative of mine—who had a substantial influence on one of the members of my family. A threshold consideration requires the distinction between power and influence. Power is positional and wielded. Influence is personal and granted. I recently met my father for the first time—a man named Preston Wilson. He told me a story about an attorney named Joe Hart, and how this man helped him save his business empire from financial disaster. Hart, however, required as a condition precedent that Wilson commit to perform an unspecified request in the future. Desperate, my father agreed.

Hart performed his magic and saved my father's business. When it came time for Hart to call in the IOU, he required my father to meet, earn the trust of, and care for some friends of Hart's, each of whom was challenged and none of whom my father would have ever chosen on his own to associate with. My father reached out to them.

He told me that Mr. Hart had exceeded his expectations and had a major influence on him.

I've interviewed Hart's secretary and actually met two of the friends (one, a mentally challenged dishwasher working in a South Carolina restaurant; the other, an eighty-year-old former yacht builder suffering from Alzheimer's).

For me, the jury's not in as to whether Joe Hart had a major or lasting influence on my father. In talking with Wilson's wife, who used the curious term "evolving" when referring to her husband's experience with Hart's "Collectibles," I had the impression that the degree and depth of influence, its endurance, and the amount of respect it has been given by my father, remains in question or has yet to be determined.

I'm going to follow this story because—as you will be happy to learn—I am emotionally involved. I'm dealing with the fundamental lie my mother told me many years ago, and all the identity issues that created—one of which is to what extent I can and want to accept Preston Wilson as my father. I'm intrigued by the core principle of the late Joe Hart's requirement and impressed with the depth and wisdom of the man. I believe he granted my father a golden opportunity to reach out to others and, in the process, examine the way he has lived his life. Whether he takes advantage of that opportunity will be at least a factor in how I choose to relate to my father going forward.

My best,
Katherine

The reply from her professor was not long in coming.

> *June 5, 2012 5:25 p.m.*
> *Katherine,*
>
> *Consider your assignment submitted and accepted.*
> *Excellent job. As to its completeness—some stories*
> *never end.*
>
> *As always,*
> *Gerry*

Katherine breathed deeply and let out an extended sigh, glad to have that behind her. She marveled at the reach of her mentor's perception.

Before she could gather up Hailey and treat herself to a celebratory drink, another e-mail popped up. Theresa Leary from the bank. Katherine quickly opened the message, which contained only two lines, Constance Shipman's name and a phone number.

She dialed the number. Constance Shipman answered. Katherine explained who she was and why she was calling and asked if they could meet. Mrs. Shipman said she had to run some errands in Easthampton and suggested they meet later at her home—and that Katherine meet her husband as well that evening. Katherine agreed and wrote down Constance's address.

Katherine took Hailey for a quick walk, dropped her off at home, plugged in Constance's address into her GPS, and drove to Easthampton. The Shipman house was a small, two-story wood frame with a single-car garage. Katherine was greeted by a thin, intelligent-looking woman in her late forties wearing a navy blue shirtwaist dress. She introduced herself, and Constance showed her into the modest living room, where coffee was waiting.

"My husband is upstairs on the phone. He'll join us when he is finished, if that's all right."

"Of course. The coffee smells good."

Constance poured a cup for Katherine and one for herself. "For a reporter, I didn't expect you to be so young."

"Actually, I've been on the job all of a week. But I have a great interest in what's happened with regard to the local bank. I appreciate your taking the time to talk with me."

"Theresa called me. She's such a nice young lady. She said you thought you might be able to help."

"I've read about the takeover of the Hamptons Bank. I was moved by what it must have been like for you and others, having worked there so long. I know what it's like to need a job. I hope you were able to find one."

"No, I haven't. I've certainly tried. It's a terrible time to be looking for a job. My husband's an attorney whose firm went bankrupt. He's been looking for more than a year. We've been careful over the years, but it's not easy. Our savings are just about used up."

Katherine could see the tightness in Constance's shoulders and the worry in her eyes.

"I'm so sorry to hear that. I'm interested in the impact a bank failure has on employees caught in a situation like yours—through no fault of their own. I'm assuming you had no idea your bank was failing."

"It was a total shock to me. That bank job—apart from my family— was my life. Twenty-seven years. I hope this story helps."

"I must tell you, I'm going to write the story, but I don't know yet whether it will be published. That's entirely up to my editor. So this could all be for nothing. But I'd like to try."

"So would I. Ask away."

Katherine questioned Constance, methodically developing her history with Hamptons Bank, her training, the depth of her duties and responsibilities as a teller. Then she delved layer by layer into the reporting structure at the bank, the oversight, evaluations of her job performance, promotions, raises, setbacks. According to Constance it was a steady, incremental history, free of any disciplinary action and a professional match between the bank's expectation and her performance. Finally, Katherine explored Hamptons' financial condition, which Constance said she knew nothing about. Katherine continued to probe what Constance did know and when she knew it.

Just as Katherine was finished, Constance's husband joined them, introducing himself and looking exactly as Katherine expected—a pleasant enough man, average height, round in the middle, an earnest but intense face. Another lawyer in trouble.

It took no prompting for him to reveal his own story with far more detail than Katherine needed—but not more than she wanted. It was a sad story, unfortunately not unique. She silently counted her blessings.

"Thank you both for talking to me—and for your candor," said Katherine when she'd concluded the interview. "What you're going through must be terrible, and I'm sure you're not alone."

"CCB let our whole department go," explained Constance. "Not at first, but it wasn't long before they brought in their own people. Not just the tellers, but the janitors, the security guards, everybody."

"I'd like to include others in the story," Katherine said. "Can you give me the names of other tellers who were laid off? Names of some of the security people or the janitors—the others you mentioned."

"I can do better than that," Constance said getting up and going to her desk in the adjoining den. She came back with a book and handed it to Katherine. "This is the personnel directory for our department—names, addresses, everything. They're all gone."

Katherine thanked Constance again and went back to the office. Although it was getting late, she called several people from the directory, and connecting with three, she felt she would have enough material to round out the story. She would begin to write it in earnest the next morning.

Katherine fell asleep that night thinking about Constance and her husband, and how fortunate she was to not only have a job—but also be working at something she had dreamed about doing all her adult life. As she cuddled with Hailey in bed, she counted her blessings, among them a mother who had encouraged her and supported her all along the way.

CHAPTER THIRTY-SEVEN

Preston's driver took him to Teterboro Airport, where a Cessna Citation X and its young captain and crew were standing by.

"Are you ready to leave?" the captain asked, taking Preston's suitcase and garment bag.

"Yes, thank you," Preston said as he boarded the plane.

During the four-hour trip to Las Vegas, bathing in the luxury of the cabin, Preston wished he were not alone. He scanned the summary of Wilson's cash position he'd asked Casey to prepare, admiring Casey's ability to distill the condition of seven stores down to three pages. He felt let down and abandoned by Casey's threat to quit. At least he hadn't actually left. They had been together for so long, been through so much, surely Casey wouldn't leave him now.

Preston's concern about Casey's leaving was bad enough. But Marcia's misgivings bothered him even more. He remembered her reaction. *If he's worried, I'm worried.* Preston hated hearing her raise the question about what would happen to Casey's shares, all the more when she told him to ask his lawyers about it. He'd thought they'd put all the old worries behind them, but now he could feel the yarn in the sweater begin to unravel.

Sitting in the quiet comfort of the private jet, Preston felt as though he were in a finely finished coffin, flying into the skies of despair. He stared out the window, registering nothing, and remained in his state of self-imposed depression until the plane landed smoothly at the North Las Vegas Airport, where he was greeted by a limousine that drove him to the Wynn Hotel.

Preston checked in, called Austin, and arranged to meet for drinks in the lounge with the Wilson team attending the JD Power conference and NADA meetings. He also called Missy.

"Hi, Preston. I take it you've landed and are settling in. How was your flight?" asked Missy, solicitous as always.

"Smooth and efficient," Preston said. "As I mentioned last week, I'm here for the automobile dealers' meetings, but I'd really like to have dinner with you and Tommy tonight if you're free. Also, Missy, I would appreciate talking to you privately if we could."

"Tommy knows you were scheduled to arrive about now, and he and I were planning to have dinner with you tonight. You're at the Wynn, right? Would you like to eat there?"

"That would be great. I'll make a reservation at Wing Lei. Say for 7:00 p.m. Will that work?"

"The earlier the better for me. I'll check with Tommy. I'm sure it will be fine."

"When could we talk?"

"Tonight."

"Privately?"

"Why do you want to talk to me privately, Preston? Marcia problems again?"

"I'm sorry. It's just that ... well, when we talked before, last year, you—gave me some insights—got me to look at things ... at Marcia, a different way. I could really use some of that right now. To be perfectly honest, Missy, that's the reason I came out here. I don't care about the auto meetings. My team can handle that."

"Well, we could have breakfast. Do you want to come to our apartment, or would you rather talk in the coffee shop there?"

"If you don't mind, I'd rather talk here."

"We'll catch up tonight."

Preston came upon Bill, Antonio, Loreen, Sam, and the other

members of Wilson's delegation gathered in the lounge. Bill rearranged the chairs and low tables to accommodate the group, while Sam gave the long-legged waitress their drink orders. They all stood and saluted when Preston arrived and pulled up a chair. Party time.

"At ease," Preston said, ordering his own drink. "I hope you guys will spend some time focusing on the courses—what you can learn and bring home to make our operations run better and help us sell more cars."

"Austin gave us that speech before we left," Sam said.

The group meeting lasted about an hour, attention to the agenda dulled by the drinks and diluted by the rambunctious environment and the shouts from nearby tables.

Preston looked at his watch and excused himself, telling his team that he had another appointment. He wished them good luck with the meetings. By the time he'd made his way through the crowds, climbed the stairs to the restaurant, and checked in with the maître d', it was 7:30 p.m.

"Your two guests are seated and waiting for you, Mr. Wilson. Please follow me," he said.

Preston shook Tommy's hand, gave Missy a kiss on the cheek, and took a seat in the booth opposite them. "It's great to see you guys," Preston said, once again struck by how Missy's natural beauty could make the perfect dress look even better.

"It's good to see you again, too," Missy said. "It's been a while. Actually, I haven't seen you since the funeral. It's been a little over a year since Joe ... I still can't believe it."

"I know. He was quite a man," Preston said.

"I always wondered why you didn't say anything, you know, at the funeral," Missy said.

"I know why," Tommy said. "He's not an all-in kinda guy."

Preston smiled. Tommy didn't. No one spoke.

"Let's celebrate. Time for some champagne," Preston said, motioning for the sommelier.

"Hold the booze for us," Tommy said, "but don't let us stop ya."

Preston ordered a bottle of chardonnay instead. "You sure you don't want anything?"

"No, thank you," Missy said. "Tell us how you're doing. Tommy tells me you have a son. Congratulations. You must be so proud."

The wine steward poured a small portion in Preston's glass; Preston tasted it and signaled his approval.

"Thank you. It's been exciting. A lot of changes."

"You named him Preston Joseph, right? After Joe. That's so nice," Missy said.

"Yeah, we call him P.J. He's ... a handful. Just starting to walk."

"Show me a picture," Missy said.

Preston reached for his wallet, pulled out a picture of Marcia holding P.J., and handed it to Missy.

Missy studied the photograph with obvious delight. "He's handsome, like his dad," she said, handing the photograph to Tommy.

"Better looking," Tommy said. "Let's eat."

Preston signaled their waiter, who immediately came and took their orders.

"By the way, congratulations to you, Missy. Tommy told me you were married here in Vegas, and I hear Harry came with his band."

Missy's face lit up like fireworks. She described the wedding in detail, the Viva Las Vegas, what everybody wore, how sweet it was, and the reception. "Harry was wonderful. It was so much fun. I'd never heard music like that. We danced and laughed ourselves silly."

Dinner was served, and they took a break from their discussion only to exclaim about the food. After dinner, Preston ordered a scotch, Tommy a beer, and Missy more hot tea.

"How's Marcia handling all of this?" Missy asked. "It's a lot of work. Is anyone helping her?"

"Her mother stayed with us for a couple of weeks after the hospital. Marcia said that helped a lot."

"Of course it helped. You don't like your mother-in-law?" Tommy asked.

Preston felt embarrassed, wishing he had put it differently, reminded once again of how direct Tommy could be. "We have a nanny. That helps."

"I don't know about nannies," Tommy said. "They ain't family. I worry the kid could tell. When the time comes, Miss—I don't want no nannies—if you're okay with that."

"That's fine, Tommy. I doubt that we could afford a nanny anyway. Besides, my mom and half my relatives will be out here—or actually in Elko."

"How's the project coming?" Preston asked. "Did you get the information Casey sent?"

"I got it," Tommy said. "My numbers guys sent him back most of what he asked for. When I didn't hear further from you, I figured you didn't like the cash flow situation, and I proceeded in accordance. We've arranged some seed money, and we've already started on the renovation."

Missy chimed in. "We hope to have the camp open on a small basis in ninety days. I'm going to start with basic dance lessons for the girls. I can't wait."

"It's quite an undertaking. I don't know how you run a dance studio for girls with special needs," Preston said.

"You run it like any other dance studio. We all have special needs, Preston," Missy said. "It's just that these girls need a little more help. I thought you might understand that now that you have a young boy who has special needs of his own."

Preston suggested they adjourn to the first-floor lounge for cigars.

"I don't think a cigar's a good idea tonight, Preston. Maybe you and I will have one while you are here—shoot a little craps," Tommy said.

"What are you talking about? You're the one that got me hooked on cigars."

"I did an introduction to you to cigars. I didn't do any hooking. Whether or not you smoke them is up to you."

"Well, let's go down to the lounge, and I'll smoke one," Preston said.

"That ain't gonna happen tonight."

"Thanks, Tommy," Missy said, nodding in agreement.

Preston was confused by the exchange, but he didn't want to upset Missy, so he dropped the subject.

Tommy and Missy thanked Preston for dinner.

"Are we still on for breakfast?" Missy asked.

"Absolutely," Preston replied. "What time would be convenient for you?"

"How about 8:00 a.m. at the Frontier Coffee Shop—where we first met."

"I'll see you then," Preston said and shook Tommy's hand while putting his arm lightly around Missy's shoulder.

CHAPTER THIRTY-EIGHT

Preston found Missy in the coffee shop at a table not far from the one where they'd first met, and a waitress came to take their orders.

"So, Preston, what's going on?"

"Thanks for agreeing to meet with me—"

"Preston, skip all that. You have a problem with Marcia. Again. Talk to me."

"Well, for a while, after Joe turned things around, everything was great. Marcia was pregnant ... we'd always wanted a child. Marcia seemed happier than I'd seen her in years. She helped me in the business, she was upbeat, and she was ... I thought she was back in love with me. Then, after the baby was born, everything seemed to fall apart."

"What do you mean, fall apart?"

"She became short with me, more distant. It was like I couldn't do anything right as far as she was concerned."

"What else?"

"That's about it."

"I doubt it. There's more. Keep talking."

"I don't know what else to say."

"I have a couple of girlfriends who are going through this. A baby—especially the first year—is hard, and that's without P.J.'s hearing problem. Do you think that Marcia feels that you did all you could to help?"

"I don't know."

"That's a problem. Do you help with the dishes, empty the garbage, make the beds, fix the formula, whatever?"

"We have a maid, and we have a nanny. I don't think Marcia's got it all that bad."

They both obviously welcomed the arrival of their food, and the opportunity to regroup.

"Okay, forget about the maid and nanny. Marcia has a one-year-old child, and that's her primary concern, and it should be. I don't want to pull teeth here, but you're not helping me help you."

"What do you mean?"

"The last time we had this kind of discussion, you admitted that you'd been holding back. Now I'm sensing a lot more walls. My guess is Marcia's tired of climbing those walls. Tell me more about P.J.'s hearing problems."

"He was born with a moderate to severe hearing loss. We ... Marcia consulted her pediatrician, a pediatric audiologist, and a highly regarded hearing and speech school. They subjected P.J. to extensive further testing and assessment, and within weeks recommended that he be fitted with hearing aids for both ears."

"That's great. That means he'll have help hearing."

"But, that's the thing. He *can* hear, some. I talked with another pediatrician who advised that we wait a while and see how P.J. develops. Marcia was so upset, you'd think I hit our son over the head. So intense about it—wanted our son to wear hearing aids, a thing in his ears with a tube and the other part hanging behind his ears—in the first six weeks. Imagine a young baby being subjected to that? He'd probably pull them off, chew them, maybe eat them. I thought it was nuts, particularly when it may not be necessary."

"That could be a problem. I'm sure Marcia has talked about it with the medical people. Has she said anything about that?"

"I don't know whether she talked with them about that specifically.

I do know she talked to her friend Ann, who visited her recently. When I came home that night, it was five degrees above zero in our apartment, if you know what I mean."

"What happened?"

"Marcia was in the wine, opened with one of her we-need-to-talk speeches. That's when she told me she was going to have him fitted. I told her we had honest differences about that."

"What did she say to that?"

"She said this was important to her and P.J. That my way could hurt him, having him fitted could only help."

"How did you respond?"

"I told her I thought we were a team on this. She said she was resigning from the team and went to bed. A few days later, after work and stopping at my club, I came home and told her I had a problem with one of our key guys leaving. She brushed that news off and told me she'd gone ahead and had P.J. fitted."

"How's he doing?"

"Too early to tell. It's a process, having him adapt to the aids. It's supposed to be a happy time when you do it."

"Are you helping Marcia with that process?"

"No, she's better at that. Besides, she knows how I feel. But it gets worse."

"I'm sure. Go ahead."

"That's when she tells me that I'm becoming an older man and that she's feeling farther away from me. She told me if I can't be an involved husband I should at least want to be an involved father. That really pissed me off. I told her I am an involved father on two fronts."

"Two fronts? You lost me."

Preston's legs were moving up and down so fast the table started to shake.

"Are you all right?" Missy asked.

"Great. Just great. Got a one-year-old who's deaf, a twenty-three-year-old daughter I never knew about, and a wife about to leave me."

"What? Hold it. A daughter you never knew about? Did you tell Tommy about this?"

"No."

"A daughter shows up after all these years, and you don't tell Tommy? He's not going to like that. Anyway, that's another problem. Anything more you can tell me about your new-found daughter?"

"Her name's Katherine. She's smart, lives in New York, and has a master's in journalism. I met her mother when I was twenty-three. She was a nurse and took care of me while I was briefly in the hospital, and I took her out after work for something to eat. It became a little more than that, but that's the only time I spent with her. I never gave it another thought, never had any reason to. Then out of the blue, she calls me, tells me I have a daughter and suggests I get to know her."

"This is probably a stupid question, but how do you know she's your daughter?"

"I went through all of that, Missy—paternity test—the whole nine yards. She's mine, and to tell you the truth, I'm happy about it."

"And how about Marcia?"

"She's fine with Katherine, likes her, been supportive on this. She told me it's not about Katherine; it's about her, our son, and me. She said something about our fabric stretching and tearing. That's the way she talks. She said we repaired it once, and she didn't know if we could do it again. I asked her what all of that meant, and she said not enough to me, and then just shut down."

"You really know how to ruin a girl's breakfast, Preston," Missy said. "I don't know if I can be of help or not. You've dug a pretty deep hole. I'll give you a few observations for what they're worth. Marcia's a fine woman. It's all about trust. It takes a short period of time to lose it and a long period of time to get it back. Tommy's really smart about these things. He says you're not an all-in kind of guy. Marcia's feeling that right now. She's protecting her cub and you're not getting it. She's right. What harm can it do to fit P.J. with hearing aids if they may help him? What are you really worried about? Is your son not looking as good to you with hearing aids? This is not about you, Preston. Kids have special needs. Your indifference to that disappoints me. It must outrage your wife. I don't know if you can fix this one."

Missy reached over the table and gently put her hand over Preston's. "You're a good person, Preston. Don't give up on yourself. It's hard to look deep inside and find the best parts, especially when you're lonely and scared. Only you can decide whether it's worth the effort. But if you want to keep Marcia, that's a place to start. And, if you want a relationship with Tommy, you can't just pretend you're his friend."

Tears slowly slid down Preston's cheeks. The coffee shop was full of people, the smell of hot coffee, excitement in the air. He was looking at one of the most beautiful women he knew, and she was giving it to him straight. He had never felt more alone.

Preston thanked Missy, paid the tab, and headed back to his hotel. He stopped by one of the crap tables, but without Tommy to watch, he managed to drop two thousand dollars in half an hour. Not a good day. He went to the spa, got a massage, stretched out by the pool, and gave Tommy a call.

"Hi, Tommy. When can we get together? I'd like to see you before I get tied up with meetings and have to head home."

"I'm over at Caesar's, watching some games, managing some accounts. Come on over."

"How long are you going to be there?" Preston asked.

"Another hour. Two."

"I'm going over to the convention center, check on my team. Then I'll find you."

★ ★ ★

Preston found Tommy talking with two men in corner seats in the large sports center, where huge screens depicted an array of basketball and baseball games, NASCAR races, and horse races.

"I'll be with you in a minute, Preston," Tommy said.

Preston sat down in front of one of the races and watched with intensity while he waited.

"You like the ponies?" Tommy asked, coming up behind Preston and catching him by surprise.

"I like to watch them run," Preston said, seeing Tommy give him a funny look.

"Nobody just watches them. Here, have a cigar." Preston followed Tommy to a nearby lounge, where they ordered drinks and lit up their cigars.

"What's on your mind?" Tommy asked.

"Just want to hang out with you a little."

"What's on your mind?" Tommy asked again.

"I had breakfast with Missy. She's quite a woman."

"For the last time, let's have it."

Preston took a long pull on his cigar and blew out the smoke. He tried to control his legs and keep his voice steady. "I'm in a bit of a spot," he said.

"The ponies'll get ya. How much you owe?"

"It's not that."

"Don't lie to me."

"That's not what I want to talk to you about. Marcia and I are having some problems. When I first met Missy, she gave me some insight, you know, how women look at things. It helped, and Marcia and I got back together. Now I'm going through that again."

"Missy's got a heart bigger than those screens," Tommy said. "But she ain't a marriage counselor. She's busy right now trying to plan the camp, talk to our contributors, line up the kids, supervise the improvements. I don't want her overworked right now, or put under any more stress."

"I totally understand, Tommy. Missy has a way of talking to you where she ends up getting it all. In the course of our discussion, I mentioned that I now have a twenty-three-year-old daughter, and she was upset that I hadn't told you about her when we had dinner in New York. So I am telling you now."

"That don't compute. How'd you find the years to make her twenty-three?" Tommy asked.

"It's a long story." Preston took another pull off his cigar.

"They all are. Make it short."

"I was twenty-three, same as she is now. Met a girl. Went out one night. Never saw or heard from her again until she called me out of the blue two months ago and told me I have a daughter living and going to school in New York and that I should get in touch with her. That's as short as I can make it."

"So you did, right?"

"Right."

"And she's a nice girl, right?"

"Right."

"And Marcia ain't going to kill ya—over this at least, right?"

"Right."

"Okay. So ya told me. How's the cigar?"

"Good."

"I gotta go," Tommy said. "Good luck with your meetings. Stay in touch."

CHAPTER THIRTY-NINE

Preston's meeting with Tommy in Vegas hung in his thoughts like a cobweb. *Nobody just watches the ponies.* The guy was uncanny. Either that or he was just taking a wild swing. Preston couldn't decide which. *It's not like I don't have enough to worry about,* Preston whined to himself, without Marcia adding his betting on the horses to her list of complaints. And what was wrong with that anyway?

Preston was reacting to all the external pressures on his life. The cumulative obligations imposed upon him by his wife, P.J., Casey's threat to leave, and reaching out to the Collectibles hit him like an allergy—his mind had all but broken out in mental hives. And the guilt. He was always feeling the guilt. He hated it, but he knew the only way to make it go away—or at least diminish it—was to do what he'd been putting off. At this point in his introspection, Harry popped into his mind.

Harry was the last Collectible on his list—the one he never got to until Joe's funeral. Tommy had told him over dinner that he and Missy didn't know Harry until then either, but they weren't under an obligation. Tommy thought a lot of Harry, a stand-up guy, said he was close to Joe. Then the photography at the wedding and the oompah band, whatever that was. *And now I have to reach out to this guy, earn his trust, and take care of him . . . forever.*

"He's not a fast response kinda guy," Tommy had said when he gave Preston Harry's number. *At what point is enough enough?* But guilt won. He made the call.

"You got the Oompah Man," a booming voice said on the recording. "Hit a note and leave it. If you're lucky, I'll get back at you."

Preston hesitated for a moment, inclined to just hang up but instead said, "Hello, Harry. This is Preston Wilson. We met briefly at Joe Hart's funeral. I would appreciate it if you would call me." Preston added his telephone number. He hoped Harry wouldn't call.

But within seconds his phone rang. "Hey, Car Man. What's happening? Are you knocking 'em dead? I see on your fancy website you're selling the big stuff. How's it going?"

Preston didn't know which question to answer first. He decided to start with hello. After that, he said, "The car business is cyclical, but we're getting along at the moment," immediately feeling that the response was too technical or, at least, too formal.

"What's on your mind, big guy?" Harry asked.

"Well, we didn't get a chance to talk much at the funeral. I spoke with Tommy recently, and he was singing your praises. I thought I'd reach out—see how you're doing."

"Tommy and Missy are good people. Man, can they dance. You should have seen them at their wedding reception."

"I understand you have a band, played at the reception."

Harry's booming voice burst into song, "*We sang at the wedding, too, we sang especially for you. We played the brass, you danced on the grass. We played especially for you.*"

Preston managed a synthetic laugh. "Where are you, Harry?"

"The great state of Buffalo. It's actually a city."

"What are you doing up there?"

"Having the time of my life. A bunch of us have a band and, to our amazement, we're in demand. VFW, Elks Club, Fourth of July picnics, Oktoberfest, school dances, private gigs, you name it."

"Are you still doing photography?"

"Once in a while, when I'm moved to take the shot." The one

thing Preston remembered about Harry was his placing a picture he'd taken of Joe on the bridge of his boat on an easel for all to see at Joe's funeral. The photograph showed Joe looking forward, with a relaxed smile on his face and a hopeful expression in his eyes, illuminated by the sun's rays.

"How about our getting together sometime, maybe hanging out?" Preston said, immediately bothered by the cavalier tone of his request.

"Why?"

Preston was stunned by Harry's response, mainly because Preston was wondering the same thing. *What is it about these people? They're all freaking mind readers.*

"So ... I can get to know you better."

"Do you play an instrument?" Harry asked.

"No"

"Hunt, fish, shoot trap?"

"No."

"Write, act, sing, dance?"

Preston said no again.

"What do you do?" Harry asked, "Other than play golf, sell cars, and drink at the country club? Just guessing on that last one."

"Well, once in a while I shoot craps and smoke cigars. Does that count?"

"Hell, yes. It shows you're human. I was doubting that for a minute," Harry replied.

"So, what do you say?" Preston continued. "Do you want to figure out how we can get together? Do you ever come to the city?"

"Joe told me about you. He spoke about you in a positive light— that's what he does . . . did. I'm not sure I want to get together with you. I have good days and bad, ups and downs. I'd hate to meet you on a down day."

Preston found himself at a loss for words.

After a while, Harry broke the silence. "If we ever get a gig in New York City, I'll let you know. You can come and hear the music, meet the boys. How's that sound?"

"Evasive," Preston said. "Frankly, I'm disappointed by the way this conversation has gone."

"I can fix that," Harry said.

Preston heard the click and then the dial tone, and for the second time that day he was left feeling like someone who'd just had a glass of cold water thrown in his face.

CHAPTER FORTY

Feeling refreshed, Katherine sat at her desk and reviewed the draft of her story. She decided it was too long and cut it down where she could, but the revisions were taking a while.

She stopped for a quick lunch to clear her head and walked down Hampton Road to the Golden Pear Café. Not a minute in the door, she spotted Marcia Wilson, two ahead in the short line. There was no way to avoid being spotted, and Katherine feared an awkward moment might be brewing. Marcia, however, made the first move, with a genuine kiss on Katherine's cheek.

"Hi, Katherine. What a surprise! It's good to see you. Are you working here now?"

"Yes—still learning the ropes, actually. Good to see you, too. Are you—what are you doing in Southampton?"

"We have a summer place not far from here. Nadine is in the city today with P.J., and Preston's away at a car dealers' shindig in Las Vegas. I wanted to take care of some errands at our place, and then I was going to treat myself to a day at the club, the spa, the whole nine yards, but, you know, I'm just not in the mood for the bitchiness some of our girls can bring to the table."

Katherine could see the strain in Marcia's neck and the tightness in her lips. "Their loss is my gain," she said. "Let's have lunch together."

"You're a dear. I'd love to," Marcia said, taking Katherine by the arm and escorting her to the table a waitress had just then signaled was free.

"I didn't realize you had a home in the Hamptons," Katherine said.

"Yes. It's a little house here in Southampton. Not on the water but comfortable. To tell you the truth, I like it better here. The Trump Tower thing was your father's idea."

Katherine reached for her pen and pad but stopped short. She thought Trump Tower was pretentious and priced for a migraine. But what intrigued her was the assignment of its choice to *her father*. Marcia could have said *my husband's idea*. Her mind swiftly scanned the implications, even responsibility, and her conscience told her to pay attention to Marcia. The scan won the battle. *Your mother's a nurse. Your father's a war hero.* Pride. Susan: *My father and mother are drunks.* Shame. *Your father's idea . . .* her conscience won the war.

"How's P.J. getting along?"

"Very well. Thanks for asking. And I mean that."

Their food came, and Katherine started to eat as she wondered why the last four words were necessary. The answer came soon enough.

"P.J. finally has hearing aids—both ears. Because they were fitted this late, there's a process we must go through to put him at ease, so that he'll accept wearing them. It must be a happy experience. We're working on it, but it would be nice if your father was interested enough to participate."

So much for a pleasant lunch, Katherine thought. She searched for a different topic. "You said he was in Las Vegas. Did he see Tommy and Missy, or was it all business?"

"Yes, he said he had dinner with them. As I think we mentioned, they are opening a camp for children with special needs. I admire that."

"So do I. Like to meet them one of these days."

"How is your job going?"

"I'm already in over my head, but, honestly, I love it."

"Can you talk about what you're doing?"

"Sure, without getting into specifics. In addition to the usual round of rookie assignments, I'm working on a story about the banking world, specifically the impact on the little guy when bank officials do what they shouldn't and not what they should."

"Are those two different?"

Katherine laughed. "A distinction without a difference? Technically, there are omissions and commissions. I'm looking into both."

"Well, I know banks can be difficult, and we need them. I hope you find what you're looking for."

"I wish what I'm looking for didn't exist."

"Careful what you wish for," Marcia said with a smile.

"Do you miss teaching?" Katherine asked.

"Yes, but I love P.J. to death, and I want to be the best mother I can. The first year or two can be a challenge ... to sleep, if nothing else."

Suddenly, as if they were discussing a nuclear bomb or the bubonic plague, a sadness appeared to overtake Marcia. Her head dropped, and out came her handkerchief from her handbag—just in time to catch a miniature Niagara Falls.

"Are you all right?" Katherine asked, getting up and putting her arms around Marcia. "Can I take you somewhere, do anything?"

"No, let 'em look. I don't care. It's been a bad few months, that's all. Sometimes it just hits me."

"What's wrong? Can you talk about it?"

"I can, but in this case I don't want to because it involves your father, and I don't want to let him down. Or you either for that matter."

Now it was Katherine's turn to feel upset. "Does it have something to do with me?" she asked in an even, low but stern voice.

"Oh no, absolutely not. If that were the case, I would not be sitting with you right now. It is definitely not about you. It's about your father, P.J., and me. But if I go into it with you—and criticize him—it would place you in an awkward position, and I don't want to do that. Your father loves you, adores you. He so wants to be your father in your eyes."

"I understand," Katherine said in a much lighter tone. Seeing Marcia regain her composure, Katherine decided to probe a bit further. "When we had dinner and were discussing Joe Hart's friends, you mentioned something that stuck in my mind. May I ask you about it?"

"Sure, go ahead. You seem trustworthy, Katherine. That's a nice quality to have."

"Thank you. You said Preston's relationship with the Collectibles was *evolving*. What did you mean by that?"

Marcia appeared to think for a couple of beats and then said, "He started out quite taken by Joe—apart from being appreciative for all Joe did for him, for us—by the concept of reaching out to help Joe's friends. We—Pres and I—were having some troubles back then and meeting these people seemed to help him. He changed the way he looked at them, at life. Then he got busy with work and his interest—I say commitment—seemed to fade. By evolving I was trying to be polite, but it irks me."

Katherine was busy taking notes on her paper napkin.

"Why are you so passionate about this subject?" Marcia asked.

"The same reason you helped Preston help Johnny. I met him a few days ago, along with Alice. Corey, too."

"You went . . . you are some young lady, young lady." At that, they both shared their first laugh of the lunch.

"Maybe, but if I don't get back to work I may be out of a job."

"I've enjoyed this immensely," Marcia said. "I'll let you know the next time I come out. And feel free to drop by. Bring your dog. Take a walk on the beach. It's not that far."

"I've enjoyed it, too."

"By the way, can we keep this conversation between us girls?" Marcia asked.

"You bet. We're not the bitchy kind." And they laughed again, this time even harder.

★ ★ ★

Back at her desk, Katherine rewrote her draft of the human-interest story centering on Constance, her husband, and three others, polished it, and e-mailed the finished copy to Sol. She debated with herself whether to send Chuck a copy, but rationalized that Sol wanted her to pursue this. *Take it to another level.* She knew Thursday started a new week, and that Chuck would be assigning her more stories. If Sol liked the bank story, maybe that would be included.

She had no way of knowing the sandstorm she had created.

CHAPTER FORTY-ONE

Katherine was at her desk as usual bright and early that rainy Thursday morning when her phone buzzed. It was Chuck; she picked up.

"Come into my office." The line went silent.

She told Hailey to stay and walked to the editor's office. Chuck was sitting behind his desk, leaning his considerable frame so far back in his chair, it appeared to Katherine he might fall over backwards. Without looking at her, he motioned to her to sit. She did.

"I was about to call you in to give you an assignment when Sol sent me a copy of your ... unemployment tear-jerker." Once again, the air conditioner blew cold. The last thing Katherine wanted was a problem with her editor. She willed herself to be calm, feeling the heat rise on the back of her neck.

"Here's the way it works," Chuck continued. "I'm the editor. Harold's my assistant. He edits the copy. If we're pressed for time, our assistant copy editor will give us a hand. Let's work backwards. Paper published Wednesday 2:00 p.m. Noon's the cutoff for production so the stories have to be edited and approved well before that. Thursday starts the new week—I make the next round of assignments. In between, we have to plug the holes, feed the Web with whatever we can. Got it?"

"Got it."

"It's a little more nuanced than that. Number one: You didn't ask me or tell me you were writing this story. Two: I didn't assign you this story. Three: It hasn't been edited. Four: You decided it should be written under your byline—Luke, our senior writer, assisted Sol when this FDIC bank story broke, and he wrote the CCB takeover follow-up under his name—all of which I approved," Chuck said. "I know it's your first few days, but we do have a process around here. I'd like you to follow it."

"Completely understood," Katherine said.

"By the way, who gave you the lead?"

"I'll tell you that if you tell me something first," Katherine said. She saw a thin, twisted smile cross Chuck's face, with no trace in his eyes.

"Are we negotiating?"

"No."

"What?" Chuck asked.

"How did you like the piece?"

"It was too long for our paper. It did catch the human interest side. Your lead?"

"Went to CCB and got the lead myself. A young teller there happened to know Mrs. Shipman."

"And how did you happen to know she would know that?"

"Because I'm an investigative reporter, and it's my job to know who to approach and how to get them to talk."

"I suggest you talk with Luke and tell him that you liked the work he did on the prior stories and that you're hoping it will be okay with him if you pursue an assignment that deals with the layoffs. We'll see what he says. In the meanwhile, cover the obits for the next week, and here's a list of five stories I'd like you to write."

Katherine looked over the list: how a community radio station was getting along after leaving Long Island's Southampton University campus and moving to Southampton Village; Southampton Village's police chief passing his exam to become permanent chief; the district attorney's office dispute with the Southampton Town Board letter on moving police records; whether the Southampton Zoning Board of Appeals would approve a Southampton pool application; and a new director taking over at Southampton's animal shelter. She tried her best to maintain a neutral face, hoping Chuck could not read her thoughts. It wasn't that she didn't know she would be starting at the bottom. She had expected that. She enjoyed meeting new people and understood the value in finding local stories of interest. The problem was the transparency of her impatience with doing such stories the way they'd always been done.

Katherine wanted to expand these stories, uncover what the men and women in Southampton and Long Island were really all about, their aspirations, their frustrations. She wanted to learn what they were particularly interested in, how they were unique, and what drove them, but why not cover the bank stories as well? They were in the *Twin Forks Press* area, too. But looking at Chuck's face and gauging his general demeanor, she knew this was not the time to debate the matter. She simply smiled and said, "Thank you."

"Get out of here," he growled. "I have work to do."

★ ★ ★

Katherine walked down the aisle that divided the partitions in the reporters' den and passed Luke's desk, saw he was busy writing and went back to her station. She thought about her conversation with Chuck and decided she needed to rein in her enthusiasm a notch, or at least its appearance. An e-mail popped up that she hadn't expected.

Angelo Bertolini. She opened the attachment.

Investigative Report

Investigator: Angelo Bertolini, P.I. #2394876 N.Y. [Former NYPD DECT GS]

Subject: Preston Wilson

White Male

DOB: 3.13.65; Age: 47

Married: Marcia Wilson; Age: 39

Child: Preston Joseph Wilson; Age: 15 months

Education: College Degree: B.A. Political Science, Hamilton College

Occupation: Automobile Dealer

Corporate: 35% Owner, Wilson Holdings Inc. (35% Marcia Wilson, 15% Alex Herman, 15% Casey Fitzgerald)

Dun and Bradstreet Rating: Wilson Holdings Inc. BA

Employees: 6 stores—127 employees in the aggregate

Financial: Credit Rating: 680

License: New York State

Violations: 2 speeding, 1 red light, 24 equipment violations (reductions)

Addictions:

Drug Use: No Arrests, No Convictions

Alcohol Related: No DWI arrests or convictions; one DUI arrest—no conviction

Tobacco: Yes—cigars

Gambling: Yes—off-line and casino-based betting—horses

Criminal: NYS Unified Court System: No record shown

Bankruptcies/Involuntary Receivership: None filed

Medical Records: Pending

Civil Matters: Wilson Holdings Inc.: Multiple lawsuits, 6 active, 3 dismissed (NY County Supreme Court Docket); other states pending, federal pending

Personal Claims: (1) Sexual harassment, employee, dismissed

Private Clubs: Union League Club, Southampton Country Club, Vail Colorado Ski Club

Business Reputation: Automobile industry-dealers (20 groups, other sources) "well regarded, successful dealer who dodged the bullet"

Personal: Appears satisfactory

Additional notes:

Note: Surveillance (Angelo)

Subject under random surveillance by Angelo from time to time. Attends Union League Club, his place of business, upscale restaurants throughout Manhattan, often frequents the 21 Club, going to and from his condo residence in New York City, usually by car with driver, occasionally walks, associations appear consistent with the car business. Behavior, associations, and those accompanying subject all appeared routine and uneventful.

Courtesy Surveillance (by reciprocal service agreement) Subject took private plane to Las Vegas 6/1-6/3/2012. Subject checked in Wynn Resort; meeting with group of men in lounge—45 min; dinner in hotel at Chinese restaurant with T. Greco (known to P.I. 10642) and unidentified female—2.5 hours; subject gamed at craps table, predominantly black chips—1 hour, lost; returned to his room alone; left his room at 7:30 a.m., took taxi to Frontier Hotel, 8:00 a.m. met with attractive woman (same unidentified female) in coffee shop, had breakfast—2 hours; went back to Wynn Resort; gamed at same craps table, black chips again—1/2 hour, lost; went to spa in hotel—2 hours; went to betting parlor at Caesar's, watched horse races, met with T. Greco, went to lounge—1 hour; T. Greco left, subject back to horse races—2 hours; end of surveillance due to prior commitment of colleague. (Photos available upon request.)

Note: Subject was subject of a sexual harassment complaint by one Henrietta Higgins, an employee at Mercedes Manhattan. This occurred February 12, 2012, at complainant's desk on the first floor of the main showroom. Subject alleged to have inappropriately touched complainant on the back and then the shoulder and made inappropriate remarks including "You look very nice this morning." These were the allegations complainant alleged to support the complaint. New York State Division of Human Rights referred investigation to the Equal Employment

Opportunity Commission. The EEOC conducted a field investigation. No probable cause was found. Complaint was dismissed. Follow-up by Angelo consistent with EEOC findings.

Summary: Client had no specific direction or inquiry for investigation. No parameters were set. P.I. used his discretion in a random surveillance, inquiry, and review of subject, avoiding contact with subject or those likely to inform subject of investigation.

Conclusion: Subject has general good reputation as successful businessman. No known addictions or infirmities. Criminal record clean. Informal unconfirmed sources suggest further investigation for potential gambling issues, particularly with offline betting.

Katherine called Angelo right away to thank him for the thorough report.

"You got it. You had me shooting in the dark so I didn't know how far you wanted me to go. A friend of mine in Vegas helped me out—no charge. If you want me to do more, let me know."

"No, this is fine. I appreciate it. But keep an eye and ear open for anything you think I should know about Preston Wilson or his company."

"You ever gonna tell me who this guy is to you—why you're interested?"

"Maybe someday."

"Is he causing you any trouble?"

"He's definitely not causing me any trouble. But thanks."

"My pleasure," Angelo said.

CHAPTER FORTY-TWO

"Hi, Marcia," Casey said, getting out of his chair, moving around his desk, and giving her a hug. "Good to see you."

Marcia sat down in one of the two chairs in front of his desk, and Casey sat in the other.

"You're probably wondering why I'm here."

"Not at all. I should have called you sooner."

"Are you sure you want to do this?"

"I don't want to do it. I have to do it."

"Why?"

"We all went through hell, but thanks to Joe, we turned things around—"

"And you think it's not working?"

"Considering how deep the hole was, we've come a long way. Our banks are still with us, our sales are adequate, and we're still generating revenue."

"But?"

"This is going to sound selfish, but ... the but is I'm not happy. It doesn't feel right to me around here anymore. I think Austin's an ass. Systemically, we're moving sideways and taking unnecessary risks."

"I get that Austin's an ass, but help me with the last one, Casey."

"If I learned anything from Joe, it's the importance of a strategic plan—a process with benchmarks or metrics to measure whether we're on course performance-wise, timing-wise, and otherwise. The otherwise is not doing anything illegal. I'm still into all of that, but I'm lonesome."

"Meaning Preston, Austin, and others aren't helping—aren't with you in the process?"

"I don't think they see the value of the process or the danger in not following the rules—and that's the risk—but it's worse than that. I honestly don't think they care."

Marcia thought about Alex, the automotive consultant Joe had brought into the negotiations with BNA in Charlotte, and thereafter, to whom Preston had given fifteen percent equity in the company. "Have you talked about this with Alex?"

"Yes. He sees it the same way. In fact, he's been pulling away from a lot of the operational oversight. I doubt if Preston will be able to keep him."

"But he owns fifteen percent."

"Of what? Besides, Alex was not driven by the equity. That was an add-on. Wilson Holdings is not his day job. He came in, helped us a lot when we needed it—honestly, because Joe asked him to. And Joe's gone."

"Does Alex not get along with Preston?"

"He gets along with him. He just doesn't get him."

"You sound like you've made up your mind."

"After we met in the mountains, what followed for me was a real change in the way we did things. I remember when I called Preston—that was when Joe was starting to work on our case—to tell Preston all the stuff he wanted from us, documents, tax returns, operating statements, audits."

"And he told you to give it to him."

"But it wasn't that simple. We needed documents from him, and as you know, from you. And the letter from the criminal lawyer—that really pissed Preston off. What Preston didn't get was that Joe needed him to be a part of the turnaround process, not a distant CEO making assignments—and to commit to a clean way of doing business."

"And you think that's all happening again. I can understand that. I really can," Marcia said, tears forming in her eyes.

Casey returned to his desk chair and reached in his desk for a box of Kleenex, which he handed to Marcia, and a Snickers bar for himself.

"This company's been good to me for a lot of years. I make two hundred thousand dollars a year and can drive any car I want. I've earned that—worked my tail off here. And I've always been loyal to your husband. What matters most to me is my wife and three children. They know I'm not happy. I told Preston I quit, but he, of course, didn't take me seriously. That's why I'm officially resigning as CFO—today."

Marcia had never seen Casey so emotional, and yet so calm. She knew how important Casey was, not only to the company, but to Preston. Casey might have underestimated Preston's reliance on him, or maybe he had it just right, maybe he understood all too well Preston's reliance on him. She would have felt better if he was ranting and raving; perhaps then there would have been hope. Under these circumstances she doubted it, however. After all, she'd been wrestling with a lot of the same issues.

What a mess, she thought. *What a serious, unnecessary mess.*

★ ★ ★

Preston entered the Manhattan store on a cloudy Monday morning, made more so when he saw Casey still in his office standing behind his desk. Preston walked in and sat down. Casey continued packing personal items in cardboard boxes.

"I learned from my wife that you're quitting," Preston said.

"Resigning," Casey said as he packed his framed diploma from Wharton. "You're the one who's quitting."

"What are you talking about? I'm not quitting," Preston said.

Casey stopped what he was doing, grabbed a Snickers bar from his desk drawer, walked around his desk, plopped down in the chair next to Preston, and put his feet up on the desk.

"How can you eat a Snickers bar at a time like this?"

"They're good."

"All you think about is food."

"We've had this discussion."

"I'm confused."

"I agree. You are."

"When did we have this discussion?"

"Roughly 1:30 in the afternoon, November 18, 2009."

"You're losing it, Casey."

"We were in a small conference room at the bank in Charlotte. Joe had just come back from lunch with the president and chairman to give us a status report. You thought we were going 'down the chute,' as you put it, and you were lecturing about 'all I could think of was food.' I told you then I wasn't going to make myself the goat anymore. I meant it."

Preston was quiet for a while trying to recall their discussion during the Charlotte workout.

"That was two and a half years ago, Casey. How do you remember all that? More important, why?"

"You were scared then, Preston. So was I. And we had good reason to be. The problem is, you're not scared now."

"And you are?"

"No. I'm no longer CFO. I don't have to lie awake at three in the morning wondering whether your prep-school buddy is going to do what I asked him to do or whether he is telling me the truth. That's your problem now."

"Do you really think Wilson is in trouble? We've worked out of tight spots before. Our sales are up. I can't understand why you're leaving me. We've come so far together."

"We have come a long way, yes, but I don't think it's really been together."

"What's that supposed to mean?"

"Wilson clearly benefited from the workout and consolidation. The bank gave us more room, and the controls Alex put in place allowed us to properly allocate the increased revenues. But there's been net profit erosion ever since you brought Disley in to handle the accounting."

"He thinks you don't get the big picture financially."

"I don't care what he thinks. And I'm tired of caring what you think. I promised myself when Joe got us out of trouble, I'd never let myself get into that position again. It's not fair to me, to my wife, or to my kids."

Preston stood up and put his hand on Casey's shoulder. "Don't leave me, Casey. I have too many problems right now. Marcia. P.J. A new daughter I really care about. Cut me some slack. I need you here."

"You should really care about each of them," Casey said as he got up and poured himself a cup of coffee. He walked around the desk, took the boxes off the desktop with one hand, set the coffee down with the other, and sat down in his desk chair. He pushed back on the chair, locked his hands behind his head, and put his feet up on the desk. "You're a good guy, Preston—deep down. But, you know what's sad? When you get cornered, you always make it about you. By the way, I'm not leaving the company—I'm just not an officer, board member, or employee anymore. As a fifteen percent shareholder, I sincerely hope you will get involved with running your company."

"I just can't believe you're going to walk out of here," Preston said. "I know you don't like Disley, but he and I have been friends for a long time, and he's smart about finances. He'll bring things around for the company."

"You're right. I don't like him. And I don't trust him. I think he's a scumbag. Do me a favor, Preston."

"What? Anything."

"Get out of here so I can finish packing. I want to get home to my wife and kids."

Preston got up and slowly walked to the door. He turned and looked at Casey, but Casey never looked up. Instead of walking to his office, Preston walked downstairs and out of the building.

CHAPTER FORTY-THREE

The weeks following her run-in with Chuck were, from Katherine's perspective, more of the same. More obituaries, more local interest stories: the untimely death of a school teacher, the town's suspension of a local police sergeant, groundbreaking for a new marine science center, the opening of a Starbucks in Southampton, and the antics of a motel clerk who had taken to dressing up at night as a Star Wars storm trooper and showing up at events, such as Superhero Day at Chick-fil-A.

On the weekends, Katherine took Hailey for long walks on the beach, checked in with her mother and grandfather, talked with Sean on a couple of occasions, did the laundry, watched Netflix movies, and did what she could to make her apartment a home. Susan came out one Saturday, a glorious weather day. After spending the day at the beach with Hailey, they went back to Katherine's apartment, and Katherine ordered two oversized corned beef sandwiches on rye from the Country Deli. Two containers of popcorn and five hours of nonstop yakking later, they fell asleep.

After Susan left on Sunday, Katherine realized she hadn't spoken with her father in more than three weeks. She called him at home.

"Hi, Preston."

"Hello, Katherine. How are you? Where are you? What are you doing?"

"I'm fine. At my apartment. Talking to you," Katherine said, hoping for at least a chuckle but hearing none.

"I've been thinking about you. I know you've started work. How's that going?"

"As I expected. I'm reporting local stories—the ones my editor considers to be of local interest, that is. I'm really calling to see how you're doing. It's Father's Day, you know, Happy Father's Day."

"Thank you, Katherine. I appreciate that."

Katherine could hear the emotion in his voice, and it touched her more than she'd expected. "I wanted to see if you, Marcia, and P.J. would like to visit me at my apartment the next time you're in Southampton—and I can fix you dinner."

"That sounds great. Hang on a minute."

Katherine assumed Preston was checking with Marcia, and she wondered how that would go—but she felt she had to invite them all, and she wanted Marcia to see her apartment, too.

"Marcia asked me to tell you that she'd love to see your apartment and would love to have dinner with you there sometime, but with all that's going on she'll have to pass for now, and she knew you would understand."

"That's fine. I do understand."

"But I'm going to be playing golf with my foursome at Shinnecock Hills Friday. I could come when we're done. Say around 6:30 p.m. How does that sound?"

"Wonderful." Katherine gave Preston her address. "I'll see you then. Don't expect anything fancy."

★ ★ ★

The door opened, and Katherine vied with Hailey to get to Preston first. "Hi," she said, holding Hailey back by her collar. "Meet my roomie, Hailey. Come in."

Preston walked in the door, gave Katherine a hug, and Hailey a quick tummy rub. Hailey returned the favor with kisses.

"I hope you like dogs."

"Oh, I do. Just never had one," Preston said.

"How was your game?" Katherine asked as she pulled Hailey off him.

"I played better than expected. That happens sometimes when one of the guys is doing well and picks up the rest."

Katherine showed her father the apartment, which didn't take long. The doorway opened into a small living room on the other side of which was a bath and bedroom. A turquoise microfiber sofa bed and matching chair, and small desk and desk chair lined the wall on the right. On the left, past a small wall which enclosed the kitchen, was a modern white round table with four chairs. The floor was covered with new wall-to-wall beige carpet. The two windows had neutral colored Roman shades.

"Not quite Trump Tower."

"I think it's great," Preston said, moving to the wall, where Katherine had hung several pictures. "These are interesting. Mind if I take a closer look?"

"Sure. Would you like a scotch? I bought some Dewar's."

"Please. Can I help?"

"No thanks. Go ahead. Look at the pictures."

Preston was drawn to a small framed picture of a young nurse in a crisp white uniform and cap. He lifted the picture carefully from the wall and sat down in a nearby chair and studied it. The warmth in her face, the bright smile, those ice-blue eyes. He was mesmerized, transported back in time. He'd kept the subject at a distance in all his discussions with Marcia, but the truth was, he remembered her very well and had thought about their encounter from time to time.

"That's my mom," Katherine said, "after her graduation. You can see how proud she was. I love that picture." She handed Preston his drink and took a sip from a bottle of Sam Adams.

Preston thanked her for the drink, not taking his eyes off the photograph. Emotions and thoughts swirled in his brain as if a small dam had burst. He couldn't speak for a few moments.

"Are you all right?"

Silence.

"Hello. Anybody home? Are you hungry?" Katherine asked.

"I do remember her. Very well."

"A lot's happened in the past few months, hasn't it?"

"Yes. A lot's happened," Preston said, still holding the picture and taking a long sip of his drink.

Katherine gently took the picture from Preston's hands and hung it back on the wall.

"Take a look at this one," she said pointing to a motorcyclist in full riding gear and helmet and covered in mud under a big banner proclaiming, "YOU FINISHED."

"Who is that?"

"Me. Having just survived my first and only Enduro cross-country motorcycle race."

"Really? That's amazing. I want to hear more about that."

Katherine and Preston looked at the rest of the pictures: Katherine at her high school graduation with her mother, grandma, and grandpa; Hailey as a puppy; Susan and Katherine in Uganda; her graduating class at Fletcher Thomas; her grandfather in his workshop; and another picture of a motorcyclist—walking away, helmet in hand, with the number 6A on his back.

"Tell me about this one," Preston said.

"That's Sean."

"That's it?"

"Maybe after dinner I'll tell you more about him. Are you ready to eat?"

"Absolutely. I appreciate your inviting me." Preston took his seat at the round table while Katherine served salads and then a chicken and rice casserole.

"Okay, I've waited long enough. Tell me about Sean."

"I met him at the race. We were in touch after that. On my way back from Braydon, I saw him again in North Carolina. By the way, the car has been a real help—going home, getting my stuff, hauling it back here to move in, and then taking my trip south. And Hailey loves it—especially the sun roof."

"SUVs are practical and good to drive—especially on long trips," he agreed. "Now tell me, what took you to Braydon?"

"You did. You know I wanted to learn more about Joe Hart—the Collectibles. Casey gave me Alice's number. She's wonderful."

"I'm impressed with your discipline and follow-through. People say they want to know about something, but you rarely see the follow-through." Preston clinked his second glass of scotch against Katherine's beer.

"Thank you. I appreciate your saying that. It was a great trip. I learned a lot."

"What did you learn?"

"For one thing, now that you've talked about being impressed, I was impressed with what Alice told me you did for Johnny—it apparently made a real difference in his speech and how he's getting along. I met Corey and his daughter Barbara, too."

"You're following in my footsteps. He was quite a man."

"He still is," Katherine said as she cleared the table. "Alzheimer's sucks."

"Tell me how your job's going."

Katherine told Preston about her relationship with Sol and how excited she was to finally be reporting. She described the slate of stories she'd been writing and how many interesting people she had met. Then she plunged into a detailed discussion about the failure of Hamptons Bank, the FDIC shutdown, and the takeover by CCB—including how many Hamptons employees were laid off. "I wrote a story on what it meant to them—the hardships they've endured trying to find jobs."

"Unemployment's a real problem. How was the story received?"

"It hasn't been published yet. I'm still waiting for a green light."

"Why not?"

"Our editor is sitting on it. He makes the assignments. He tells me to keep my focus on local interest stories, reminding me that, after all, this is a weekly. To me, it's all local. I'm still investigating the banks and writing the stories."

Katherine talked about the FDIC's ten million dollar suit against the Hamptons Bank officers and board members for failing to follow bank policy in making a series of loans with willful disregard for a borrower's ability to pay. She told him about Alice's misfortune, too. "This is happening all over the country. It's unbelievable," she said.

Preston was moved by Katherine's passion. He discussed some of his own experiences with banks, keeping matters quite general. He was happier than he had been in a long time. He got a real kick out of sitting with his daughter, having dinner, and listening to her talk. She was so smart; it scared him.

Katherine brought in a lemon pound cake she had baked, a fresh pot of coffee, and set everything up on the coffee table in front of the couch. They sat, ate dessert, and talked into the night.

"Have you been in touch with Johnny lately?" Katherine asked.

"No. It's been over a year."

"Corey?"

"Same."

"How about Missy and Tommy?"

"Saw them recently in Vegas. I was there for a meeting. They're doing great."

"How about Harry?"

"Funny you should ask about Harry. I called him just last week."

"How'd that go?"

"Not well, to be honest."

"What happened?"

"Well, I'm getting a lot of static from Marcia about not reaching out to the Collectibles—not doing enough. I hadn't gotten to Harry before Joe died. Met him at the funeral. Haven't seen him since. So I decided to call."

"And?"

"And he shut me down. It was ridiculous."

"How did he shut you down?"

"You really want to know all of this?"

"Yes, if you don't mind. I find it fascinating."

"Okay, so I called this guy—and I got a message, 'You've got the

Oompah Man ... leave a note.' Can you believe it?"

"The Oompah Man. I love it. So what'd you do?"

"I left a message. He calls me right back. He says, 'Hey, Car Man. What's happening?' Calls me 'big guy.' I tell him I understand he has a band, that he played at Tommy and Missy's wedding reception. You know, trying to get through to the guy. I suggested we get together sometime. And he asks me, 'Why?' I was asking myself the same thing."

Katherine, obviously enjoying the story, had propped her feet up on the coffee table and was slipping pieces of cake to Hailey. Preston didn't know whether to keep going or not. He didn't think it was so funny.

"So what happened next?" Katherine asked.

"You don't want to hear this."

"I do, I do."

"I told him so I could get to know him better. Says he's not sure he wants to get together with me—that he has ups and downs and would hate to meet me on a down day—and then he hung up."

Katherine thought she understood what might be going on.

"Harry's bipolar, isn't he?"

"Yes, now that you mention it."

"So ... you're taking this as a rejection?"

"Well, I didn't think it was a very nice conversation."

"Probably wasn't, but that's not my point. Sounds to me like Harry was going through a cycle. It's not about you. I wouldn't take it personally."

Preston thought about that for a while. He couldn't get over sitting with his daughter, having an honest, nonjudgmental discussion.

"I can't thank you enough for having me here tonight, Katherine. You're so easy to talk to. And the dinner was delicious."

"Thank you. I enjoyed it, too."

"I can see you're frustrated about not getting your stories out there. It's only been a few weeks. I'm amazed at how well your job is going. I wish you worked for me."

"Thanks. I know I am impatient. My grandpa always kids me about having a four-leaf clover under my bonnet. Maybe something will come up soon, turn things around, who knows."

Preston gave Hailey a pat and a kiss on the head. Then he got up and gave Katherine a sincere hug. Katherine walked him to the door, Hailey following, tail wagging.

"Good night, Preston. And thanks for the fatherly advice."

"Good night Katherine. Maybe one of these days you'll call me Dad," he replied with a smile and a wave as he walked out the door.

★ ★ ★

Katherine walked slowly back to her couch, inviting Hailey to jump up and join her.

"We need to talk."

Hailey stretched out on the couch with her head between her front legs, lifting first her right eyebrow and then her left. Katherine took that as a sign to be succinct.

"I shouldn't have made the fatherly advice remark. Not smart. But it was good advice, and it was from my father."

Thoughts about Preston had been percolating in the back of her mind for months. She felt intuitively that he cared about her, even loved her, and his actions so far backed up his words.

"I've moved a long way from that, Hailey. He is reactive and practical as contrasted with intuitive and introspective, but what difference does it make? He's a good man. He cares about people. He cares about me. I'm not holding back, Hailey. Are you listening?"

Hailey opened her eyes, did the jig with her eyebrows three or four more times, then sighed a dog sigh and closed her eyes again.

"You're being impossible. Forget it, I'm going to bed. You can stay right here."

Hailey closed her eyes more tightly.

CHAPTER FORTY-FOUR

The phone call came like a bolt of lightning. Preston hadn't heard from the president of Bank North America in Charlotte since the workout more than a year ago, and now Tom Gallagher was on the line.

"Hello, Mr. Wilson. We haven't talked in a while. How y'all doing up there?"

"We're fine, thank you. What can I do for you?"

"You may have heard that BNA has completed a few acquisitions up your way, and we've expanded a good bit. We'd appreciate your paying us a visit here in Charlotte to go over things, and then we're going to move your file to our Manhattan office where it'll be handled by Arthur Goldberg, vice president, commercial finance."

"Okay, when do you want to meet?"

"Hard to believe we're soon to start the third quarter. We'd like to review your financials, operating statements to date, go over the transition. Sometime in September that's convenient for you and Casey if you can work that out."

"Of course. Austin Disley has taken Casey's position as CFO. I'll bring him along."

"That's fine, Preston. Just let me know the date as soon as you can so I can have Mr. Goldberg come down and join us for the meeting. Floyd Ritter, our general counsel, may want to stop in, too. And please give my best to Casey. He's a good man."

"I'll do that, Mr. Gallagher," Preston said. When the line was clear, he buzzed Austin.

"Can you come in, please?"

"You bet."

In a couple of minutes, Austin glided into Preston's office, adjusted his bow tie, poured himself a cup of coffee, and took a seat. Without Casey as a foil, Austin was positively cocky.

"What's up?"

"BNA is expanding, and our account is being moved to its Manhattan office."

"We've been dealing with the Manhattan office all along."

"New York has been handling our banking transactions, and that office is our landlord, but the floor plans have always been out of Charlotte's distressed asset division. See what you can find out about Arthur Goldberg, a vice president with BNA here—particularly whether he's in risk management or underwriting."

"Who's he?"

"Let's slow this down. I just got off the phone with Tom Gallagher, president of BNA in Charlotte. To ensure an orderly transition, he'd like to meet with me next month, review our company, and introduce me to Mr. Goldberg, the vice president here who will be handling our account."

"And you want me to check out Artie Goldberg?"

"Do you know him?"

"No. Just guessing they call him Artie."

"Austin, get serious."

"Come on, buddy. I was just going to suggest that you lighten up. Ever since Casey left, you've been acting like the world's coming to an end. Wilson Holdings is doing great, if that's what you are worried about."

"I'd like to schedule the BNA meeting the third week in September ... " Preston stopped talking and checked his calendar " ... the eighteenth. I'm taking you with me. They are going to want to see everything in detail. Gallagher talked about financials and operating statements, but he means everything."

"Great. Are we taking the Gulfstream?"

"Yes. But, Austin, I need you to focus. I want to go into that meeting fully prepared. I want a summary report well before the meeting showing exactly where we are. And I want to know all I can about Mr. Goldberg. I know you were glad to see Casey go, but I wasn't."

"Okay, buddy. I'll handle it. I won't let you down," Austin said, for the first time that morning without a smirk on his face, and walked out the door.

★ ★ ★

Not too long ago, Preston couldn't wait to get to the office and couldn't wait to come home. He was happy, and he'd felt a sense of harmony in both places. Over the last few months and too many times, he'd asked himself where that sense of happiness had gone. He knew the drivers, of course. They were obvious. Marcia's frostiness. Discontentment. Disappointment in him to the point of anger, really. The whole P.J. issue. He wished she realized how much he loved his son. And now Casey. The one bright spot was Katherine, and while he knew Marcia liked Katherine, she somehow saw his strong feelings for his daughter as a threat. He couldn't understand how that could be.

Missy had helped before, but this time her advice didn't work. It was like taking pain pills that didn't make your headache go away. Preston knew that he could not lose Marcia or P.J. No matter what. He had to solve this on his own. He arranged for a car to take him home.

Preston walked in the door and immediately sensed the quiet. He felt dizzy, recalling a time not that long ago when he had found a note on the credenza from Marcia telling him she had left. He searched the credenza and was relieved to find no note. Just then the door opened, and in came P.J. in his stroller, being pushed by Marcia.

"Marcia!" he exclaimed. "I am so happy to see you and P.J."

Marcia stood in place, staring at him for a moment. "You thought I'd left, didn't you? Just packed up P.J. and left."

"Yes, I did. To be honest, it scared me."

"Get used to it. You'll be okay," Marcia said, lifting P.J. out of the stroller, taking him into his room, placing him gently on the changing table. Preston followed her. She changed P.J.'s diaper and repositioned his hearing aids while talking to him in a happy, buoyant manner. It dawned on Preston that he had yet to touch P.J.'s hearing aids. He silently cursed himself for the oversight.

Marcia took P.J. to the kitchen, put him in his high chair, prepared his dinner, and fed him.

Preston sat in an adjoining chair at the table, looking on and feeling stupid. "This probably isn't a good time to talk."

"Correct."

"I really need to talk to you. When can we talk?"

"After he has dinner, I give him a bath."

Preston cursed himself again. He'd watched the bath routine, but he hadn't really given P.J. one himself.

"Then, I put him in his cuddly sleeper, and we sit on a blanket in the living room while he stacks the cups and then puts the rings on the plastic post. Then he crawls over every inch of our condo floor, explores all the outlets to see if they still have the plastic safety covers, pulls himself up on the TV, hits the bottom of the screen with his hand, and gives me a look that means he wants to see cartoons again. But I don't fall for that because it will keep him awake. Instead, I read him a story, put him to bed, sing to him, and, if I'm lucky, he goes to sleep."

Preston had a routine of his own. He retreated from the table, went to his den, grabbed the cut-crystal decanter, poured himself a four-finger scotch, and collapsed in his leather chair, talking to himself.

CHAPTER FORTY-FIVE

"Hi, Marcia. Am I getting you at a bad time?"

"Katherine. Nice of you to call. No, it's fine. P.J.'s napping."

"I'm in the city, not too far from you. I wondered if this might be a good time to stop in and see you and P.J today. I haven't had a chance to spend much time with him. How's he doing?"

"He's wonderful. He'll be up shortly. Come over. We'd love to see you."

"Great. I'll be there as soon as I find a place to park."

When Katherine arrived at the condo, she knew P.J. was up. She could hear his screeches through the door.

"Come in, Katherine. It's good to see you," Marcia said, giving her a hug. "P.J.'s practicing for the opera."

"Everybody in the lobby and the elevator was clapping for him."

"Really? Was he that loud?"

"No, just kidding. I heard him at the door and was glad he was up."

Katherine went over to P.J., who was in his ExerSaucer Activity Center playing with an assortment of animals mounted on springs, and gave him a kiss on the cheek. "How're you doing, little guy?"

P.J. continued to squeal and screech, waving his arms in the process.

Katherine sat on the floor next to P.J., and Marcia joined her.

"As you can hear, P.J.'s having a great time making noises and, to the extent he hears them, getting used to his voice," Marcia said. "What brings you to the city?"

"I had some shopping I wanted to do—some specialty items for my kitchen—and it's easier to drive in on a Saturday or Sunday. Mrs. Bergner, my neighbor, is looking after Hailey. I don't know what I'd do without her."

"I can't believe it's been more than a month since we had lunch. You look like you're having fun—enjoying your job."

"I'm sorry you couldn't come to dinner a few weeks ago—but I understand. I did have a good talk with Preston."

"He told me he loved spending that time with you. You've made quite an impression on my husband. Me, too."

"Thank you. It's been quite a year. A lot of surprises. A lot of new things. You're right; I am enjoying my work. It's unfair to call it work. I'm living my dream."

"I'm truly happy for you, Katherine."

"Marcia, I remember you telling me when we had lunch that P.J. was fitted with hearing aids, but I don't see him wearing them. You mentioned it was a process. I'm interested in how that works. How's P.J. coming along?"

"I think we're making progress. It's only been a month and a half. It's important for me to remember that, while sounds began to be amplified for him at fourteen months, he's starting at one month. The aids will help him, but he has to catch up."

"Catch up?"

"The audiologist talks about an auditory age and a listening age. A newborn with normal hearing has a head start."

"I'm not sure I understand," Katherine said. "I assume it has something to do with his ability to develop the sounds."

"This is all new to me, too. The audiologist stresses distinguishing between what P.J. hears and what he understands. Before the aids, he could hear some sounds—a dog barking, loud sounds from the television, a horn blaring in traffic. Now he has to begin to learn how to form an understanding of what the sounds mean. We have also had intervention from a language therapist, too."

"I want to understand this. Do you mind if I take notes?" Katherine asked.

"Of course I don't mind. I'm grateful for your interest. I wish your father shared a little of it."

"Is he really not interested?"

"If he is, he's doing a good job hiding it. At the very least, he's passive. He's leaving all the process to me."

"That must be so frustrating and lonely," Katherine said.

"More than you can know. It's not just that he doesn't help. It's that he doesn't seem to *want* to help. It's a pattern with him."

"Is the process working, with P.J.?" Katherine asked.

"Yes. Here's how it works. I put the aids on when it's a happy time—something he wants to do. When I read him a story. When I let him watch cartoons on TV. They stay on for about an hour, or as long as that activity takes. Then I take them off. Hearing those sounds associated with what he's learning is a big item. Now he's getting upset when I take them off."

"When do you expect he may talk—say words like 'dada' or 'mama'?"

"In a normal hearing boy, that would begin about now. Girls can be a little earlier. It starts with the vocal play. Actually, what you've been hearing P.J. do today. But the yelling has no meaning. As he hears, they're imitations. He babbles. *Bababa.* I say *bababa* back. I say *boobooboo.* He imitates that. Before the aids, the vowels sounded louder than the consonants . . . "

"Can you go a little more slowly?" Katherine asked, taking notes as fast as she could.

"Sure. That's what P.J. is going to be saying to me one of these days! I'm probably getting overly technical."

"Not at all. Keep going."

"It's just that I don't have anybody to talk to about this. It feels good. I guess the short answer to your question is maybe I'll hear 'mama' in four to six months. But I will hear it."

Marcia picked P.J. up and took him in the kitchen and placed him in his high chair while she cut up a banana, sliced a cucumber, and added some yogurt for his lunch. "I'm sorry, Katherine. Would you like some coffee? Can I get you anything to eat?"

"I'd love a cup of coffee if you're going to have one."

Marcia and Katherine sat at the kitchen table and talked for another hour. Katherine brought her up to date on the stories she had written and the ones she was working on now, and how much she enjoyed her colleagues at the *Twin Forks Press*, especially Sol. She avoided questions about how Marcia and Preston were getting along, and Marcia kept quiet on that subject as well.

Katherine looked over her notes about P.J.

"You mentioned that Preston is leaving the process to you. And then you said it was a pattern. Do you mind if I ask you what you mean by that?"

"I don't want to let Preston down, but, honestly, I'm worried. He leaves P.J. to me. He leaves difficult issues at the office to Casey, well, he did before Casey quit. He now leaves them to Austin. It's a passive-aggressive denial thing."

"Casey quit?"

"Yes, a few weeks ago."

"I really liked Casey," Katherine said.

"Me, too. Preston pushed him farther than he was willing to go. I'm with Casey."

"And that's the trouble you're worried about?"

"I don't want to say any more about this, Katherine. I hope you'll understand."

"Of course. I didn't mean to pry."

"Not at all, I'm the one that brought it up."

Katherine decided to change the subject.

"Before I leave, Marcia, could I peek in on P.J.'s room? The lights were off, and I didn't get a chance to get a good look last time."

"Oh, my goodness certainly! Go look now."

The door was open, and the first thing Katherine noticed was the wooden crib with a natural finish on the left against the wall. There were white sheets printed with colorful lions, tigers, elephants, and giraffes. The zoo theme included a mobile hanging above the crib. There was thick blue soft carpet and draperies that matched. On the opposite wall were a changing table and a row of shelves. Near the window was a large sliding rocker with padded cushions. Katherine sat in it, leaned back, and closed her eyes. She could smell the baby powder. The overall room was comfortable, quiet, and peaceful. Katherine snapped a picture on her iPhone to show Susan and her mother, and went back to the kitchen.

"What a wonderful room. I'd like to have a rocker like that myself."

"Thanks. It was a gift from my friend Ann. I'd like you to meet her sometime."

"I'd love to. I have to go now, but I've enjoyed the visit." She walked over to P.J. and gave him a soft kiss on the top of his head. He looked up at her with big blue eyes and smiled. Katherine felt as though she would melt. "Good-bye, little guy. I'll come see you again," she said and brushed a strand of his soft hair out of his eyes.

Marcia walked Katherine to the door and hugged her again. "Thank you for coming to see us, Katherine. I can't describe how much I've enjoyed spending this time with you."

Katherine could see the moisture in Marcia's eyes.

"Me, too, Marcia. Me, too," she said.

CHAPTER FORTY-SIX

Katherine and Hailey arrived at the newspaper at their usual early hour on Monday morning. Hailey made her customary rounds of the office, sniffing the coffee in the break room and checking out the reporters' stations to see who had arrived, while Katherine opened her computer to check her e-mails, messages, and to-do list.

She'd jotted herself a note that she wanted to call Alice and ask her if she would share her scrapbook.

"Hi, Alice. It's Katherine Kelly. Hope I'm not calling you too early."

"Hello, my dear. I've been up for two hours. It's good to hear your voice. How are you and Hailey doing?"

"I'm doing well. Hailey's wistful. I think she's in love with Buck."

Alice laughed. "They all feel that way. She'll get over it. How's the reporting going?"

"I've been writing obituaries, filler for the Web, local interest stories—a school board member arrested for drunk driving, the firing of a local police sergeant—that sort of thing. I've also written several local bank stories, but my editor is sitting on them."

"Oh, dear. That must bother you so. I'm sure it takes time."

"I'm calling to ask if you would be willing to lend me your scrapbook—you know, the one about your bank situation in Braydon?"

"Of course. I'd be pleased for it to have some practical use. And

I've found some pictures of Joe I think you'd like—Joe and Harry fishing in Joe's boat, a picture of Joe and Corey in Corey's shop, and a picture Harry sent me of Joe ... which is so special. I'll send them along in the package."

"Thank you, Alice."

"Before you hang up, I'd like to tell you a little story if you have time."

"Absolutely."

"This came to mind when you told me about your reporting. Fishermen are always worried about the weather, always talking about it. No one wants to be caught in a storm. But how will you know when it comes? The joke around here used to be, 'It starts when you say no to Joe.' You remind me of him."

"Thank you for telling me that, Alice. It says a lot about Joe. I'm flattered that I remind you of him in any way. And thank you for sending the package along."

"You're welcome, my dear. Give Hailey a kiss for me, and tell her Buck gives her a tail wag. Keep writing and good luck."

The point Alice was making was not lost on Katherine, who marveled at Alice's light touch and sensitivity. What a gracious woman. She had to find a way to help her.

Katherine reviewed her strategic plan for the bank stories, mindful that she had to maintain strong focus on the coverage area for *Twin Forks Press*. So far, her first five stories fit—at least, to her way of thinking.

She felt she had plenty of room to drill deeper into those stories, given the broad scope of the wrongdoing of Hamptons Bank alone. Material false entries on the books, reports, and statements. Overvaluation of the assets supported by artificial appraisals and flipping of the real estate. Unqualified investors. Inadequate review of borrowers' financial condition and capacity. The list went on and on. It was criminally and civilly wrong.

And the problem wasn't limited to Suffolk and Nassau counties. It was all over the country. The damage was an equal-opportunity provider—leaving a big wake.

What Katherine needed now was for her stories to reach Chip Reider from Long Island's first congressional district, and Brian Quinn from the second district. One was a Democrat and the other a Republican, and each had a long history of respected service to his constituents. Moreover, Quinn was on the House committee for financial services and had been an outspoken critic of the failure to aggressively go after the wrongdoings of the bank. Neither would be insensitive to the local outcry that Katherine hoped would result if her stories were ever published.

Katherine completed the week's obituaries, fine-tuned her local-interest stories, and developed several more stories to meet *Twin Forks'* website demand. As soon as those tasks were completed, she continued her research.

Alice was right.

CHAPTER FORTY-SEVEN

Thursday morning. Assignment time.

"Good morning, Chuck," Katherine said. "How are you this bright and cheery morning?"

"Fine. And you?"

"Fine, as well, and ready for the list."

"Sol would like a word with us before I do that. He's waiting in his office."

Katherine had gotten used to the chilly nature of their discussions, and the unaccustomed warmth of Chuck's tone, genuine or synthetic, was beginning to make her sweat. She followed Chuck into Sol's office, realizing just how tall the man was. He'd been seated every time she'd talked to him. She hoped she hadn't underestimated him in other ways.

Sol directed them to the round table, and they all sat.

"Good morning," Sol said. He retrieved a stack of papers piled on the floor and laid them on the table. "I have here five stories written by Katherine: First, a story about tellers and others who after years of experience with Hamptons Bank were terminated when CCB took over. Second, a piece on FDIC's ten-million-dollar suit against the Hamptons Bank officers and board members for failing to follow sound policy in lending. Third, an article about a group of Southampton citizens who invested in Hamptons Bank only to lose their life savings when it failed. Fourth, a piece on the fall of Henry Wilkins, former president and CEO of Hamptons Bank, who was named U.S. Banking Industries' Community Banker of the Year in 2007 and now facing a possible lifetime in prison. And fifth, an account of Henry Wilkins refuting the charges." Turning to Chuck, he said, "I assume you've read these."

"Yes."

"Did you like them?"

"I thought they were interesting and well written, but not a good fit for our reader base. Not the kind of local interest stories we write. Not only are they not relevant, but they're too long, they're overly comprehensive, and they exceed our capacity. It's not what we do."

"And that's why you have not assigned these stories to Katherine."

"Precisely."

Katherine could feel her heart pound in her chest and her blood course through her body. She willed herself to remain calm while she jotted down some notes in her pad.

Sol turned to Katherine. "Kiddo?"

Katherine looked at her notes. "It's not what we do," she read aloud. "That to me means let's do what we've always done." Katherine looked up at Chuck. "I'm the new kid on the block, and I've made it clear that I respect your position as editor. What I found at the root of my cost-containment study of Florida's Medicaid department was bureaucratic inertia—taking refuge in established routines. I suppose this can happen anywhere, even creep into the culture of journalism."

"Chuck?" Sol said.

Chuck shook his head. Sol got up and looked at Chuck and Katherine. "Can I get either of you some coffee?"

Chuck nodded and Katherine shook her head. Sol went into the break room. Katherine studied her notes; Chuck studied the table. In a few minutes, Sol returned with two coffees.

Chuck looked directly at Katherine and met her assessment head-on. "I'll tell you what I think. Bureaucratic inertia—refuge in established routines—that's a lot of corporate babble. I don't even know what it means. I'm not sure you do. My focus is on local content. That's what our readers want, and that's what keeps us in business."

Katherine felt the heat in her back rise through the back of her neck and into her head. She leaned over the table and returned Chuck's stare, wishing she were a few feet taller so she could get a few inches closer to his bulbous nose. She ran through her mind what she wanted to say to him. *You want to write about a dog pissing on a fire hydrant. I want to write about the president of a bank—a local bank—pissing on his board, his employees, his customers, his investors, and the country.*

"I agree content matters and my stories are local," she said instead. "I just don't want to miss the parade."

"I like the stories," Sol said. "I find them comprehensive and compelling." He got up and paced in front of his desk, then turned to the table.

"Katherine could have gone anywhere she wanted. The reason she came here, apart from believing in me, was because she was impatient and eager to be given a real chance to show what she could do. I promised her I'd give her that chance. In fact, I told her I'd start her on a story I just broke about the FDIC closing Hamptons Bank."

Sol stopped talking, and no one else spoke for a few beats.

Chuck broke the silence. "Okay, Katherine, consider all five stories assigned to you. They may have to be cut a bit to get them on the front page. We'll run them one a week under your name and see what happens."

Sol addressed his editor first. "Thanks. You make the trains run around here."

He turned to Katherine. "Anything else you want to say, kiddo?"

"Not a word," Katherine replied, with a smile that said it all.

"I think we're done here," Sol said.

CHAPTER FORTY-EIGHT

Preston's cell phone buzzed, and he caught the caller ID.

"Hello, Missy. How are you doing?"

"That's the reason I called. I told you about our hope to have the camp open in a few months."

"A dance studio for girls with special needs," Preston said.

"That's where I wanted to start. The renovations in the main building were finished three weeks ago, and today we had our first classes. Fifteen girls signed up, and I divided them into three classes, five girls in each class."

"Were you the only teacher?"

"Yes, for now."

"How can you teach three classes?"

"Why not? I'm in good shape. Each class lasts about forty-five minutes, with a break of fifteen minutes in between."

"Sorry. That was a stupid question."

"You had to see their faces. It was wonderful. The concept's going to work. And the mothers and grandmothers who came were ecstatic."

"Well, I'm happy for you. How's Tommy?"

"He's right here. Hang on. I'll put him on."

Preston heard Missy tell Tommy, "It's Preston—he's asking about you." There was silence for about a minute.

"Tommy, are you there?" Preston asked.

"Ah, hello. Preston?" Tommy mumbled, his voice rising on the name.

"Hi, Tommy, how's it going?"

"Going good. I'm with Missy in Elko. She's doing great with the girls. Big day here."

"Yeah, she sounds excited," Preston said.

"We're all excited. It's a *pivotational* moment."

Preston wanted to talk to Tommy further, but had trouble thinking of what else to say. The pause was awkward.

"You done?" Tommy asked.

"Well, no. It's good to talk to you, Tommy."

"It don't sound good for you. Lot of dry spots. How're the ponies treating you?"

"Is Missy listening?"

"It doesn't matter, Preston. You can't hide forever. People bet and people know. There's a guy in Vegas that's been checking on you."

Suddenly Preston was interested in the conversation. "What? Who? Why?"

"Now you sound like one of those ace reporters. All I can tell you is a friend of mine at Caesar's saw me talking to you and gave me a tip that a PI he knows was asking about you. Somebody wants to know more about you."

"What do you think that means?"

"That somebody wants to know more about you. But don't worry. You probably know more about you than he does."

"I'm not borrowing to cover anymore."

"You do what you do."

Preston decided to change the subject. "My daughter, Katherine, is doing well. She got a job as a reporter with a weekly newspaper on Long Island, and she's already writing stories under her name. We've been spending time together, and I'm really proud of her."

"That's good to hear. How are things going with P.J.? I love that name."

"Great. P.J.'s almost seventeen months, and he's walking all over the place."

"Get to the tough stuff, Preston," Tommy barked.

"What do you mean?"

"It's always uphill talking to you. You told me he has a hearing problem. I want to know how he's getting along. Missy mentioned hearing aids. How's that going?"

"He's got the aids. Marcia is working with him every day. He's doing better. It's hard to know where he is compared to where he should be."

"A lot of people I know have that problem. I'm glad he's doing better. I hope you're doing all you can to help. Be *compassionated.*"

Preston chuckled. "It's always good to talk to you, Tommy."

"Wait a minute. Missy's telling me she wants to talk to you some more. Big mistake."

After a beat, Missy came on the phone. "How's it going with Marcia?"

"Not well—but we're still together."

"I heard Tommy talking to you about P.J. I'm sure he'll tell me how he's doing. I hope well. And, apparently, you mentioned your daughter, too. I can't wait to hear about her. Thanks for taking the call. I just wanted to share the news from Elko. Wanted you to be the first to hear about it."

"Thank you for calling, Missy. I haven't forgotten what you told me at breakfast, and I haven't given up on Marcia. Katherine's been a joy. Great news about the camp. I mean the dance studio. The progress."

"Thanks, Preston, good luck and keep in touch," Missy said, and the line went dead.

CHAPTER FORTY-NINE

When Katherine's cell phone buzzed, she was surprised to see her grandfather's name. She couldn't remember when he had called her last.

"Hi, Grandpa, are you all right?"

"Hi, Kitten. I'm fine. Have you got a minute? I hope I'm not bothering you."

"Of course. I've always got time to time to talk to you, Grandpa."

"I'm standing in the Rod and Gun Club with a guy who wants to say hello to you. His name is Harry Klaskowski."

"Harry . . . on the wall Harry?"

"One and the same. Only now he's here in person. I've been bragging about you, and he wants to speak to you."

"That's wonderful. I do want to meet him—for a lot of reasons. Please put him on." Katherine grabbed her notepad and pen.

"Hello, Miss Kelly. Harry here. Your buttons must be popping the way your grandfather goes on about you. I'm pleased to talk to you."

"Likewise Mr. Klaskowski. More than you know."

"Cut out the Mr. Klaskowski stuff. It's Harry. Your grandfather and I have been friends too long. He tells me you're burning the world up as a journalist down there. Congratulations."

"I don't know about the 'burning the world up' part, but I am—finally—a reporter, and I love it."

"That's great. This old coot I'm with tells me that you shot twenty for twenty-five, right here, a couple of months ago. Nice going."

"That old coot tells me you're a state champion. Nice going to you. But I have a report for you when you're ready."

"Go ahead. Shoot. No pun intended."

"I spent time with a friend of yours in Braydon, South Carolina, not too long ago."

"Really? Who?"

"A lovely lady named Alice Hawkins."

"How in the world did you get together with Alice?"

"It's a long story, but it's a story that includes you. I bet you can figure that out."

"You're a pistol. I can see why Adrian brags about you so much. Okay, I'll play the game. We'll see how good you are. Is it about having heart?"

"Yes it is—if you spell it H-a-r-t."

"I'll be. You win. We have to get together."

"I agree. Do you ever get to New York City?"

"Funny you should ask. Me and my oompah band have a gig down there a week from Saturday night. You have to come. It's at the Heidelberg Restaurant in Germantown. Do you know where that is?"

"I'll find it. Can I bring my friend Susan?"

"Sure can. Bring whoever you can. We need to pack the room."

"I have one more person I'd like to bring if I can get him to come."

"Your boyfriend?"

"No, my father."

"That's not funny. Adrian told me about your father years ago."

"I wasn't trying to be funny, Harry. It's just that the man you were told about—to my grandfather's surprise and mine—turned out not to be my father. My father is a man I think you know. His name is Preston Wilson."

The line was silent for a few moments.

"Preston—the big-shot car dealer in New York—is your daddy?"

"That's correct. Can he still come?"

"Absolutely. As a matter of fact, I talked to your father not too long ago. He called me wanting to get together, and I told him if we ever had a gig in New York, I'd let him know. I didn't, but I should have. Thanks for helping me out."

"Thank you. My father told me that he talked with you. He really does want to get to know you better."

"Well, we'll see about that, but I can tell you right now, I can't wait to meet you, young lady. In fact, if you come a little early—like in the afternoon—I'll buy you lunch."

"You're not hitting on me, are you, Harry?"

She could hear his laughter. Harry and Katherine exchanged telephone numbers.

"Your grandfather wants to talk to you again. I look forward to seeing you in New York. When you get in, you can call me on my cell. Here's your grandpa."

"Hi, Kitten. That was a long conversation. I know you're busy. I hope I didn't do the wrong thing putting him on the phone."

"Not at all, Grandpa. In fact, it's ironic, but I really wanted to meet him and talk to him for a lot of reasons that I'll explain to you another time. Maybe you could come down for Harry's gig and stay with me."

"I'd love to, Kitten, but I need to look after your mom and take care of things up here. When you get a chance, give me a call."

"I will. I love you Grandpa."

"You, too," Adrian said.

Katherine was pleased beyond words. Another of the Collectibles— and she couldn't wait to meet him.

CHAPTER FIFTY

Katherine was intrigued by the description of the symposium to be held in East Hampton, Long Island. The participants would include bankers, financial regulators, and local lawyers looking to rack up continuing education credits and provide their clients access to the regulators. What especially interested her was the array of law enforcement on the program: The New York External Fraud Committee, the Long Island Fraud and Forgery Committee, the Westchester External Fraud Committee.

She knew how difficult it was to permeate the institutional web of protection. Turfs were protected and information was held close. That was changing with Homeland Security demands and its current emphasis on inter-agency cooperation, but still, success in uncovering information came down to personal relationships. In addition to learning about the bank fraud investigative policy and process, Katherine knew she had to find a friend on the inside. That was one of several reasons she'd persuaded Sol to let her attend and to spring for the hefty registration fee. Professional development, he'd called it. *A fishing expedition was more like it,* she thought.

Katherine arrived early and watched the attendees come in. Some went to the refreshment table to seek the breakfast they hadn't had yet. Others milled around looking for connections to their personal network. The ones who had not had the opportunity or inclination to study the materials ahead of time were going through them now.

When Katherine scanned the meeting room, she saw a thin woman with black hair, dressed in a summer-weight slacks ensemble seated in the end seat, three rows from the front, with a large wheel-aided briefcase on the floor beside her. Katherine sensed a no-nonsense air about the woman, estimating her to be in her late thirties. Katherine entered the empty row from the left and stood behind the seat next to her, watching as the woman poured through a stack of files and waiting for an opening.

"Hi, I'm Katherine Kelly. I hope I'm not disturbing you."

"I'm preparing for the first session," the woman replied. "But that's okay. Have a seat. Carol Martin." She offered a hand to Katherine.

They shook, and Katherine sat down, took out her fresh note-pad and pen, and stared at the blank paper, focusing on how she could get the most out of this day. Ideally, the day would provide a window into the minds, and perhaps some of the files, of a host of current and former government prosecutors, agents, and investigators. She was determined to make the most of it.

Katherine had already studied the four-inch-thick notebook of symposium materials, noted her questions in the margins, and flagged areas of specific interest. She was impressed with the diversity of commitment—all directed to economic fraud. One of the areas she had flagged was an article about Secret Service involvement in an investigation. From the list of contributors and sponsors, it looked like representatives from the FBI, IRS, SEC, DEA, TARP, the Federal Reserve, the Postal Service, and the U.S. Attorney's Office would be there, along with local district attorneys.

"What brings you here?" Carol asked. "Are you an attorney on Long Island?"

"No, I'm a reporter working with the *Twin Forks Press*."

"Reporting on ... "

"Trying to learn more about bank fraud—how institutions deal with it."

"That's interesting. I don't remember ever encountering a reporter at one of these conferences before," Carol observed.

"I hope it stays that way," Katherine said.

Carol smiled. "What drew you to bank fraud?"

"Willie Sutton."

"As in 'Why do you rob banks?'—'That's where the money is'?"

"Yeah. Exactly. Wow. You're fast, Carol. A lot of people are getting hurt from bank fraud. One way to fight it is to expose it—particularly the greed that drives it."

"And you've written stories about that?"

"Several."

The room began to fill in, and the speakers took their places at a long table up front.

"Are you going to stay all day?" Carol asked.

"I plan to."

"If you like, let's have lunch together. I'd like to hear more about your bank fraud stories."

"Sounds good," Katherine said just as the moderator brought everyone to attention to begin the introductions and keynote address. "To be continued," she whispered.

At noon the conference broke for lunch.

"There's a good diner five minutes from here," Katherine said. "Or would you rather have the sandwiches and drinks provided?"

"Diner," Carol said.

"I'll drive."

Over lunch, they discussed the morning's presentations—who captured their interest and who didn't and why.

"I'm glad I came," Katherine said.

"If you're into bank fraud, this one is worthwhile," Carol said. "I've been chasing perpetrators in this area for some time—they get more slippery every day."

"How long have you been with the district attorney's office?"

"Twelve years. Before that, I worked for JP Morgan Chase."

"What drew you to the DA's office?"

"A choice. Security and money or making a significant difference."

"Believe me, I get that," said Katherine. Their allotted time for lunch nearly up, they split the check and headed back.

The afternoon sessions were divided into three parts. They heard attorneys from the eastern and southern districts of the U.S. Attorney's Office and in-house counsel from UBS and Bank North America. Next was a presentation on the difficulties of financial compliance in a borderless economy presented by representatives of the Federal Reserve, the Manhattan DA's office, and the DEA with in-house counsel from Morgan Stanley, John Hancock, and JP Morgan Chase. Then came a provocative PowerPoint presentation by the special inspector general for TARP.

The dialogue was lively, and Katherine developed a strong sense about the distance and, at times, tension, between the institutional side and the private side. Katherine especially appreciated the insight into the way the various parties viewed each other and their roles.

When it was over, Katherine and Carol went for coffee.

"What do you do with your golden retriever on days like this?"

"Fortunately, I have a neighbor who loves dogs."

"My husband wants a dog, but I can't see how it can work in the city. By the way, we should try to get together sometime."

Katherine agreed. They exchanged business cards and promised to call each other.

★ ★ ★

Before Katherine knew it, a week had flown by, and she found herself enjoying a free Saturday. Late August in Southampton was a delight, except for the locals who resented the traffic and could no longer get reservations for dinner or go out for a quiet movie with friends. Temperatures in the high seventies, walks on the beach with Hailey, salt in the air. When they got back to her apartment, Katherine caught up on her personal phone calls, including one to her father.

"Hi, Preston. Am I getting you at a bad time?"

"Hi. Not at all. I'm headed to the club—looking to get eighteen holes in and check on one of our dealerships on the island. How are you?"

"Good. I messed up though. Should have called you earlier. A week and a half ago my grandfather called me. He was at the Rod and Gun Club shooting skeet when he ran into an old buddy he wanted to introduce to me on the phone."

"What are you talking about?"

"Harry Klaskowski."

Preston was quiet for a moment.

"You're full of surprises, Katherine. Your grandfather knows Harry."

"Yeah. They're old hunting and shooting buddies."

"Harry's obviously a man of diversity," Preston said. "When I talked to him last, he was the 'Oompah Man.'"

"I remember. That's why I'm calling. He's performing with his band at the Heidelberg Restaurant on Second Avenue at Eighty-Sixth Street."

"Really? When?"

"Tonight. That's where I screwed up. I should have called you earlier. Susan and I are going, and we'd really like you to come, too."

More silence.

"Come on. You either have a conflict or you don't want to go. It's a great chance to bond with Harry—and have a good time. I can't wait. Neither can Susan. We need a date."

"I'll talk with Marcia."

"How's that going?"

"Don't ask."

"How's P.J.?"

"He's walking now—all our outlets on the floor are plugged," Preston said with a laugh.

"Try to come tonight," Katherine said. "I hope I see you later. Give Marcia and P.J. a hug for me."

"Good to talk to you, Katherine. I'll give it a try."

★ ★ ★

About a half an hour away from the club, Preston decided to call Marcia and tell her about his phone call from Katherine. He couldn't get over the irony of Harry being an old friend of her grandfather and his putting Harry on the phone to talk to Katherine.

Preston hoped that Marcia was in a better mood than when he had left home. She used to encourage him to play and to spend time with his golfing buddies. Now, her whole world revolved around their son. He hit his condo number on the Bentley's communication system. Marcia answered and Preston launched into a detailed description of Katherine's call.

"What are the odds?" Preston said.

"How is Harry doing?"

"He's coming to New York City with his oompah band."

"Playing here? That's great. Where? When?"

"Tonight actually. A restaurant in Germantown. Katherine's going. With her friend Susan, and she wants us to come."

"I can't go, obviously."

"Can't or don't want to?"

"It's too short notice to get our sitter. But you should go. Support Harry and have fun with your daughter."

"I think we should go together."

"Think again. I have to go now. Have a good game," Marcia said and the line went dead.

Preston wondered whether he would ever get his marriage back on track. Could he dismantle the wall Marcia had built between them? Rebuild what they once had. He'd done it once before. Why couldn't he do it again? He certainly was spending more time with P.J., or at least trying. Marcia didn't seem to resent Katherine. In fact, she was all for his spending *father time* with her as she called it, and she was getting close to Katherine herself. At the same time, she continued to drift away from him. *Why was she doing this? How do you deal with a woman who thought in terms of "stretching and tearing fabric"?*

Missy's words came to mind. *Don't give up on yourself . . . look deep inside and find the best parts . . . if you want to keep Marcia, that's a place to start.* He'd thought about those words many times, trying to figure it out. Maybe he should see a shrink. He told himself he was willing to do whatever it took. As he pulled into the club's parking lot, he pushed all of this to the back of his mind. Playing golf always helped.

★ ★ ★

Katherine arrived at the restaurant a little before 5:00 p.m., as Harry had suggested. She went through the dining area and was directed by a waitress to a large room in the back to the left, finished handsomely in dark wood with a two-foot-high platform at the end.

She saw five burly men in their late forties dressed in green Bavarian lederhosen with red trim and wide suspenders adorned with folk print detail moving speakers, instruments, and chairs around on the stage. Each wore a white shirt, with matching tall white socks inside high leather lace-up tasseled boots, and a green felt hat with a red feathered band.

As Katherine approached, the largest of the men bounded off the stage with surprising agility, came over to her, and placed his huge arms around her. He easily lifted her off her feet while exclaiming, "You must be Katherine." When he finally let her down, and she got her breath back, she said, "And you have got to be Harry."

Harry led her by the hand to a table in the back of the room on which a number of authentic Bavarian beer steins were waiting. Katherine could see the droplets of water on the pointed cover, spilling over the elaborate carvings on each mug. She could not wait to taste the cold beer inside.

Harry handed her a stein, grabbed one himself, and proposed a number of toasts each followed by hardy swallows of beer. They drank to Adrian. They drank to Joe. They drank to Alice. Harry asked Katherine to tell him everything she knew about Joe and his friends. She told him how she had gotten to meet Johnny and Corey and wanted to meet Missy and Tommy. She talked about how respectful Marcia and Preston were of Joe, how much he had done for them and their family, how they had named their son after him. She said she was fascinated by all she had learned about Joe, his impact on others. How she only wished she could have known him.

"Are you hungry?" Harry asked.

"Starving."

Harry went to the doorway of the dining room and spoke with a waitress. In a few minutes a robust woman with long blonde hair, also in German folk costume, came to the table, placed a blue-and-white tablecloth over the white one and soon returned with two servings of consommé with spätzle, a salad, and knackwurst with potato salad and sauerkraut.

They ate and talked and drank. Katherine asked Harry a hundred questions. Where he came from, what he'd done, whether he was married, his relationship with her grandfather, how he had met Joe.

"I can't believe how many things you've done, Harry. What an exciting life. Grandpa tells me you are an excellent photographer."

Harry told her what he liked to shoot and turned the subject around to Katherine.

"Your turn. I know you're a hotshot journalist. Give it all to me."

"You know where I grew up. I went to college in New York City and always sort of knew I wanted to be a reporter. Insatiable curiosity. Born nosey, I guess." Katherine told Harry about her master's program and her job with the *Twin Forks Press*.

"Your father must be proud."

"You're a cagey guy, Harry. I know where you're going."

"This may not be the place. We're here to have fun tonight. Sometime, though, I would like to ask you about the whole newfound father thing. It must have been really something for you to go through. Adrian wouldn't tell me much. He loves you to death."

"You're right. I have some questions for you, too, but this isn't the time or place."

"We'll talk again. I see why he loves you. Is your friend coming? What's her name—Susie?"

"Susan. She'll be here. I'm going to call her. I didn't know what time to tell her."

"We start to play after the room fills and dinner has been served. Probably around 7:30 p.m. The wait staff has to set up, and the guys have to place the speakers, do the sound check, and have their own meal. When we're done eating, I'd like you to meet them. Great guys."

Katherine asked Harry to tell her how he had assembled the band, where the other guys were from. Harry complied, and then he took her over to meet his four bandmates. She counted an accordion, trumpet, trombone, baritone, tuba, guitars, and drums. How could they play so many instruments? Each of the men, following Harry's cue, gave her the same warm welcome he had. Katherine loved the attention, especially after a few beers. It was like having a whole roomful of convivial, musical uncles.

Harry joined the men for rehearsal while the room was being arranged. Katherine took advantage of the moment to go to a more quiet place and and call Susan.

"Come now. You're going to love it."

Susan said she was on her way.

About thirty minutes later, Susan arrived. Katherine introduced her to Harry and the other members of the band, and then Katherine joined Susan at one of the tables while Susan had dinner. The room was starting to fill up, with several tables pulled together to accommodate various sized groups. The common denominators were drinking beer and having a great time.

As Susan enjoyed the German food, Katherine told her about Harry, his connection with her grandpa, and what more she'd learned about the Collectibles. Finally, the band started to play and the crowd burst into applause. Katherine grinned, judging by the looks on the faces around her, no matter how old you might be or whether you had a liking for the *Volkstümliche Musik,* if you had a pulse, your arms couldn't resist swinging, your feet couldn't resist tapping, and your heart couldn't help but sing along.

The band played on, the audience singing and swaying in harmony. The beer flowed, while Susan was obviously having a great time with her St. Pauli non-alcoholic brew. Katherine was smiling, singing, and toasting Harry and the band when, for a moment, time stopped. She watched her father walk into the room and over to their table. She jumped up, threw her arms around his neck, and gave him a kiss on the check.

"I'm so glad you came, Preston. Meet my friend, Susan."

Preston shook Susan's hand, joined them at the table, and signaled their waitress for a beer.

He pointed to the man playing the accordion. "There's Harry," he exclaimed.

"He's so cool," Katherine said, "and he can play every instrument up there."

Preston's beer arrived, and in no time, he was clapping and joining in the fun. Katherine had never seen him like this. So happy, totally, in the moment.

When the band finally took a well deserved break, Harry came over to the table and gave Katherine another huge hug.

"I can see you're loving the music," Harry told her. He turned to Preston and gave him a hug. "Car Man. Glad you came," Harry said with a wide smile.

"How could I turn down an invitation from you and my daughter?" Preston asked. "I love the music, too. You guys are great."

Katherine introduced Harry to Susan, and he gave her his signature Harry hug.

"Any friend of this pistol is a friend of mine," he said and waved for another round. Katherine whispered in his ear what Susan was drinking. Harry nodded.

Before long it was time for Harry to rejoin his men on stage. He had been so much fun at the table, they were all sorry to see him go but equally eager to hear him play and sing again. The band went on playing for another two hours. The fortitude of the musicians was unbelievable. By the time the band began to play its last number, the entire room had become one, with everyone on their feet, clapping and singing along with the band.

Katherine, Susan, and Preston rushed to the stage afterward and hugged Harry and the other men in the band. Harry took Preston aside and thanked him again for coming.

"It meant a lot to me to have you here," Harry said, "and even more to see you get over yourself and have a good time."

"I wish Joe was here tonight," Preston said, his eyes moist.

"He was here, Car Man. He was here."

Harry said good-bye to Katherine and Preston.

The band had a large van and one of the men would be driving them to their hotel. They had offered to drive Susan home and she had accepted. Katherine gave Susan a hug and said good-bye.

When Katherine walked outside, she was surprised and happy to see Preston's driver waiting. She'd been wondering how in the world she was going to get home. She was glad Hailey was with Becky.

"Why don't you stay with us tonight? After my driver drops us off, he'll pick your car up and have it parked in our garage."

"Are you sure I won't be disturbing anything?"

"I'm sure. You'll be good in our guest room."

They climbed in the back seat of the limo.

"This is a good idea," Katherine said. "I definitely shouldn't be driving."

"Me either," Preston said looking out of the window.

Katherine put her hand on Preston's arm and tugged until he turned her way. "Can I ask you a question?"

"Sure. Fire away."

"Do you think Joe would have picked Table Number Two or Table Number Thirty?"

"What are you talking about?"

"If Joe was here, or I mean, at the 21 Club, would he have had lunch at Table Number Two or Table Number Thirty?"

"I don't know which he would have picked. I like Number Two because Gecko once sat there and I can see who comes in the room. Why do you ask?"

"Can't help myself," Katherine said. "But, I've been wanting to ask you that for a long time." Then they both burst out laughing.

The driver must have been able to hear their laughter, but it didn't seem to matter. They were having such a wonderful time.

CHAPTER FIFTY-ONE

Katherine and Preston entered the condo as quietly as they could, but Marcia was still awake. Preston showed Katherine the guest room. Marcia greeted her warmly, brought in fresh linens, and asked her if she would like coffee or anything to eat before she went to bed. Marcia wanted to hear about their night, and while Preston turned in, they had decaf coffee and apple pie and talked for another hour or so.

Marcia was delighted with Katherine's description of Harry, the band, and especially the part about Harry taking Preston aside and talking with him.

"I love that you invited him. I've been trying to get him to reach out to Harry and the others. I don't know why he holds back."

"Me, either, but he came, and he clearly had a good time. Hopefully, he'll do more of that."

Marcia was conflicted. She wanted to say so much more to Katherine, but she also did not want to let her husband down. What good would it do to involve Katherine in her marital problems, which she had determined were severe? She didn't want to rehash her feelings about Preston's attitude toward P.J., and as much as she'd tried, she could not close the gap. She thought about marriage counseling. That's what she would have recommended to someone else. But this was her, and deep down, she had no faith that things would change.

She hated the way she felt and knew that P.J. would ultimately be hurt if his parents separated. She felt she and P.J. were trapped in the benefits of luxury and security but without genuine love. In a sense, it was like a magnificent, hollow tree. She tried to choose her words carefully.

"He's really into you—he loves having a daughter. I think you're helping him in ways that I don't fully understand but greatly appreciate. It must be challenging for you."

"I don't know about challenging. Between us ... "

"I promise you that. Absolutely."

"I think about Harry. All the ups and downs. Life's like that. It sure has been for me. The last few months have been the happiest I've ever been. I feel more complete. I have a father now—something I've wanted all my life. My family's grown. And that includes you and P.J. I have to learn to trust it all. Challenged makes me feel selfish, ungrateful."

Marcia marveled at this young lady and wondered if she was being selfish.

"I guess challenged was the wrong word. I'm sorry."

"No. There's nothing to be sorry about. These are my issues ... I've always held back. But that may be changing."

"How? Why?"

"I met a guy. I spent time with him at Wrightsville Beach. He made me feel special. I may be crazy, but I trust him."

"Tell me about him."

"His name is Sean O'Malley. He's twenty-nine. In the Secret Service. Easy to look at and makes me laugh."

Marcia thought about her early days with Preston. How much she had loved him. She suddenly felt robbed—the chill of years gone by.

"I'd like to meet this young man."

"I don't know when I'm going to see him again."

"Why don't we fix that? We're having a picnic in Southampton on Labor Day. You're family, and you should be there. Call him up right now and invite him."

Katherine looked at her watch. "It's one in the morning."

"So what? He's in the Secret Service. They're trained to adapt, I'm sure." Marcia saw the wheels turning in Katherine's head. "Do it. Call him."

Katherine picked up her cell phone and punched in the number. "Am I calling you too late?" she asked.

Marcia left the kitchen to give Katherine some privacy. When she came back, the conversation was over.

"Well?" Marcia asked.

"He was really good about the call. He said he'd check with his team leader in scheduling. He couldn't promise anything, but he said he'd try."

"I think it's time for you to get some sleep. Me, too," Marcia said and gave Katherine a hug.

★ ★ ★

Sean pondered the phone call. He was glad to hear from Katherine. Her concern about the timing of the call underlined the difference in their worlds. His schedule changed rapidly with time zones and assignments.

Katherine, like so many others, thought of the Service as largely occupied with protecting the president, the vice president, and other high-level officials, past and present. But there were multiple threats—equally dangerous—including invasion of cyberspace security. The agency increasingly needed staff with the capacity to understand both computers and the mindset of those driven to disrupt and destroy lives.

Sean wanted to be one of those agents and was excited to be assigned to the financial institution and telecommunications fraud unit. The post had its practical limitations. The work of agents involved in investigating financial institutions was little known by the public, and the Secret Service preferred to keep it that way. There were many people he couldn't talk to about what he was doing—and that included Katherine.

Until now, it had been easy for Sean to manage the women in his life, keep it simple. The Service came first, but there was still time to play. But his feelings for Katherine ran deep. She was honest and open. He didn't want to betray that. She couldn't know that he'd been following her articles on the banks in the Hamptons. There was even a file on her. And one for her father and Wilson Holdings, too. This was not a time for him to show up at the Wilsons' Southampton home for hot dogs on Labor Day.

★ ★ ★

It was partly cloudy, with temperatures in the low seventies, when Katherine and Hailey arrived for the picnic. The smell of hot dogs and hamburgers permeated the air and drew her to the spot before she spied Preston at the grill surrounded by a group of men—all wearing loud Bermuda shorts, with Preston in a blue-checkered apron and white chef's hat.

Marcia and another woman about the same age were sitting in lounge chairs sipping drinks and talking. Hailey went to Preston and with a nudge of her nose let him know she was ready for lunch.

Preston waved his long-handled spatula, and Marcia introduced Katherine to Ann. Marcia made sure that Katherine felt at home. Katherine met Bill and his wife, Sam and his wife, Antonio, and Loreen. Austin, who had come alone, was holding court with the other male guests, which was fine with Katherine.

Katherine followed Marcia into the kitchen, gave her a bottle of merlot she'd brought, and asked if there was anything she could do to help.

"No, this is pretty low-key. But I'm glad you're going to get the chance to get to know Ann."

"Is there any chance that Casey may be coming?" Katherine asked.

"I think he's tied up with his children this weekend," Marcia said. "At least that's the position we're taking."

Selfishly, Katherine had been hoping Casey would be there. She wanted to see him again and have him meet Hailey, but that seemed unlikely now.

When lunch was ready, the men sat in a group at one end of the long picnic table; the women, at the other. Katherine sat next to Ann and enjoyed getting to know her and talking to the other women. Hailey made the rounds, accepting contributions from all the guests. Katherine could hear enough of the men's conversation to know they were talking shop and golf.

After lunch and a walk on the beach, the guests began to leave. Katherine and Preston relived their night with Harry and the oompah band.

"That's the first time I've seen you let go," Katherine told him. "I loved it."

"What about now?" Preston said pointing to his Bermuda shorts.

"Not so much," she said. "But the shorts are nice."

Katherine could not help but notice that Preston and Marcia had not spoken to each other all day, and she could feel the chill hanging in the air between them. It made her sad and uncomfortable. But she felt there was nothing she could do about it.

She thanked Preston and Marcia for a wonderful day, and she and Hailey headed for home. She was glad she'd gone, but worried about Marcia and Preston. And there was that empty feeling from Sean not being there. She knew it was short notice, and in any event he probably had other plans. She hoped it was work and not something else, but she also felt she had no right or at least no basis to expect that he'd be there. She argued with herself all the way home.

As she parked her car in the back, and they walked to her apartment, Hailey, to Katherine's surprise, began wagging her tail and barking, running ahead of her to the door. When Katherine caught up, she saw why.

Without a word, she dropped what she was carrying, rushed toward the man she'd just been thinking about, wrapping her arms around his neck and her legs around his midsection. Sean held her tightly but kissed her gently. Hailey jumped up, put her front paws on Sean's back, and licked his neck—almost knocking them both over. Sean and Katherine burst into laughter as Katherine pushed Hailey down and composed herself.

"Hi," Sean said. "Guess you're glad to see me."

"Pretty much."

"I know I'm too late for the picnic."

"But you're here."

"Are you going to let me in?"

"Well ... okay," Katherine said.

Sean gave Hailey a pat as they went inside, and then he looked around the apartment. The pictures on the wall caught his eye, and he carefully studied each one.

"I like your apartment."

"It's small but it's ... cozy."

He focused on the picture of the racer's back and smiled.

"He's a good guy," Katherine said. "I followed him in a race. Still following him."

"And he's following you."

"Hungry?"

"Yes."

Katherine reached in the bag of leftovers Marcia had sent home with her, quickly arranged a plate of potato salad and reheated the hamburgers and hot dogs.

"Would you like something to drink ... beer, wine?"

"I'll have a beer, thanks."

Katherine brought the food to the table and then a couple of cold Sam Adams. Suddenly, she realized she was hungry again and fixed a hamburger for herself.

"How long have you been here, and how did you know where to come?"

"I'm a Secret Service agent. I'm supposed to know these things, or at least be able to figure them out."

"I can't tell you how happy I am that you did."

He reached over and put his hand on hers. "Me, too." He raised his beer and clinked it with Katherine's. "A toast to Kat—who, despite the obstacles, always finishes the race."

Katherine raised her bottle. "A toast to a man I would follow anywhere."

Sean took the dishes to the kitchen and started washing them. Katherine joined him.

"We can put these in the dishwasher," Katherine said.

"I like doing them. Tell me about the picnic."

Katherine described the house and its proximity to the beach and gave Sean a rundown of the people. "It was nice. The girls took a walk on the beach, and you could tell they all got along great. But there was a bit of tension between Preston and Marcia."

"That bothered you."

"It made me uncomfortable. Marcia made a point of inviting me as part of the family. They're not getting along."

"Why do you think that is?"

"A lot of things. It's complicated. I just hope I'm not adding to it."

Hailey sauntered into the kitchen with her rubber bone toy and dropped it at Sean's feet. She then headed to her favorite spot on the carpet in the living room, circled it a couple of times, and lay down. Sean accepted the invitation and followed.

Katherine joined them on the floor. Sean asked her about how her work was going, and Katherine told him about her job and how happy she was with Sol and the opportunity to pursue the kinds of stories that interested her. She talked about her grandfather's call and the good time they had had with Harry.

It was getting dark outside, and from where they were sitting they could see the waning moon through the window. Sean put his arm around Katherine, gently pulled her to him, and kissed her.

Sean continued to watch the moon.

"I wonder if we can see it from in there," Katherine said, indicating the only other full-sized room in the place.

Katherine told Hailey to stay, as she led Sean to her bedroom. Hailey ignored the command and followed them in. Katherine and Sean ignored Hailey, as they gently sat on the bed. Katherine stretched out on her back and placed her hands together on Sean's face. She stared at him for a full minute. His eyes locked on hers, and she felt their hands begin to undress each other, slowly, deliberately.

The next thing she felt was a warm, soft kiss on her left eye and then her right, making her smile. She opened her eyes and felt herself kissing Sean back, harder and deeper than she had ever kissed before. She felt the weight of his body first along her side and then on top of her, enveloping hers.

Katherine held her arms tightly around Sean's neck with the intent to never let go. She felt a lifetime of defenses being stripped away until suddenly, they disappeared, frightening her and releasing her at the same time. She felt the power of a man, more powerful than she had known. The rhythm of their movements became stronger, each setting off a new fire, adding more fuel of desire, more naked need, until finally she felt their hearts burst together.

Later, after they slept in each other's arms for a time unknown, they woke and looked deeply into each other's eyes, not saying a word.

"How are you feeling?" Sean asked, pulling the bedspread over her. "Are you warm enough?"

"I've never felt so warm in all my life. I've dreamed about feeling like this forever," Katherine said, her eyes misty.

"Tell me what you are thinking right now," Sean said.

"I'm not sure I can. Thoughts are buzzing through my brain in all directions like trains rolling in and out of Grand Central Station. Sean, so much has happened—major stuff—in the last six months. You're the most major of all. I think you're my Joe," she said.

As they lay there, cuddling together under the warmth of their bodies and covers, for once in her life Katherine had no questions and only one answer. She knew at that moment she wanted to spend the rest of her life with this man.

Sean looked to Katherine as if he were reading her mind. "There's one thing you need to know," he said. "In the Service, I will be gone for long periods of time, not knowing when I will return, and often, not in a position to communicate with you, or if I am, to tell you where I am or perhaps more importantly, what I'm doing."

"I guess that's why they call the Service 'secret.' Is there a question in there?"

"Inherently, yes. It's an old question. Will you wait?"

"Forever."

CHAPTER FIFTY-TWO

For Katherine, the July financial summit meeting with Sol and Chuck swiftly changed everything. The men and women she had come to know and like in the newsroom suddenly had an interest in what she was doing and wanted to have coffee with her in the break room. Some even took a new liking to Hailey. Chuck ratcheted down his inherent condescension, and the temperature in his office warmed a few degrees. But the main thing was, her stories were getting out there—and the incoming reactions were positive.

Readers e-mailed, called, and even stopped in to talk about the injustice of what had happened to Constance Shipman. The news got better when Constance called Katherine to tell her she'd been offered a senior teller's job with Golden Shore Bank. When Katherine's thoroughly researched piece about the FDIC lawsuit hit, audience response tripled. Readers were beginning to connect the dots. In the third week, when readers of the *Twin Forks Press* learned of the collective millions lost by investors—many of whom were their neighbors—response increased ten-fold.

The reaction—verging on small-scale celebrity—fueled Katherine's determination even more. What happened next exceeded her wildest expectations.

Congressman Brian Quinn called her at the newspaper office the week after Labor Day. Of course she knew he was up for reelection and likely trying to change his image anyway he thought he could to make a difference, but his concern also seemed genuine.

"I want to congratulate you on the stories I've been reading," he told her. "You may know, as the ranking member of the House Financial Services Committee, I have a keen interest not only in the health of our financial institutions, but also in the way they are run."

"Apparently for some at the top, avarice is a way of life." Katherine asked him point-blank, "How do you propose to change that?"

"We've already done a lot. Investigations are going on, as we speak, on multiple levels—numerous federal offices and all the state agencies. It's also the focus of several of our committees in Washington."

"Why did you call me, Congressman?"

"I was particularly interested in your story about local investors and the money they lost when Hamptons went down. Many of my constituents have contacted me about this, asking what we can do to help. I'd like to sit down with you and go over how we can work together—help each other."

"I'd like that. When and where?"

"I'm in Brentwood today. Can we meet this afternoon?"

"Yes, what time?"

"How about 2:00 p.m.? I can send a car for you, if you like."

"Can my golden retriever come along?"

"Are you serious?"

"Yes. She's here at the newspaper office with me, but, of course, I could drop her off at my apartment if need be."

"Bring her. See you then."

"At what number may I reach you, if something comes up?"

He provided her with the number.

Katherine went straight to Sol's office. The door was open, and he waved her in.

"Hey, kiddo. What's up?"

"I'd like to ask your advice. Congressman Quinn just called me. Said he liked our stories, particularly the one on the Hamptons Bank investors. Said many of his constituents have been asking him for help in connection with their losses. I asked him why he called me, and he said he wanted to meet and discuss how we could work together and help each other."

"Really? He has a high profile."

"Several questions come to mind. For one thing, nothing in my stories has been political. He's a Republican. Chip Reider, our congressman in the first district, is a Democrat. What are the ethics? Should I talk to him at all? Should I try to talk with Reider and Quinn together or separately? Give equal time? I'm digging deeper and deeper into the bank issues. Obviously, Quinn has deep investigative resources—on a national level. Either could be a big help."

"Talk to him. Record everything—with his permission. Ask a lot. Say little. Keep me in the loop. It's getting interesting."

A couple of hours later, Katherine and Hailey stepped out of the limo at Representative Quinn's local district office.

"It's nice to meet you, Miss Kelly, and your dog as well," said the congressman.

"Thank you. It's Katherine. This is Hailey's first ride in a limo. She's very appreciative. She told me she'd be happy to wait quietly in your reception area while we talk, if you like."

"No, I think she should hear this. Bring her in."

When Katherine saw a picture of a blonde golden retriever on the congressman's trophy wall—among the pictures of famous people—she understood.

They sat at one end of a large conference table.

"I'm pleased to meet you, Congressman," said Katherine. "I've followed you more closely since I moved to Southampton, and I'm under the impression that you truly care about your constituents, as does your neighbor to the east, Congressman Reider."

"Nicely done, Katherine," Quinn said with a smile.

"Do you mind if I record our conversation?"

"I'd rather you didn't. In fact, I'd like your agreement that this conversation will be off the record—at least until we can agree on what we want to be on the record."

"This may be a short conversation then, but we'll see how it goes," Katherine said. "We both share an interest in the banking industry, but our constituencies are obviously different. How do you see our helping each other?"

"You're a young reporter and you have gotten your teeth around a juicy bone. We can identify and pursue our common interests. Press—depending on how the story's written—can be an incentive for those in the banking world who want to do the right thing and pressure on those who don't.

"In fact, it can cause the worms to come out of the woodwork. That can lead to better evidence, stronger testimony, and more political capital to achieve banking reform," said Congressman Quinn.

"I won't be able to provide you with my sources, and I won't do anything to compromise my stories."

"I may have information that can add to your stories. You can decide what you want to use. I won't interfere with what you write or ask you not to write it. If you have information you feel may be helpful to what we're trying to do, and providing it to us is not a problem for you, we'd like to receive it."

"Do you ever work in conjunction with Representative Reider?"

"We often work together. There are always bipartisan issues where cooperation can help. There's no exclusively Democratic or Republican way to defraud a bank."

"I'd like to talk with my publisher about all of this. May I have your permission to tell him what we talked about—providing it will remain off the record?"

"You have it, and give Sol my regards. By the way, I'm not sure if you've heard that Bank North America's acquisition of CCB has been finally approved. I've enjoyed talking with you, Miss Kelly. I think we should be able to find a way to work together."

"I certainly hope so. I have enjoyed meeting you and appreciate our conversation. I'll be back in touch."

Congressman Quinn walked her to the door, gave Hailey a pat, and asked his driver to take them both back to the newspaper.

Katherine reported her conversation with the congressman in full to Sol back at the office.

"What did you think of him?" her boss asked.

"Smart. Cagey. Committed. He had so many layers, I thought I was talking to an onion."

Sol smiled.

CHAPTER FIFTY-THREE

Katherine was always searching for the nugget—the little acorn—seemingly innocent or sometimes made invisible which, if picked up, dusted off, and examined carefully could lead to or even grow the tree. Quinn had dropped the nugget about the CCB merger with BNA. Why? What did he know that she didn't? What was he telling her? What was she missing?

It started with her curiosity about CCB's responsibility, if any, in taking over Hamptons Bank. Katherine reviewed her file. Did CCB bring in its own people because it wanted to keep its own culture and for economic reasons, or was it also for prophylactic purposes?

Another piece that intrigued Katherine was how many of the Hamptons employees who were terminated pointed out that CCB was doing the same things that had brought Hamptons down. Apart from how they knew that, which was important, was it true? And if CCB was dirty, would the FDIC have facilitated its takeover of Hamptons?

In an effort to unbundle the potpourri of bank wrongdoing, she turned her attention to the CEO of Hamptons, Henry Wilkins. The indictment was self-explanatory. Multiple charges of bank fraud, conspiracy, providing false information, overvaluation of bank assets. But what lay underneath? She wanted to understand the schemes and with intense focus, finally sorted it out.

Wilkins's real estate department had loaned money to Ronton Real Estate Development, Inc., to finance Ronton's purchase of lots. Ronton then had the lots appraised based on current sale prices—which were inflated because the lots were resold at the closing to investors looking for large returns when they developed and sold them. Wilkins and his loan officers knew the appraisals were inflated, because the lots were flipped for twice Ronton's purchase price, but they were happy to arrange the mortgage loans based on false qualifying information and even happier to receive a fifteen percent kickback. While Wilkins's scheme forced many properties into foreclosures causing lenders, insurers, and others to incur millions of dollars in losses, Wilkins pocketed more than eight million dollars.

How pervasive were schemes like this? Katherine wondered. Her research showed that the Manhattan U.S. Attorney's office nearly two years earlier had secured the first conviction against a bank president and CEO for attempting to steal eleven million dollars from the taxpayer funded TARP, and it had continued its investigation into the misconduct at the bank, vowing not to tolerate fraud or those who stole from taxpayers for personal gain.

Katherine knew from her off-the-record discussions with SIGTARP's special inspector that those investigations were getting hot and likely to break at any time. The hook there was that a bank CEO had conspired with others to falsely represent that he had invested $6.5 million in the bank in order to convince regulators that the bank had improved its capital position, and then later tried to get $11 million in TARP funds.

In April of that year, Reginald Harper pled guilty in U.S. District Court in Louisiana to conspiracy to commit bank fraud. Harper, the former president, CEO, and loan officer, and his co-conspirator Fouquet, a Louisiana real estate developer, had orchestrated a fraudulent scheme to conceal delinquent, non-performing loans at First Community Bank by creating new "sham" loans. Harper arranged for First Community to provide more than two million dollars in loans to Fouquet to purchase land and build houses on it. When they couldn't find enough qualified buyers, Harper and Fouquet devised various cover-up schemes to avoid reporting the delinquent loans. They used "nominee" loans and "straw" buyers to apply for new loans, and the bank submitted a false "call" report to hide the institution's true financial condition.

Katherine's research showed conviction of bank presidents and CEOs on a variation of these fraudulent schemes in small or regional banks all over the country, including, as she had already learned, Braydon, South Carolina. So why not CCB? That would be her next target.

Katherine placed a call to CCB's vice president, commercial real estate development.

"Mrs. Stacy Bowers?"

"Yes."

"My name is Katherine Kelly. I'm a reporter with *Twin Forks Press*—"

"I know who you are."

"I'm working on a story that involves CCB and certain real estate transactions. May I ask you a few questions?"

"No, you may not," the bank executive said and hung up.

CHAPTER FIFTY-FOUR

Preston felt like he was in a time warp when he walked into the BNA conference room on the thirty-ninth floor. Through the all glass floor-to-ceiling wall across from the entranceway, on a clear day similar to the one when he'd been here over a year ago, he saw the gleaming, New-South city of Charlotte. He recalled perfectly the light brown wallpaper on the remaining walls, and the one with a large white board and a tray of markers. Only one difference bothered Preston. He wished Joe were here.

"Good morning, gentlemen," Tom Gallagher said with a broad smile, walking around the table and extending his hand. Preston thought he was reliving the past. "Let me introduce Floyd Ritter, our vice president and general counsel, and Arthur Goldberg, our vice president, commercial finance in New York City."

Preston shook their hands and introduced Austin Disley as his CFO. The five exchanged business cards and took their places around one end of the conference table.

"I hope you had a nice flight," Ritter said. "Did you use the corporate jet?"

"Absolutely," Austin said. "We flew the G5. It was almost too fast."

"It's not our corporate jet," Preston interjected before Austin could go any further. "We have an arrangement for hours with Marquis Jet."

"Help yourselves to coffee or whatever you would like on the credenza," Gallagher said. "If Mr. Casey were here—and I'm sorry he's not—I would have asked for some sandwiches and maybe a couple of Snickers bars," he said with a chuckle. "Good man."

Preston decided to leave it alone, feeling both the same way and overexposed without Casey present. "It's your meeting, Mr. Gallagher," he said.

"Mr. Ritter?" Gallagher said.

"Thank you for coming down," said the vice president. "There are two purposes for this meeting. One is to formally let you know that your file will from this point be transferred to our Manhattan office. Arthur?"

The other VP picked up the ball smoothly. "Gentlemen. We already are handling several of your bank accounts, and we are, of course, the lessor of Wilson Holdings' office space—"

"Do you know Teddy Thompson?" Austin interrupted.

"Yes, I know Mr. Thompson. We understand you've had some dealings with him."

"Yeah, great guy. Real asset to you guys."

"If you don't mind, I'll continue," Goldberg said.

"No, sure, go ahead," Austin replied, oblivious to the disdainful looks from others around the room, including Preston.

"One of our questions in looking over the current financials and other materials Mr. Disley has submitted is whether you have reviewed your real estate appraisals provided in support of the office lease renewal," Goldberg said.

"I know they were submitted and met Teddy's requirements. I'm under the impression that BNA has its own appraisals as well," Austin said.

"And what causes you to be under that impression?" Goldberg asked.

"I assume you must have," Austin replied.

"As you know, these appraisals state the value of the underlying single-purpose real estate pledged as additional security for the floor plan exposure and to support your capital loans."

"I'll look into those," Preston said.

"I'd appreciate that," Goldberg offered. "After you return to the city, I'd like to meet with you and do a more exhaustive review of all of your capital notes, our current floor plan arrangements, and the financial statements—Wilson Holdings, your joint personal financial statements with Mrs. Wilson, the consolidated operating statements, and your 2011 personal and corporate state and federal tax returns."

"Certainly," Preston replied.

"Thank you. That covers my end of things for the time being," Goldberg said. "Back to you, Floyd."

"The other purpose of the meeting is to identify the steps necessary and the process required to complete the twelve-month review, assessment, and audit required under the terms of our Workout and Forbearance Agreement," Ritter explained.

"I thought all of that was behind us," Austin said.

"It's an ongoing process, Mr. Disley, as set forth in the agreement. I'm sure you understand, as I said earlier, BNA wants to fulfill its due diligence requirements in connection with the workout process. We have regulators and others to whom we are required to report. You are, after all, still classified as a distressed asset, although we recognize how much you've accomplished in the last three years."

The conversation continued for another thirty minutes or so, with the bank officers gently but firmly detailing all the steps required in the process. Preston was greatly relieved when Austin stopped asking questions and started taking notes. Within two hours, the meeting was completed.

"Again, thank you for coming down," Gallagher said. "I'm sure you'll be in good hands with Mr. Goldberg up there in the big city. I would like to have a word with you privately, Mr. Wilson, if I may."

"Of course," Preston said as he followed Gallagher out of the large conference room to a smaller one around the corner.

"What happened to Casey?" Gallagher asked. "Is he in good health? Is he okay?"

"He's fine. And his health is good—still a little overweight. He wants to spend more time with his wife and three children. They're growing up fast, and he supports them in their baseball activities and whatever else they do. I guess he's had enough accounting for a while."

"He did a lot more than accounting," Gallagher said. "He was a full-blown CFO with oversight over all your operations. Those are pretty big boots to fill. Are you sure Disley's going to hunt?"

Preston looked at the bank president with a quizzical expression.

"What I mean is, will Austin be able to do the job? That's your call, of course. I'm not meddling, but I am asking."

Preston didn't know what to say, so he said nothing.

"Well, we all have our jobs to do, Mr. Wilson. I don't have to tell you there was a man missing in this room today. And he'll be missed for a long time by a lot of people. My suggestion to you is that you take all of this morning's discussion seriously. I wish you the best of luck. Please give my regards to Mrs. Wilson and be sure to tell Casey I asked about him."

Preston thanked Gallagher, shook his hand, and joined Austin in the hallway in front of the elevators. It was a quiet ride down, neither one saying a word.

On the flight back, it wasn't so quiet.

"Austin, what's the story with you? You interrupted Mr. Goldberg. That stuff about the appraisals. Have you even read the forbearance agreement? It sure didn't sound like it. I must tell you, I was not only disappointed, I was embarrassed."

"I think you're getting worked up over nothing, buddy. And I think you're scared, because Casey wasn't there. I have this thing covered. We can't let these guys push us around. They know damn well that our appraisals are higher than the current values. You know that, too, don't you? It's no secret that the market collapsed in a lot of the cities where Wilson owns property. That's not our fault. We can't control that. Lighten up. We'll get through this."

Preston was disgusted. Austin was right about one thing. He was scared. He decided his best strategy for the moment was to have a scotch and sleep for the rest of the flight.

CHAPTER FIFTY-FIVE

As soon as they landed back at Teterboro, Austin placed a call to Teddy Thompson. "We need to talk. Not at your office."

"Let's go to the club, play a little racquetball," Teddy said.

"Let's not. Let's go for a ride in the new Porsche Cayman I helped you purchase. Pick me up at 3:00 p.m. sharp."

"I'll be in front of your office," Teddy said.

Austin was waiting outside. Teddy was prompt. When they were out of New York City, and on the Jersey Turnpike heading toward Atlantic City, Teddy demanded to know what the hurriedly called meeting was all about.

"I want to get a few things straight," Austin said. "To begin with, you did accept the appraisals I gave you, correct?"

"The appraisals ... for ... to back up the renewal of your lease?"

"Yeah, plus to augment our balance sheet to support the cap loan renewals."

"Sure, we accepted those. What's the problem?"

"Did you have appraisals of your own?"

"What are you talking about, Austin? You hired the appraiser I gave you."

"Don't screw around with me, Teddy. I'm talking about the financials you asked for to support the cap loans—appraisals as backup to those financials."

"Why are you asking these questions now?"

"Why aren't you answering them?"

"I'd like to know where you're going with this, Austin. You're Wilson's CFO. It's your job to give BNA accurate information. It's my job to ask for it."

"What's Arthur Goldberg's position?"

"VP, commercial finance."

"What exactly does that title mean? Is he in risk management? Is he an underwriter?"

"Why do you want to know that?"

"Because my boss asked me to find out."

"What it means to me is that finance covers a broad area, and he's got a lot of clout."

"Is he involved in automobile floor plans?"

"Probably not directly—they're asset-based, but it's all part of the strength of the borrower and the quality of the loans."

"Do you report to him?" Austin wanted to know.

"Not directly. He's pretty far up the food chain. I started out in the transactional side of lease financing as a lease portfolio manager. I'm now a vice president in our New York City real estate leasing division."

"So what are your duties?"

"You know what they are."

"Just answer the question."

At that point, Teddy reached over and ran his right hand from Austin's neck to his groin.

"What are you doing?" Austin yelled.

"I thought you might be wearing a wire."

"Don't be stupid. You'll wreck this car."

"Asking these questions is what's stupid," Teddy said, and turned his concentration back to driving and the questions. "I'm in the marketing side. My job is to increase our lease finance portfolios."

Austin was at the end of the questions he could think to ask. They sat quietly for a while, Austin trying to figure out how difficult their situation was. He told himself it was the bank's responsibility to get its own appraisals, and in any event, it was the appraiser's responsibility to provide a fair and accurate evaluation. Appraisers differed on value all the time. It wasn't in the interest of the bank, any more than it was Wilson's, to dispute past appraisals anyway.

"Where are we headed?" Austin asked his friend.

"Atlantic City. We have no choice. What else can you do with the cash?"

"Yeah, practice is over. Time to have some fun."

CHAPTER FIFTY-SIX

The big fish eat the little fish and to get to the top, start with the guy at the bottom. From a tactical point of view, these two understandings were, to Katherine, fundamental. And they were why she approached Maria DeSanto, a transactional level CCB employee under bank vice president Bowers.

Maria was a talker. She had information. And she was scared. It didn't take long.

"Maria, from what you have told me, you were following Mrs. Bowers' specific directions in accumulating the financial statements, appraisals, and other information from Weaver Construction Ltd. for the mortgage loans and then processing the loan documents to complete these transactions," said Katherine, laying things out as clearly as she could.

"That's right."

"And you didn't have direct knowledge that the appraisals were bogus?"

"Correct."

"You told me you know what's going on from overhearing conversations between Mrs. Bowers and her supervisor in Manhattan."

"That's the truth, I swear it."

"Why didn't you discuss this with Mrs. Bowers?"

"Because I thought she'd fire me," said Maria. "You'd have to know the woman. I can't lose my job. And I don't want to get in trouble. What should I do?"

"I'm a reporter and I can't tell you what to do." Katherine believed Maria, wanted to help her, and didn't want her to have a break down. "Is there someone you can go to for advice—a family member, a lawyer—someone you trust?"

"I don't want to talk to my family about this, and I don't want to talk to a lawyer either," Maria said, reaching for a tissue.

"I attended a symposium with people from law firms, the Long Island Fraud and Forgery Committee, the FBI, the DEA, and the U.S. and local district attorney's offices. They were there to network and better understand each other's role in dealing with financial fraud and white-collar crime. I became friendly with a local assistant district attorney named Carol Martin. You may want to talk to her."

"What would I say?"

"Again, this is all up to you. You could just tell her the truth. She may already know about this. In any event, she'll be looking for the same thing I am—stronger evidence of wrongdoing as high up the chain as she can go. If she believes you will cooperate and will be helpful, that may turn out to be your best protection."

"Will you go with me?"

"Absolutely. Whether Carol wants me there will be up to her."

"Arrange it, please. As soon as you can."

★ ★ ★

Katherine had the opportunity the following day. She arranged for Maria to meet Carol in private, to arrive at a different time at the public library, and to use a study room at the back. Katherine introduced the two women. "Carol, this is Maria DeSanto. She works in the transaction department of CCB—now BNA—in Southampton. Her supervisor is Stacy Bowers, vice president of commercial real estate."

"Nice to meet you, Maria."

"As I explained, I spoke with Maria in the course of my ongoing bank fraud investigation of CCB, and I suggested to her that she might want to talk with you. She asked if I'd come with her and I agreed, but it's up to you whether I stay."

"Let's see how it goes. Do you have an attorney, Maria?" Carol asked.

"No, Miss Kelly suggested I might want to talk with one, but I haven't. I haven't done anything wrong. Still, I don't want to get in any trouble."

"Do you have information that somebody has done something wrong?" Carol asked.

"I've overheard Mrs. Bowers talking to her supervisor at BNA in the city. It involved work that I, and others in my department, did in processing loans."

"Can you be more specific?"

"Are you familiar with loan processing?" Maria asked.

"Prior to coming here, I closed hundreds of commercial real estate loan transactions."

"Well," Maria continued, "what bothered me was talk about appraisals being phony and financial statements being built up to look better—to meet minimum standards for the loan."

"Was this one conversation or more, and over what period of time?"

"Many conversations over the last six months or more."

"Was there anything in writing about the appraisals or the financial statements not being accurate?"

"No. Not that I've seen. But the appraisals and the financial statements were often signed off on by the appraisers and borrowers, and then they would be changed—big changes—and then they would have to be signed off on again. That might happen once or twice but not a lot. Then it started happening more frequently. Eventually, I started to think something was wrong."

"Did you talk with anyone in the bank about it?"

"I mentioned it to one other girl who does transactional work with me. She was bothered, too, but she was afraid if she said something, she'd get fired. I felt the same way."

"So why are you talking about it now?"

"Because I'm scared—and I don't want my mother and family to read about me in the paper having done something wrong. I've read some stories that Miss Kelly has written. I don't want to be in one."

Carol turned to Katherine. "Is she going to be in one of your stories, Katherine?"

"I hope not. I'm interested in getting to the heart of whatever schemes are going on and exposing the bad guys, preferably the ones leading the parade."

"I can understand that," Carol said. "At this point, I'd like to talk with you, Maria, further and alone. Our investigations have to remain confidential. I'll want to take a statement from you, and if you are willing to cooperate with us, we may well be able to work something out for you. I want you to understand that you always have a right to counsel at any point you wish. Is that understood, and do you want to continue?"

"It is and yes, I do."

"Would you excuse us for a moment, Maria? I'd like to talk with Katherine, privately, if you don't mind."

"Sure. No problem," Maria said.

Katherine followed Carol out into the hallway, where she lowered her voice.

"Thank you for bringing Maria to me. She may be of real help. I should be able to arrange immunity for her. Just between us, we have a BNA real estate connected fraud investigation going on now, and like you, we want the big fish."

"I'm glad I could help. I realize your investigations are confidential. However, if there comes a point as you go up the line, where you can pass information on to me, either on the record or off, I would appreciate you doing so. I'd rather be the first to know, if possible."

"I will, to the extent I can. And, I'll be clear what's for publication and what's not."

"Thanks, Carol. I'll say good-bye to Maria."

CHAPTER FIFTY-SEVEN

It was Katherine's favorite time of year. Leaves changing, still warm, Halloween coming. But this fall in Southampton was especially exciting. She was well into a productive rhythm at *Twin Forks*, she loved the people there, and she felt satisfied with the depth and progress of her stories and pleased that they were being so well received.

On the personal side, she had never been so content. She was able to spend more and more time with Preston and with Marcia and P.J., though usually separately. She talked with her mother and grandfather often, had fun with Susan when they could get together, and loved relaxing and playing with Hailey. As if that were not enough, Sean had called several times, and each conversation with him seemed better than the last.

The only thing that worried her, more than she knew it should, were reports of Tropical Storm Sandy churning in the Caribbean. She knew she was being silly, living where she did, but she'd never been through a hurricane. The accounts of the havoc wrought by Katrina had been horrific. She told herself not to worry. But as the days went by, updates on Sandy occupied more and more time on the weather channels. What seemed different about this storm were indications from early models that it could actually reach the Northeast—New York City and Boston. She blocked the storm out of her mind and tried to focus on maintaining a balance of work and play, never having felt greater fulfillment from either before.

By now, there was a real symmetry and incremental growth in her bank stories. An unexpected boost came from a press release Congressman Quinn put out in mid-October. Calling for the elimination of fraud and curbing the wrongdoing in the banking system, he had cited two articles on specific bank schemes of misconduct involving real estate loans and mortgages written by Katherine Kelly of the *Twin Forks Press*. Katherine suddenly found herself not having to nose around for leads and sources—instead they came to her, even on a national level. She soon realized—and reported—that the schemes she was unearthing at Hamptons Bank had been used elsewhere as well in both community and regional banks, and Sol let her run with the story. Her stories had wings, and they soared.

And, thanks to the rapid growth of her relationships and corresponding leads, she was able to increase her weekly story contribution to double digits. Sure, there were some twelve-hour days in there, some missed meals, and some work on Saturdays and Sundays, but she didn't care, because readers (and Sol) were giving her positive feedback. Still, the hurricane occupied more and more space in her mind as the media increased the Sandy drumbeat: why Sandy was a different kind of storm and the widespread devastation it could cause.

As families across America were preparing for Halloween, those in the Northeast were busy making other preparations. New York City's Mayor Bloomberg dispensed pre-storm advice and precautions, as did officials in New Jersey and other areas falling within Sandy's projected path.

When Sandy slammed into the East Coast October 29 around 6:30 p.m., it was clear that the breadth of the storm—a thousand miles wide—was extraordinary and exacerbated by eighty-mile-per-hour-plus winds. The slow-moving nature of the hurricane and the anticipated rainfall prompted experts to predict extreme flooding. When Katherine heard that Mayor Bloomberg, for the first time in history, had preemptively closed sections of the New York City subway system, there was no doubt how serious the situation was.

That Monday and Tuesday convinced the rest of America as images of flooding and destruction too terrible to imagine were viewed day and night. During the worst of the "superstorm," as the TV had taken to calling it, Katherine remained with Hailey at the newspaper offices, with most of the other key personnel. They watched the televised images of devastation, as the rest of America did, for as long as their electric power and generators lasted, and they worked to update their online edition. They knew that subways had flooded, boardwalks and piers had vanished, and people in many places in the five boroughs, New Jersey, and Connecticut had lost their homes. Lower Manhattan was partially under water; lives were lost on Staten Island. Southampton suffered as well. While the flooding on Long Island was, for the most part, in the low-lying coastal areas along Dune Road and in Flanders and Sag Harbor, electric power losses were far more widespread, affecting some ninety percent of utility customers across the Island. The residents' misery was made all the worse by the cold, wet weather.

For some reason, Katherine's apartment had retained power, as had the *Twin Forks Press*. Susan had power, and so did Preston's condo. Too many others were not so fortunate. When Sol had renovated the *Twin Forks Press* building and upgraded its emergency generators a few years earlier, he'd added a stall shower in the men's room—mostly for employees who cycled to work. But now, a few of Katherine's fellow employees and their families were waiting in line to use the shower in the early morning hours.

Katherine and the other three full-time reporters met with Sol and Chuck urgently to discuss what they could do to help. Thankfully, countless citizens in the Northeast metropolitan area and from all over the country provided money and assistance in whatever way they could. The power companies were trying to restore power as quickly as possible, but too many went without help for too long.

Many without power or other help in parts of Staten Island, New Jersey, and Long Island felt abandoned, even though the President, himself, as well as FEMA, the governors, and many others appeared to be vitally concerned and had promised to do all they could.

Sandy and a subsequent snowstorm on November 7 knocked out power to more than eight million customers in twenty-one states, including two million in New York. A week later thousands on Long Island and elsewhere still were without electricity. Many of Katherine's readers called, and some wrote to her—telling her they knew she had their interest at heart and that they needed her help now more than ever.

As the water receded, some even came to the *Twin Forks Press* office to talk with her in person. One was Norman, a pudgy, middle-aged pool-company employee who covered his balding hair with a red baseball cap. Norman told Katherine he was planning to organize a protest later that day outside National Grid's offices and dispatch center on Montauk Highway in Water Mill. A growing number of customers were outraged at what they saw as the company's inadequate response and failure to replace outdated or obsolete management systems to handle large-scale outages such as this one. Norman wasn't sure how many people were going to show up, so Katherine was the only reporter he'd told so far. Another protest against National Grid in Hicksville had drawn large crowds, and he was hopeful the same thing could happen in Water Mill, too.

It was still early, and most of the other reporters were either not in yet or busy taking care of their own homes and families. Katherine found Sol and Chuck in the break room and told them she wanted to cover the protest.

"A lot of our people are without power. You've seen the protests. They feel ignored, left out, and that no one's listening to them. Let's give them a hand, help them be heard," Katherine said.

"Thoughts?" Chuck asked.

"Let's go out there and get video of some of the protesters. Push out the videos on our website and our YouTube channel, too. Let the protesters tell their own stories," Katherine said.

Chuck hesitated, arguing that they'd already covered the story from numerous angles and they were operating with a reduced staff. Sol listened to Chuck's objections but in the end gave her the green light. "Go ahead. Take Esther along to help. You do the interviews, and she can do the editing and uploading on site."

Katherine checked her watch, called Norman on his cell, and told him she wanted to try to interview some of the residents at the protest. She asked if he'd be willing to help.

"You bet. These people have had enough, and they feel like no one's listening to them." She arranged to meet him and his group at 1:30 p.m. and go over everything. She asked Sol if he would mind looking after Hailey.

"Okay, kiddo. Happy to be both your publisher and your dog sitter."

Katherine went in the break room, downed a couple of cups of black coffee, and thought through what she wanted to cover and how. She wanted subscribers who did have power and Internet connection—even on mobile devices—to like and share the videos on Facebook, drawing attention to what was happening in their own backyards. Much of the attention from the New York media, even WABC-TV and the other local TV outlets, had been focused on Staten Island and other places near the city. Frankly, it was far easier for the outlets to send reporters and TV crews there. Even Newsday, the big Long Island daily newspaper, barely covered the North and South forks of Long Island. The Hamptons had largely been forgotten by everyone but the local weeklies, and Katherine was determined to change that.

CHAPTER FIFTY-EIGHT

When Katherine and Esther arrived at National Grid's offices, Norman and some of the protesters were already out front, carrying picket signs and demanding the company restore their power. They immediately went to work, using Katherine's SUV as their impromptu office. Norman first introduced them to a young guy living in an apartment that had no power. Katherine and Esther shared a knowing glance; they'd interview him, sure, but they'd also keep looking for a deeper human interest angle.

A half hour later, Norman introduced them to Dottie Everheart, a young mother who had three children at home—and no power, heat, or water. Like many South Fork residents, the Everhearts depended on well water, and that meant that when her electric pump was down, there was no water for cooking, drinking, cleaning, anything. Katherine shook hands with the woman, and immediately recognized her as someone she'd interviewed once before. Dottie was one of the out-of-work former employees from Hamptons Bank, and she'd already been struggling even before Hurricane Sandy hit. This was a story Katherine wanted to tell. Esther put a fresh memory card in the video camera, and the pair went to work.

Katherine interviewed Everheart for about twenty minutes, asking her about what it was like to care for her three young children in a cold, dark house without water. The fact that she was trying to hold it all together after losing her job as a security guard at Hamptons Bank made the story all the more poignant.

Within the hour Katherine and Esther had uploaded the video to the *Twin Forks Press* site and continued to seek out other interviews during the daylight hours. They picked a total of four videos for posting, but the unemployed mother of three, they knew, would draw the most attention.

Katherine had been so focused on her work that she hadn't noticed that the crowd had swelled to more than four hundred men, women, and children, some standing, some walking a picket line, many carrying handmade signs. A News 12 reporter was talking to a camera, with the crowd behind her, telling her audience that National Grid was doing all that it could and promising to get the power turned back on as quickly as possible. Katherine had been told the very same thing by a utility company spokesman. Still, she wondered why she rarely saw utility company trucks on local streets.

Katherine's video was getting plenty of hits on the *Twin Forks Press* site, and dozens of people had started sharing it online. Dottie Everheart's awful situation left many viewers in tears. Many simply forwarded the link to their friends without comment; the story spoke for itself.

★ ★ ★

One of those who happened to visit the *Twin Forks Press* website that day was the *Today Show*'s Nat Mauer, who owned a summer house in Southampton and spent many weekends there, even during the off-season when many of the local boutiques, restaurants, and art galleries were closed. The summer house was his personal refuge away from the city, the place he retreated to for quiet dinner parties with friends. Mauer hadn't been out to the Hamptons since the hurricane hit, and he'd been concerned about the extent of damage in the beachfront communities. The caretaker for his sprawling home had assured him that everything was fine there, except for the loss of a tree in his backyard. But he had no sense of what Southampton or Bridgehampton looked like. Poking around on the Web, he came across the *Twin Forks'* site and Katherine Kelly's video featuring the single mom. Dottie was both pretty and well-spoken, and she related a heart-wrenching tale.

Mauer clicked on the video so that he could watch it again. What she said about the hurricane was interesting. But what piqued his curiosity most were the woman's comments about the closure of the bank where she'd worked to support her family. The *Today Show* producers had been anxious to do a piece about banking fraud, and they envisioned building the piece around the plight of a victim—someone who'd been impacted by a bank closure. They'd been on the lookout for a local subject to build the story around. The *Today Show* host clicked on one of the links next to the video, taking him to the package of banking stories that Katherine had produced.

"Hey, Robert, take a look at this," Mauer shouted to the producer who had been working on the banking segment.

★ ★ ★

Katherine drove back to her office, gave Sol and Chuck a report on the successful video shoot, picked up Hailey, and headed home, where she heated up some soup and sat down to watch the news. She was still half-frozen from the shoot and welcomed Hailey's warmth when the dog hopped up on the couch to snuggle with her.

The local News 12 showed pictures of some damage along the shore, including some massive flooding and beach erosion that had left close to sixty thousand residents of South Fork without power; several local schools had been closed for as long as a week. It showed an interview with Mayor Brian Gilbride, who highlighted the work of the Sag Harbor superintendent of public works as well as the fire department volunteers who had pumped out more than four million gallons of water.

Pictures of damage caused by "Superstorm Sandy" to other areas in Long Island were shown, too, along with footage from the protest in Water Mill and an interview with Norman, the protest organizer.

Later that evening, Katherine's iPhone rang. A producer from the *Today Show* had shown up at Dottie Everheart's door—and what should she do? She'd never given a TV interview before, no less one that was going to air across the nation. She was embarrassed to say that she didn't have a job and was on unemployment.

"You should do it," Katherine told her. "If you talk on camera, you'll help expose some of these banking issues and—hopefully—prevent more banking failures and more victims, like you."

The next day, a driver in a black Lincoln Town Car drove Nat Mauer east to do the interview with the former bank employee. The woman's story was just what the *Today Show* needed for the segment that was scheduled to air two days later. The producer would have to work halfway through the night to complete the segment. The show also booked Congressman Quinn for an interview in the studio.

Mauer told the producer to link the *Today Show*'s online story on banking back to the *Twin Forks Press'* coverage. It was unusual to link to such a minor site, but Mauer liked Katherine's coverage and felt it made sense to feature the stories. After all, without the weekly's local coverage, they would never have found their victim.

The *Today Show* segment on banking—its look at Hamptons Bank, the single mother's plight, and the website's link back to *Twin Forks'* coverage—prompted thousands of people to read Katherine's stories about Hamptons Bank. Suddenly, the whole world seemed to know her byline, and Katherine's cell phone wouldn't stop ringing.

Within an hour, she talked to at least ten of those millions, starting with her mother, her grandfather, and Susan, followed by telephone calls from Sol, Alice, Esther, Marcia, Casey, and Sean. Even Chuck had called to congratulate her.

The next morning, the *Twin Forks Press'* server temporarily crashed from all the traffic, but all Katherine could hear was the applause she received when she and Hailey walked into the newsroom.

Sol called her into his office.

"Nice job, kiddo. I hope you're having fun, because I am. This is what it's all about. It's been a miserable hurricane, but at least we've done our jobs. Take the day off and relax. You've certainly earned it."

Katherine went home with Hailey, fixed them both dinner from what groceries she had on hand, and then went for a long walk on the storm-littered beach with Hailey. She had experienced one of the happiest days of her life. Unfortunately, the euphoria would be short lived.

CHAPTER FIFTY-NINE

When Katherine and Hailey arrived at work the next day, the voice mail on her office phone was blinking with dozens of messages. Among them was one from Carol Martin. She moved it to the top of her call-back list.

"I have some information I believe you will find interesting. Not on the phone. Where can we meet?"

"I can come to your office."

"I'm in your area. If you're available, how about I pick you up, and we'll go for a drive—say in about half an hour?"

"Fine. I'll be out in front."

About twenty-five minutes later, Katherine told Hailey to stay at her desk, grabbed her pen and notepad, and walked outside. Carol was waiting in a small, two-door Volvo. Katherine hopped in, and Carol headed east, making her way carefully through streets still strewn with debris.

"You're becoming quite the celebrity, Katherine. Congratulations."

"Thanks. My fifteen minutes, I'm sure. What have you got, and what are the terms?"

"I'd like to bring you up to speed on our CCB/BNA fraud investigation. For now, let's call it on background—without attribution. You can use it, but you can't quote the source."

"Agreed."

"Maria was very cooperative and helpful. She even agreed to wear a wire. Bowers is dirty. She and a few others in BNA's real estate department got in bed with a real estate developer with a scheme to create artificial value in commercial lots in the Hamptons, flip them, and sell them to over-eager buyers looking to make a killing on the other end."

"Sounds like others I've investigated."

"The extent of the fraud on the transactional side was bad enough—trumped-up appraisals, false financial statements, lying on loan applications. But the scheme went further. We were able to link the conduct of a BNA business borrower with the conduct of a BNA VP in the real estate leasing division. And the borrower was a tenant of the bank."

"How did it work?"

"An ostensibly independent real estate developer borrowed money to buy the lots, then brought its buyers to the bank for financing. Bowers made that easy. The VP in the leasing division made it easier by supplying phony appraisals. BNA's borrower was a CFO of a big car dealership in the city. He and the real estate VP had an arrangement to allow the developer's buyers who became BNA's borrowers to buy upscale cars at wholesale—and then he and the VP shared a kickback from the developer."

"How did you get them to talk?"

"We went up step by step. Employee Seven talked and named Employee Six. Six ratted on five and so on. We're not done yet, but indictments of Bowers, the VP Thompson, the developer Easy Buy, Inc., and the auto CFO Disley will be announced shortly. To be safe, you could refer to them as under investigation for multiple counts of conspiracy, bribery, and bank fraud."

Katherine felt a buzzing between her ears and a twinge in her stomach. "Tell me the name of the auto executive again?"

"Austin Disley. A hard name to forget. Great stuff, huh?"

Katherine remained silent, frozen in the seat of Carol's car.

"Unless you have more questions, I'm going to take you back. I have to get into the city."

"No. Thanks, Carol. Well ... just one. What is the name of the auto dealership?"

"Manhattan BMW-Mercedes. At the moment, the CEO is a person of interest. Could end up as an unidentified co-conspirator, though, or worse."

Katherine said nothing more on the return trip but thanked Carol for the information, went inside the newspaper office and straight to the ladies' room, and threw cold water on her face. The wavy lines had already started. She closed herself in a stall and sat with her head in her hands—waiting for her vision to return to normal, fighting nausea the whole time.

A half hour later, she went back to her desk, retrieved Hailey, who was waiting patiently for her, and drove to her apartment. After Katherine took Hailey for a brief walk, she went back inside, poured herself a glass of water, and stared at the pictures on her wall. She reached for the small square box of tissues on the coffee table. Ten minutes later, she got up and threw the empty box in the wastebasket and started on another.

After a while—how long, she didn't know—she got up, fixed herself a fresh cup of coffee, and called Susan.

"What's going on?" Susan asked.

"Not my best day. What are you up to?"

"Same you-know-what, different day. You sound funny. Why are you calling?"

"Do I need a reason?"

"In the middle of a weekday? Yes."

"Can you talk?"

"Yes."

"Okay. Strictly between us."

"What else?"

"Think of a reporter investigating bank fraud. She gives a crony in law enforcement a whistle-blower. In return, her buddy tips her off as to the investigations, and tells her she can write about it on background." Katherine stopped for a minute.

"Good for you. Right?" Susan looked closer at her friend.

"There's more."

"There always is. Go on."

"One of those under investigation is a business executive allegedly acting in concert with a bad guy at a bank."

"Not good."

"Right. Possible conflicts of interest, too."

"You know more about that than I do."

"Tough decisions."

"No doubt. Now you know why I get drunk once in a while."

"Any ideas?"

"You're the most thoughtful person I know. You'll figure out the right thing to do. I don't know what else to say."

"I don't either. But, thanks, Susan."

"That's why you pay me the big bucks—call me anytime."

Katherine laughed bitterly. "I'll talk with you later."

She sat on the couch and forced herself to think it through. Nothing forced her to write anything. She could simply let it play out. Should she tell her father? She was under no duty to do so nor any restriction not to. After all, if she wrote the story on background, she could tell her father as long as she didn't reveal her source.

On the other hand, if she wrote the story, her father would learn about it then. But what would that do to her relationship with him? She had finally come to accept him as her father, even love him. So he wasn't perfect; who was? Besides, there was no evidence, at this point, that Preston Wilson had done anything wrong, at least, legally. But he was her father. *I hope you're happy, Gerry. Doesn't get any more to the core than this.*

Katherine got up and went to her computer. She sat for a full twenty minutes without touching a key. She felt so alone, a feeling that she had largely managed to escape over the past few months.

She remembered flagging the reference to the Secret Service at the symposium, surprised with its involvement in institutional bank fraud. She thought about calling Sean. How much help could he be? And should she even be talking to him about this? Maybe it would only make things worse. There were too many hats. But she ought to be able to talk to him on a personal level. That's if she could reach him.

This was going nowhere. She stood, pacing the floor. She could see Hailey thought she was acting strange.

"What do you think I should do?" she asked her faithful friend.

Hailey wiggled her eyebrows several times.

"What kind of answer is that?" Katherine asked.

Hailey gave her a sigh, extended her front legs, and lowered her head in between, ultimately resting it on her right paw.

"So it's my problem. Big help."

Katherine continued to walk the floor. Finally she decided that she'd argued with herself long enough. She called Sean. To her surprise, he answered on the first ring.

"Hi, Kat. What's going on?"

"Am I getting you at a bad time or place?"

"What do you need?"

"Nothing. Well, I mean I just wanted to talk if we could."

"I can talk but not for too long. Go ahead."

Katherine felt that she'd intruded and immediately regretted making the call.

"I'm working on a bank fraud story and wanted to run the facts by you if I could."

"That's not a good idea."

"I just want to hear your take on what I should do."

"Isn't that a conversation for you and your editor or somebody at the paper?"

"It's a personal matter ... I'd rather talk with you."

"Is the subject related in any way to you?"

"I'm the reporter."

"Is that all?"

"I'm not sure what you mean."

"Katherine, does what you want to discuss with me relate directly or indirectly to you, apart from your role as a reporter?"

Katherine thought for a bit. "Yes."

"Then I don't want to discuss it."

"What? I really need to talk to you right now. It's important to me."

"I have to go. I'm sorry," Sean said.

Katherine was speechless as she heard the click. She sat down at her kitchen table and tried to figure out what had just happened. The more she thought, the worse she felt. She blocked Sean out of her mind. She would deal with that later. If she was going with this story, she knew she had a small window of opportunity. How small, she wasn't sure—but she'd come too far to let another reporter take her story.

She called Carol Martin.

"Hi, Katherine."

"Thanks for taking the call. Quick question. When will the indictments in this BNA case take place?"

"The arrests come first. Warrants have been signed. Then an arraignment for each defendant. A judge will determine whether to hold them over for a grand jury. Off the record, we expect it to go that way. But you never know what the defense may come up with and what witnesses may be out there with knowledge. I can't give you more right now, and I didn't give you this."

"Thanks so much, Carol," Katherine said and clicked the phone off. She took Hailey for a long walk, fed the dog and herself, and called her mother.

"Hi, dear. How are you?" Beth asked.

"Can you talk?"

"Yes. I'm home. About to fix your grandpa some dinner. What's up?"

"I feel like one of those clay pigeons Grandpa shoots."

"Uh-oh. I thought the bad guys were the targets."

"This has got to be strictly between us."

"Not even Grandpa?"

"He's part of us. But you can't talk about this, Mom."

"Okay."

"You know about my bank fraud stories."

"I've collected every one of them in a scrapbook."

"I'm considering writing one you may not want to keep. I wanted to give you a heads up. It involves a bank Preston's company deals with and could name one of his high-level employees as being under investigation—maybe even arrested."

"And you can't tell me more, right?"

"I could, but I'd rather not because I haven't decided whether to write the story."

"Does the 'more you can't tell me' involve your father?"

"Trick question, Mom."

"How's he doing? He had a great time with you in Germantown."

"And you would know that . . . how?"

"He told me."

"What? When?"

"I wrote a note to Preston to thank him for all he has done for you. He called to thank me and said you have changed his life. He loves you so much."

Katherine searched for words.

"Are you there?" Beth asked.

"Yes. Sorry. It's been a long day, Mom. Is everything all right with you? How's Grandpa?"

"Everything's fine. Grandpa's getting hungry. He's giving me one of his 'What's the deal?' looks."

"Give him my love. It's been helpful just to hear your voice, Mom. I'm glad Preston's been in touch. He's been good to me."

"He certainly has. I hope whatever it is you're wrestling with works out. I love you."

"I love you, too, Mom."

Katherine cuddled with Hailey on the floor. She tried to anticipate what Sol would say if she opted to go with the story. She could not escape the gnawing feeling that she didn't have enough, but that point would be academic if she decided not to write it. There were plenty of reasons to go either way.

The kitchen clock told Katherine it was 7:15 p.m. If she was going to do it, it would be better to call him at home. She checked the white pages, found the number for Austin Disley, and made the call.

"Hello," a male voice said.

"This is Katherine Kelly. Is this Austin Disley?"

"Yes. What is it?"

"I'm a reporter with the *Twin Forks Press* in Southampton, New York. I'm writing a story about bank fraud, and, in the course of my investigation, I learned that you have been arrested, or are about to be. I thought I would give you an opportunity to respond. Would you like to comment?"

"It's ridiculous. My lawyer is already on top of it. We plan to fight it all the way, and he's confident that, when all the facts are known, I will be totally vindicated."

"Would you like to comment on what those facts are?"

"No. I've said enough." Yes, Katherine agreed, he had.

"Thank you, Mr. Disley," Katherine said, happy to end the call with no further questions. She went to her computer and typed the conversation word for word, noted the time on the memo, ran off a copy, and placed it in her file.

Then she went to the bathroom, took a Tylenol PM, and went to bed.

CHAPTER SIXTY

Katherine woke early, had a cup of coffee, and filled Hailey's water dish. That's when she noticed the thin brown envelope under the door. She picked it up, noted the "personal and confidential" stamp, and carefully opened it.

Supplemental Investigative Report

11/13/12

Investigator: Angelo Bertolini, P.I. #2394876 N.Y. [Former NYPD DECT GS]:

Subject: Preston Wilson

White Male

DOB: 3.13.65; Age: 47

Wilson was subject of a sexual harassment complaint February 12, 2012 by one Henrietta Higgins, an employee at Mercedes Manhattan. No probable cause was found and complaint was dismissed.

Contacts known to this investigator state that the NYPD has interviewed Henrietta Higgins, former employee at Mercedes Manhattan, in connection with current, known fraud investigations of major Manhattan bank. Inquiry prompted by disgruntled employee flag on Higgins as potential whistleblower.

Additional informants advise this investigator of financial and reporting problems at Wilson Holdings of which the ADA's

office may not be aware and that other investigations exist on a
federal level. Further investigation indicated.
Note: This report delivered in hand due to sensitivity of content.

★ ★ ★

"Can you believe this, Hailey? Let's go for a walk."

When they returned, Katherine had breakfast and then sat at her
computer. She opened the "pros and cons" document she'd prepared
and added the new information. If the NYPD/ADA investigation
had reached Higgins, they were looking for more than what they had
on Disley alone. If Disley was a lone-wolf wrongdoer—acting without Preston's knowledge or authority—that would help Wilson. But
what if Higgins had information to the contrary, or could offer other
evidence of wrongdoing? Katherine was acutely aware of what she
didn't know, but compelled to focus on what she did. Arrests were
probable. Indictments were possible. Her story could bring out more
facts, fuel further investigation. It could make a difference. It could
also ruin her father.

Katherine poured herself a cup of coffee and flipped through the
pages in her notepad until she found Stacy Bowers' direct work line
number and extension.

"Ms. Bowers, this is Katherine Kelly, and before you hang up on
me again, I want you to know that I've been informed that you may
be under arrest in this matter. I thought I would give you the opportunity to respond before I write my story."

"My lawyer is handling this. They have arrested the wrong person.
I've done nothing wrong. I have nothing further to say."

"Thank you, Ms. Bowers."

She had to write the story. See how it would come out. Turning it
in would be another matter—one that required another call.

Katherine wrote the story in little over an hour. It didn't need extensive rewrites. In fact, it was too clear. The problem was it was all true.
She read it again and then created a draft e-mail to Sol and Chuck,

attaching the story. She printed copies for them and herself and placed them in separate envelopes, saved the draft, and shut down the computer. She picked up the phone and dialed Preston's cell.

"Hi, Dad. It's Katherine."

"Hi, honey. Just to make sure I'm not dreaming, did you actually say 'Hi, Dad'?"

"I did."

"That's wonderful. When can we get together?"

"Right now. We need to talk."

"Sounds serious."

"It is."

"Okay. I'll be glad to help. Where do you want to meet?"

"Some place where you will feel comfortable having a heart-to-heart discussion."

Preston was silent for a moment. "Well, we could talk at the Union League Club. It's private there. Or, I'll meet you wherever you like."

"That's fine. I'll drive in. I'll be at the club by noon."

"I'll see you then. Cheer up. We'll get you through this."

"We'll see," Katherine said.

The traffic into the city was light. Katherine arrived in about two hours and parked her car. Preston was waiting for her at the door, and they walked upstairs to the large sitting room on the left. They sat in two oversized leather chairs in the far corner with no one around.

"Would you like a drink?" Preston asked.

"No."

"Are you feeling all right? Are you warm enough in here? You look a little pale."

"I'd like to talk to you about some information I've received in connection with a story I have been pursuing. I'd like you to listen to it first without asking me any questions, and I'm not going to tell you where this information came from. Can you do that?"

She saw her father sit back in his chair, suddenly looking very uncomfortable.

"I hate being told what I'm supposed to do when I don't know what

I'm about to hear," said Preston. "If you have a problem with a story you're writing, I don't know how I can help. If you're in some kind of trouble, tell me. I'll do whatever I can."

Katherine proceeded to tell her father the story. She started with the conduct of CCB. Traced how it evolved to BNA. She wondered whether Preston was still in the dark about Disley's arrest. She described the scheme and the role of each of the players without mentioning any names. Preston's legs tapped faster and harder against the floor as each layer was explained, and he appeared to unravel at the description of the CFO's conduct.

"Let me stop here and ask you a question," Katherine said.

Preston nodded.

"How does all of this strike you?"

"It's a horrible story. I'm sure there are more sides to it than I'm hearing now. Because you won't tell me where you are getting this, I have no way to evaluate the source."

"Assume, for discussion purposes, the sources are accurate."

"Then I think it's serious. Someone is in deep you-know-what."

"What would you advise that someone to do?"

"I don't know. Get a lawyer."

They sat quietly for a while.

"Before I go on, there are some personal things I'd like to say. The last few months have been unusual for me. I guess, looking back, I've led a pretty placid life in some respects. Then suddenly, I find out I have a father. I hear about a man named Hart who helped you and, in return, required you to take care of a number of his friends. That intrigued me, as you know. I was trying to figure out after all these years if I needed a father. I wanted to see how you handled that promise. I've learned a lot about you since then. I learned a lot about myself, too. At first, I was pretty self-absorbed about what all of this meant to me. I was mad at my mother for lying to me for all those years. Wondered how I could believe her after that. But after a while, I came to accept the fact that she loves me and always has— without reservation. Whatever she did, she did it for me. I owe her a lot. Starting with an apology for the way I've treated her.

"As to having a father, I have come to believe and feel that you are a good man—even if you like the ponies."

"Where did you get that?"

"Doesn't matter. I shouldn't have brought it up. You're not perfect, but who is? You're the best father I have, and I'm fortunate to have you. And I believe you do love me."

Preston stopped squirming, stood up, walked to Katherine, put his arms around her, and gave her a long hug. She could feel his heart beating through his chest. Tears flowed from her eyes. After a while, they broke away and each sat down again.

Katherine reached for some tissues she had brought with her and blew her nose.

"You asked how you could help me. Here's my dilemma. I've written this story. The question is whether to turn it in. Your CFO is in trouble either way. So are the other co-conspirators involved in any wrongdoing. The criminal investigation is ongoing. If I turn this story in, it will add to the investigation. The digging will be deeper. Wilson Holdings will feel the impact, and it won't be good. It could bring down your empire.

"If I don't turn the story in, I won't be telling the whole truth. A known truth untold is the worst form of a lie. Not going forward with this story would be contrary to everything I believe is important about being a journalist. In a sense, I would lose my soul. What would you advise me to do?"

Preston considered the question. He stared at his shoes, either in deep thought or from a lack of any idea about how to respond. After several minutes, he looked up at Katherine. "I honestly don't believe Austin could have done any of that. I know he's no Casey, and I'm sure I've been overly protective of him. He's my oldest friend. But I'm certain he wouldn't be disloyal to me, and I can't imagine him intentionally committing a crime."

"My experience is that little in life is certain," said Katherine. "Again, for the purpose of this conversation, let's assume Austin did do these things. If he didn't, my story won't matter. If he did, this story will matter—at least to me. You could, in some way, be dragged into this. Do I protect my father or tell the truth? I've written the story, and it's ready to be turned in. What's your advice?"

Katherine watched her father get up, walk over to a large mahogany table covered with neatly placed newspapers and magazines where he remained standing stock-still for several minutes, appearing to be staring at all of the publications at once, but reading none. He turned, walked back, and addressed her.

"I understand your commitment to journalism, but I'd like to think you also feel a commitment to me. Your family. I don't know why you feel you have to be the one to pull the trigger, break a story that could hurt me and all I've worked for. But it's your call. Personally, I think blood is thicker than principle."

"I don't see why there isn't room for both," Katherine said. "And I'll love you whatever happens."

Katherine got up, hugged her father again, and walked out of the club alone.

She retrieved her car from the nearby parking garage and drove to the *Twin Forks Press*, hoping to get there at least by 4:30 p.m. She hoped Sol would still be there. She made it on time, saw Sol's parked car, grabbed the envelope, and went to his office. The door was shut. She stood there clutching the envelope, fighting extreme nausea. She knocked on the door.

"Come in."

She walked in. Sol stood up and stared at her.

"What's wrong?"

Katherine tossed the envelope on his desk. "I wanted to deliver this to you personally. I'll e-mail it, too. I want to talk about it," she said in a choked voice.

Sol picked up the envelope, opened it, took out the material, and sat at his desk. He motioned to Katherine to sit down. She did.

"There's something I need to tell you. An employee of CCB that I met in connection with my bank investigations decided, at my suggestion, to cooperate with the Manhattan District Attorney's Office. Someone from that office recently informed me, on background, of the status of the investigation, and that a series of arrests were imminent. One of the suspects works for Wilson Holdings, a large automobile dealer in the city."

"I've heard of them. They have a branch not too far from here."

"Preston Wilson is the owner. He's my father."

Sol slowly read the copy, apparently unaware that Katherine's eyes were following his, line for line. When he finished, Sol looked up at Katherine.

"When that person from the district attorney's office gave you the information, did he know that Mr. Wilson was your father?"

"I have no reason to believe that person did."

"Who besides this person has independently confirmed the investigation leading to arrests?"

"Stacy Bowers and Austin Disley."

"You talked to them?"

"On the phone."

"They acknowledged their arrests?"

"Yes."

"You really turned the rock over this time. This is going to raise a lot of serious questions."

"Yes. It is."

"You realize your father may somehow become involved—and if he does, and if you're going to continue with these stories—you're going to have to disclose your relationship with him?"

"I realize that."

"Well, congratulations, kiddo. This is great reporting. Precise. Provocative. Powerful. You wrote it with your heart and signed it with your soul. But, there will be more investigations. Are you sure you want me to run it?"

"Yes," Katherine said, quietly but firmly. "Some stories never end."

∞

James J. Kaufman

An attorney and former judge, James J. Kaufman lives with his wife, Patty, in Wilmington, North Carolina. The author of several works of nonfiction and the novels, *The Collectibles,* Book One of The Collectibles Trilogy, and *The Concealers,* Book Two, he is now writing the final book in the trilogy. Visit him at **jamesjkaufman.com**. For additional copies of this book or other information regarding *The Collectibles* and *The Concealers,* please e-mail the publisher at **downstreampublishing@gmail.com** or write to Downstream Publishing at P.O. Box 869, Wrightsville Beach, NC 28480.

**The author with Charley, his golden retriever, who passed
to Rainbow Bridge December 2012**

GENERAL BOOK CLUB QUESTIONS FOR *THE CONCEALERS*

By James J Kaufman

1. The novel begins with reference to Morton's Fork. What is the relationship between this reference and the characters and situations in which they find themselves?

2. What were your thoughts when you first read Mark Twain's quote, and did they change after you finished reading the novel? If so, how and why did they change?

3. The prologue, through a critical scene, makes a connection with *The Collectibles,* Book One in The Collectibles Trilogy, and gives a glimpse of several significant scenes later in the book. Did this act as a spoiler or whet your appetite for the story? Why do you suppose the author included the scenes in the prologue?

4. Why the title *The Concealers*? Who are the Concealers in this story?

5. Given the circumstances, do you feel that Beth was justified in not telling Katherine the truth earlier about her relationship with Larry Manning and the identity of her real father? Should she have told Katherine, and if so, when—in point of time and circumstance?

6. Susan tells Katherine that everyone lies. Is that true? Is it ever right or acceptable to lie? If so, under what circumstances? Is withholding the truth the same as a lie?

7. Has Preston fulfilled the commitment that he made to Joe Hart? If so, when and how? Has Preston's commitment to Joe been altered by Joe's death? Preston's frustration about his commitment was expressed in a question he asked himself, "How

deep is the duty to the dead?" Can you name any instances in which anyone you know has made a commitment to a living person, and then failed to follow through after the person died? How do you assess this duty?

8. Should Katherine have done more to help her friend in connection with Susan's alcoholism? If so, what should she have done and when? Was Susan a "Collectible" of Katherine's?

9. Should Katherine have discussed with Preston his failure in Marcia's eyes to do more for P.J.? For the Collectibles?

10. In Chapter Two, the reader is introduced to the difficulties of hearing impairment in a young child, and in subsequent chapters, the readers learn how Preston and his wife each deal with these difficulties. How would you characterize Preston's understanding of the difficulty? How would you characterize his response? How would you characterize Marcia's understanding and response? Which approach would you have taken? Could you understand the alternative approach? How serious did you find these issues?

11. In Chapter Twenty-Eight, Katherine rides with her grandfather in his pickup truck, and she discusses Adrian's visit the preceding day to a Catholic church to light a candle. What impressions and feelings did you have from their discussion?

12. In Chapter Thirty-Eight, did you find that Tommy was annoyed with Preston? How would you characterize Tommy's attitude toward Preston and what do you think drove that attitude?

13. Did Carol Martin breach any ethical responsibilities with respect to telling Katherine about the results of her investigation?

14. Should Katherine have disclosed her relationship with her father in her first story involving the arrest of Austin Disley?

15. Should Sean have responded more to Katherine's outreach with her desire to run the facts by him in connection with her bank fraud story?

16. Did Katherine make the right decision in turning the story in? Why or why not?

17. Assuming *The Concealers* is the second act in a three-act play, and now that Katherine has made the decision to go with the story, what is your expectation in Book Three of the Trilogy? What do you think will happen to Preston and his company? What will happen to *The Collectibles*?